THE SHADOW BOX

Books by
John R. Maxim

Novels

PLATFORMS
ABEL BAKER CHARLEY
TIME OUT OF MIND
THE BANNERMAN SOLUTION
THE BANNERMAN EFFECT
BANNERMAN'S LAW
A MATTER OF HONOR

Nonfiction

DARK STAR

THE SHADOW BOX

John R. Maxim

AVON BOOKS ◆ NEW YORK

FOR JOHN KEEDLE
... WHO TURNED OUT TO BE AMAZINGLY RIGHT

THE SHADOW BOX is an original publication of Avon Books. This work has never before appeared in book form. This work is a novel. Any similarity to actual persons or events is purely coincidental.

AVON BOOKS
A division of
The Hearst Corporation
1350 Avenue of the Americas
New York, New York 10019

Copyright © 1996 by John R. Maxim
Author photograph by Susan McCann, Island Photography
Interior book design by Kellan Peck
Published by arrangement with the author
Library of Congress Catalog Card Number: 96-6789
ISBN: 0-380-97300-6

All rights reserved, which includes the right to reproduce this book or portions thereof in any form whatsoever except as provided by the U.S. Copyright Law. For information address Howard Morhaim Literary Agency, Inc., 841 Broadway, Suite 604, New York, New York 10003.

Library of Congress Cataloging in Publication Data:
Maxim, John R.
   The shadow box / John R. Maxim
      p.   cm.
I. Title.
P3563.A8965S53   1996   96-6789
813´.54—dc20   CIP

First Avon Books Hardcover Printing: September 1996

AVON TRADEMARK REG. U.S. PAT. OFF. AND IN OTHER COUNTRIES, MARCA REGISTRADA, HECHO EN U.S.A.

Printed in the U.S.A.

FIRST EDITION

Q 10 9 8 7 6 5 4 3 2 1

Avon Books are available at special quantity discounts for bulk purchases for sales promotions, premiums, fund raising or educational use. Special books, or book excerpts, can also be created to fit specific needs.

For details write or telephone the office of the Director of Special Markets, Avon Books, Dept. FP, 1350 Avenue of the Americas, New York, New York 10019, 1-800-238-0658.

The killing was to be done just so.

Exactly as ordered. Any improvisation would be punished.

This man, this Jake Fallon, would leave his nephew's apartment building some time between ten and midnight. He would be without a bodyguard. The taxi was to be waiting for him. During the ride back to Brooklyn, the driver was to talk to him of baseball. First of baseball, and then of the driver's wife and children. Nothing else.

But when the time came, when this Fallon climbed into the taxi, and had waved goodbye to his nephew, he was clearly in no mood to talk of baseball. The driver had been warned that this might happen.

"He'll probably have a lot on his mind about then," said the man who had sent the driver. "Just keep saying your lines. He'll rise to the bait soon enough."

Jake Fallon, however, had said nothing at all except to give his address and to say what route should be taken. The driver knew these things already. Last night and this morning he had practiced the run from the nephew's building—it was high on Manhattan's West Side—to Fallon's fine brownstone in Brooklyn Heights. He had rehearsed, each time, what he would say in the taxi. He rehearsed what he would say when Fallon knew he was to die. He had worked very hard on his English. He had to learn many things about baseball.

The driver turned south on the FDR Drive. The bridge to Brooklyn was ten minutes away and the Pierrepont Street house was only ten minutes more after that. It was time to try again.

"Such a wonderful game is baseball," he said.

From in back there was only a grunt.

"Only two years have I been in this country and already I am a fanatic. But here it is November. Until April there is no more baseball. Waiting so long will be hard."

The man in the back only shrugged. He had been expected to agree.

The driver reached into a bag at his feet. He pulled out a baseball and held it to the partition where his passenger could see it.

"Do you know what this is?" he asked his silent passenger. "It is a home run that was hit by the great Barry Bonds of the San Francisco Giants and I myself caught it. You don't believe? It was on television. Millions were watching when I caught this ball."

His passenger managed a smile.

"I know," said the cab driver, sadly. "I talk too much when I am nervous. My wife tells me this all the time. It is why she told me to work tonight. She says please don't come to the hospital. She says I'll drive everyone crazy."

"Hospital?" The man raised one eye. "She's sick?"

Now about children. "Not sick. She is at last going to give me a son. She thinks it's a daughter but I know it's a son."

"Either way, you should be there."

A sigh. "Of course you are right. I will call when I get you home. Are there pay phones near this Pierrepont Street?"

"Not at this hour. You can call from my house."

This time it was the driver who smiled.

He had studied this man as he entered the taxi. This man known as Big Jake Fallon. The one who had sent him said, "This guy is no pussy. Don't take him head on." But he did not seem so dangerous. In years past, perhaps, but now he was old. He was a man in his sixties and he had a big belly.

The nephew, who had come down with the girl to see him off, was younger and fit. His turn would come soon. He might at least make it interesting. Also the bodyguard. But that one would be someone else's job. His death was also to be done just so. They meant to bury the bodyguard alive.

"That was your son?" he asked Big Jake Fallon. "From his looks he could hit home runs for the Yankees."

"My nephew. And no, Mike mostly played football."

"That beautiful girl was his wife?"

"She's . . . his fiancee."

"They will have handsome children. Perhaps, one day, their sons and mine will play for the—"

"Yeah . . . maybe. That's my house on the left."

This was almost too easy, thought the driver.

The man had punched out a code that unlocked the door and turned lights on all over the house. There was no wife. No one else would be home. Jake Fallon entered and bade him to follow. A ceramic umbrella stand stood in the hall. A baseball bat sat among the umbrellas. To the right was a room that was nothing but sports. Photos of boxers and basketball players and men wearing football helmets. All with autographs and words of friendship toward Jake Fallon. But much of the room was baseball. There were bats on the wall and a few under glass.

Fallon pointed toward the phone at one end of the room.

"Make your call," he said. "Then feel free to look around if you like."

He turned and walked to a book at the room's other end. It was a dictionary, a large one, that rested on a stand. Fallon leafed through the pages. As he did so, he muttered one word. The word was "Adler." The driver heard it clearly.

His instructions from this point were clear. It is to be slow, it is to be painful, and the weapon must be a bat.

He is to be given the hope that begging for his life might save him. Make him plead. Try to make him soil his trousers. Tell him then, and only then, why he is to die. Say, "This is from Armin Rasmussen." It was a name that the driver did not know. But this Fallon, he was assured, would remember it well.

The driver took a bat from a trophy case. He caressed it with his hands, reading the names of the players who had signed it. Jake Fallon glanced back at some sound that he'd made. He was not alarmed. He was accustomed, no doubt, to his treasures being touched. He turned back to the book, flipped one more page, and found what he was looking for. Cursing softly, he straightened. He took a long breath. By the time he released it, the driver had crossed half the room.

His instructions were to start with the knees. But the shoulders were better. You can't draw a weapon if your shoulders are smashed.

The driver raised the bat. He swung it with all his might.

2

His housekeeper found the body the next morning. She had to be treated for shock. The police sent a car for his nephew, Michael. He was needed to make the identification.

Michael Fallon had to do so by the suit that his uncle had worn that evening, and by his rings, and by the Knights of Columbus pin on his lapel. There was little left of his face.

"I'm real sorry, Mike," said one of the detectives.

Michael could barely speak.

"Where was Moon, by the way?"

Moon was Jake's friend, his bodyguard. More than that, he was family.

"He's . . . up in the Catskills," Michael managed to say. "Uncle Jake had a piece of some middleweight. Moon's helping to train him."

That Moon should have been here was left unsaid.

The detectives could only guess what had happened. Jake would have arrived there some time before midnight. They would pin it down further from the cab company's records. He walked in on a burglar who was looting his collection of sports memorabilia.

The detectives had known Big Jake Fallon. It was just like him, one said, to fight. Forget his age. Man to man, he said, Jake could probably have taken his assailant. But the burglar had one of Jake's baseball bats. It was probably what he'd gone there to steal.

The police said he must have been an amateur. Maybe some strung-out junkie. Maybe some local kid who had seen it while delivering groceries. A pro, they said, would have known that much of Jake's collection—especially a bat signed by all of the 1969 World Champion Mets and inscribed to Big Jake Fallon—would be impossible to sell. And a professional would not have panicked. This one did.

He went into a frenzy. Big Jake had apparently tried to ward off the blows with a heavy oversized dictionary that he kept on a stand in his study. Perhaps, thought one of the homicide detectives, he'd gone in to look up a word. He heard a noise behind him, turned, probably saw the bat and grabbed the dictionary to use as a shield. It did no good. It was knocked across the room, smashed out of its binding. Then the man with the bat broke both of Jake's arms.

Jake must have kept fighting. He knew how to use his feet. He must have hurt the burglar, maybe marked him. The police could think of no other reason that the thief went so berserk. He kept pounding Uncle Jake long after he went down. His ribs, his shoulders, his head. He stopped, from the look of it, only when the bat split in two.

Michael's fiancee, Bronwyn, arrived at the house. He had asked her not to come but she did. She said this was no time for him to be alone. She took him away from there.

It was Bronwyn who helped get him through those first few days. She took charge of arrangements for the funeral. She had met Uncle Jake only once. And Moon not at all. Neither knew that she existed until he called his uncle to announce that he was engaged. Jake had come that night to meet her.

The engagement had been a sudden thing. He'd known Bronwyn for barely three months. He had kept her a secret from Jake and Moon because he still could not believe his own luck and because he didn't want either of them grilling her. Moon, especially, had a history of making some of his woman friends want to grab their coats and run. Moon could be scary. And he happened to be black. Bronwyn said that Moon's absence was all the more reason to have his uncle over now. Without Moon to encourage him, she said, he might be on his best behavior.

And he was. In fact Bronwyn, by dessert, had him wrapped around her finger. The dinner she prepared was part of it. She said the easiest way to a man was through his stomach. Bronwyn did it all from scratch. She'd been planning the menu for a week.

She didn't do his ego any harm either. She told him how thrilled she was to finally meet him. She said that before coming here she'd read everything she could about New York City and there was scarcely a book that failed to mention the notorious Big Jake Fallon. She got him telling stories about New York pols, about the fight game, about his "handsome nephew," and especially about Moon. She heard the sanitized versions of most of them.

She was so beautiful that night. She wore a simple black sheath, bare at one shoulder, with very little jewelry because the dress didn't need it. No jewel could compete with her eyes. They were violet in color, the only violet eyes he had ever seen. The dress showed off her flawless skin. Her dark hair was cut in a modified shag with the ends teased forward to frame her face. She was tall and sleek and her every move showed a dancer's grace.

The major hurdle, Fallon had thought, would be the fact that she was English. Jake was not overly fond of Brits. Nor was he likely to be thrilled at the prospect of his nephew marrying a Protestant. But in Bronwyn's case, he seemed ready to make an exception.

After dinner, the dishes cleared, she sat down to play a nocturne by Chopin. To her gratified surprise, Jake recognized the piece. And Bronwyn played it like an angel.

If it bothered Jake at all that this had happened so quickly, or that the wedding could not be in the Church, he gave no sign. His eyebrow went up only once. That was when he saw Bronwyn's things in the bathroom and realized that she'd already moved in. She'd moved in, in fact, only two weeks after he met her.

Jake would have given his blessing. Michael was sure of it. But toward the end of the evening, a change had come over him. Bronwyn noticed it. She asked him if anything was wrong. He assured her that it was nothing, another matter entirely that he had suddenly remembered. Apologizing to them both, he said that he'd better call a taxi.

There was no need for that, Bronwyn told him. There were always plenty of cabs cruising down 82nd Street. They walked him down and flagged one at the curb. He was dead an hour later.

Moon was not at the funeral either.

He was in Mount Sinai Hospital. He had suffered a mild stroke within hours of being told that Big Jake Fallon was dead. It was Bronwyn who had him brought down from the Catskills and saw that he had the best of care. Thank God for Bronwyn.

She arrived at the service with the entourage from Lehman-Stone, the investment banking firm for which they both worked. It was where they met.

Bart Hobbs, their boss, was in the lead.

Hobbs was a slight but elegant man, old money, all the right schools. He had always seemed nice enough, Fallon supposed. But his niceness had a scripted feel to it. It was as if someone had written down for him what he was expected to say in a given situation. He came with several top executives, all in identical dark suits, all with grim but bewildered expressions. Even Avery Bellows, a former senator, now head of their Washington law firm and a lobbyist for Lehman-Stone's clients, had flown up from the nation's capital.

The cause of their bewilderment was the rest of the crowd. It must have seemed that below a certain social level, every name in New York was there. There were the deputy mayor, two councilmen, several sportswriters and columnists, theater people, ballplayers, many priests and nuns. At least a dozen prizefighters showed up, including three former champions. Big Jake Fallon had known them all.

Brendan and Sheila Doyle came in with two carloads of hoods up from Brooklyn. Brendan Doyle was Jake's lawyer. He was also Michael's. Jake's estate, it turned out, was to be evenly divided between Michael and Moon after a list of smaller bequests was distributed. His longtime housekeeper got a generous pension.

Bronwyn mixed easily. She always did. In the church and at

the reception afterward, the Lehman-Stone delegation had formed a tight little knot, counting the minutes until they could decently retreat to a world they understood.

Bronwyn would not permit it. In her gentle way, she chided them, forced them to circulate. Perhaps as punishment for his being standoffish, she led a horrified Bart Hobbs into the thick of the Brooklyn crowd and, through Doyle, introduced him to the Giordano brothers, the elder of whom had sixteen indictments, no convictions, unless you'd count a couple for simple assault. Actually, they had something in common: an interest in finance. The Giordanos were loan sharks who, in addition, pretty much controlled the Brooklyn docks.

Hobbs, having survived that encounter, was getting new instructions from Bronwyn. He caught Michael's eye, called him over, and made a show of handing Bronwyn a set of keys.

"Michael, I have given Bronwyn an order," he said. "She is to take you to my home in Palm Beach. She is not to take no for an answer. Your flight is tomorrow at noon. You two are to stay there as long as you like, soak in my pool, take walks on the beach, hold on to each other, take care of each other. I don't want to see either of you until you *both* feel ready to come back to work."

Bronwyn studied the ceiling, looking pleased with herself. She had probably written that out for him.

But Michael declined with thanks. He could not leave New York because he wouldn't leave Moon. Two nights later, Bronwyn Kelsey was dead.

She died because at the end of the second day, the sadness and the exhaustion having caught up with her, she wanted a cigarette. Her first in a year.

He urged her to forget it, just go to bed. But she reached for her coat. There was a convenience store, not far, just over on Columbus Avenue. She said that if she left now, she could get there before it closed. He could not very well let her walk there alone. They arrived at the store five minutes before closing, just as another New York lowlife was getting ready to rob it.

She should not have died that night. What made it all the harder to bear was that, if anything, it should have been him.

The robber had been standing by the cooler, waiting for them to make their purchase and leave. But Bronwyn had lingered at the magazine rack. The robber pulled a cap down over his face and a sawed-off shotgun from his coat. He aimed it at the young Korean counterman who stood frozen. The shotgun then swung toward Michael.

He had made no move other than to motion Bronwyn down. She dropped to a half-crouch behind a display of junk food. Yet the robber seemed to feel threatened by him, perhaps because he was bigger and stronger. Perhaps because this bum, probably so much like the one who had killed Jake, had seen the contempt in his eyes.

What jerked the gun wide . . . what then pulled the trigger . . . was a dying spasm of the robber's brain as the Korean counterman blew it apart with two hollow-nosed bullets from the pistol he kept near the register.

The shotgun's blast caught her full in the chest. Fallon ran to her side. She died staring up at him. One eye had changed color. Or he imagined that, maybe. What he did not imagine was that she was blaming him, hating him. For not protecting her. For letting this happen.

3

Bronwyn's service was small and private. The only people in attendance were from Lehman-Stone. Moon still wasn't up to it anyway.

Hobbs, this time, was terribly shaken. He brought with him the firm's chief of security, a thuggish-looking man named Parker, who posted guards to keep reporters from entering. They waited with their cameras on the sidewalk outside. Several of the executives could barely look at Fallon. A few seemed angry. It was as if they too blamed him for not taking that blast himself.

But not Hobbs. For all his grief, he tried as before to be comforting. Hobbs took him aside at the door to the chapel and explained to him, gently, that Bronwyn had already been cremated. It was done, he said, at her parents' request.

Her parents were British subjects who had retired to Portugal's Algarve. Fallon was to fly there and meet them over Christmas. The mother, said Hobbs, was too frail to travel and so had asked that Bronwyn's ashes be sent back to England, where they would be interred in a family plot.

Cremation. Fallon could not bear the thought of it. But neither, said Hobbs, could her parents bear the thought of looking at their daughter's ruined body.

"You can't know, Michael, how sorry I am."

He supposed that he could. It was Hobbs who had brought her over, borrowed her from Lehman-Stone's British affiliate. It was Hobbs who had introduced them and assigned her to work on his team. He had even encouraged their romance and now, quite likely, wished to God that he had not.

"Get away from this town, Michael. You'll be seeing her everywhere you turn. The Palm Beach house is still yours for the asking."

But his answer was the same. Not until Moon is stronger.

He kissed the urn that held Bronwyn's remains. It was placed in a shipping container. He put a rose in with it. He went home, numb with grief, only to find out that his apartment had been burglarized.

The building's doorman had seen no one enter or leave who was not a resident, but that in itself meant little. Burglars, in the past, had entered through the garage or by crossing from adjacent roofs.

The door to his apartment had not been forced. The interior, however, was a shambles. Missing were his laptop computer, a watch, and a few other pieces of gold jewelry. The thief had also gone through his desk and a file cabinet, but Michael had kept nothing of value in either place.

Some blank floppy disks and a few that held data appeared to be missing. The data, job-related, was no loss. It would be of no use to anyone else and, in any case, he had copies of it at Lehman-Stone. His most grievous loss had been on top of the desk. It was his only picture of Bronwyn. She had given it to him the week before she died. She'd had it mounted in an antique shadow box frame that she said had been in her family for more than two hundred years. It was trimmed in gold filigree. Someone stole it for the gold.

The police came in force. Two uniforms first, then two detectives. This, it became clear, was because Michael Fallon's name was still fresh in their minds from the killing at the convenience store and from the newspaper accounts, a few days prior, of the funeral of Big Jake Fallon.

The police were not surprised that he'd been robbed.

"They watch for funerals," one of the uniforms told him. "Funerals and weddings. Miserable pricks."

Fallon, in his state of mind, could not swear that he'd locked the door or even that he'd shut it securely. The doorman suspected another tenant, a troubled young man who lived on the twelfth floor with a widowed mother. He was nineteen, had been arrested several times for petty theft, and had been in drug rehab twice. The detectives checked his apartment and found property that other residents of the building had reported stolen. But nothing of Michael's.

Ten days later, he was out of a job.

It was done suddenly. It was done brutally. No reason was given.

For those ten days he had taken at least part of Bart Hobbs's advice. Don't think about work. Give yourself some time. But having that time made it worse. He had done nothing but take long walks, go to movies without seeing them, and sit with Moon at Mount Sinai.

Moon was in his late fifties. Although solidly built, he was not an exceptionally large man except for his hands. He had the hands of a man twice his size. Uncle Jake had often said that he'd never met a tougher or more dangerous man than Moon.

"Or a kinder, wiser man," Big Jake had added. "It's as if there's two of him."

Now, however, he looked anything but tough and his floor nurse had her doubts about his wisdom.

Physically, he seemed much better. His speech was not as slurred and his left hand had pretty much stopped shaking. But he had also taken an unauthorized walk through Central Park. He said he needed to fill his lungs and to be out where there was life. The nurse had chewed him out for it but she let him keep his clothing if he promised to behave.

It was his mental state that troubled Michael. He had a lost and haunted look about him. Michael worried that a world without Big Jake Fallon was not a world that Moon would want to live in. At other times his eyes would take on a peculiar and almost frightening shine. He was imagining, Michael supposed, what he would do to the man who had beaten Jake Fallon to death. If he ever got those hands on him.

Moon understood that he needed to get himself together. He said it himself.

"When you hate," he said, "but that hate can't find a place to go, it turns inward. You start hating yourself for the things you wish you'd done. You want to hurt yourself."

"Yeah, well, I'll hurt you if you don't quit talking like that."

The threat brought a welcome smile. "You're gonna try me *now?* Now that I'm old and had a stroke? Why don't you wait another year or two, Michael? Maybe I'll have cancer by then."

"Just don't you leave me, Moon."

Michael's own need was to get back to work, get busy.

He called Bart Hobbs to say that he'd be in the next Monday. Hobbs argued. He thought it was too soon but Michael insisted. In the end, Hobbs couldn't say no.

On the Friday preceding, however, he found a call on his answering machine from one of Hobbs's assistants. Don't bother coming in, was the message. We've cleaned out your office. Your personal effects are being sent to you by messenger. With them, you will find a document. Sign it, and you will receive a check in the amount of one hundred thousand dollars. Refuse, and you will be paid through the last day you worked. Nothing more. No severance. No year-end bonus. This offer is final.

He tried to call Hobbs. Hobbs would not speak to him.

On Saturday, he went to Hobbs's apartment building. It was on Fifth Avenue, facing the park. The doorman would not let him past the lobby. On Monday, he went to the World Trade Center, to the offices of Lehman-Stone. Security guards stopped him. They escorted him from the building. He was furious. Humiliated.

The document in question was in effect an admission that he had been transferring customers' money into a dummy account and had been using inside knowledge to enrich himself. He read it, stunned, and of course refused to sign it. He gave it to Brendan Doyle, demanding that he file a lawsuit at once charging slander and wrongful dismissal.

"What have you been up to there, Michael?" asked the lawyer.

"Nothing, damn it. It's a goddamned lie."

"First let me have a talk with them," said Doyle.

That same day, he received a letter from Moon. Moon had asked him not to visit for a few days and now he understood why. Against his doctor's advice, Moon had checked himself out of Mount Sinai. The letter said that he had been to the cemetery, had a good long talk with Jake. Right now he needs to do some traveling. Maybe go someplace where it's warm.

Moon, like Hobbs, thought that Michael would do well to do the same. Like Hobbs, he knew that the city would be too full of ghosts.

"I'm real sorry, Michael," the letter ended. "You got twice my sorrow and here I'm running out on you. But there are things I need to settle in my head. I can't do that where everything I see is full of memories and where I lie awake all night wanting to put a real bad hurt on someone."

Fallon took *someone* to mean almost anyone. Any Brooklyn burglar. Anyone who had ever been less than a friend to Uncle Jake. He would worry about Moon and he'd miss him. But he was glad to see him back on his feet. And especially out of New York.

Moon didn't write again. For the next two months, December and through most of January, he didn't call either. Michael tried a few places where he thought Moon might have gone. New Jersey, where he still had family. Or Naples, Florida, where Uncle Jake owned a condo out on Marco Island, half of which now belonged to Moon. But no luck. If Moon called or wrote after January, Michael didn't know it. By that time he was running himself.

New York had killed Bronwyn. New York had killed Jake. And then it turned its attention to him.

"Michael . . . it is not New York that was doing all this."

"That city kills, Doc. That city eats its young."

"And Bronwyn, incidentally, did not die hating you."

"You weren't there, Dr. Greenberg. You didn't see her eyes."

It *was* New York that killed Jake and Bronwyn. You can blame those crimes on society, the breakdown of family values, the decline in church attendance, or just on the lowlife bastards who committed them. But at bottom it's the city. It breeds a meanness, a predatory mindset that you find nowhere else in this country.

New York killed Jake, it killed Bronwyn, and it made a wreck of Moon. You'd think it would have been satisfied, but then, a few days later, it set its sights on the last of the Fallons. It began by firing him.

"Michael . . . it was not New York that fired you."

"You're not listening, Doc."

"Sure I am. You said the city breeds meanness. Your firm was in the city. Ergo . . ."

"Doctor . . . you grew up in Wisconsin, right?"

"Just outside Madison."

"Yeah, well . . . in Wisconsin, tragedy is missing the first day of deer season. It's seeing the Packers get blown out by Tampa Bay."

"Michael . . ."

"New York fired me and then it blacklisted me."

"Michael . . . listen to me . . ."

"And then it tried to kill me. It tried to kill me twice."

4

The first attempt came on a January evening.

Fallon had barely left his apartment since Bronwyn's service. The holidays had come and gone. He had done nothing to celebrate them, had sent no cards, and had ignored the few invitations he had received.

On that day in mid-January, Brendan Doyle called him, got his machine, yelled, "Pick up, damn it," and insisted that Michael join him for dinner. They needed to talk. They needed to discuss the pending action against Lehman-Stone.

"No, it *can't* be done over the phone. You blew us off for Christmas dinner and you didn't show at our New Year's party. You're feeling sorry for yourself, Michael. If Moon were here, he'd kick your butt for you."

Doyle said he'd be waiting at his regular table in the dining room of the Algonquin Hotel.

"I'll wait fifteen minutes. Don't make me come get you."

Brendan F. X. Doyle was a trim and dapper little man, far smaller than his temper. He had flaming red hair, worn long and in waves, white at the temples and sideburns. For years, Michael thought he owned only one suit. He owned many but they were all light gray and double-breasted, and like Jake he wore a

Knights of Columbus pin in the lapel. He stood when Michael entered and offered his hand. He was reading Michael's eyes, not liking what he saw.

The setting, if anything, had added to Michael's gloom. It made him think of his mother. She had run off when he was eleven. It was at this same table, more than twenty-five years earlier, that Doyle and his Uncle Jake had set him down to tell him what they had learned about her and to brief him on their efforts to find her.

She had written only once. The letter, postmarked Chicago, asked Michael to forgive her. When he was older, it said, he would understand how little time we have on earth. She had been given a chance at a new life. She was going to take it. His father had showed him the letter, written on his mother's stationery, but would not let him read it for himself. He read parts of it aloud, wept silently over others, then slowly tore the letter into strips and flushed them down the toilet. He was drunk for three days afterward. In fact, until the day Michael's father took his life, he was never quite sober again.

A waiter had appeared at the table.

"What are you drinking?" Doyle asked.

"Dewar's and water. A double."

"He doesn't need a double," Doyle said to the waiter.

Fallon chose not to argue. It would have brought on a lecture. His mind was still on his mother. Through Doyle, a pain in the ass even then, Uncle Jake had hired a private detective agency to try and track her down. In part, this was to appease her side of the family, which consisted largely of Irish cops and perpetually pregnant women named Kate or Irene. They could not accept that one of their own, a woman who attended daily Mass and received the sacraments, could possibly run off with another man.

The detectives started in Chicago. They reported, however, that she had stayed only long enough to write and post that letter. They traced her to Nevada, where, at a roadside wedding chapel, she married a man who was said to be a former Catholic priest. She did so without benefit of divorce. On hearing this, the Kates and the Irenes could only gasp and make the sign of the cross over their breasts.

The two were subsequently seen in California and later in Oregon, where the trail grew cold. Jake tried again a year later, prior to adopting Michael, but this was to satisfy the courts. No trace of her could be found. She had vanished, totally, into the new life she had chosen.

"Michael . . ."

Fallon blinked himself back to the present.

"They're gone, Michael," the lawyer said gently. "It's time you accepted that."

Doyle had assumed, Fallon realized, that he was thinking of Bronwyn and Uncle Jake. He did not correct him. He reached for the weak scotch and water that the waiter had left at his elbow. The lawyer sipped from his own.

"Michael . . ." He studied the ice cubes in his glass. "Have you thought any more about buying a boat?"

"A boat?"

"A sailboat. You've talked about it."

Yes, he had, but not lately. And not for anytime soon. He'd done a fair amount of sailing, as weekend crew, with friends who lived up in Connecticut. He'd taken lessons on Cape Cod. Like half of New York City, he'd made wistful visits to the boat show at the Javits Center. Someday. The great escape. Either that or buy a ski lodge. Everyone he knew had probably dreamed of doing one or the other.

"What brings that up?"

A shrug. "You have the means and, like it or not, the leisure. Recent events notwithstanding, there are those who would envy your situation."

Fallon studied him, frowning.

"Mr. Doyle . . . have you spoken to Lehman-Stone?"

"That's another thing. You don't need their money."

"Need isn't the issue."

Doyle rubbed his chin. A sigh. "Michael . . . they're talking criminal charges."

The frown deepened. "Charging me with what?"

A shrug. "They won't say. But they claim they've got you cold."

Fallon's color rose.

"And you believe them?"

"Michael . . . you've done *something*. What is it?"

Fallon threw down his napkin, pushed back his chair. The smaller man seized his arm and hissed. "Sit, Michael. Sit down like a grown-up and talk to your lawyer."

"My lawyer? You sound more like theirs."

Doyle reddened. "You'll apologize for that."

"Like hell I will. It's a frame or it's a bluff. Either way, here's you of all people telling me to fold and blow town. You can kiss my ass, Mr. Doyle."

"They hate you, Michael. Tell me why."

Fallon hesitated. "Now it's personal?"

"The way they're behaving . . . it's how people act when someone has betrayed their trust. What might you have done that could be perceived in such a way?"

"Like using privileged information? Nothing."

"No dummy accounts? No ripping off pension funds?"

"Fuck you, Mr. Doyle."

"On a personal level, then. This Hobbs. Could he have been jealous of you and Bronwyn?"

"Hobbs? He introduced us."

"There was nothing between them?"

Fallon frowned, then shook his head abruptly. "If anything, he encouraged the relationship. A month after we met, he had us up to his ski lodge in Maine. He put us both in the same bedroom. Then at Uncle Jake's funeral he practically ordered us to fly down to his house in Palm Beach. Does that sound like jealousy to you?"

"Might he blame you for her death?"

Fallon considered this, then shook his head once more. Some of them did, he supposed. And he certainly blamed himself. But he'd seen no indication that Hobbs shared that view. Whatever had happened, whatever they found or thought they found, had come well after the night Bronwyn died.

The lawyer drummed his fingers. He wet his lips. It seemed to Fallon that whatever question was now forming in his mind, he was reluctant to ask it. He blinked it away and took a sip of his drink.

"For the record," he said at last, "in your whole life, I never heard you tell a lie. I never knew you to steal a dime."

"That means you'll take them on?"

He made a face. "You could lose more than you'd gain."

Fallon waited.

"Think of a nasty divorce, Michael. Think of a custody battle. The husband, who might be the nearest thing to Jesus Christ in terms of actual behavior, will hear that he's a drunk, a philanderer, a wife-beater, and if, God forbid, the children at issue are girls under ten, he'll hear that he had his hand up their dresses."

"You're saying I'll get dirty."

Doyle nodded. "Win or lose. The whispers will never stop."

And now that look again. As if he were toying with another subject.

"Michael . . ."

He waited again.

"Your uncle . . . never thought much of your career choice. You being on Wall Street, I mean."

"No, he didn't."

"Did he ever say why?"

"Sure. He thinks all rich white Protestants are thieves."

The lawyer smiled, in part at Michael's use of the present tense.

"I have pointed out to him," said Doyle, "that one finds the odd Jew on Wall Street. Even the odd Papist. His reply was that the Jews invented commerce but the Protestants invented greed."

The smile flickered at the memory, then faded.

"And . . . you pushing drug company stocks. He didn't much like that either, did he."

"There's nothing wrong with drug companies."

"But with all the industries you might have specialized in . . ."

"Mr. Doyle, what's your point?"

The lawyer shook his head quickly. "None. None at all."

Doyle signaled for the waiter.

Big Jake's advice, given while Fallon was in college, was to do what you love and the money will follow. Unless they won't pay you. In that case, go where the money is, make your pile, then go do something useful with the rest of your life.

Good advice. The kind uncles give. But Jake definitely hadn't meant Wall Street because Uncle Jake was not a fan of the financial community. He said that the Mafia in its best year never pulled off scams such as are concocted every day on Wall Street. Not just the savings and loan robbery either. Not just the legalized piracy of corporate raiders, throwing tens of thousands out of work to further enrich a few. He said the traffic in heroin and cocaine wouldn't exist if a bunch of rich white Protestants hadn't put up the money in the first place. He wasn't far wrong.

Eventually, Fallon did go where the money is. But he did it his own way and with a nod, he thought, to his Uncle Jake's misgivings. Almost from the beginning, he had specialized in drug companies of the legitimate kind. First as an analyst at Shearson and later as a trader with Lehman-Stone. Lehman-Stone had held positions in Merck, Pfizer, and all the major pharmaceutical giants, but mostly, of late, in European firms such as Glaxo and Germany's AdChem.

To hear his Uncle Jake talk, however, none of these companies was any great improvement over the Medellin Cartel. In fact, during that Tylenol scare a few years back, when cyanide-laced bottles were turning up on supermarket shelves, Jake said that he would not have put it past a rival drug company to have planted them.

An outrageous accusation. But Jake wouldn't back off. At the very least, he said, these companies test each other's products all the time, hoping to find some contaminant so they can blow the whistle and force a recall. Why? Because dropping a dime on a competitor can mean a windfall increase in market share and their own stock shoots up in value. For that matter, it wouldn't surprise him if some of those Wall Street bozos had planted the poisoned bottles themselves. Two or three people die, the stock drops like a stone, and they make a killing because they've been shorting it for weeks.

Fallon couldn't deny that it was possible. Absurd, unfair, and slanderous, but still remotely possible. Maybe they also killed President Kennedy. Maybe they're aliens out to control us by drugging us. It's possible, right?

It was no use trying to tell Jake how many people are alive and functioning today because of the products Michael's clients had developed. All the jobs they've created. All the grants and scholarships they've awarded. Uncle Jake didn't want to know, nor would he explain his antagonism.

But Fallon thought he knew the reason. A shrug from Moon, during that tirade of Jake's, had as much as confirmed it. It had to do with Fallon's parents. Both of them, his father in particular, had worked for a drug company that was run, almost certainly, by white-collar criminals.

Even so, thought Fallon, it was flat-out ridiculous to mention that rinky-dink operation in the same breath with the Mercks and Pfizers and AdChems of the world. For one thing, all it made were veterinary products. It was a small manufacturer/distributor named Eagle Sales, based over in New Jersey, long since out of business.

His father had been their accountant. His mother, as he recalled, had worked there first. It's where they'd met. She quit just before he was born but she would go back every now and then, filling in for vacations and the like.

The only possible connection, and the reason that Doyle was tapdancing around it, was that the owners of Eagle had skimmed the hell out of that company and his father had probably helped them do it. No one ever said so straight out but it had to have been true. That last year, after his mother left, there was just too much money, all of it cash, lying around that apartment.

So what?

Like father, like son?

Is that what Doyle was getting at?

Or does he think that going into a marginally related field was rooted, somehow, in some deep inner urge to make amends for whatever his father had done? Or maybe to succeed where his father had failed?

That was total horseshit. All of it. Doyle, in any case, did not return to that subject.

The upshot of the dinner was that Doyle would file suit but he would then lie back and wait for heads to cool. No one wants this to go to court. No one wants the SEC in this. Be patient and they'll settle.

Doyle did have one theory as to what was going on here. It had to do with corporate image. Lehman-Stone was a very conservative firm and so were its clients. But suddenly they're getting a lot of unwelcome press. Their name was mentioned, repeatedly, in the newspaper accounts of Big Jake Fallon's murder, if only in connection with Jake's adopted son and heir. Several of the stories mentioned that Big Jake's younger brother, Michael's father, had taken his own life.

Then, after Bronwyn was killed, one tabloid did a story on what amounted to the Fallon curse . . . how Big Jake's nephew seems dogged by tragedy and death. Even the burglary made the papers. To make matters worse, that same story reported that the Giordano brothers of Brooklyn had placed a bounty on whomever killed Jake. The younger Giordano, called Johnny G., was said to have been a boyhood friend of Michael's.

The long and the short of it, said Doyle, is that Lehman-Stone now sees that one of its traders is related to the notorious Big Jake Fallon and the infamous Giordano brothers. They decide to disassociate themselves, and fast.

"But they don't want to look like pricks, either," said Doyle, "dumping a guy who's taken some really hard shots. They won't if they can make him look like a crook. He's Jake Fallon's nephew, right? He's Johnny G.'s pal. How straight can he be?"

"You think that's what happened?" Fallon asked.

"It's a theory."

"Mr. Doyle . . . Bart Hobbs has lied about me. I want his ass in court."

Outside the Algonquin, an unexpected snow had begun to coat the sidewalk. It gave Doyle another excuse to argue for that boat.

"I'm tempted to go in on one with you," he said. "We'll find a nice island, swim in to the beach. Who knows? We might even trip over some sleeping native and he'll turn out to be Moon."

"You still haven't heard from him either?"

"Not a word."

"I'm worried about him."

"You worry about yourself." Doyle squeezed his arm and grunted. "Get back to the gym, Michael. You're letting yourself go soft."

He squeezed him once more, this time with affection, then turned and walked off toward the cab stand at Grand Central Station.

*   *   *

Fallon looked for a cab of his own. He did not have high hopes. The off-duty lights of New York taxis are known to wink on at the first flake of snow. But the Sixth Avenue subway was only a block and a half away. He reached it, missed one train, and stood waiting, deep in thought, for the next.

Witnesses told of a thirty-ish male, Hispanic, smelling of alcohol, who had been dozing against a platform pillar. The train came in. The roar jarred him awake. He suddenly lurched into Michael, shoving him into the path of the oncoming train. A large black woman, God bless her, slammed a forearm across Fallon's chest and then clawed at his hair. She slowed him, almost stopped him, but one arm had flailed out and the lead car struck it. The impact snapped his arm at the wrist.

Fallon was knocked to the platform. The drunk, they said, tried to slip away. The black woman grabbed him, told him to wait for the police. He threw a punch at her. She smothered it and proceeded to slap him silly until two transit policemen arrived and, seeing a large black woman swinging a smaller white male by the hair, ordered her to let him go.

She and other witnesses tried to explain. But the cops pulled the smaller man free and threatened to arrest her. The man bolted for the stairs but another subway rider tripped him, and the woman pounced on him again. The transit cops then seized her, pulled her off, and cuffed her hands behind her back. Other riders, most of them black, tried to intervene and were threatened with arrest. The drunk, the man who caused it all, disappeared in the confusion.

Fallon knew that the woman had tried to help him but he was too dazed, in too much pain, to make himself clear. He was taken to the emergency ward at St. Vincent's Hospital, where he spent most of the night waiting for a lull between stabbing and shooting victims so that his arm could be treated. But his head had cleared and he used the time to find out where the woman had been taken. He was reluctant to wake Brendan Doyle over a broken arm. A hospital orderly told him how to post bail, by phone and credit card, for the woman who had probably saved his life. Her name, he learned, was Lena Mayfield, forty-six, a widow. She worked part-time at four different jobs.

He called Doyle the next morning. A week later, they went to court with her. Fallon spoke before the judge, and the charges were summarily dismissed. Fallon wrote out a check and asked Mrs. Mayfield to take it. She whistled when she saw the amount but shook her head.

"Taking money for doin' right," she told him, "crosses out the doin' of it."

He was determined to find some way to thank her, to at least make up for the clothing she ruined and for any lost earnings. But he didn't get the chance. New York wasn't finished with him yet.

5

Only three days after the hearing, while his forearm was in a cast, two muggers decided that Michael looked easy.

He had gone to see a movie near Lincoln Center. The weather had turned milder and he chose to walk home. It was just after ten, not late; Columbus Avenue was well lit and he could see other people out walking. By the time he reached the mid-seventies, however, there was no one within two blocks of him except two approaching black males. They had crossed from the other side of the street and came toward him from the opposite direction.

Fallon tried to believe that they meant him no harm. They were black, but so was the woman who had saved his life. Nor did these two look especially dangerous. They were not young kids on a prowl. These two seemed close to Fallon's own age and they looked too healthy to be junkies. He'd be damned if he would cross the street like some frightened tourist from Toledo.

But as they neared, he realized that he was probably in trouble. The one on the curb side, his hair worn in dreadlocks, was looking around, glancing over his shoulder as they walked. The other, his head bald or shaven, thick mustache, would be nearer to

Fallon when they passed. That one kept his eyes straight ahead, both hands in his pockets. His skin was the lighter of the two. Perhaps not a black man after all. But not Hispanic either.

The bald one, Fallon knew, would walk past and then suddenly turn. He would aim a sap or a fist at the back of Fallon's neck and then throw him to the pavement. He would ask, "You okay?" as if speaking to a fallen drunk. He would strip him of his wallet, search for any separate cash, and then look in vain for a watch. The other would be waiting, standing lookout, ready to kick him if he resisted. They would be finished and on their way within ten seconds.

Fallon didn't wait. The bald one was abreast of him when Fallon wheeled, his left arm out ready to parry, and swung the cast on his right. The bald one had indeed been turning. The rough plaster cast thudded high against his cheek. It tore the flesh open. He yelped and raised both hands to his face. The right hand held no sap or weighted glove. It held a knife. The long thin blade glistened at his ear. Fallon lashed at it with a downward backhand blow of his cast, driving it into his assailant's face. It cut him terribly. The knife slipped from wet fingers. He tried to call to his companion for help. Air and blood blew through his cheek.

The one in the dreadlocks was clawing at his belt. Fallon spun the bald one and shoved him at the other. He followed, low, and aimed the edge of his shoe at the second man's knee. The hard chopping kick tore at his tendons. Fallon heard them pop through an agonized shriek. The man was going down but a gun had appeared in his hand. A revolver. Big, heavy, chrome-plated. Fallon moved in quickly. In a single motion he jammed one shoe against the gun and raked the man's eyes with the rough edge of his cast. Another scream. With his good hand he seized the revolver, gripping the cylinder so that it couldn't be turned. He wrenched the gun free. He brought it down across the nose of the man who would have shot him and then against his collarbone. A third blow broke his jaw. He stopped when the one in dreadlocks could no longer raise his arms.

He turned to the bald one who was on his back, rolling, trying to hold his face together. As Fallon approached, this one tried to kick up at him. Fallon seized the kicking leg, placed a foot on the other, and heaved upward as if to tear the man in half.

Another shriek, cut short, and then a high-pitched hooting sound. From across the avenue, a woman's voice said, "Someone call the police."

Fallon turned the gun in his hand and cocked it. The bloody knife was at his feet. He kicked it under a parked car then stood over the one in dreadlocks. He was semiconscious, moaning. The other now mewed like a cat.

Fallon pointed the gun at the second man's leg. A voice in his mind said, *Cripple them, Michael. No use doin' this twice.* But the woman was still yelling and suddenly, in the distance, he saw the strobe of blue lights. *Time to go,* the voice told him. *Just walk away slow.* Fallon obeyed. He reached the next corner and turned toward Central Park.

"Michael . . . where did you learn to do that?"
"Do what?"
"Hurt people."
"Moon. Moon taught me."

He supposed that he should have waited there. And explained what happened. But he'd had enough of the police. Enough of the media.

Doyle had been right about that. Fallon had, over a period of eight weeks, figured in two major homicides. He'd had microphones stuck in his face at Uncle Jake's funeral and again after Bronwyn was killed. He had managed to duck them after the subway incident but that one made the papers all the same. And they were waiting for him outside the courthouse when he appeared for Mrs. Mayfield. A reporter asked him whether he had considered that there might be a Fallon curse.

The next day, that same reporter's tabloid ran a photo it had found in its morgue. The photo was a shot of his parents' old apartment house. On it, they had traced a dotted line from a sixth floor window to the sidewalk below, showing where another Fallon had leaped to his death.

He didn't need them hearing about this new episode. He didn't need to see his face on a television screen, an object of pity. Some street reporter wondering aloud how one man could attract so much trouble. Or how it was that he took those two so easily.

Those were his main reasons for not waiting.

"Was another that you wanted to keep that gun?"
"Yes, it was, Doc. Enough was enough."

He had walked toward Central Park, and into it, because to go straight home would have been foolish. One of those witnesses might have followed and then told the police where he lived.

Once in the park, he did have second thoughts about the gun. If the police were to find him, it might be hard to explain. What did you intend, Mr. Fallon? A little more hunting? Otherwise, who in his right mind would walk through Central Park at night? Seen too many Charles Bronson movies, Mr. Fallon?

"Would they have been right?"
"Doc . . . I don't know."
"The truth, Michael."
"If someone had come at me . . . I guess so, yes."
"You guess what? Say it."
"I would have killed him."

And that was what scared him.

The person who came at him might just have been some poor homeless slob startled out of his sleep. It's why Moon has never liked guns. With guns, you do more damage than you have to. He knew that he'd done more than enough already. While in the park, his heart still pounding, his hands balled into fists to keep them from shaking, he did consider ditching it. Maybe throwing it in the lake. But he didn't.

He exited the park well above 82nd Street, doubled back, then watched the entrance to his building for a while. No police cars appeared. At half past eleven, a tenant pulled up in a taxi and the doorman helped her with her bags. Fallon seized that moment to enter the building through the parking garage, using his magnetized card. Should anyone ask, the doorman could not say when he arrived or even be sure that he'd been out. Nor would he see the blood that glistened on Fallon's sleeve.

He ran cold water on it, scrubbing clots with a toothbrush.

THE SHADOW BOX ■

Some blood had splattered the plaster cast. He washed it off as best he could and used Clorox to bleach out the rest. His wrist throbbed painfully. The cast had cracked. He dried it and secured it with masking tape. That done, he washed and examined the gun. A Colt Python, 357 Magnum. If he'd shot that man in the leg as he'd intended, this thing would have blown it off at the knee.

He emptied a Weight Watchers dinner package, concealed the Python in it, and placed it in his freezer. The package bulged considerably but it would serve. He poured himself a scotch and turned on the television, searching for a local news program.

There was nothing yet, of course. There might be something in the morning. In this city, a mugging is hardly headline news but this one, he thought, might get a mention. The media likes victim-turns-the-tables stories.

He sipped his drink and flipped through the channels. On one of the cable stations, he found a program about boxing. He watched it for a while. Oddly, it calmed him.

He did not see boxing as violence. Not mean violence. Not random violence. He saw it as a fair test of skill and courage between two men, well witnessed, with a referee ready to step in should one have too great an advantage. He was more than a fan. Fighting, he supposed, was rooted in his genes.

His great-grandfather, according to family lore, had been bare-knuckle champion of three counties: Cavan, Roscommon, and Meath. His grandfather, the first to emigrate, was more of a saloon brawler, but his father, Tom Fallon, had gone eighteen and two as a light heavyweight and had been promised a shot at Billy Conn before they drafted him to fight the Germans instead. He became a tank commander. Fought with Patton's Third Army through half of France, all of southern Germany, and well into Czechoslovakia. Won several campaign medals plus a Bronze Star for valor and two Purple Hearts for shrapnel wounds. Fallon could never understand how a man like that, so strong, so brave, could decide that life was too hard and kill himself. Or maybe now he could. A little.

Uncle Jake had never fought in the ring. But he had been a fight judge, served on the boxing commission, and helped to promote some major bouts. These, however, were sidelines. Full-time, he was a Brooklyn Democratic Party boss and deal-maker who seemed to know every police captain and headwaiter in the city.

As for Fallon himself, he had hoped to enter the Golden Gloves tournament as soon as he turned sixteen. Get Moon to train him. But his Uncle Jake told him to forget it.

"That string ends with your father. You, you're going to be a gentleman."

"Uncle Jake . . ."

"Tennis is good. We'll get you started on tennis."

"Not polo?"

"Don't get smart. But golf is good too. They have summer camps these days where all you do is learn golf."

"Uncle Jake, what's wrong with learning how to handle myself first?"

"That's all you want?"

"I've been beaten up twice. Twice is plenty."

Jake thought about this for a day or so.

"Tell you what. A good street fighter will take a boxer every time. Moon says he'll teach you street fighting."

"I know street fighting. That's where I got beat up."

"Yeah, well, Moon's never even been down. A guy needs to be hurt, Moon gets it done quick. Ten seconds or less."

Young Fallon made a face.

"What?"

"Nice to know I'm going to be a gentleman."

"Ten seconds, Michael. It's a kindness if you can think of it that way. Less damage needs to be done."

Fallon poured himself another scotch.

The boxing program was about Jack Dempsey. Dempsey had lost his title to Gene Tunney because he couldn't get used to the neutral corner rule, which was still fairly new. He had Tunney down. The referee kept pointing to a neutral corner but all Dempsey wanted was to run and club Tunney the instant he tried to get up. So Tunney got his famous long count and he was able to recover. Before that rule, if you knocked an opponent down you could stand over him waiting to hammer as soon as his knee cleared the canvas. What Dempsey did to Willard, for example, was horrendous. He broke every bone in Jess Willard's face.

New York is like Dempsey. There's no neutral corner. You let down your guard and it drops you.

He had a bad night.

Twice he dreamed about the two muggers and woke up in a sweat. Being awake, in the dark, was worse. That knife. What if he hadn't turned when he did? What if he hadn't moved first as Moon had drilled into him? What if those two weren't muggers at all? And that drunk on the subway platform. What if he wasn't so drunk? And that burglar who killed Uncle Jake. What if . . .

Fallon cursed.

He saw what he was doing to himself and it was stupid. They're all on someone's payroll, right? Someone who hates him. Which, if we believe Brendan Doyle, means Bart Hobbs. Okay, then what? Did Hobbs have that man follow him from the Algonquin just in case it snows and he decides to take the subway? If so, wouldn't he have picked someone a little bigger to try to push him in front of a train? Big enough, for example, that he wouldn't get the shit kicked out of him by a woman like Lena Mayfield?

And those two muggers. For them to have been on someone's payroll, for them to have been out there waiting for him, they had to have known he'd be coming. But he'd gone to see that movie on a whim and he took a cab to get there. What did he think? That someone had a whole surveillance team out there watching his every move? Here he comes. Uh-oh, he's heading home on foot. Let's go to Plan B. Call in the fake muggers.

No way.

All it is, it's this rotten city. Predators on every street corner and behind almost every desk. He'd been one himself. On Wall Street when he started out. The way they all start out. Making a hundred cold calls a day pushing stocks that he knew damned well almost no one but himself and his brokerage house would ever make a nickel on.

Maybe that's what it is. Justice. The city . . . God . . . somebody . . . handing him a bill. But he couldn't start thinking like that either because next thing he knows he'll be afraid to leave the building without that Python in his belt. And God didn't kill Uncle Jake and Bronwyn just because Michael Fallon sold stocks that went down.

Mr. Doyle was right about one thing. What Michael Fallon needed was to stop moping. Start seeing some people. Get a job and keep busy. There were at least three firms that had been trying to recruit him for years.

But not anymore.

They were polite enough. They were sympathetic. They said let's get together, we'll have lunch. But they never called. He'd try them again and they suddenly weren't in.

No brokerage firm, no bank, wanted to touch him. He tried as far west as Los Angeles and as far east as London. Two or three people leveled with him, after a fashion, and strictly off the record. They said what Brendan Doyle said.

"Mike . . . even if you're clean, even if you win your lawsuit, we just don't need that kind of baggage."

"Baggage? I was a top producer at Lehman-Stone. You guys have hired traders who were under indictment."

"True, Mike. But nobody ended up dead. People who get close to you have a way of getting killed."

"Who? My uncle? Bronwyn? What did that have to do with me?"

"Mike . . . do yourself a favor. Go buy that boat and see the world."

That was as much as anyone would say. That and "We hear things. What we hear is bad. But no one's going to spell it out for you because no one wants to put his hand on a Bible. Sorry, Mike. Buy that boat."

It also struck him, at about this time, that his phone had developed an echo. And hang-up calls became more frequent. Sometimes twice an evening.

6

And there were more bad nights.

After a while, it was getting hard to tell where the nightmares ended and reality began. In his dreams he'd see people he knew . . . from Wall Street and from the neighborhood as well . . . going about their lives as if he weren't even there. These had been his friends. A few of the women had been more than that. But now they didn't want to know him. And he couldn't find out why.

But always, lurking in the background, watching, is this man who wants to kill him.

Fallon had no idea who he was. The face kept changing. You'd think it would be Bart Hobbs but it never was. In one dream it was even his father. In another it was Bronwyn. Most often, it was a face or faces that he'd never seen before. But there was never any doubt, in these dreams, that it was always the same man underneath.

This man wants to kill him but not right away. He wants to destroy him first. See him lose everything. Every friend he ever had. Every dollar. Get evicted. Slink out of town with his tail between his legs and find a bridge to sleep under. That's when this man will come walking up and start smashing him with a bat. With Michael helpless, bleeding, but still conscious, the man will drag him to a grave and throw him in it. That's when he'll show his real face. He'll tell Fallon why as he's pouring gasoline over him. Then he'll strike the match.

> *"Listen to me, Michael. This isn't all that unusual."*
> *"What isn't?"*
> *"Feeling isolated. Feeling that no one wants to know you. Ask anyone who's ever lost a job."*
> *"This is different."*
> *"Of course it is. You've also lost two loved ones, both to violent deaths, and you've been extremely moody ever since. People are genuinely sympathetic but they just don't know what to say to you so they keep their distance."*
> *"What about being blackballed?"*
> *"That's probably nonsense."*
> *"They were ducking me, Dr. Greenberg. I didn't imagine it."*
> *"No, you didn't. But would you hire you? In your present state of mind?"*
> *"I was a top producer, Doc. These guys would hire Jack the Ripper for the kind of commissions I generated."*

Fallon and Dr. Greenberg agreed on at least one point. He, Michael T. Fallon, was getting seriously screwed up. What ultimately made him decide to bail out, however, that final straw, was something else. The police were looking for him after all.

On the evening of the day before he ran, he had walked to his local dry cleaner. The shop was on Columbus Avenue, three blocks south of his apartment and some eight blocks north of where the encounter with the muggers took place. The owner's name was Stanley and he was sort of a friend. For the past two summers, Michael had played softball with him in Central Park. Stanley brought out his shirts and took him aside. He asked if Michael, by chance, "had anything to do with carving up two jigs a couple of weeks back."

"Me? Why are you asking me?"

A grimace, a raised hand. The gesture said don't waste your breath. Two detectives, he said, have been around asking if anyone knows a well-dressed white male, middle thirties, about six-one, who, at the time, had his right arm in a cast. The dry cleaner hooked a thumb at the four inches of plaster sticking out of Michael's sleeve.

"The story," said Stanley, "is that this white guy, armed to the teeth, suddenly attacks these two jigs. Or maybe one's a semi-jig. Anyway, this guy goes after them, a knife in one hand, this chrome-plated cannon in the other. For a change, the jigs had nothing. White guy cut and pistol-whipped the first one, turned the second one's knee into rubber and then smashed his face in with the gun butt. Next he grabbed the first one's leg and made a wish.

"Basketball's loss," Stanley added.

"This white guy," the dry cleaner went on, "was about to finish it, blow them both away, but some woman screamed and he took off. Cops got there. Two ambulances. Cops said it was drug-related, which they always do, which in this town it almost always is. They figured that's two less of them on the street and they wouldn't have made a big deal. But the mayor's office got wind that they never found any drugs or weapons on those two, said it must have been a racial thing and made a stink. Fucking liberals. Guy should get a medal. For the time being, however, the heat's on to find him so he should probably make himself scarce."

Fallon took his shirts and left.

So much for eyewitnesses, he grumbled, walking home. He could understand, he supposed, why they thought the gun was his. He was the only one seen with it and those two would hardly admit that he'd taken it from one of them. But he had never actually touched the knife. It would have the bald one's fingerprints on it. But they must not have found it. Maybe it was still under that car the next morning. Maybe someone else found it and kept it. All the bald one saw of it, he would have said, was when that crazy white man reached out and cut him with it.

Would the cops have bought all this? White assailant has a weapon in each hand and still manages to toss these two around? When one of those hands is injured? Has a knife but doesn't stick anyone with it? Has a gun but only uses it as a hammer? Fallon didn't think so. But his temples were pounding all the same.

In his mind, he saw the police appearing at his door, pushing their way in, going straight to his freezer. He saw himself in handcuffs. Mobs of reporters in a feeding frenzy. *Stalked by tragedy, Fallon nephew snaps . . . Turns vigilante . . . Next on "Current Affair."* He saw the Reverend Al Sharpton leading a march to his apartment house. He saw two bedridden thugs, their legs in traction, pointing fingers at him. And then telling their friends where he lives.

He reached 82nd at Columbus and started across. A car turned the corner, no headlights, tires squealing. It barely missed him. The driver lowered his head and kept going. It's nothing, he told himself. Happens every day. But by the time he reached his building, he was looking over his shoulder. He saw that, behind him, a man had rounded the corner and then stopped. Ahead, in a car double-parked at the curb, he saw the glow of a cigarette. Even the doorman was looking at him strangely.

He walked through the lobby to the elevator. The doors opened as he approached. A man stepped out, Fallon didn't know him, he didn't live in this building, but Fallon thought he saw a flash of recognition in his eyes. The man looked away and hurried on.

Fallon stepped into the elevator, then hesitated. An elevator was a perfect trap. They could be waiting as it opened. He took the stairs instead. Reaching his floor, he found no one on the landing, no one in the corridor, but it struck him that they might already be inside.

Michael . . . don't do this to yourself.

He knew that he was as near to mindless panic as he had ever been. He forced himself to stop, take a minute to settle down. He found his keys, worked one lock, then the other. He pushed the door open and, on a sudden impulse, threw his shirts into the middle of the room.

No one shot at them. No one leaped on them thinking they were him. He felt his color rising. Embarrassment more than fear. He shut the door quickly and walked through to his kitchen. He opened the freezer. The Colt was still there in its Weight Watchers box. He pulled it out. The cold steel stuck to his fingertips. He dropped it and it fell to the floor. He used a dish towel to pick it up, then stepped to a window to see if that double-parked car was still there. It was. He rushed back to bolt his door.

He sat, watching the door, the heavy Colt across his lap. If the police did come, they would knock. They would show identification. But if anyone else came . . . if they tried to force the door or pick the lock . . . he would . . .

"Michael . . . make a long story short."
"I fell asleep. The next morning, I ran."

His telephone woke him that morning. He answered and heard a click. That click pushed him over the edge. He would get far away from this city. He would go to Cape Cod. He tapped out the number of a hotel that he knew in Hyannis and booked a room for an indefinite stay.

Twenty minutes after that he was gunning his car up the ramp of his parking garage. A car with two men still sat at the curb. Fallon blew past it. He lost it in traffic on Central Park West.

He would need cash. He doubled back to Columbus Avenue, where he waited for his bank to open. Two hours later he was stopping for gas on Connecticut's I-95. He used a credit card to call Brendan Doyle. Doyle was out. He left a message telling Doyle where he was going.

It dawned on him then that making those calls had been stupid. His home phone might well have been tapped. But even if no one was listening when he called that Hyannis hotel, he had guaranteed the room on his gold card. All someone had to do was punch up his credit history and, presto, there he is. Michael T. Fallon, Member since 1985. Booked a room in Hyannis, stopped for gas at a rest stop near New Haven, made a credit card call to his lawyer.

Add to that, the garage attendant had seen him come down with a suitcase. The doorman had seen him just miss a delivery truck as his car shot out of the garage. Garage attendants and doormen. Slip them twenty bucks, they'll tell you anything you want to know.

And then there's his bank. The cashier had stared at him, saw the way he kept looking over his shoulder as he cleaned out two accounts. More than twenty thousand dollars. Much of it in cash.

They would know he was running.

If he went to Hyannis, they would have him by morning.

"Michael . . . you do know how this sounds, don't you?"
"It gets worse."
"Who would have found you? Who are 'they'?"
"I'm not sure."
"But you're convinced that they mean to kill you."
"Doc . . . they tried twice."
"If that's so, why didn't you go to the police?"
"You're not listening again. The police are after me, too."

It had started to snow as he reached Rhode Island. The snow became heavy as he crossed the Massachusetts line. By this time he was totally paranoid.

A van, two men in it, had been on his tail for at least twenty miles. He couldn't see their faces through the snow. Abruptly, he veered up an off ramp. The van followed. All he could think was that *they* had called ahead. The men in the van were hired killers.

The road sign said Route 24. Fallon followed it south. He stepped on the gas, the van stayed with him. Then, on a straight stretch of road, no other cars near, it tried to pull out abreast of him. He jerked his wheel left, blocking it, as he groped for the big Colt Python that he'd hidden under his seat. He had trouble gripping it. His right arm had been broken at the wrist, and the plaster cast, although crushed and crumbling, left only his fingers free. He glanced back at the van through his mirror. The man in the passenger seat had rolled down his window. He was leaning out.

Fallon found the heavy revolver, managed to cock it, then lowered his own window. He eased his car to the right and waited. Let them try. This time he was ready.

But a shout of "Asshole!" was all he heard.

The van sped on.

Fallon pulled off the road and sat until his heartbeat slowed and his cheeks were no longer burning. If that man had reached his hand out, if only to flip a finger, Fallon might have fired before he saw that the hand held no weapon. But his mind, at least, had started working again.

The signs said this new road led to Falmouth. He would go there, find a motel, give himself time to think. But approaching

Falmouth, other signs said that eight miles farther, off to the right, was the town of Woods Hole and the ferry to Martha's Vineyard. The ferry ran year-round. He followed those signs.

Martha's Vineyard would be better. Much better.

For one thing, it was an island. So was Iwo Jima but the idea of a place surrounded by water seemed comforting all the same.

For another, he had never been to Martha's Vineyard so they'd have no reason to look for him there. In fact, when he fails to show up in Hyannis, they'll think that booking that room, even making that gas purchase, was a calculated ruse. They'll never imagine that his true destination would be so close to the one he faked. They'll think he's long gone in some other direction. Not in Massachusetts, not even in New England. More likely, they'll guess that he went south. Moon had gone south. They'll think he went down to find Moon.

At Woods Hole, the ferry was just coming in. Only three cars were waiting for it. Fallon bought a ticket and followed them on board.

The sun had begun to set as the Woods Hole ferry docked at Vineyard Haven. Michael drove up the ramp and pulled over to a kiosk marked *Information*. He wanted to ask about hotels but it struck him that he couldn't stay here either. He knew that, in his state of mind, he would be down here at the landing every day watching for cars with New York plates. He looked at a wall map of the island, got back in his car, and followed the signs to Edgartown on the far side of the island.

He recognized the waterfront area. It was a picture postcard setting that he had seen before in photographs but the rest of the town was unfamiliar to him. A pleasant-looking woman was towing groceries on a sled. He stopped to ask her what hotels were open. Her smile faded when she saw his eyes but she also noted the small Mercedes he was driving and decided that he was probably too rich to be dangerously deranged. With the car in mind, she pointed him toward the Harborview Hotel, a luxury Victorian on the west end of town.

The desk clerk had looked at him curiously as well. Fallon couldn't blame them. A man, middle thirties, turns up alone in the dead of winter. Clothing rumpled but expensive. He hadn't shaved or showered. A filthy cast poking out of his right sleeve. It left crumbs of white plaster all over the front desk. But it could have been worse. The big Colt Python had tumbled from his lap as he climbed out of the car. Luckily, no one had seen it.

Even so, there would be talk. He knew that he shouldn't stay too long.

"But you did."

"Not there. After the first week I rented a house. From that same lady."

"The one with the groceries?"

"It turned out she's a real estate agent. Her name's Millie Jacobs."

"What . . . it said so on her sled?"

"She dropped by the Harborview. I think she smelled money."

"Michael . . . isn't there someone you should call? Someone who'll be worried?"

"I did. I called Doyle."

"But that's when you were headed for Hyannis. He'll know you never got there."

"I'll call him. But not just yet."

"You don't trust him either?"

"I . . . trust him."

"You hesitated just then. Why?"

"I don't know."

He did trust Mr. Doyle. He'd been the Fallon family lawyer for almost forty years but, more than that, he was a friend. More than that, Brendan Doyle was his godfather. He'd been to his christening, his first communion, and, after his father died, he had arranged Michael's adoption by his Uncle Jake. Like Moon, he was practically family.

It was only that . . . the last time they spoke . . . he thought he saw something in the lawyer's eyes. Something he was holding back.

But Fallon shook that thought away. He had to stop this. This grasping at shadows. There was no way in the world that Brendan Doyle had turned against him.

The message he left said he needed some time to himself. Later, in a week or so, maybe longer, he would call, tell Mr. Doyle where he is and maybe where he's going next. Who knows where. All he knew was that he was never going back to New York City. New York would kill him if he did.

"Now it's New York again."

"Doc . . ."

"First it's New York. Then it's a 'them.' And now it's New York again."

"That city, Dr. Greenberg, killed everyone I ever cared about. Except Moon and my mother. And I'm not even sure about them."

"And except this lawyer?"

"Yes . . . And except Brendan Doyle."

7

The doctor's full name was Sheldon L. Greenberg. His doctorate was in psychology. Fallon found him easy to talk to because he wasn't real.

Actually, he *was* real. He just wasn't in Martha's Vineyard.

He was in a book that Michael found.

During his first lonely weeks on the island, he had hardly spoken ten words to any of the locals except Millie, the real estate lady, and the bartender at the Harborview Hotel. To forestall speculation and to explain his black moods, he concocted a story about a fiancee who had broken their engagement when her former boyfriend drifted back into town. He said he got angry, punched a wall like a jerk, ended up fracturing his wrist. Damned cast itches. Poked holes in it so he could scratch it with a wire coat hanger and now it's falling apart.

It seemed a serviceable, leave-the-poor-guy-alone kind of story. He said he wasn't sure how long he'd stay. Long enough to get her out of his system. He felt no rush, he told them, to get back to work. No real need either. In ten years on Wall Street he'd done fairly well.

Millie Jacobs's eyes brightened at the mention of ready cash. She reached for her book of pricey listings. She also mentioned that she had a niece on Nantucket, bright girl, honors grad from

Radcliffe who plays a good game of tennis and writes wonderful poetry. Fallon told her that the niece and the listings would have to wait. He wasn't ready. But he did agree to rent a small house from her. His hotel room had begun to close in on him and it was only a matter of time before a chambermaid found that pistol.

But he still spent most of his evenings at the Harborview bar because Kevin, the bartender, had moods that were even darker than his own. He was a dour, defeated-looking man of about fifty who had taken this job to wait out a recession. But for him, that recession never ended. He had been a systems analyst with IBM until his dreams of a comfortable retirement went up in smoke.

Kevin also knew, firsthand, what faithless bitches women are. His wife, a dental hygienist, had served him with divorce papers on the very day his severance had run out and a week after the bank had repossessed their condo. Kevin hated bankers and divorce lawyers just as much as he hated women. And he hated fat-cat senior executives who tell you one month not to leave, your job is safe, and then dump you when they've found some kid who'll do your job for half your salary.

It struck Fallon that the next wave of serial killers might well come from the ranks of the white-collar unemployed. Kevin's view of the world was so bitter, his future so bleak, that Fallon found himself starting to count his own considerable blessings. Perhaps the healing process had started after all. That aside, Kevin's primary appeal was that he poured the only decent drink in Edgartown.

Every other bar and restaurant measured a precise ounce and a half of scotch because that was state law. The same law forbade bartenders to serve doubles. Kevin paid no attention. His idea of measuring was to pour until all the ice floated. He didn't like politicians either.

On slow nights, as most of them were, Kevin would retreat to the far end of the bar reading books that had wistfully pathetic titles such as *Starting Over* and *Jobs on Cruise Ships*. But the books started Michael thinking. It was time to consider his options. Where to go from here. A book might have some ideas.

*   *   *

He spent an hour in the Edgartown bookstore at the shelf marked *Self-Help*. Several of the titles dealt with being fired and how to land back on one's feet. All of them had keep-your-chin-up sections aimed at people in their fifties whose jobs had been their identity and who were scared to death that they might never find another. None of these had much relevance to his situation.

For one thing, they hadn't been blackballed. No one had set out to destroy their careers. No one had tried to kill them.

And Fallon was, after all, in good shape financially. His investment portfolio was worth almost half a million. Doyle had been managing it for him. And he would inherit a lot more from Jake. There was Jake's house in Brooklyn, a condo in Florida, and all that sports memorabilia, much of it pretty rare. Even after splitting it with Moon, and after taxes, Jake would leave him at least another million or so.

But that was later, this was now. He still needed someone to talk to. That someone became Sheldon Greenberg. Fallon found his book on the bottom shelf.

Greenberg's book was about big-time stress. Severe emotional trauma. There were chapters devoted to people who've been mugged, burglarized, stalked, and shot at. Most of which fit. There was even a section on people who had lost a loved one to violent crime.

Fallon read the book in one day. It said, basically, that he was suffering from post-traumatic stress disorder. Well, no shit. He almost tossed it away because Dr. Greenberg promptly began nagging him about getting off his ass and getting treatment. And about boozing with Kevin every night.

"For one thing, you're turning into a drunk. For another, Kevin hates you."

"He hates me? For what?"

"For having money. For still being young. Face it, Michael. You're not going to get much sympathy."

Fallon realized that this was a little nuts. Talking to a book. Having the book talk back. But people talk to God and dead saints. Why not to a psychologist who isn't nearly as far away?

Anyway, the book seemed to help him. The book and the passage of time. By the end of his first month on Martha's Vineyard, so different, so quiet, New York seemed a continent away. He had almost convinced himself that maybe he'd been running from shadows. Someone is *always* double-parked on 82nd Street. There were *always* strangers in the building.

Those detectives, however, were real. They were reason enough to get out of town until the city gives them something more pressing to think about.

What helped as much as the passage of time was finally being rid of that cast. One evening when he could bear it no longer he pried it apart with his fingers and burned the pieces in his fireplace. The skin underneath was deathly white and had the smell of sewage. Dried blood, not his own, caked the back of his hand. He scrubbed it raw. The muscles had atrophied and he could barely flex the wrist without pain but the arm felt as cool and as light as air. He almost felt reborn.

If that felt so good, he asked himself, why stop with the cast? The next thing he burned was his suit.

He spent a day buying all new clothing. He bought what the islanders wore. Woolrich shirts, crew neck sweaters, Timberland boots and boat shoes. He began running again, working out, drinking less, eating balanced meals. Day by day, the wrist regained its strength. He bought a bicycle and began exploring the island on it. He bought several books about its history, its geology, its architecture. He read about the great whaling ships, the looting of the island by the British, and the pirate ships that had once prowled these waters. The islanders hanged a few pirates. The British hanged a few islanders. After that, however, things settled down nicely. Derring-do gave way to farming and then to marking up prices for tourists. High crime, these days, was clamming without a license.

But it was, no question, a beautiful place. Edgartown in particular. Many fine old homes and gardens, brick walks, delicate wrought-iron fences. His book on architecture said there were three principal styles: Federal, Greek Revival, and Early Victorian. He learned to recognize and appreciate the subtleties of each. It seemed a gentle thing to know.

New York, by mid-March, seemed as far away as Pluto.

*   *   *

The pain of losing Bronwyn had begun to ease a bit. No day went by without some thought of her, but her face, in his mind, had begun to blur. That seemed somehow indecent but he had known her, after all, for less than three months. They had had no time to store up memories and there were no snapshots of happy times to torment him. The one photograph he had of her had been stolen for its frame. It was just as well. He needed to let her go.

Jake would take longer. In his case there were too many memories. But day by day, a few of them were starting to bring smiles. What he began to feel worse about was Moon. He missed him and was worried about him, and yet here he'd allowed six weeks to go by without even asking whether he was still alive. People do have multiple strokes. As much as he dreaded it, he would have to call Doyle.

But he kept putting it off. A dozen times he'd picked up the phone and begun to dial. It was disgraceful of him not to call, to let Doyle worry and wonder. He realized that. It's just that it was so peaceful here.

He considered taking the ferry back to the mainland, driving up to Boston, and making the call from there. He would not have to say where he's been living all this time. While there, he could rent a post office box so that Doyle could send him his mail. He could open a bank account so that Doyle could send his money to Boston as well. When he needs it, he'll drive up and get it. All Doyle had to know is that he's safe. He doesn't have to know where.

"Michael . . . call him."

"Stay out of this one, Doc."

"Tell me that this man is your enemy. If you can't, there is no decent way of refusing to give him your address."

"I didn't say he's my enemy. All I said . . ."

"Call him, Michael. This minute."

Fallon gritted his teeth. He punched out the lawyer's home number. Doyle was shocked into silence at the sound of his voice. But only for a moment.

A whispered "Where the hell are you?" asked and answered, was followed by a blowtorch of personal abuse. Boiling Doyle. Michael had been a thoughtless, irresponsible, self-pitying son of a bitch. A full minute went by before the lawyer ran out of the more profane modifiers for "son of a bitch" and "little shit." Sheila Doyle, Fallon assumed, must be out for the evening.

"Mr. Doyle . . . I almost got killed."

"What you *got* was a broken wrist. You fell apart over *that?* That's how Jake and Moon raised you?"

"Have you heard from Moon?"

"You just get your sorry ass back here."

"I'm not coming back. Now calm down and hear me out."

Michael told him about the muggers, one with a gun, the other with a knife, and why he wanted no part of the police. He mentioned the car that had almost run him down. He agreed that it might have been nothing, but it was one near-miss too many. He told of getting to the point where he thought his phone had been bugged and people were watching him. Following him.

Silence on the other end.

"Mr. Doyle?"

"Give me a minute."

Another long silence. He had a sense that the lawyer was pacing.

"Mike . . . you still should have called," he said at last. "I could have handled the cops for you."

"Mr. Doyle, where's Moon?"

"I don't know. Moving around. He sent me one letter but no return address. He doesn't even know you've been missing."

"Where was it postmarked?"

"Miami. But it said he's just passing through. If you're thinking Jake's condo, I already checked."

"Did he say when he'll be back?"

"He says one of these days. Michael . . ."

"Have you been picking up my mail? Maybe he wrote to me too."

"I have and he hasn't. I've paid all your bills, incidentally."

Fallon had assumed as much.

"You can give up the apartment. I won't be needing it."

"Michael . . . does anyone else know where you are?"

"No."

"Have you used any credit cards, made any long distance calls?"

"Only this one."

"Let's keep it that way for a while. I'll see if the police are still looking."

"Mr. Doyle . . . have you been straight with me?"

"About what?"

"Anything. Everything."

"You can ask me that? Jake Fallon was my best friend in the world and I'm your fucking godfather."

"Yeah. Look . . . forget it."

"Forget it, my ass. Say what's on your mind."

"Nothing. It's just . . . it's been a rough few months."

There was more to the conversation. Much of it had to do with going easy on the booze, not calling attention to himself, walking away from arguments. All things considered, said the lawyer, maybe getting away from New York was for the best.

"But you're still a little shit. Sheila lost ten pounds worrying."

"Mr. Doyle . . . these things that have happened since I got fired, could Hobbs be behind them?"

"The guy's a worm, Michael. Worms call their lawyers, they don't send hitters."

What it was, he said, was that Michael was right the first time. It's just the city. If his mind had not been on Jake, on Bronwyn, on getting canned in such a crummy way, he would have done a better job of avoiding stumbling drunks and ducking muggers.

What eased Fallon's mind the most, and made him glad that he'd finally placed the call, was when Doyle had already said goodbye but added this:

"Michael, listen," said the lawyer quietly. "If there's anything I haven't told you, anything I'm holding back, this would be the reason. It's just none of your goddamned business."

"It's about Uncle Jake?"

"He had a life of his own, Michael."

What made that reassuring, Fallon supposed, was that the lawyer didn't have to say anything at all. He was afraid, however, that he knew what it was. Big Jake Fallon made *deals* with people. Big Jake Fallon *fixed* things. Somewhere along the line, one of these deals had involved either the financial community or the pharmaceutical industry or both. He could think of no other reason that first Jake, and then Moon, and then Brendan Doyle had been so negative about his entering a field that combined the two. Maybe they thought he might hear something, stumble across something. And it's probably why Doyle would have liked to see him drop that suit against Lehman-Stone.

Well . . . to hell with it anyway.

To press it, he would have to go back to New York. It just didn't seem that important anymore.

8

For several long minutes, Brendan Doyle stared at the telephone.

His fingers drummed slowly against the surface of the desk. His expression was one of sorrow. Of regret. But as the rhythm of his drumbeat quickened, as fingertips gave way to knuckles, his expression changed as well. Regret had given way to anger.

He reached for the phone once more, but hesitated when he heard voices from the floor below. His front door had opened and closed. Sheila had come home. The other voice was that of Clara, their housekeeper.

Doyle reached under his desk for a black leather briefcase and, walking softly, carried it from the room. He climbed two carpeted flights and then a steel spiral staircase leading to his roof. He walked to the edge, set the briefcase down, and opened it. It contained a cellular phone.

The Doyle town house was on Pierrepont Street in Brooklyn Heights. Jake Fallon's home, now jointly owned by Moon and Michael, was three doors down and across the street. Doyle couldn't look at it. He kept his face averted but he could not keep his mind from seeing it.

"Ah, Jake," he whispered. "Damn you for your soft heart. You should have finished this twenty-five years ago."

He picked up the handset of the cellular phone. It was a Priva-Fone, virtually untappable, nor could it be picked up by a scanner. He dialed a number. A male voice answered.

"Marty, it's Brendan Doyle."

Marty was Captain Martin Hennessy, Detectives, Manhattan South. Doyle had reached him at his home in Bay Ridge, Brooklyn.

"I need to know about a felonious assault that happened in January." He recited the details as he knew them. "In particular, I want the names and addresses of the victims and all that is known of their assailant."

He listened. Then, "No. No, this has no connection with whomever killed Jake. First thing in the morning, Marty? . . . Thank you . . . What? . . . No . . . Still no word from Michael."

Doyle grimaced as he broke the connection. It had probably occurred to Hennessy that Michael's apartment is only a few blocks from the scene of the assault. But Marty would keep that to himself. Marty and Jake go back a lot of years.

He punched out a second number. It had several more digits than the first. A softer male voice answered.

"Moon? It's Brendan. Michael is alive and well."

On the other end, a hissing sound. It was like a balloon deflating.

"Where?" Moon asked him.

The lawyer told him. He recounted, in broad strokes, the incident that put Michael in fear of arrest if not of his life. Doyle told him of his call to Captain Hennessy. He said he should know more in the morning.

"Martha's Vineyard. That's up off Cape Cod?"

"Moon . . . just leave him. Let's keep him out of this."

"How much does he know?"

"Almost nothing."

"I didn't raise him stupid, Mr. Doyle."

"And he isn't. But for the moment, at least, he blames the city for Jake and the girl."

"So did I. Until I started remembering."

"Hey . . . we're still not sure. Go slow, okay?"

"We *been* goin' slow. Five months now."

"You're still healing, Moon. Give it time."

"It's Rasmussen, Mr. Doyle. I can close my eyes and see him doing it. It's Armin Rasmussen killed Jake."

"Moon . . . he'd be seventy-five years old now. We don't even know he's still alive."

"He's alive. And old men swing bats. Come down here to Florida and you'll see. They don't run the bases so good and they can't chase down flies. But they can damned well swing a bat."

"Well . . . let's see what we find out from Hennessy."

"Mr. Doyle?"

"It's Brendan, for Christ's sake."

"I'll call you Brendan when I feel more friendly toward you. You were supposed to look after Michael or I wouldn't have left."

"If you stayed, and you're right about Rasmussen, you'd be just as dead as Jake."

Moon said nothing for a long moment. "Mr. Doyle?"

Jesus.

"Yes, *Mister* Moon."

"You won't ever tell Michael, will you?"

"Like you said, he's not stupid. He'll have to know some of it."

"About his mother, I mean."

"I'd cut my tongue out first."

The lawyer had one more call to make. He hit a memory code for the number of Villardi's Seafood Palace on Ocean Parkway, Brooklyn. The restaurant was owned by the Giordano brothers. He left a message for them. Brendan Doyle, it said, has some interesting news. Kindly join him for lunch there tomorrow.

One floor down, Sheila was calling his name. He replaced the handset and closed his briefcase. He would not tell his wife that Michael is safe. Let her worry awhile longer. If she drops a few more pounds, she might even thank him for it.

Doyle, like Moon, had thought of Rasmussen the instant he was told that a bat had been the murder weapon. Like Moon, he had imagined that fat Kraut bastard standing over Jake. Bat in hand. Just as Jake had stood over him on that night twenty-five years ago. When Jake called him to account for what he'd done to Michael's parents.

But Jake, in the end, let him live. Rasmussen, ruined, broke and bleeding, had fled back to Germany. And then he simply vanished. During the five months since Jake was murdered, Doyle had skip-tracers here and in Europe trying to pick up his trail. So far they'd found nothing.

On a rational level, Doyle had trouble believing that Rasmussen had a hand in this if only because so much time had gone by. Who would wait that long for revenge? And, more to the point, why then go after Michael . . . if indeed that subway thing and the mugger had been deliberate attempts on his life?

Still, he did wish that Jake had finished it back then. If he had, they would all be able to believe that Michael is right. That it's just the city. Accept it, lick your wounds, and get on with your life.

But Moon won't accept it. And now Moon blames him for this latest attack on Michael.

Doyle could have told him, he supposed, that he had people tailing Michael ever since that subway thing. But they'd managed to lose him on several occasions. The evening when he walked home from that movie, got jumped by those two muggers, was obviously one of those times.

Moon would have asked, "What people? Who'd you put on him?"

He would have answered, "I asked Julie Giordano to lend me some of his." Plus the guy who sweeps Julie's house for bugs. Doyle had him put a wire on Michael's phone just to see how much Michael *did* know. And he paid Michael's doorman to keep tabs on him and to change the tapes twice each shift. He would not tell Moon about that part because Moon wouldn't like the idea of bugging Michael. He would not be much happier about the tail.

Moon would have said, "You used Giordano's people? Those are leg-breakers, *Mister* Doyle. A leg-breaker and a bodyguard are not the same thing."

Well . . . we live and learn.

Not only did they lose Michael that night, they lost him on the morning when he split for Hyannis. In fact, to hear Michael tell it, seeing Julie Giordano's goons down in the street and even strolling through his fucking lobby was one of the things that made him run for his life.

So now, thought Doyle, he understands the difference.

A goon is a goon and a shadow is a shadow. But for some things, you still need goons. With luck, by lunchtime tomorrow, he would have another job for the Giordano brothers.

9

Three more weeks had passed on Martha's Vineyard.

March had rolled into April, Easter had come and gone. The whole island was a soft green. A mild winter with a lot of rain had caused the flowers of spring to come early. They came in a profusion unlike any that Fallon had ever seen. Showy white flowers, called shadbushes, bloomed in great cascades on every street, along every road. There were tulips and jonquils that had been forced in greenhouses and other wild flowers called beach plums. There were chirping little pond birds called pinkletinks. Michael liked the sound they made almost as much as the name.

The whole of Edgartown smelled of paint and sounded with the banging of hammers. It seemed that all at once, every house in town was getting a clean, fresh coat after a winter of wind-driven salt. Every boat was being scraped and caulked. Fallon felt reborn.

He was no longer lonely because, aside from Brendan Doyle calling once or twice each week, more of the locals were seeking him out.

Even Doyle had lightened up. Moon still hadn't called but Doyle thought he understood why. All it was, he suggested, was that Moon had too much pride to let anyone see him while he was less than a hundred percent. He didn't want people, even family, offering him chairs and watching his hand shake while he eats. That, Michael agreed, did sound like Moon.

Doyle had also determined, through discreet inquiry, that the New York police were no longer interested in finding him. No warrant, no nothing. They had been unable to match a name to his description and had gone on to other matters. The racial issue, advanced by city hall, had been mere political rhetoric that had barely survived the press conference. Al Sharpton won't be marching on Edgartown either.

What made him more attractive to the locals was that he told Millie, the real estate lady, that he was ready to look at those houses and maybe some local businesses. A restaurant, perhaps. A hardware store. Maybe he'd breed and raise pinkletinks.

Steady, Michael.

But he had definitely decided to settle here. Live in Edgartown year-round. Great place to raise a family someday. The trick was to find something that would keep him occupied for more than just the summer.

She asked him for a price range. He said that price would be no problem.

Millie Jacobs was married to Dr. Emil Jacobs who was the first-string local dentist. Fallon learned, in short order, that the only gossip mill that is more efficient than a real estate office or a dentist's office is a combination of the two. Within days, everyone in Edgartown knew that Michael had recovered from his broken heart, had a pot of money in the bank, was a serious buyer, and was definitely on the lookout for a wholesome, sincere, Martha's Vineyard sort of woman.

Kevin, the bartender, confided that Millie's Nantucket niece was a bowser. His own niece, however, had won a Miss Lobsterfest pageant; came with a ready-made family, two cute little girls from the prick she divorced; and was still a size seven. The grocer had a piece of land that had a water view. Millie said forget it. It's where the gallows used to stand and it's nowhere near the sewer. The barber had a jeep for sale. Four-wheel drive. Can't live on this island without one, he said.

"That Kraut car of yours is nice for saying I got mine, but it ain't worth a damn after a half-inch of snow. Anyway, out here we buy American.''

''Michael . . .''
''Wait a second.''

That was another thing. He was feeling less of a need for his telepathic therapy sessions with Dr. Sheldon Greenberg. The price was right—hours of them for the cost of one book—but as long as it was all in his head, he would just as soon talk to Uncle Jake. Besides, the Greenberg thing showed signs of getting strange. The other day he asked Greenberg what he thought of the idea. Buying property here. Settling here. Greenberg answered that he was *''on the fifteenth hole at Sea Pines, two strokes down, playing a ten-dollar Nassau. Don't bother me now.''*

Fallon took that to mean he was getting better.

He also learned something about real estate people. Other, that is, than that telling one a secret is cheaper than placing an ad. He learned that the minute you suggest that you're ready to buy, and they think they have your price range, *guaranteed,* a house will come on the market at an unbelievable steal of a price. But you must act now. Wait a day and it's gone.

One such house did appear. Millie called it a miracle. The hand of God and the luck of the Irish combined.

''This isn't just a house,'' she said in hushed tones. ''This is the *Taylor* House.''

''Michael . . . think long and hard.''
''Are you kidding? It's gorgeous.''
''It's an inn, Michael. You're not an innkeeper.''
''All the help said they'd stay. The place even makes money. Millie says it's been fully booked for years.''
''All the same . . .''
''And people who come to inns are nicer, by and large, than people who go to hotels. They'll cut me some slack while I'm learning.''
''Quoth Millie Jacobs?''
''Doc . . . you never did anything crazy?''
''Sure. But I was sane at the time.''

"Now you're being a shit."
"Good luck, Michael."

The Taylor House wasn't just any inn, either. Fallon, on his walks, had stopped to admire it many times. Especially at night. He would stand and look in the windows at the carved woodwork and the antique furnishings inside. You could do that in Edgartown without someone calling the cops.

The Taylor House stood high on North Water Street looking out over the harbor. An absolutely prime location. The architecture was Federal style, solid and square but softened by a graceful baluster along the roof, arched fanlights, and a columned portico entrance that had its own little balcony on top. It was three stories tall, painted white with black shutters, and it had a widow's walk on the roof. There was a small formal garden in front and a larger one in back. The front garden was all boxwoods and clipped yews, enclosed behind a delicate white fence at the edge of a red brick sidewalk.

Captain Isaac Taylor was a nineteenth-century whaling ship captain who, having made his fortune, decided nothing was too good for him. He brought carpenters and shipwrights all the way from Boston, had wallpaper shipped from France, fabrics from Italy, and furniture from England. Spend two or three years chasing whales, Fallon supposed, and you want something nice to come home to.

Built in 1829, the house became an inn shortly after the turn of the century. It had six large rooms that were strictly for guests, a dining room, and a library, plus two smaller rooms for seasonal help. All the rest of it was private. The master suite took up most of the third floor.

The wife of the present owner, one Polly Daggett, had been crippled in a hit-run accident during a visit to Boston. She would need long-term care and a hip replacement, said Millie Jacobs, which was why they had decided to sell.

Fallon placed a call to Brendan Doyle, who agreed with Sheldon Greenberg. It sounded nuts. But Fallon had already put a binder on the house, using most of his cash and travelers checks, and Doyle, in the end, relented. He would liquidate some of Michael's securities and advance whatever else was needed until the will was probated. He would transfer sufficient funds to the Main State Bank of Edgartown and would have the title search done through a Boston law firm.

"Michael . . . you're sure you want to do this?"

"You know who used to stay there? Jimmy Cagney."

"Um . . . relevance, Michael?"

He knew damned well what the relevance was. Brendan Doyle was a lifelong Cagney fan. Had his picture taken with Cagney once. It's hanging in his office. And Cagney did stay at the Taylor House before he bought a place of his own in Edgartown.

"You can have his room if you come up."

Silence.

"Sit on the very same toilet."

"Michael . . . why do I hear your heart thumping?"

"Because I'm psyched about this."

"And your voice is up an octave. I make note of these things, Michael, because this is the way you've sounded, all your life, when you've tried to put something over on your elders."

"Like what?"

"Have you told me everything?"

Look who's asking. "Scout's honor."

"You've left nothing out?"

"Come on up, Mr. Doyle. You've been in New York too long."

Fallon did leave one teensy thing out.

The place was supposed to be haunted.

10

Jimmy Cagney.

In Cagney's day, thought Doyle, gangsters knew how to get things done. If they needed answers they'd pull a snatch, hang the slob from a meat hook, and let him ripen for a day or two until he was ready to cooperate.

But Cagney, to be fair, didn't have to worry about wired phones, bugged restaurants, video cameras, and RICO statutes. Three weeks after getting that police report, after lunching with Johnny and Fat Julie Giordano and handing them a copy with the names, addresses, and even mug shots of the two black muggers who tried Michael, between them they still had zilch.

Well . . . zilch isn't fair either.

We now know some interesting facts. They are not, for starters, your ordinary street hoods. One of them isn't even black. The one with the dreadlocks is Jamaican but the one with the mustache who shaves his head is a Pakistani. Mohammed something or other.

The Jamaican is a parole violator who, even if he could talk through a jaw that still takes only liquids, is now back in custody. But wonder of wonders, whom did he list as his employer?

Parker Security Services, Inc.

And how many clients does Parker Security have? Only two

of any size. The firm of Lehman-Stone and the firm of Adler-Chemiker AG.

Knowing this is one thing. Getting at the Jamaican to ask a few questions is another. Fat Julie Giordano was somewhat more hopeful of getting at the Pakistani who is an illegal alien and is currently in the custody of the Immigration and Naturalization Service. Word is, however, that he is to be given a conditional release by this weekend because they're short of jail cells and because risk of flight is minimal. Michael did a good job on him. Word is he walks like a duck and still farts through his cheek when he talks.

Fat Julie's plan is to intercept him between Riker's Island and the welfare hotel where they got him a room. That done, Julie will ask him if he'd care to fill in a few gaps or is he ready to play make-a-wish again.

It had better work.

Moon is hard enough to keep down as it is. This one clear connection, tying those two muggers to Lehman-Stone, would be all he needs to hear. Short of pumping him full of Thorazine, there would be no stopping him.

Michael's pen had been poised over the binder agreement when Millie Jacobs said, "By the way . . ." These three words made him freeze.

According to Sheldon Greenberg's book, when people say, "By the way . . ." whatever follows is almost always the key issue at hand and, chances are, they're about to try to diddle you.

"Not that this would bother you, Michael . . . a worldly young man like yourself . . . educated . . . however . . . full disclosure and all that . . ."

Wouldn't bother you, my ass.

It was almost a deal-breaker. He had to take a long walk to think about it.

On the one hand, he didn't need this. He had enough ghosts of his own. On the other, it wasn't much of a haunting. No blood oozing up through the floorboards or anything like that. All it was, it seems that over the years quite a few guests have said they've heard the laughter of children coming from empty rooms.

"Hey, Dr. Greenberg?"
"I told you so, Michael."
"No, wait. This could even be good."

That, in fact, was Millie Jacobs's argument. For openers, she said, everyone who lives here has heard the story and no one gives it much thought. The truth is, any number of Martha's Vineyard houses are said to be haunted. Try to find a town in all of Massachusetts that doesn't have at least one ghost.

"Watch out for 'The truth is . . .' as well."
"Will you listen for once?"

Most of the guests who've stayed there, Millie went on, either didn't know, didn't care, or assumed that any children they might hear were those of other guests. But here's the good news. Quite a few have come *because* the place is thought to be haunted. The Taylor House is listed in *Haunted Houses of New England* and a number of other such books. Those listings, she said, are as good as a four-star rating in the Mobil Guide. If the sort of clientele they attract are a bit eccentric, she asked, what's wrong with that as long as they keep coming and tell their friends?
"And they're very quiet, of course."
"Quiet?"
"The better to listen."
Ask a silly question, thought Fallon.
"Are there any theories? Any legends about who these children are?"
"Several. But Polly Daggett invented them."
"Why several?"
"So her guests could have charm or horror depending on what turned them on."
"Polly, I take it, was not a believer."
"She knew a good thing when she saw it."

Fallon bought the place.
Or at least he signed the binder. The closing was three weeks off but he decided to move in. The Daggetts could not object as long as he paid the full off-season rate.

For the first time in months, he needed nothing to help him sleep. No Dalmane or Seconal washed down with a scotch. His stash was running low anyway. He decided that he would risk the return of the nightmares and the four-in-the-morning gremlins. If the place was going to spook him, let it be now while there was still time to back out.

He heard no laughing children.

His bed never levitated, he felt no sudden chills, nor did he wake from a sound sleep to see a beautiful young woman floating near the foot of his bed. But he had no nightmares either. Just a minor amount of tossing. Perhaps he no longer needed drugs to sleep. Or a Colt Python kept within reach. Still, after all the talk, he was a little disappointed.

On the third night, he had retired early. Something woke him near midnight. He wasn't sure what. He lay there, listening for a while. The only sounds were those of the oil burner kicking on and a faint low whistle that seemed to be in the wall that faced front. Fallon got out of bed, crossed to the wall, and put an ear up against it. He heard it clearly, more so near each of the windows. He smiled.

"Dummy," he murmured. "It's the shutters. Just the wind off the ocean blowing through the slats."

But he was awake now. He slipped into his robe and sat by the window, elbows on the sill, looking out over the harbor and at the dark mass of Chappaquiddick just beyond. It struck him that if any place on this island should be haunted, it would be Chappaquiddick. That Kennedy mess. The Kopechne girl who drowned. He wasn't here three days before he heard the absolute, guaranteed true story about what really happened that night. Everybody hears it. Same story. It seems that there was a second girl . . .

Movement on the sidewalk below caught Fallon's attention. He leaned closer to the pane and looked down. There was a man there. Just standing. He was dressed in a hooded black slicker and he seemed to be staring at the front entrance. His hands were raised to his temples as if to hide his face. Fallon felt a weight in his stomach. His mind, the rational part, said it was only another tourist admiring the house. But the darker part of his mind saw the faceless man of his nightmares. That man had found him.

Fallon backed away. He stepped to his night table and slid the Colt Python from the drawer. Fear was replaced by anger. This was his new life, goddamn it. He made his way to the staircase and started down. He moved slowly, pausing every several steps to listen. One of them, for all he knew, could already be in the house.

In his mind he saw those two from New York. The bald one, the taller of the two, could be the man outside. They're walking again. It's been three months. It's possible that they've healed by now.

But by the time he reached the front door and looked out through the side light, the man in the slicker was gone. He heard an odd grinding sound. It came from the street, just off to the right. Fallon fumbled for the latch and pulled the door open. He took a breath and ducked through. He followed the Python, held with both hands, and aimed it at the source of that noise. The man in the slicker was leaving. On a bicycle.

A bicycle?

He had climbed on, shifted to a lower speed, and started down the hill toward the center of town.

"That would be Parnel," said Millie Jacobs.

Fallon had stopped by her office, said yes to a cup of coffee, and was almost out of small talk when he blurted a reference to the man in the hooded black slicker.

"Parnel?"

"Tall and skinny? Rides a green twelve-speed with two wire baskets?"

Fallon remembered the baskets. Mounted over the rear wheel like saddlebags. He also remembered realizing, after his heart stopped pounding, that on the first day of assassin school they probably teach you not to take your bike on hits. He answered her question with a nod.

"Parnel Minter. He builds lobster traps mostly, but he's also a sensitive."

"Sensitive?" Fallon repeated stupidly.

"It's like a psychic. He gives readings during the tourist season.

Goes into a trance and leaves his body but he's back in five minutes with the keys to your success. Likes to tell that body leaving's how he met his wife. He was flying over Marblehead one day, felt her psychic energy, and swooped down for a look-see. Liked what he saw, came back to get his body, and drove back up to court her."

"Millie . . ."

"Wife reads Tarot cards when she's Madam Cassandra. When she's just Helen Minter, she stacks produce over at the A&P."

"Um . . . why would Parnel Minter have been . . ."

"Staring at the Taylor House? Hands up like this?" She mimicked his pose. "He's listening for the children."

Fallon blinked.

"A few days of that and you're bound to come ask him what he's up to. That's when he'll tell you who the ghosts are and offer to get rid of them. He tried that with Polly Daggett. She wasn't interested, even when he cut his price to fifty dollars but she let him paint her fence for that amount."

Fallon felt a headache coming on.

"Millie . . . am I going to get much more of this?"

"Oh, Parnel's harmless."

Yes, but a Colt Python isn't. Fallon winced at how close he'd come. If he had been a little more frightened, if his adrenaline had been pumping any harder . . .

"And he's not exactly a fake. I mean, Parnel does hear voices but my husband thinks they come through his dentures. The barometer falls enough, he can pick up NOAA Weather Radio."

Fallon closed his eyes. He rose to his feet.

"If you want the real thing," Millie said, leaning back, "you might try to see Megan."

"Megan?"

"She's close by. Lives over in Woods Hole."

"Thanks all the same."

"Of course, your happy little ghosts wouldn't interest Megan. She's big time. The Massachusetts State Police use her when they're stuck. One time she described a murderer for them. All she did was walk around some woods where two of the victims were found and she told them what he looked like, the house he lived in, the kind of car he drove, and even part of his name."

Fallon's skepticism showed on his face.

"It was in all the papers, Michael."

"What papers? The rags at the A&P checkout?"

Millie's eyes became cool. "If you're done with your coffee, Mr. Fallon . . ."

He spent the next five minutes apologizing.

No, he told her, he was not some smart-ass New York know-it-all who thinks all islanders are rubes and all realtors are talking heads. He had no doubt that much of that murder story was true—the papers, it turned out, were the *Boston Globe* and the *Providence Journal*—and that certain people do seem to have unusual gifts. His apology offered and accepted, it seemed only polite to show a modicum of interest in the subject that led to it.

Millie softened as well. She told him that she had never given much credence to ESP either, especially when its primary practitioners were Parnel and Cassandra. But if there *was* a genuine article, it would have to be Megan. For openers, the man she described had been totally unknown to the police. That means she could not have been influenced by some investigator who already had a suspect and hoped to panic him into confessing by getting a psychic to finger him.

"You'd never guess, to look at her," Millie added. "She's such a pretty little thing."

Fallon arched an eyebrow. "You know this woman?"

Millie shook her head. "Seen her on her boat, is all. She lives on it. Seen her handle it, all by herself, in weather a gull won't fly in."

She's pretty and she sails. Fallon was instantly intrigued. "Megan what?"

"Just Megan. They don't use last names."

"Show biz, right? Like Cher or Madonna?"

The realtor shook her head. "Makes it harder for the weirdos to find them."

This exchange had aroused Michael's interest because, until now, he had envisioned another Madam Cassandra. Probably fat, wearing a tasseled shawl, a turban, about two pounds of rings on her fingers, and at least one hairy mole on her lip. Certainly not pretty and not athletic. Nor gutsy enough to drive a good-sized boat through a gale.

"Where did you say this boat is?"

No, Michael. Don't even think about it.

He spent that day and the next trying to clear his head of the pictures Millie Jacobs had put there.

"A pretty little thing," she said. And a hot sailor. Out of that dim sketch, Fallon had begun to create a total image. There are no fat sailors. Pretty little Megan, therefore, would be about five-three, a hundred eighteen pounds. Living on a boat, she'd have a year-round tan. Her hair, bleached by the sun, would be a dirty blond and she'd wear it in a low-maintenance cut. A ponytail, most likely. Fastened with a simple rubber band. Megan would be about twenty-six years old. Her eyes would be . . . what? Dark and piercing? No . . . something softer. Her eyes are gray, the color of a winter sky.

He saw those gray eyes dancing as she drove her boat through a dangerous blow. It's gusting to fifty. She knows she's carrying too much sail. She ties off the wheel, then scrambles forward onto a pitching bow to set a storm jib and reef in the main. She moves like a cat. Keeps her whole body flexed and fluid. Now she's dancing back to the cockpit. Back at the wheel, jaw set, she's brave and purposeful, ignoring the salt spray that's stinging her face.

But those eyes. There's pain in them. A longing in them. She's thinking . . . if only the right man would come along. Someone to share this with. Someone like Michael Fallon. Even now, she sees him in her mind just as he sees her. She's picking up his psychic energy. But she has no idea that he's this close. And that he's coming to Woods Hole to meet her.

Yeah, right.

In your dreams, Michael.

More likely, she'd tell him to get lost. That was Millie's opinion as well.

Millie said that over the last two summers, several of the Taylor House regulars, all of whom had heard of her, had tried to arrange consultations with her. A couple of them offered some fairly big bucks for just a thirty-minute session. She had turned them all down. Nor would she talk to reporters, doctoral candidates doing theses, psychic researchers, or representatives of any federal agency.

"Feds? What would they want with her?"

"They probably never got a chance to say."

"Hmmph."

About the last person she would speak to, therefore, is a New York dropout whose inn makes funny noises. She was probably a pain in the ass anyway.

11

The Pakistani had been released on a Friday morning. A Department of Corrections van delivered him to the homeless shelter floors of the old Lenore Hotel in time for breakfast. He was last seen hobbling outside for a smoke. Two days later, it was the Giordano brothers' turn to ask Brendan Doyle to lunch.

Doyle arrived at Villardi's Seafood Palace to find them already seated. Fat Julie, imposing, immense but not actually fat, sat on the right. He was dressed in leather sneakers and warm-up suit of green velour because he played handball on Sunday mornings while Connie, his wife, and the children were in church.

People wonder, thought Doyle, how mobsters get their nicknames. Julie, who was nearing fifty, had been seriously overweight while in his early twenties due to two years of inactivity while recovering from an attempt on the life of his father, whom Julie had shielded with his body. Big Julie became Fat Julie.

Fat Julie, however, was a clear improvement over Queer Julie, which the kids his age called him before that. Not that he was queer either. The thing was, a movie came out, *Carousel*, starring Shirley Jones as Julie Jordan, and there was a song in it entitled "You're a Queer One, Julie Jordan."

Julie Jordan . . . Julie Giordano. Kids pick up on things like that.

His father finally put him to work on the docks so that he could turn that fat back into muscle. He was also to observe how longshoremen steal so that Rocco, his father, could more profitably organize their efforts and also build a loan-sharking operation for purposes of maintaining cash flow between major cargo heists.

Julie did lose the weight. He also felt called upon to resolve the occasional challenge to his father's authority. He did so with the aid of the stevedore's box hook that, for a time, he carried everywhere in the hope that people would get the message and start calling him Julie the Hook.

Rocco, his father, thought this was dumb. Julie the Hook was a very good name for an enforcer but a rotten name for a loan shark. Loan sharks don't *make* people borrow money from them and they're scary enough as it is. Why would anyone want to borrow money from a *Julie the Hook* when he could go a couple of blocks and get it from some guy named Willie or Ernie, for example, both of which are nice friendly names? "It's like," said old Rocco, "if they could get it from a bank, they wouldn't go to one named First Foreclosure Savings and Loan."

The name never caught on in any case. While certainly dangerous if provoked, he was, on the whole, simply too good-natured to sustain such a handle.

His brother, Johnny G., sat on the left. Johnny G. was ten years younger, closer to Michael in age and build, and, in fact, had been Michael's friend since high school. Johnny G. favored dark Italian suits and subtle neckties. He could have passed for an attorney. Between them was a nervous, dark-skinned man in a soiled windbreaker who kept his eyes on the table. For an instant, Doyle thought they had brought the Pakistani with them. But this one wasn't bald.

"Meet Mohammed Yahya," said the younger Giordano, rising to shake hands. "Born in Pakistan, runs a crane for us down the docks, deals pills on the side."

Fat Julie raised a finger as if to say, That last part will keep.

"Past couple of days," said the elder Giordano, "he's been our interpreter. We're all done with the other guy."

Doyle grimaced. This statement, if it meant what he thought

it meant, had just made him an accessory to murder. "You're sure this table's clean?" he asked.

"Place gets swept twice a week."

The lawyer was less than reassured. He looked up at the ceiling, which was decorated with fish nets and colored glass floats, any one of which could hide a surveillance camera.

"Trust me," Fat Julie said impatiently. "Except don't say nothing near the bar."

Doyle glanced in that direction. There were two bartenders working it, one in his twenties, the other about fifty. They wore red jackets.

"Don't gawk either." Fat Julie rapped the table to get Doyle's attention. "Kid on the left? He's wearing a wire."

Doyle sighed audibly. He brought his hand to that side of his mouth.

"The one you're 'done with,'" he said quietly, "what's his name, again?"

"Mohammed Mizda. Half of Pakistan is named Mohammed."

"Tell me that Mohammed Mizda is still among us."

Fat Julie understood. "You asked Hennessy for a sheet on the guy. You don't want him all of a sudden floating past Hennessy's window. Relax. He's on ice."

That phrase covered many possibilities. Doyle chose not to try to narrow them. He pulled up a chair and sat.

"We needed Yahya, here," said Fat Julie, "because the other guy knows about six words of English. One of them is heroin, by the way."

"I'm listening."

The younger Giordano produced a notebook. Fat Julie made a face that showed mild displeasure. He did not approve of writing things down but Johnny G. had gone on to college, graduated from Villanova with a degree in business, and knew the value of taking good notes. Some of them, Doyle saw, were in English. These were neat and bold. Johnny's writing. The others were scrawled in a different hand and in a language that Doyle presumed to be Pakistani.

"It's called Urdu." Fat Julie had followed his eyes. "Johnny knew that from crossword puzzles."

Fat Julie was proud of his educated brother.

Johnny G. cocked his head toward the notebook. "I'll tell you . . ." He took a breath. "This has been one hell of a learning experience." His expression said that he was only just beginning to believe some of it himself. "Mizda—the guy we interviewed?— started off as a smuggler."

"You're gonna love this," said Fat Julie.

"Guy's whole clan were smugglers. I mean, it's like a caste thing. You could go back a thousand years and you wouldn't find one who ever did anything else."

Fat Julie made a series of circles with his finger. The gesture said skip to fast-forward. Johnny G. made a face but complied.

"What they'd do lately," he said, "they'd bring this chemical out of India on the backs of camels. They'd haul drums of it over deserts, mountains—whatever they got there—to drug factories in Pakistan, Afghanistan, even all the way down to Myanmar."

"That used to be Burma," added Fat Julie helpfully.

"Um . . ." Doyle raised a hand. "Could we start at the top? Mizda and the Jamaican attacked Michael. Was that a hit or not?"

"Oh, yeah," Johnny G. answered as if that had been obvious.

"Who ordered it?"

"Guy named Parker. Runs that security service where both those guys work. All Parker told them was that Michael's a spy who could get them deported and they should make it look like a street crime. He said they had two, sometimes three teams out trying to catch Michael alone. They started using teams because they blew two chances already just sending one guy."

"One blown chance was the subway incident?"

"And before that, the Korean's. That was them too."

Doyle drew a deep breath. He let it out slowly. Until now, he'd been unwilling to believe that the convenience store killing was anything more than a botched random stickup.

"He volunteered all this? He mentioned Bronwyn's murder with no prompting from you?"

Johnny G. stared. "We know how to do this, Mr. Doyle."

"My apologies."

"You ready to hear about the camels?"

Doyle was rubbing his eyes. He tossed a hand as if to say that at this moment, he had scant interest in any subject but the attempt to murder the last remaining Fallon.

"You want to hear it," said the younger Giordano. "You really do."

"Let's get some drinks first," said Fat Julie.

Young Johnny Giordano had always been bright. His father, now dead, would carry copies of his report cards and read off his grades to anyone who would listen. If old Rocco were here now, thought Doyle, he would probably read them aloud to that wired bartender just to get them into the record. Fat Julie might do the same thing.

A big difference, however, is that old Rocco Giordano would then break the man's head. At one time Fat Julie might have done so as well but that was before Johnny G. came of age. Through Johnny G., he became more circumspect. A bug, once discovered, is better left in place. They should look for ways to use it. There is no better way to drop a dime on a rival or to discredit a bothersome judge than to be overheard talking about them.

Doyle had seen all the report cards. He had even attended Johnny G.'s graduation and had noted some of the more enlightened business practices that he had subsequently brought to the family business. Loan-sharking, for example, was now computerized. During the course of this luncheon, however, the lawyer would develop a whole new appreciation of the younger Giordano. He showed a mind that was both inquisitive and patient. Far more patient than his brother would have been. The interrogation of Mohammed Mizda had been thorough.

The camel story was this. Mizda, along with most of the men of his clan, would deliver drums of a chemical called acetic anhydride to the drug factories over the border. Acetic anhydride is essential to the production of heroin. The camels would come back loaded down with high-grade heroin, automatic weapons, gold and silver. Most of the Golden Triangle dealers were now moving their heroin in this fashion, which is to say through India, because of increased pressure from local and Western drug enforcement agencies.

Johnny G. thumbed forward through several pages of notes. He found what he was looking for.

"Oh, yeah," he said brightly. "This is interesting about the gold."

Inquisitive, Doyle would note later, but discursive. He had an unsettling habit of leaping between subjects as if indifferent to the one that was of immediate interest to his audience.

"You want to bring gold into India," he began, "you have to smuggle it. Otherwise they tax the hell out of it to protect their own gold fields which are down around Madras."

"Madras," echoed Fat Julie. "Like in Madras shirts."

"Thank you."

"Kid's smart," said Fat Julie proudly. "You listen to this."

"Yahya here," Johnny G. continued, "says one time a car drove in, they searched it and came up empty until a border guard scratched it by accident. The whole damned body was made of gold." He shook his head as if in wonderment. "I mean, this is *India*. Didn't you always think India was poor?"

Doyle closed his eyes. "The chemical, Johnny. Finish about the chemical."

Johnny G. smiled. "You already guessed, right?" He flipped back to the beginning and read from the page. "It's manufactured by a company in Akra, which is near Calcutta. It's called Bhatpara Chemical. Bhatpara Chemical is a wholly owned subsidary of . . ." He smirked expectantly at Doyle.

Doyle frowned. "AdChem?"

"Give the man a cigar. That's also where the gold goes."

As Fat Julie signaled the waiter to bring menus, Doyle looked across at the nervous Pakistani, who had not uttered a word. He wondered why they brought him. He threw a questioning glance at Johnny G.

"Just wait," said the younger Giordano. "We'll get to the good part in a minute."

12

Michael Fallon, at that hour, was on the ferry to Woods Hole.

He had not, he told himself, set out to see the famous Megan. The most she had to do with it was that she started him thinking about getting a boat of his own. Nothing big at first because he probably wouldn't have the time to enjoy it, let alone keep it up. Maybe a Boston whaler that he could use to buzz around the island. Whalers have a shallow draft. Perfect for clamming and for running up onto quiet beaches.

A used one had been advertised in Saturday's paper. It was up in Vineyard Haven sitting at the town dock. He drove over to see it on Sunday morning.

The town dock happened to be near the ferry landing. The ferry to Woods Hole just happened to be in and was taking passengers. On an impulse, similar to the one that brought him here, Fallon bought a round-trip ticket and walked aboard.

This had nothing to do with Megan. All he wanted was to sit out in the sun with a cup of coffee, enjoy the crossings, then wander around Woods Hole, which he still had never actually seen, until it was time to catch the next ferry back. But he just *might* amble by her slip if he can find it. Check out her boat. See what she really looks like.

*   *   *

Fallon saw her before the ferry reached the landing.

He spotted her boat first. Millie said it was a ketch, blue hull, white top, with hatches and rails of richly polished teak. He saw only one ketch. It fit that description.

There was no one on the deck but suddenly, near the stern, a diver in a wet suit broke water. She, if that was Megan, had been down cleaning her bottom. Fallon watched as she rinsed off a scouring pad and tossed it aboard. Next, without the aid of a swimming ladder, she launched herself up and over the gunwale. Fallon held his breath. She unbuckled her SCUBA tank and stowed it in the aft locker. She stripped off her hood and shook out her hair. The hair was blond but a bit darker than he'd imagined and it wasn't tied back. But everything else was the same. The height, the weight, even the way she moved. He couldn't see the eyes.

She slipped out of the wet suit and draped it over the railing. Underneath, she wore a one-piece bathing suit that was nearly backless. The front of it covered her entire chest and tapered to her throat. She reached behind her neck to undo it. A male voice near Fallon said, "Hey, check that out." Another said, "Man, I'd like some of that."

Fallon felt a flash of anger. He threw an annoyed glance toward the source. Three young men of college age had been watching as well. One of them met his eyes and nudged the others. "You got a problem, buddy?" he said.

Fallon wanted to say, "Yeah, I've got a problem with your mouth." But he didn't. He remembered Doyle's warning and, that aside, he knew that getting into a brawl over a girl he'd never met would be terminally dumb. He looked away, back toward the boat, but by then she was gone.

He stayed on the upper deck watching, hoping that she would reappear. Ten minutes went by. Passengers were walking off. Some had already reached the parking lot. He was about to turn away, hurry down to the gangway deck, when she emerged from the cabin hatch. Now she wore short cutoff jeans and a loose-fitting blouse. She was knotting its ends at her waist, leaving the midriff bare. Her stomach looked rock-hard. And she had tied her hair back. Dried and straightened, it was now a lighter shade. She was, to his astonishment, just as he had envisioned her.

Fallon, he told himself. *Get a grip. You have about as much ESP as a banana.*

The phrase "pretty little thing," he realized, tends to narrow the field in terms of height and weight. It suggests that she's young. Women who live on boats, and who single-hand them in any weather, do not look like couch potatoes. And they would have good color and their hair, unless black, would be some shade of blond from the bleaching effect of the sun. It's the same with women skiers. Downhill racers. They all look like Megan for most of the same reasons. They might be pretty little things but any one of them could run ten miles cross-country without breaking a sweat.

Anyway, he still hadn't seen her eyes. Maybe he was wrong about the eyes.

"Pretty boat," he said.

"Thank you."

She was busy replacing a block on her traveler. She had not looked up when he approached. But when he spoke she seemed to stare, for just a beat, at nothing. Fallon saw the logo of the boat's maker.

"A Cheoy Lee," he said. "It's what . . . thirty-six feet?"

"Thirty-four."

"Full keel?"

She shook her head. "Shoal draft. Centerboard."

"Um . . . my name is Michael Fallon."

She paused for a moment, chewed her lip. She nodded slightly but did not volunteer her own.

Another stare. She seemed to be concentrating. She would still not look at him but now he could see her eyes. They were not gray. They were an olive color. Why, he wondered, does he have this thing about eyes? But he was right about them being sad.

"Fallon," she repeated. "You're the man who bought the Taylor House?"

He was startled. But pleased.

"Could I ask how you knew that?"

"Small island, Mr. Fallon. And you're wasting your time."

She went back to her work on the traveler.

"I . . . didn't come about the laughing children. If that's what you think."

"They're called starlings."

"Starlings?"

She nodded.

"Um . . . What's that? Some psychic term for lost juvenile spirits?"

She looked at him at last.

"It's a *bird* term, Mr. Fallon. You have starlings in your attic. Sometimes they get in the walls. It can sound like giggling."

She turned away again.

"Then the house isn't haunted?"

"It wasn't until now."

For the second time this morning, Fallon was getting steamed. He moved a step closer to ask what the hell that crack was supposed to mean. Suddenly, the muscles in her shoulders tightened. She dropped the block and spun to face him, the screwdriver in her hand as if it were a weapon. He stepped back quickly, both hands raised, his expression one of bewilderment. At this, she seemed to catch herself. She let out a breath and lowered the screwdriver to her side.

"I have work to do, Mr. Fallon."

He stood for a moment, slowly shaking his head. "Have we met before?" he asked.

"No."

"I mean, were we enemies in some other life? Did I do something rotten like take your parking space?"

She ignored the sarcasm.

"So if all I did was walk down here and admire your boat, why are you being such a rude little shit?"

She glared at him. Another deep breath. For an instant there, her eyes almost softened. When she spoke, her voice was husky.

"You're a violent man, Mr. Fallon."

He blinked.

"And you're a dangerous man. Excuse me, but I don't find *that* so attractive either."

This was when he walked away.

He had tried to respond but he began to stammer. And she was about to say something else. It would have been one more good twist of the knife or some sophomoric crack like "That's easy for you to say."

If she had, he might have hit her after all.

No, he would not have.

Because he was *not* violent and he was *not* dangerous. Somehow, however, that rap had been following him since he was in his teens. But just because you know how doesn't mean you do it. Except for those two last January, and except for working out with Moon, he hadn't hit anyone since his freshman year in college. Unless you'd count . . .

The hell with it.

Small island, huh? That probably explains it.

Someone, probably Millie Jacobs, had passed the word that he might be popping in on Megan who is, incidentally, not so goddamned pretty after all. Well . . . she is. But only until she opens her mouth.

Or maybe Millie just told Madam Cassandra, in which case the word could have spread to Bangkok by now. But what frosted him the most, and concerned him the most, was this stuff about his reputation. It meant that Millie had checked up on him. Or maybe the Daggetts' lawyer had. He would have to find out whom they talked to. And, since he's here, he might as well start with Megan.

Fallon turned back toward the boat.

"You're right. You did nothing to deserve that."

She said this as he approached. She was sitting in the cockpit, her knees drawn up against her chest. He saw that sadness again.

"Thank you," he managed.

"But I still can't help you, Mr. Fallon."

"It's Michael, and I don't think you can either. So why don't we try starting over?"

She looked at him. The eyes were definitely olive. They seemed to be asking what's the point. But she acknowledged, with a sigh, that maybe she owed him one.

"I'm out of beer," she told him. "But I might have some wine in the cooler."

*   *   *

Fallon stayed until the next ferry back began boarding. She assured him, over that glass of wine, that she'd heard almost nothing about him. Then, looking away, she asked what he'd heard about her. He told her the truth, or most of it. A good gutsy sailor who owns a great boat and was also a "pretty little thing" made coming for a look very hard to resist.

That made her smile. It also made her blush.

As he stepped from her boat, she reached a hand to help steady him. Her touch sent a curious thrill through his arm.

"Michael . . . it's good that you came," she said to him.

He answered, "I'm glad we met too."

"I meant to the island. It's good that you came here when you did."

Fallon boarded the ferry with a glow on his face. But his mood had begun to darken by the time it reached mid-channel. By the time it docked he was muttering to himself.

Here he was, he told himself, just having gotten his head half-way straight, suddenly letting himself get interested in a witch named Megan. Witch, or wacko, or con artist. One or all of the above.

Forget it, Michael. You don't need this. Here's a girl who can't say goodbye without telling you your fortune. She's the absolute polar opposite of Bronwyn and that's probably why you were drawn to her. It's called overcompensating, or negative rebounding, or some damned thing like that. Except that you both like boats, you have zero in common with her.

He knew what his Uncle Jake would have said.

"Keep walking, Michael. She's setting you up."

"Yeah, but why?"

"Because that pretty little girl runs a scam. She'll keep lobbing these little soft ones at you, mixed in with those distant stares, until you beg on your knees to be a paying customer."

He wasn't sure he believed that. At least he didn't want to.

But even if she's straight, he thought, you just *know* that she'll turn out to be a loon. And delusional. What will we bet that she's ridden in a UFO? She's probably been to Venus. Snuck off there for a weekend with Parnel Minter.

Millie's niece from Nantucket was sounding better by the day.

Back in Vineyard Haven, he checked out the whaler, put a deposit on it, then drove straight to Edgartown and Millie Jacobs's office. Millie swore that she had never spoken to Megan.

He could not very well ask Millie who else on the island might have said that he was violent or who else might have been looking into his past. That would be like sending up a flare. Instead, he changed the subject, chatted for a while about the real estate market, then asked if she had a copy of his credit history handy. Millie pulled the report from her desk and handed it to him. She said it showed a perfect record. He saw nothing in her eyes that said she wondered why he's asking.

Credit reports list inquiries. He knew that he could be traced to Martha's Vineyard by anyone who wanted him badly enough. But the only inquiry had been by Millie's firm after he put down his deposit.

No one, he decided, had told Megan much of anything. She had merely seen steam rising. She had seen his temper and could not resist laying a little mysticism on him. That was all there was to that.

"Okay," said Johnny Giordano. "You want to know why we brought Yahya."

The Pakistani straightened in his chair and dabbed a napkin to his lips as if he knew that his moment was at hand. It was now his turn to be the teacher.

"One reason," explained the younger Giordano, "is corroboration. Mizda talked to Yahya, Yahya talked to me. I wrote down what sounded important but you might have questions of your own. The second reason is you're not going to believe the rest of this unless he's here to swear to it."

"I'm listening," said the lawyer.

"A couple of years back, Yahya spent eight months in a federal pen. Tell Mr. Doyle what you got busted for."

He set down the orange juice that Fat Julie had ordered for him and pulled his chair forward. But Fat Julie put a hand on his arm. He turned to Brendan Doyle.

"You know I'd do anything for Jake, right?"

The lawyer shrugged and nodded.

"Same goes for Moon and Michael. This Parker character, this Hobbs, anyone you think was involved in killing Jake, going after Mike, I'd dust them in a minute. Johnny here never popped anyone but he feels the same way."

Doyle waited.

"The thing is, we smell money here. Very serious money. I'm going to say this real clear so you won't have any doubt on where we stand. We're doing this for Jake and we don't want nothing from your pocket. But if there's a way to score, I know you're going to find it. Me and Johnny want in."

"You have my word."

"You gonna tell me why Jake died?"

Doyle looked away. "I'm not sure yet."

"But Jake and Mike . . . they're both connected?"

"That's not clear yet either."

"Then you're fucking blind, Brendan. Either that or you're jerking us around."

Doyle held his temper. He chose his words carefully.

"Julie . . . if they *are* connected, the reason why Jake died is private. It stays in the family."

The gangster studied him. "You won't tell me?"

"No."

Fat Julie rubbed his chin. "If I ever found out," he asked, frowning, "is it anything that would make me and Johnny feel . . . I don't know . . . like disappointed?"

"You're asking me if Jake was dirty?"

"Big money, Brendan. Anyone can get tempted."

"Not Jake. Not for one damned second."

Fat Julie nodded slowly. He patted the Pakistani's arm. "Tell Mr. Doyle how you make your living."

In the beginning, it was Doyle who was disappointed.

That the man was a street dealer had already been established. His story had the sound of a routine drug arrest. But he realized, as he penetrated Yahya's singsong accent, that this was not about heroin, not about cocaine. This man sold pharmaceuticals.

The crime for which he actually served time, he said, was the selling of anabolic steroids. But he sold many kinds of pills. He said that Indian and Pakistani doctors, not all, but some, who had immigrated to this country and found it difficult to build a practice except as abortionists, would establish what are known as prescription mills. Patients, none of them actually ill, would come in and these doctors would write prescriptions. The patients would pay them three or four times the cost of a normal office visit, fill the prescriptions, and turn the drugs over to the street dealers.

Then, of course, there were the salesmen who worked for the major drug companies. All of them had thousands of sample packets that they were to distribute to the doctors they called on. Some would hold out these samples and trade them to street dealers in return for recreational drugs. A sealed sample packet would command a premium price because the buyer could be confident that it was genuine.

"Genuine as opposed to what?" Doyle asked.

"We'll get to that."

"Okay, these sales on the street. This is a specialty? I mean, you're telling me this is a whole separate breed of drug dealers?"

Johnny G. rocked his hand. "Your local pusher can pretty much get you any pills you want. But for some, yeah, I guess you'd call it a specialty."

"Suicide stashes, for example," said Fat Julie. "For them, you want to buy from someone reliable."

"Suicide stashes?" Doyle repeated blankly.

"Say you got cancer like my old man had. You want to be able to pull the plug when you're ready but maybe your doctor has scruples about this. A lot of them *say* they'll help but, time comes, they get cold feet. So you want to have something handy that'll put you to sleep, no mess, no fuss."

"Wouldn't I have pain pills? Sleeping pills? Wouldn't they do the job?"

"Washed down with vodka, right? That might make you throw up. And even if you knew the right dose, it could take hours. Someone might drop by, find you, and you'd wake up in the hospital with your stomach pumped out and feeling stupid. Worse, from then on your wife might lock up the pills."

Doyle grunted. "So what's in a suicide stash?"

The younger Giordano read from his notes.

"Darvon, two thousand milligrams, you're dead in an hour. Darvon sucks as a pain killer—you're better off with aspirin—but it's toxic as hell. The stash comes with two Seconals because Darvon won't put you to sleep either."

He read on.

"Dilaudid's good. You only need two hundred milligrams but that can be a hundred pills. Same with Amytal. However, you're dead with fifty Seconal and only thirty Nembutal. Darvon's also only thirty. By the way, don't let anyone sell you morphine or methadone unless you take it intravenously. The next morning, all you'll be is rested."

"Johnny . . ."

"And take a Maalox. Like I said, you don't want an upset stomach."

"Johnny, it's fascinating. But this is big money?"

"Since AIDS? It's getting there. Then you got the clinically depressed, the white-collar unemployed, the—"

A skeptical frown.

"Mr. Doyle . . . this is not about *doing* it. It's like with abortion. It's about having the choice."

Johnny G. returned to his notes. "You heard of a drug called Xanax?"

Doyle nodded. "For anxiety, right? Sheila takes it now and then."

"If she takes it, Brendan, it's not just now and then. And Xanax is *the* anxiety drug. Annual sales, worldwide, just this one drug, are about two *billion* a year. Maybe much more, but I'll come back to that. The drug's a gold mine because it's pretty much addictive. You try to quit taking it and the withdrawal symptoms are worse than what made you start taking it in the first place. Start taking Xanax, you're on it for life."

Doyle was confused. He wanted to ask what this had to do with AdChem but he was reluctant to break Johnny G.'s rhythm.

"You're going to tell me it's become a street drug?" he asked instead.

Giordano nodded. "But why, right? Why not just go to your doctor? Mohammed, tell him who buys Xanax from you."

"Those who do not have a doctor. Many cannot afford one."

"Come on. Who else?"

"Heroin addicts. Those on methadone maintenance programs."

"Tell him why."

"Methadone by itself gives no high. Methadone taken with Xanax gives a high very much like heroin."

Doyle reached inside his jacket. He pulled out a notepad of his own. He wrote, *Flush Sheila's pills.* He began to make a second note but could only draw a question mark.

"Here's the thing," said Fat Julie Giordano. "Johnny here could go on for an hour about this. He's got for instances up the ass. Now . . . we don't touch drugs, we don't deal drugs, but we *know* drugs. We're wise guys, right? We're supposed to know what's going on. And yet, until Johnny scrounged up Mohammed Yahya here, looking for someone who could talk Pakistani, we knew shit about this."

"Mohammed," said his brother, "tell him about the steroids you were selling."

"They were fake."

"Did you know that when you were selling them?"

"No."

"What were they really?"

"The pills were only caffeine tablets. The liquid steroids were corn oil. It came in vials of the type used for blood samples. A little camphor was added to give it a medicinal smell."

"Any customers catch on?"

"No."

"Because they wouldn't, right? The stuff looked and smelled legit. And since no one expects steroids to work overnight, they just keep buying more."

"Yes."

"The people who made the fake steroids. Did they get caught?"

The Pakistani nodded. "A man and his wife. From Kansas, I think. They went to prison."

Johnny G. touched Brendan Doyle's arm to alert him to what was coming.

"Mohammed . . . how do two hicks from the Midwest, running this mom-and-pop operation, go about lining up street dealers in New York City?"

"I did not buy from them. I bought from legitimate distributors."

"Which is how you got fooled, right? I mean, you said 'legitimate,' right?"

"All things are relative, Mr. Giordano."

Johnny G. smiled. He turned to Doyle. "He's saying that even legal companies lie and cheat. No shit, right?" He turned back to the Pakistani. "How many of these distributors did they sell to?"

"Many."

"Give Mr. Doyle a number. The one from your indictment."

"One hundred and sixty. In twenty-eight states."

Doyle did ask, finally, how all this connects with AdChem.

"Patience," said Johnny G. He flipped a few more pages.

"Anyway," he said, "I did a little homework. The drug business, worldwide—just prescription drugs now—is around two hundred billion. I mean, think about that. The gross national product of *Switzerland* isn't two hundred billion."

"And . . . where there's that much money . . ."

"There's crime. The black market in anabolic steroids alone, in this country alone, is a hundred million dollars. That figure comes from the Feds."

"Fake or genuine?"

The younger Giordano smiled. He sat back, folding his arms.

"Mohammed," he asked, "of all those black market steroids out there, what percent are bogus?"

"Not so much, I think. Less than one percent."

Johnny G. seemed disappointed. He recovered. "Wait, I asked it wrong. Forgetting the caffeine and corn oil, what percent are the real thing? By *real*, I mean made by legal drug companies."

"Almost all of it is real. But almost none is legal. It comes from many secret laboratories in Europe . . . Mexico . . . my country . . ."

"But steroids is all they make, right?"

The Pakistani had to laugh.

"Tell Mr. Doyle what's funny."

"They make everything."

"Pills for anxiety, for ulcers, for arthritis? Anything a lot of people use. Anything they can't *stop* using."

"That is so. Yes."

"And they're all counterfeit."

"Of course."

"Tell Mr. Doyle . . . wait . . . Give Mr. Doyle your best guess on this. What percent of all prescription drugs, sold in this country . . . not just on the street . . . I mean through drugstores and hospitals . . . is counterfeit."

"I would say half."

* * *

Mohammed Yahya had been sent to wash his hands.

"I'm going to ask you again," said Fat Julie Giordano. "Did Jake have a piece of this?"

"No."

"But Michael did."

"Julie . . . *no.*"

"I want to believe you, Brendan. But someone at AdChem, or at Lehman-Stone, has a serious beef with Michael and we both know they killed Jake."

Doyle blinked. "Mizda confirmed that?"

"He didn't know. But *you're* confirming it. Your face, right now, says that you think they killed Jake and I want to know what he was into."

"Julie . . . I swear before Christ. It is *nothing* like you think it is."

"We know that AdChem supplies the gooks who make heroin. Are they also making counterfeit pills?"

"To hear Mohammed Yahya, who isn't?"

"Was the Parker guy right? Was Michael some kind of spy, you know, like . . . what do they call that in companies?"

"Industrial espionage," his brother answered.

Doyle grimaced. He shook his head, but slowly.

"You say no. But you don't look so sure," said Fat Julie.

He shook it again, more firmly. "Truth is I wondered. But now I'm sure. If you got him talking you'd see he's proud of all the good their products do."

"Brendan . . . you have to help me out here."

"Okay, listen to me," the lawyer said quietly. "While Michael lives, I can't and won't tell anyone what I *think* might have led to this. I'll only tell you that it goes back to a time when Mike was a little kid. There's just no way that he could know what happened then."

"Does Moon know?"

"Yes."

"Gimme a number. I want to talk to him."

"He won't tell you either. Him most of all."

"Then he'll say so. Gimme a number."

14

Three days had passed since Michael's visit to Woods Hole. He had awakened each morning with Megan on his mind. Megan of the tied-off blouse and rock-hard belly. Megan of the sad and distant eyes.

He also woke with a measure of guilt because there in the background each time was Bronwyn. Bronwyn of the violet eyes. They were saying, "How could you? How could you so soon?"

Well he couldn't and wouldn't. Megan was exactly what he didn't need right now. Even if she had started to like him a little, even if she was not a fraud, she was probably more than a little nuts. No young girl lives so reclusive a life without having been seriously damaged somewhere along the way. Any idiot could see that any relationship with her was bound to be destructive. She would only make him crazy again just when his own scars were starting to heal.

"A very mature assessment, Michael."
"Butt out, Dr. Greenberg."

Three days.

And at the end of each of them, every night at midnight, he would look out his bedroom's front window and there would be

Parnel, standing in the street below, his fingertips held to his temples. Parnel would announce his arrival by letting his bike fall over with a crash that could be heard a block away.

Days starting with Megan were bad enough. He didn't need them ending with Parnel. By the third night he had pretty much decided to take Millie's advice and invite Parnel in. Michael would listen to his pitch and be done with it. Then give him some work to do. The gutters needed cleaning anyway. Michael made himself a scotch and waited for the bike to fall over.

The crash came and he looked out. There was Parnel going into his act but suddenly something was different. He wasn't looking at the house. He was looking back down toward the docks and his hands were not at his temples. He was wringing them as if in supplication.

Fallon pressed his cheek against the window and followed Parnel's line of sight. His heart started thumping again. There, walking up, was Megan. She was dressed in a foul-weather jacket, a thick turtleneck underneath, and jeans. She was walking with her hands in her pockets but she pulled one of them out and raised it. This was apparently to calm Parnel who was already moving toward his bike. She reached him and put a staying hand on his shoulder. He seemed to go limp. He stood there, nodding vigorously in response to whatever it was she was saying. Abruptly, Parnel left. He didn't mount his bike. He walked it. Twice, Michael saw him turn and make a jerky little bow in Megan's direction.

Holy shit, thought Fallon. There should have been thunder. All bow before Megan, Queen of the Netherworld, fashions courtesy of Sperry and Levi Strauss.

But a part of him was glad to see her.

Michael would never tell anyone what happened next. After she rang the bell, that is. After he let her in. He would not have believed it himself.

Fallon greeted her, dressed only in a robe and slippers. He told her he was out of beer but the wine was cold. He lied about the beer. Just something to say. She ignored him.

She began moving through the first floor, each room, very slowly. He told her that the murders had been upstairs. Where the lady in white appears. Except on Halloween when she's out eating children. But Megan didn't smile. There was no response at all. She behaved as if he weren't there.

His next move was to step in front of her, take her by the shoulders, and say, "Hey. Remember me? I live here. Michael Fallon?"

Nothing.

With one hand he lifted her chin so that she would have to look at him. He looked into those eyes. There was nobody home. The pupils were dilated. He saw hardly any green.

Amphetamines had to be the answer. Megan was stoned. But if so, her heart should have been running away and he could barely feel a pulse at her throat. Fallon stepped aside.

It was this way all through the first and second floors. She would linger at the oddest places. She would stop to touch an old portrait, for example, or an antique clock. This, he assumed, was to contact someone who had lived here. But she also stopped at a writing desk which Fallon knew to be a recent purchase. She would cock her head, as if listening, and then move on.

The third floor, Michael's floor, took the longest. He had time to pour a second scotch and nearly finish it. In his bedroom she found the Colt Python. She had touched the nightstand, moved away, then cocked her head and made a bee-line back to the drawer it was in. She opened it. Using the tips of her fingers, both hands, she picked up the big chromed revolver and brought it to her lips. She was tasting it, smelling it, he wasn't sure which.

Something else in the nightstand seemed to draw her attention. She reached a hand back in. It found his bottle of Seconal, another of Dalmane, and a third that contained his last two Valium tablets. She had shown no fear of the gun but the pill bottles clearly frightened her. And yet, wide-eyed, she brought them to her cheek. She listened to them. Then, suddenly, she threw them. She threw them back into the open drawer, then wiped her fingers against her breast as if the pills had made them unclean.

She stood for a moment, gathering herself. She looked once more at the heavy revolver. She squinted at it. A slight nod, then another, and one more.

"Three," she whispered. "But not you."

It was the first time she'd spoken.

"What does that mean? Three what?"

She gave no sign that she heard him. But she crossed the room in his direction, moving sort of sideways the way you might approach a ledge, and she reached out to touch him. He offered his hand but she pushed it back down. She touched his chest and listened.

She said, "Two . . . no . . . more than two. Many."

She looked up at him. Abruptly. Eyes widened. "Hundreds?"

It was a question. Fallon could only shrug and shake his head. The eyes, he saw, were not in focus.

She lowered them, then placed both palms against his chest. She brought her face against it. His bathrobe bothered her. She opened it to feel his skin. She stood that way, not moving. Fallon raised his hands to her shoulders, more for balance than to embrace her. She stiffened at his touch, then slowly seemed to melt. Minutes went by. Neither moved.

Fallon had no idea what to do. Talking was no good because she wouldn't answer. He tried sitting her down but she resisted. Steering her toward his bed seemed totally inappropriate because this was as unpromisingly unromantic a situation as he had ever been in in his life. It was like, one time, there was a girl left over at a party. She was too stoned or drunk to be sent home and was clinging to him. The opportunity was there, even some interest. But to act on it would have been crummy.

And yet sex was clearly what Megan wanted. She steered *him,* first pausing to turn off the light. He tried, gently, to break free of her but she tightened her grip. Megan-the-deck-ape was amazingly strong. He tried again.

"No," she hissed sharply. "Don't."

She raised one finger as if ordering him not to move.

Fallon threw up his arms in frustration. "Hundreds," he hissed back at her. "What does 'hundreds' mean?"

He asked this as the foul-weather jacket slid to the floor and the turtleneck was being peeled off. She shook her head sharply, then reached to undo her bra while kicking her deck shoes aside.

"Listen . . . Megan . . ."

That finger again.

The jeans and panties came off together. But with effort. They knotted at her feet and she tore free of them. Almost angrily.

She guided him to the edge of the bed and, with her free hand, pulled back the comforter. She climbed in first and pulled him down with her. They lay together. Neither moved.

This was not lovemaking. This was not even sex. That girl at the party would have been a transcendent, soaring joining of hearts compared to this. This reminded him more of his first dancing lesson, aged thirteen and shy, when he could not bring himself to touch the Arthur Murray lady's waist with more than his fingertips and kept arching his back lest he chance to come in contact with her bosom.

Megan rolled over him. She straddled him, sitting upright. Fallon, for the first time, felt himself rising. Until now, he did not think it would happen. Megan felt him as well. She took him in her hand and then the damndest expression crossed her face. It was sort of a what-am-I-supposed-to-do-with-this look followed by an oh-yeah-I-remember.

They had sex, sort of. And of the unsafe kind. Not a moan out of Megan. Not a hint of heavy breathing. It took Fallon quite a while to make his plumbing work. To make it work at all, he had to envision Megan setting that storm jib, dressed in her cutoffs and that blouse tied off at the waist. To Fallon, in this circumstance, that picture was infinitely more erotic than Megan astride him, totally nude but a zombie.

Afterward, he went into the bathroom and closed the door. As he toweled himself off he looked in the mirror, grimaced, and began to have one of those listen-you-asshole conversations with himself. He did not get very far because he heard Megan's voice, outside in the bedroom, saying, "Wha—what? Oh, no. Oh, God." She was, he assumed, getting new instructions from the mother ship.

Fallon stayed in the bathroom, gathering himself, compiling in his head the list of explanations he would now demand of her. No more oblique little references, no more mystical bullshit. That done, he opened the door and came out.

Megan was gone.

Of course she was. Why should that have surprised him? The last he heard of her, from somewhere downstairs, was an agonized groan and the sound of her jacket being zipped.

*   *   *

That, Fallon swore, was it.

He would absolutely, under no circumstances, have anything further to do with that fruitcake. He'd just had the worst and emptiest sexual experience since Onan. He'd been a victim of date rape. And first she'd done her best to try to mess up his head. So why did she take off? Why didn't she stick around and really make a night of it by grabbing the Python and blowing his brains out?

The gun. The Colt Python. What was that business with the gun?

"Three," he imagined, meant that it had killed three times. That came as no great shock. It doesn't have to mean, however, that the man he took it from was a triple murderer. In New York, street dealers rent these things out for the night. The going rate, according to Moon, is forty dollars. But if you use it in a crime you pay another sixty dollars and that's only if you don't shoot it. Those two were just street bums out looking for a score. That's all they were.

What did "But not you" mean? That he wasn't one of the three? That's too obvious. Maybe she was saying that she knew it wasn't him who killed with it. She could tell that by the taste. Think of all the money that's been wasted on ballistic tests and on fluoroscoping hands to see if they bore traces of powder. Think of all the innocent men rotting in prison because their lawyers never thought of bringing Megan in to lick the murder weapon.

She's even better if she gets to touch your chest.

"Two."

Fallon's first thought was that she meant Uncle Jake and Bronwyn. But he refused to give her that much credit and, besides, she immediately said, "No . . . more than that" and then, "Hundreds."

He must have caused a plane crash somewhere along the line. And then gone into denial.

Uncle Jake was right. She started lobbing soft ones and quickly worked her way up to hand grenades. But nothing she said or did was in the least bit impressive. The physical part least of all. Okay, she found the Python but it was in his night table. Open enough of them and you'll find a few guns. You didn't find one? No sweat. You can do just as good an act with an old condom

wrapper. You hold it against your forehead and say, "I feel . . .
a woman. She is . . . hungry. She is . . . searching."

It's all a scam. It has to be.

She shows up here again, she's going out on her ass.

15

Doyle had those same three days in which to think about his lunch with the Giordano brothers. He still found much of it hard to believe.

But parts of it, certainly, left little room for doubt. There was no question that Mohammed Mizda and the jailed Jamaican worked for this man. Parker, along with some fifty other men, most of them illegal aliens, none of them Boy Scouts, almost all from third world countries. In addition to this small army of thugs, according to Mizda, Parker is said to have retained a number of Americans who were specialists in the black-bag arts of wiretapping and burglary. The Pakistani, however, rarely came in contact with the latter and had no real knowledge of their mission.

What seemed indisputable, however, was that Parker had sent Mizda and the Jamaican, among others, after Michael. He had done so either at the behest of Lehman-Stone, which meant Bart Hobbs, or on instructions from someone at AdChem.

It had also been established that Mizda, before being brought here from Pakistan, had been in the pay of that AdChem subsidiary, first as a guard with those camel caravans and then as a disciplinarian of sorts. His people were warned that if they stole from the camels that were bringing back the gold, Mizda would stake them out in the Pakistan sun, place a large copper bowl on their bellies, put two thirsty rats under it, and let them dig their way out.

This gem was related by Mohammed Yahya. He told it as he spooned chocolate ice cream into his mouth.

It was not so much that Doyle doubted the story. Parker had not recruited Mizda for his love of humanity. But it just didn't seem the sort of detail one volunteers when one is hoping not to be tortured any further. Given his admission that he tried to murder Michael, the Giordano brothers were feeling less than lenient toward him as it was.

Mohammed Yahya, more likely, had simply thrown it in. Perhaps he's seen it done. Perhaps he's done it himself. God knows what else he had invented, but claimed that Mizda had said, in his zeal to impress Fat Julie Giordano.

On the other hand, he said that Mizda knew nothing of Jake Fallon's murder. Was it therefore unrelated? He said, further, that Mizda had no knowledge of any involvement by anyone at Lehman-Stone or AdChem. That it was strictly this Parker character. Which is, of course, impossible.

Unless . . .

Unless Parker had reasons of his own. Could it be, Doyle wondered, that Parker is running an outlaw security firm that has been robbing AdChem blind, diverting its products to the black market. If so, however, he would surely need someone on the inside. Someone who could doctor their production and inventory figures so that the shrinkage wouldn't show. That would explain the need for black-baggers. But how would Lehman-Stone fit in? What is Bart Hobbs's role in this? Mohammed Mizda had no idea.

No use asking him again. No good asking to take a deposition from him either because, if Fat Julie's past behavior is any guide, he's probably in the hold of some cargo ship by now. Sealed in a fuel drum. Ready to be deep-sixed far out at sea lest we discomfort Marty Hennessy by having him bob to the surface at the foot of Wall Street.

Fat Julie had smelled big money.

All those counterfeit drugs.

But Doyle found Yahya's claim so extravagant that it rendered his overall credibility moot.

Half?

Half of all prescription drugs are counterfeit? Half of two hundred billion dollars?

"Okay," Johnny G. had said afterward on the sidewalk outside the restaurant. "Say it *isn't* fifty percent. Say it's five percent. That's still ten billion dollars which is, to give you an example, about twice the size of the whole movie industry. And with counterfeits, your costs are real low so maybe ninety percent of that is pure profit. There's also not that much risk. You get caught . . ."

Fat Julie tapped a finger against the table, then cupped both hands in the manner of a poker player breasting his cards. Doyle recognized the gesture. It said, "Never tell everything. Always keep something in your pocket."

It was the second time he'd done that. The first was when Johnny G. wondered aloud why Bart Hobbs needs so many homes. The question came as he was flipping through his notebook to see if he had forgotten anything. It had no apparent relevance to the subject at hand. But it clearly had significance because Fat Julie waved that finger at his brother again.

Whatever.

In the end, at least, he agreed to wait a few days before saying anything to Moon. No use getting Moon's blood up. There were too many things that needed to be sorted out first.

That Sunday, Doyle had taken a taxi home.

On arriving, the first thing he did, other than checking the labels of Sheila's prescription bottles, and flushing the contents of two of them, was to place a call to Arnie Aaronson.

Arnie was his investment counselor. He handled Michael's portfolio as well. Before going into business for himself, however, Arnie had spent twenty years at Merrill-Lynch, was still well connected, and knew his way around the pharmaceutical industry. Upjohn and Pfizer, in fact, were part of Doyle's portfolio, and Arnie had urged him to hold them.

As for AdChem, come to think of it, Doyle didn't remember them even being listed. He asked Aaronson, whom he had awakened from a nap.

"They're not," Aaronson told him. "Not on the big board. They're listed on the Frankfurt exchange."

"Why not here?"

"This sounds more slippery than it is," he explained with a yawn, "but any company wishing to trade on the American exchanges must abide by what are known as the Generally Accepted Accounting Principles."

"And AdChem, I take it, does not."

"Not just AdChem. German accounting permits companies to have silent reserves. Those are cash accounts with undisclosed balances. So, except for big banks with clout, German investors can't find out the earnings, net worths, assets or liabilities of the companies in which they have invested. This is unequal access to information and that's a no-no with the SEC."

"Fertile ground, I would think, for insider trading."

"Exactly. Germany has no rules against it. That's not a market for the small investor."

"And ours is?"

"No. But we pretend it is. The Germans don't bother."

Doyle grunted. "What do you know about counterfeit pharmaceuticals?"

"German products or anyone's?"

"Anyone's."

"It happens. I remember Searle had a problem a few years back with some counterfeit birth control pills. What brings that up?"

"Just something I heard. Made me curious. How widespread is the problem?"

"Drop in the bucket, probably."

"Why do you say so?"

"That industry is big bucks but it's very well policed."

"Okay . . . if someone told you that fully half of all prescription medications sold in this country are counterfeit, what would you say?"

Aaronson snorted. "That's total bullshit, Brendan."

"Do me a favor? Ask around a little."

"Brendan . . . it's a waste of time."

"Bill me."

The investment counselor stifled another yawn. "You in a hurry? I could see what the FDA has on the subject."

"Sure, but ask around the industry in the meantime. Arnie?"

"Yeah?"

"Ask around about AdChem, too."

Doyle had that conversation on Sunday evening. On Thursday morning of the week that followed, three things happened.

First, Fat Julie Giordano made a decision. The promised "few days" had passed. He would talk this over with Johnny G. first, but he thought it was time he asked Moon a few questions. In trade for the answers, he would now tell Moon what he had chosen not to tell Doyle.

All Fat Julie knew was what the camel man had told Yahya.

The soon-to-be-late Mohammed Mizda said the man in the subway, the one who pushed Michael, was a Mexican named Hector who also runs pills from Tampico to Brownsville in speed-boats. He swore, however, that he knew nothing about Jake. Or about who killed him or why. But, scared and hurting, he said maybe it was Walter.

Walter was another Pakistani. His real name was Ayub but his father was a Belgian mercenary, killed in the war against India. Ayub could pass for a European so he took his father's name. Mohammed Mizda said that back in November, the time they were talking about, Walter had suddenly been sent away. But before he went, he could not resist a little bragging. Walter flashed a big roll of bills that he said was a special bonus. He said that while the rest of them freeze their tushes in New York all winter he will be in Palm Beach with the rich people.

But someone else, a Punjabi Hindu who had no use for Walter, said don't listen to all the big talk. He said that all this pig will be doing is guarding the house of Mr. Hobbs and living in a little apartment that is over the garage and keeping to himself. Getting drunk or high, even having a woman, all these are forbidden to him.

Walter became indignant. After smashing the Punjabi's face against a locker, he said that shows how little a stupid Hindu knows. He said that he is free to use the pool and the white BMW that Mr. Hobbs keeps there and he can bring a woman to his room as often as he wishes as long as he can get rid of her quickly if there is work to be done. No drinking and no drugs is only for a little while because Mr. Parker said that he might have another job for him soon and it would be in Florida.

None of this, not even the phrase "another job," proved that it was Walter who had taken the baseball bat to Jake. But, thought Fat Julie at the time, if it *was* this guy who killed Jake, the other job must have been to get Moon.

Johnny G. thought otherwise.

He reminded his brother that Moon was still in Mount Sinai when this Walter was sent to Florida and that it was a few weeks after that before anyone but Doyle knew where Moon had gone.

However, Johnny G. also remembered that back after Jake's memorial service, Bart Hobbs had told Michael and the English girl to go stay at his house in Palm Beach. Maybe the other job was Michael. Maybe it was both of them. Maybe, because Michael wouldn't go, they decided to hit them in New York and make it look like a stickup that went bad.

"And I'll tell you something else," Johnny G. told his brother. "The cab that Jake took home that night? Yellow Cab? Hennessy told Doyle that no Yellow Cab logged a fare that night from West 82nd in Manhattan to Pierrepont Street in Brooklyn. But he said such a cab had been stolen the day before and it was found a few days later at JFK. Same cab? Who knows? All Hennessy could say for sure was that it was probably used in a crime because the cab was washed clean of prints. A cab should have hundreds of different prints all over it but this one had none."

"The cab was out waiting for Jake? With this Walter driving?"

Johnny G. shrugged. "Why don't we go ask Walter?"

"Where is he? He's still down at Hobbs's place?"

"Camel guy says he thinks so."

"I want Moon to go ask him."

Johnny G. frowned. "You think he's up to it?"

"It might get his juices flowing. But let's still don't say anything to Doyle."

"How come?"

"Because he's a fucking lawyer, that's how come. You think he'd go for this? Lawyers are for talking to *after*. Talk to them *before* and you never get anything done."

Johnny G. had looked at him doubtfully.

"Come on, Julie. How come?"

His brother grunted. "It's five months since Jake got killed. I think he knew, all that time, who might have done it and he hasn't done shit."

"Give him a break. It's only three weeks since he had a name and it's only three days since we picked up Mizda."

"It was you who got hit, you think I'd sit on my ass five months?"

"Doyle isn't you."

Julie took out the phone number Doyle had given him.

He had recognized it immediately. Jake's condo down in Naples. That was another thing that bothered him. If Doyle was stashing Moon there to protect him, it seemed a very obvious place for someone to look.

The smart one might have been Michael. He stashed himself and he took his sweet time telling Doyle where. You don't do that with family unless you have a real good reason. Maybe he's got the same bad feeling about Doyle. But now that he did tell Doyle, nothing better all of a sudden happen to him or it'll be Doyle who gets hung up by his balls.

Julie punched out the number.

On that same Thursday morning, in the Taylor House on Martha's Vineyard, Fallon fought to clear his head of a lingering dream and of the pills he'd taken to help him sleep. The bleat of a ship's horn jarred him awake. He sat upright. His eyes darted, stared stupidly, then darted again.

He began to realize, slowly, that it had been no dream. She *had* been there last night. He could smell her on the sheets.

The anger washed back over him. He bolted to his feet, nearly losing his balance from the lingering effect of the drugs. He staggered to the bathroom and there, on the floor, was the towel he had used to wipe himself. He snatched it up, held it for a moment, then hurled it in the direction of his bedroom fireplace.

He thought of the sheets. He crossed to his bed and tore them free. He would boil them. Boil her out of them. Or burn them in that fireplace. But he did neither. He knew that he was being hysterical. He indulged himself all the same.

He stood, for several long moments, with the bedding gathered against his chest. What he wanted to do was strangle her. Or paddle her tight little ass so raw that she'll never come within a time zone of this island again.

What he did *not* want to do was what he knew he was doing. Standing here with her. Still feeling her.

Missing her.

The third thing that happened on that Thursday morning was that an agitated Arnie Aaronson appeared unannounced in Doyle's office. He was dressed in jeans, loafers, and a white golf jacket. Arnie had not worn a suit since Wall Street. This was less a question of lifestyle than the consequence of having gained fifty pounds.

"Sit, Arnie. Want coffee?"

The bigger man sat but ignored the offer. He set a briefcase across his lap, toyed briefly with the latch, but did not open it. Instead, he reached into the pocket of his shirt and drew out a slip of lined paper, small and folded, that looked as if it had been torn from a notebook. He stared at it for a long moment. He spoke without looking up.

"Brendan . . . you want to tell me what's going on?"

First Fat Julie, now Arnie. "Why do you ask?"

"Why?" He waved the slip of paper. "Because everyone I spoke to said those same four words. 'Why do you ask, Arnie?' Brendan? Why did I ask?"

"I'll tell you when I'm sure. They wouldn't discuss it?"

"What, that half of all drugs are counterfeit? Sure they would. They said it's impossible."

"Tell me why."

Doyle listened as Arnie Aaronson took him through a litany of industry practices and safeguards, FDA spot checks, even appeals to common sense.

"The question you have to ask yourself," he said, "is who would knowingly buy this stuff? A drug chain wouldn't. A hospital of any size wouldn't. Even if they were tempted by the prospect of windfall profits it wouldn't begin to be worth the risk. They get caught, they'd get sued up the ass. A doctor wouldn't because, unlike in Japan, for example, doctors don't get a cut on the prescriptions they write."

"You said *knowingly*. What if the hospital doesn't know it's counterfeit?"

"Theoretically, that's possible. Hospitals buy from distributors or from pooled buying groups. The distributors, and now the HMOs, buy direct from the manufacturers. In the case of counterfeits, however, the distributor would have to buy from some third party. To do that, he would have to be getting a very good price. But the second he sees that price—well below what it's been costing him to buy direct—he would know right away that this stuff is bogus."

"So? He's greedy. He buys it anyway."

"But again, if he gets caught, he's out of business and there's a chance he'll go to jail. And he could very well get caught because, aside from the FDA doing spot checks, the major manufacturers have *thousands* of salespeople out there keeping tabs on how their products are selling. If a distributor, say, has more of a given product than that salesperson's computer says they ever bought, the red flag goes up like a rocket."

Doyle had to look away. The image of those salespeople, some of them, trading samples for nose candy left him less than convinced of their proprietary zeal.

"Um . . . back up a second."

The subject of drug dealing reminded him of something that Johnny G. had started to say. That there's very little risk in this. And his uncompleted "even if you get caught . . ." He asked Aaronson about that.

"Compared to what? Pushing hard drugs?"

"For instance. Yes."

"Well . . ." Arnie began counting on his fingers. "You don't have three thousand DEA agents kicking doors in all over the world. Add two thousand FBI agents who work full time on illegal drugs. You don't have the coast guard stopping boats at sea or the air force tracking planes. You don't have dogs sniffing luggage at airports. You don't have all those local narcs that you see on 'Cops' . . . the ones who bring film crews on busts . . . and you don't have undercover cops either. You don't even have the regular local cops because this is strictly the FDA's jurisdiction. The FDA can call in the FBI but unless it's high-profile, the FBI won't get excited."

"What *do* you have?"

"In the FDA? Maybe thirty-five full-time, unarmed criminal investigators."

"For the whole country?"

"For the world."

Aaronson continued counting.

"Unlike with hard drugs there are no mandatory minimum jail sentences. There are probably no sentencing guidelines either. That means it's easy to work out a fine and maybe do some community service. The fines, by the way, run about five hundred bucks for a first offense. Informers get half of any fines levied but at those prices there's not much incentive for whistle-blowers either. The laws are soft because it's not a sexy subject. It doesn't get headlines. You don't see outraged politicians doing talk shows on it and rushing to put their names on legislation."

He paused for a breath.

"Brendan?"

Doyle nodded.

"These people I talked to . . ." The slip of paper again. "I called seven. Out of the seven, five called me back a second time to give me even more reasons why it can't happen. How's that for cooperation?"

Doyle's eyes narrowed.

"And also to ask me again. Why am I so interested?"

The lawyer's antennae started to rise. "Arnie . . . do you believe them or don't you?"

"No."

"Because the question shook them up?"

"Because three of them tried to buy me."

Aaronson, having said that, instantly wished he hadn't.

"Come on, Arnie. Talk to me."

"Forget it."

"Arnie . . . if three multinational drug companies want to shut you up with money, doesn't that tell you . . ."

"Brendan . . . it doesn't tell me shit. Forget it."

Doyle let it drop, if only to keep Aaronson from leaving. He spent the next ten minutes settling him down. Arnie, like Michael, had a lot of respect for the industry. Maybe not so much for the marketing people but certainly for the technical side. They're the people who'll cure cancer one day. And AIDS and MS and cystic fibrosis. It's personal with them, he said.

Aaronson, in their earlier conversation by phone, had mentioned some counterfeit birth control pills from Searle. He had since refreshed his memory. He didn't mind talking about that because it was fairly common knowledge and because it served to support his point that these companies are very responsible.

The product was Ovulen-21. When it was discovered, the company acted instantly to recall two entire lots at a cost of over a million dollars. What was scary, said Aaronson, was that normally a counterfeit product is chemically identical to the original. That's simply good business. A chemically identical counterfeit is that much harder to detect. Further, because counterfeiters don't pay R&D or taxes, the cost of making a good copy is relatively small versus what the real thing would cost. In fact, the difference can run as high as two *thousand* percent.

But if the counterfeiter should run short of an essential chemical, or, say, he doesn't want to leave a chemical trail by buying each of the correct ingredients in bulk, he might decide to use a substitute. In the case of the counterfeit Ovulen, the Guatemalan lab that made it substituted a progesterone hormone for one of the real active ingredients—enthynodiol diactate. They also reduced the estrogen component by half.

"So the pills didn't work."

"Oh, they might have. It's not like they used oatmeal. Other oral contraceptives use progestins. They just wouldn't have worked as well."

"How were they distributed? Did Searle know?"

"I didn't get this from them. In fact, none of the majors would talk except to tell me how things like this can't happen."

"Then what's your source? Newspaper accounts?"

"This stuff never makes the papers. For obvious reasons, the big drug companies like to keep it quiet."

"I can imagine."

"Brendan . . ." Aaronson's voice was pained. "Don't look for cover-ups here. These people try very hard to nail counterfeiters. When they do nail them, their attitude is, what the public doesn't know won't hurt them as long as we stay on top of this. By and large, I think that's fair. Why should they let a good and useful product go under, its reputation destroyed, just because some Guatemalan sleazeball tried to make a buck off it?"

Doyle could appreciate that, he supposed. It certainly explained their sensitivity to Arnie's even asking about it.

Nor were the drug makers alone in opening new horizons for counterfeiters. Aaronson went on to point out that dozens of prestigious brand names are copied all the time. Cartier, Adidas, Christian Dior. Walk along Canal Street in New York and you'll find Rolex and Patek-Phillipe watches for fifty bucks each. At a glance, most people couldn't tell an eight-thousand-dollar gold Rolex from the fifty-dollar fake unless they compared their weights. The real one would be much heavier. In the same block, he said, you'll find counterfeit videotapes, music tapes, and computer software. One company had the balls to run an ad, he said, in *Women's Wear Daily* offering immediate delivery of designer labels.

"This is just the labels, you understand. You buy them and sew them into a carload of dresses you picked up in Taiwan."

"Arnie . . . I keep asking. Where do you learn all this?"

"No secret. Some of it's gossip. But mostly, there's a magazine called the *FDA Consumer*. You can't find a consumer who's ever heard of it but it's in any good-sized library."

Doyle scribbled a note.

"If consumers don't read it, who's it for?"

"It's more like a house organ. The FDA uses it to pat itself on the back."

He made another note. "What about AdChem? You checked them out?"

"No."

"They weren't one of the seven? Why not?"

A long breath. "Because Michael worked with them, Brendan."

"So?"

"So I hear he skipped town."

Oh, for Christ's sake.

"And I hear things about him."

"From who? Lehman-Stone?"

A nod. "I hear things about them too."

"And Michael just might sue the shit out of them. He's clean, Arnie. Word of honor."

"Where'd he go? He still in the country?"

"Arnie . . . read my lips. He's dead honest, he's clean, and he's not down in fucking Brazil. He's up buying some dumb-ass hotel on Martha's—" He stopped himself.

A slow nod from Aaronson, then a quicker one. It said that Aaronson believed him. He also pushed back his chair, which said that this discussion was over.

Arnie still held his little sheet of paper. He seemed about to crumple it but he hesitated, then placed it on the edge of Doyle's desk. Doyle could see that it was a list of names and numbers.

"Do me a favor, Brendan," he said, rising. "You have any more questions, ask them yourself." He walked toward the door, where he paused.

"Say hello to Michael, okay? Tell him my heart goes out."

Doyle said he would. He watched Aaronson go, saw his brief-case clunk against the door frame as Aaronson walked through it. It sounded heavy. But Aaronson had never opened it. He had fingered the latch a few more times. But he never opened the briefcase.

16

The rest of Michael's week went by. Megan never came back. Parnel never showed up again either.

When Sunday arrived, he did one more thing that he would never admit to anyone. He took another ferry ride.

He did not disembark at Woods Hole. He had sworn to himself that he wouldn't. But he did stand at the railing of the upper deck, looking for her. She wasn't there. The slip was empty.

Michael was furious with himself. This was high school. This was being so smitten by Mary Lou McCarthy that he would take the subway up to Washington Heights just to walk down her street and look up at the windows of her apartment hoping to get a glimpse of her.

"Michael . . ."
"Doc . . . just lay off, okay?"

By the time he got back, Harold and Myra Lovelace had reported for duty. They were the full-time help and had worked for the Daggetts, in season, for more than twenty years but this would be their last. Their home was a trailer in West Tisbury but Myra's mother had died and left her an almost new double-wide down in Fort Myers. They intended to retire there come October.

Meantime, Myra was the housekeeper. Harold was the handy-man, gardener, and bellboy, and had occasionally worked the desk.

"I'm also what they call a concierge," said Harold with a grin.

"Oh. Really?"

"If I ain't heard of it, when and where it's happenin', head back to the ferry 'cause you got the wrong island."

Harold's grin was a permanent fixture. It was there while he ate, while he changed light bulbs, and very probably while he dreamed. Fallon had given them a raise and an up-front bonus because they would be carrying more of the load than usual while he learned to be an innkeeper.

"All it takes is a good heart," Harold told him brightly.

"Head for figures don't hurt," Myra added.

"Michael knows about figures. Big investor from New York."

"Ain't New York," Myra reminded him.

Harold and Myra stayed for only two hours. They'd come mostly to count the linens and draw up a list of preseason chores. After that, said Harold, they'd be on their way because Sunday night was Beefsteak & Bingo Night at the First Congregational Church in West Tisbury.

They were at the front door. Harold helped Myra with her coat.

"You're a nice-lookin' fella, Michael," Myra told him. "Break a lot of ladies' hearts, do you?"

"They're not beating down my door."

"I know one who might. Pretty blond girl? Wears it tied back?"

His expression darkened. "Does everyone on this island know Megan?"

"That her name? I don't, but she's standing, all cow-eyed, right across the street."

Megan hadn't moved.

Harold and Myra walked to their car. Megan watched them go. She stood at the edge of the glow of a streetlight, dressed in white jeans and a cable-knit sweater that was at least two sizes too large and had one of those extra wide necks. Her hands met at her chest. They held what looked to be a bottle of wine. It was wrapped in blue foil.

Fallon watched her from inside the front door. He'd be damned if he would open it until she made up her mind whether to stay or go. If she turned and left, he would try not to call after her.

At last, she heaved a sigh and stepped off the curb. He waited. He made her come to the door and knock. He opened it, saying nothing. She looked up at him, then dropped her eyes.

"Hello, Michael," she said, very softly.

He tried to remember the words he'd rehearsed in case this moment ever came. Like . . . Hello, Megan. Get lost, Megan. Like . . . I figured out why you live alone. Your parents threw you out, right? They pay you to stay away because it's cheaper than paying your shrink bills. You're a neurotic, spaced-out, and manipulative little bitch. Did I mention that I'm HIV positive?

But Fallon said nothing at all. She held out the bottle. He made no move to take it. She brought it back against her chest and sighed deeply. She hunched her shoulders. The neck of her sweater fell away, partly baring one of them. She looked so very small. So vulnerable. Not at all like the Megan who . . .

Hold it, Michael. Don't even start.

"Megan . . ." he said quietly. "Enough is enough, okay?"

She glanced up North Water Street. Two young girls were walking down in her direction. They were looking at her. One whispered to the other. Megan's color began to rise.

"Do you have to humiliate me, Michael?"

Fallon saw the girls who were trying not to stare. They knew rejection when they saw it. He stepped back from the lights of the portico entrance and beckoned Megan to follow. She hesitated, then stepped inside.

"Two minutes," he said as he closed the door behind her.

The remnants of a fire still glowed in the sitting room. She walked toward it and stood near it, holding the wine. She started to lower herself to the carpet.

"Don't get comfortable," Fallon told her. He remained standing at the sitting room's entrance.

She turned a part of her face toward him.

"If you feel the need to hurt me," she said quietly, "could you try to get it all out at once?"

Hurting *you?*

Fallon could only blink. In your head, this is about hurting you? But he said nothing. She turned to face him fully.

"Michael, I can't make you understand what happened the other night. Not in the time you'll give me."

"Good, because I don't want to hear it."

Another sigh. She nodded slowly, resignedly. She reached to place the foil-wrapped bottle on the mantel. The sweater bared part of her shoulder again. She shrugged it into place and walked past him toward the door.

Fallon set his jaw. Just once, he told himself, leave well enough alone. Let her go.

She reached the front entrance, put her hand on the latch, then hesitated. She leaned her forehead against it.

"Michael . . . believe me. I don't need this either."

"Then why did you come?"

She spun to face him. "And anyway, screw you," she blurted angrily. "You think that was *my* idea of a good time? Why did *you* have to come to my boat?"

He had told her why he came. Because he was intrigued. Because from what he'd heard, he thought she was someone he might like. But that was before he learned that there were two of her.

Her eyes seemed to soften as he had these thoughts. It was almost as if she could hear them. And now she cocked her head slightly and her eyes glazed over as if she were trying to hear more. Her eyes narrowed slightly. She looked up at him.

"You came again, didn't you? You came again this weekend."

Say nothing, Michael. Not a word.

"This morning," he told her. "Your boat was gone."

Jesus, Michael.

She looked away. "I needed some time alone. I . . . sailed down to Newport yesterday."

Fallon sensed a certain pregnancy in that announcement. "Newport. Should that mean something to me?"

She flicked a hand, waving the subject off. "Michael, you went there again for some answers. Do you want to hear them or not?"

"Okay, answer this. Can you read minds?"

"No."

"No, or only sometimes like I think you just did?"

"I can't read minds. No one can."

"And yet you knew that I went back to see you."

An exasperated snort. "If you're asking if I'm perceptive, yes. More so than most? I wish to God I wasn't. Do I know that you *do* want to hear this? *Yes.* Do I know that you don't really want me to leave? That you wish there was a way in hell that we could try to be friends? *Yes.* That doesn't make me a fucking witch, Michael. Those girls who walked past us knew that much."

She was pacing the room. She spoke slowly, haltingly.

"That first day, I said that you were dangerous. You are."

She had made him promise that he would say nothing. Not a word until she indicated that he could speak. He was already having difficulty.

He busied himself stoking the fire. He had opened the wine. It was a decent Chablis. She said that reds do not do well on boats. Megan took the offered glass and set it aside.

"I felt violence all around you, Michael. Even when you were being nice. I also felt terrible pain. It was fading, it had started to ease but it was all still there."

She looked at the wine glass, decided she could do with a taste.

"These feelings I had . . . a thousand other women could have had them. They'd meet you and think, 'This guy is really smoldering. He's carrying a lot of baggage. I don't need this in my life right now.' "

Fallon had drained his first glass. He poured a second. Except for the violence part, he'd had exactly those thoughts about her.

"But here's where I'm *not* like a thousand other women. When you stepped off my boat . . . when I reached out and touched you . . . I felt so much more . . . awful things . . . things that frightened me."

Fallon grunted. Dead bodies, he remembered. Hundreds of dead bodies.

"I'm not always right," she went on as if she'd heard him, "even when I feel it that strongly. So I came here that night to make sure. The best way to do that is to touch. But for that to work . . . it's not a trance but it's like a trance. Everything has to be blocked out. Everything that's me, I mean."

She squeezed her eyes shut. She hugged herself as she paced.

"I sure as hell touched you, didn't I, Michael?"

Megan covered her face with her hands. He could see that she was mortified. She needed a moment to collect herself. She swallowed hard and continued.

"Have you ever, like the next day, said, 'I can't believe I did that'? Just shake your head or nod."

He nodded.

"Were you disgusted with yourself? You can answer."

"I . . . wondered about myself."

"If it happened often enough, not every day but still too often, you might decide you'd be better off living alone. I did. Did you, Michael?"

"Something like that."

"You didn't want anyone else hurt."

"Hold it. Who says anyone was?"

She chewed her lip. "It's all around you, Michael. People hurt. People dying. Some of it is through violence and that's the part that's clearest. But most of it . . . many people . . . all kinds of people . . . was not violent, exactly. I want to say poison. People who were poisoned."

"Um . . . Megan."

She waved him off. She stopped pacing and sat, still hugging herself.

"Megan . . . I know nothing about lots of people dying. Poisoned or any other way."

She rocked in her chair. Eyes closed. She seemed to be struggling. "Yes, you do," she blurted. "Or you should. Or someone thinks you do. Or . . . oh, Christ, I hate this."

Fallon pushed to his feet. He walked to her chair and lowered himself in front of it. For an instant, she seemed frightened of him. He backed away.

"Megan," he said gently. "That part is nonsense. It just didn't happen."

Silence. Tears welled in her eyes.

"Okay," he said wearily. "Let's say it did. I either know about it, I should know, or someone thinks I do. Which is it?"

The tears spilled over. "I think you know."

He took a breath. "And if I swear to you I don't, will you believe me?"

"I do believe you. But you *do* know."

They had finished the bottle.

Michael sat on the carpet by her chair. She had asked if she could touch him again but only with her fingertips. She did, but she could feel nothing else. Michael hadn't thought she would. There was nothing to this poisoning business. Megan said it herself. She was not always right.

Wait a second.

"I work . . . I *did* work . . . with a number of drug companies. When you talk about a poisoning, about all these people dying, could you be talking about . . . I don't know . . . a manufacturing error? A bad batch?"

"Has that happened?"

"In this country? Not that I know of. And I *would* know. Everyone in the industry would know."

She pursed her lips, then shook her head as if to say, "Then that can't be it."

"Why, by the way, did my pills upset you?"

She looked away. "They just did."

"Megan, I'm looking for a connection here."

"Michael . . ." She flared at him. "I just don't like pills."

Uh-oh.

"They numb the mind. Why do you take them?"

"I stopped, actually."

"Then get rid of them."

He whistled inwardly. What was she? he wondered. A former addict? Suicide-prone? Or maybe psychics just like to keep all their circuits clear. Whatever. Her reaction had been extravagant and she knew it. She turned her head and gave a jerky little wave as if asking for a moment's grace. The hand settled on his arm.

"Michael . . ." She squeezed it. "Go sit over there."

"Why?"

"Because you're going to be mad at me. Go sit."

Fallon obeyed.

He thought that he was about to hear what she had against pills. Perhaps some clue to what made her the way she is. But she had shifted gears entirely.

She began by telling him that on the night she rushed out of there, she had never intended to come back, hoped never to see him or speak to him again. When she came to . . . realized what she'd been doing . . . she was so humiliated that she ran all the way down to the Edgartown dock, started her engine, and nearly plowed into a forty-foot Bertram.

And she was frightened. The physical stuff aside, there was that gun. Awful things had happened around it. It was all a stew in her mind but she felt certain that she'd seen him mixed in with it. She had not seen him using the gun, not actually firing it, but she felt that he wanted to, planned to, hoped to. One of those.

And there was still some of that anger in him, she said. And fear. Not as much. Just some. But the house, this house, seemed okay. It had been a happy house. Always. There were no dumb ghosts. He would be fine here.

"So where do I get mad?" he asked her.

She wet her lips. "Never mind. That's not important."

Fallon groaned aloud. Yup. That'll do it. Someone asks, Michael, do you know what's wrong with you? . . . No, what? . . . Never mind. Someone asks, Michael, do you know what women say about you? . . . No, what? . . . Never mind.

"Megan," he told her, "there is a poker by the fireplace. I'm about to pick it up and hit you with it."

She almost smiled. "Okay. Give me a second."

Another grimace as in here goes nothing.

"Michael, I know about Bronwyn Kelsey. I know how she died."

He felt his head go light.

"And your uncle. I know where you lived, where you worked. I know how you broke your arm."

He stared, disbelieving.

"It was from the newspapers, Michael. I went to a library."

He began to understand. "Your sail to Newport?"

She nodded. "They've got a big microfilm section."

She had not intended to research him, she said. She'd simply taken the boat out because she had a sense that he might come that weekend to confront her, attack her, say all the hurtful things he must have been saving up. She wanted to be someplace else when he did. But she couldn't get away from him. Even out on the water. There was this great bubbling stew that she mentioned. And all those dead that she felt.

She knew that he had come from New York, that he seemed to be running from something, and anything that big, she reasoned, had to have been in the papers. It was no more than a hunch. But she spent last evening and early this morning scanning back issues of the *New York Times* and the *Post.* Then she spotted the name. His uncle's name, actually. And his own a few issues later.

"I'm very sorry, Michael. About your loss, I mean."

He said nothing.

"Are you angry?"

"I don't know."

"I'd never say a word. And I won't mention it again unless you feel like talking about it."

"I don't. At least not tonight."

She peeled back her sleeve, turned her watch to the light. She drummed her fingers, then rose to her feet.

"Do you . . . need a ride?" he asked her.

She shook her head, cocking it toward the Edgartown marina. It was only a two-minute walk.

"Megan, if you'd care to stay over . . ."

"No, Michael."

"This is an inn, Megan. I didn't mean with me."

She dropped her eyes. "I'm sure you didn't."

Michael looked for sarcasm. He didn't see it. He saw sadness.

"Megan, you explained that. The other night . . . that wasn't you, exactly."

She said nothing. The shoulders seemed to come together again. She looked small again.

"What if we just sat here?" he offered. "We have the fire. You can tell me where you've been with your boat. The Caribbean, maybe. I've never been there myself."

Still nothing. But she did look tired.

"We can lay out some cushions. You take one side of the fireplace and I'll take the other. I'll get some quilts and pillows, make a couple of Irish coffees . . ."

She shook her head. She seemed ready to cry again. Now what?

"Megan, tell me what's wrong."

"You wouldn't see much difference," she blurted. With that, she turned toward the door.

He went after her. He reached to touch her shoulder, then drew back when she recoiled.

"Are you going to tell me what that means?"

A weary sigh. "Come on, Michael. You're not that dumb."

"You'd be amazed. Tell me."

"I freeze up, okay? I'm good at one thing and it isn't screwing."

Oh, boy.

"Megan, can't we just . . ." He almost said can't we be friends? "Can't we just sort of be with each other without that coming up? I mean, no one pinned any medals on me, either."

She wavered.

"Stay for one more log. And one Irish coffee."

"One log?"

"Scout's honor."

She did fall asleep by the fire.

Michael fetched a pillow and comforter. He covered her. Carefully, he eased the pillow under her head and straightened the arm that it replaced. He was relieved that she didn't stir. Lying there, finally at peace, she really was a lovely woman.

He had kept his word and his distance with some difficulty. He found himself wanting to hold her. But if he did she might read his thoughts and get them wrong again. He'd be thinking, *Go ahead, Megan. Doze off. You're safe here with me,* but she'd hear, *Come on, tootsie. Let's get naked and give it another shot.*

One eye fluttered. It opened just a bit.

She whispered, "You're a nice man, Michael."

And then she was asleep again.

The fire was down to a few glowing coals.

Fallon took off his jacket and shoes. He lined up some cushions well to his side of the fireplace and eased himself onto them.

Megan was snoring softly. One arm was stretched out where he left it. Her hand was within reach. He wanted to touch it. He hesitated, for fear of waking her again.

But he did reach out. Very lightly, he placed his hand over hers. The part of it nearest the fire was warm. He could feel her heartbeat through it. Her hand did not move or otherwise react until he started to take his own away. Her fingers arched, just a little. He waited. Then her hand slid out from under his and came to rest on top of it. Ever so lightly, she squeezed his hand.

"I freeze up," she had said to him.

He would like to have tried. He would like to have had the chance to show her that he could be patient . . . encouraging . . . kind. He had no idea whether he could ever get her to trust him or, more importantly, to trust herself. Maybe not. It probably wouldn't happen.

But whether or not it did, even if they never made love or even touched again, he knew one thing. He knew that this, right here and now, was as tender a moment as he'd ever had in his life.

17

Brendan Doyle, like Megan, had been to the library.

On that Sunday afternoon, he had photocopied every page from Moody's, Standard & Poor's, and the Dun & Bradstreet World Business Directory that made reference to AdlerChemiker AG and one from Moody's Financial listing the officers and owners of Lehman-Stone. He had also used the library's Wilsondisc computer to find any and all recent articles on the subject of counterfeit drugs. There were only a few and Arnie Aaronson had been right. Most of these were in the magazine called *FDA Consumer*. He photocopied those as well. Once home, he arranged them in two stacks and made himself comfortable.

Before he began, his yellow Hi-Liter in hand, he tried the number of Jake's Florida condo one more time. Moon still wasn't answering. It had been two days now.

Doyle regretted lying to Michael. But if he'd told him where Moon was, Michael might have been on the next plane to Naples. And it wasn't strictly a lie. Moon's primary address these past several months had been a neurological ward up in Fort Myers and then a rehab and therapy clinic in Naples. He got worse before he got better. It had been only three weeks since his therapist said that he could try living alone.

Jake's apartment had seemed a safe enough address. Anyone who thought to look for him there would have done so months ago.

But now Doyle was worried.

He wished now that he hadn't given Julie Moon's number. It's just that it was hard to say no, all things considered. All Julie wanted to hear, he said, was that Michael and Jake were clean. He would have believed it, coming from Moon. No one ever believes a lawyer.

But what Julie had also said was "Always keep something in your pocket." Doyle knew what he hoped that *didn't* mean. He hoped it didn't mean, "Doyle's okay but he's slow. He's too legal. Doyle likes to see proof. Fuck it. Let's just give this to Moon."

Yeah, well fuck you too.

You want to see speed? I'll show you speed. I'll show you how fast Moon's brain explodes if you get his blood pressure all pumped up.

But first things first. AdChem.

Let's see what Michael was into.

AdlerChemiker AG, according to Moody's, was mostly a holding company, created in 1982 under German law. It was actually a merger of several smaller firms, some of which had been in business since before World War Two. Of these, the centerpiece was Arznei-Fabrik GmbH, wholly owned by the von Scharnhorst family of Munich. Doyle half expected to see that they made poison gas for death camps but all they ever made were vitamins. Later, after the merger, Arznei-Fabrik branched out into pharmaceuticals, buying up two more R&D companies, a printing and packaging firm, and a mail order drug firm.

Rapid growth through the eighties. Heavy investment in R&D, which apparently paid off. They now sell about sixty different product lines and hold over three hundred new drug patents. Until the past few years, relatively few have had FDA approval for sale in the United States but they made up for it in the rest of the world where standards are far less rigid.

This, Doyle knew, did not mean the products were crap, necessarily. The FDA requires that a new drug be effective ninety-five percent of the time. That means ninety-five out of one hundred patients must benefit from it or it can't be sold in this country.

It's a dumb standard. It sounds fine as long as you're not suffering from some nasty disease and there's a medicine that will help it, say, eight times out of ten. It's why Tijuana, just over the border, has become one big supermarket for drugs that you can't buy here. And where some drugs you *can* buy here sell at a tenth the cost.

But getting back to AdChem . . .

They have subsidiaries, it says here, in over twenty countries. Most of them third world. India, Pakistan, Cambodia, Egypt. Several in Central America. And there's Guatemala again, where Arnie said the bogus Ovulen was made. The legitimate reason for all these exotic subsidiaries is, of course, the low labor cost but it's also the freedom from burdensome controls. Some of them have no standards at all concerning product contamination, safety in the workplace, or even for the disposal of toxic waste. If they did make counterfeits, thought Doyle, you wonder who'd notice.

Adler.

It struck Doyle as odd that none of the companies in the AdChem group ever had Adler in its name. None of the directors had that name either. Most of them are von Scharnhorsts by blood or marriage. Among them, they control almost seventy percent of the stock. The largest single stockholder is the Countess Anna von Reisch und Scharnhorst. Her husband and her cousins run the company. No Adlers and no Rasmussens either. Moon is really reaching on that one.

He found a profile on the Countess. It had photographs. One dated back to the war when she had volunteered at a civilian aid station. During the Allied bombings of Munich she was twice cited for heroism, pulling injured victims out of burning buildings. This says she saved dozens of lives.

Doyle thought she had a good face. Very correct, very Prussian. Never pretty, exactly, but strong. The war ended and, with the help of the Marshall Plan, she started putting the family business back together. She gave jobs to hundreds of destitute Germans, sold ancestral land to pay their salaries until the company could start earning money. In her later years she spent less time on the business and more time on her charities. No kids of her own. She still worked three days a week as a volunteer in a children's hospital.

Looks . . . profiles . . . can be deceiving, thought Doyle. But if this woman had a venal bone in her body, he couldn't see it. Even so, Doyle had no doubt that AdChem had routinely skirted the law. That, after all, was the point in having so many subsidiaries in so many places. What is criminal here is legal there. It is also a way to hide the very large profits that are made on some of these products.

Take an ordinary blister pack of a given medication. The raw materials are bought here, there, and everywhere, usually from a company's own subsidiaries, and each ingredient is marked up separately. Another plant mixes them, marks up the result. The mixture is sent to still another plant that presses it into pills. That's another mark-up. They go from there to the packaging plant for assembly. One last mark-up is added but this is the only mark-up that shows on the books. Little if any tax is paid on all those other profits.

For all that, Doyle still couldn't see where AdChem is doing anything that all the others don't do. Johnny G. sees big-time counterfeiting and even big-time heroin trafficking. Doyle couldn't see that either. Just because one plant in India sells a chemical that's essential to making heroin—among many other uses for it—that does not a criminal organization make. And if there's still all that money in their regular drugs, and if you keep the right kind of books, why should they bother with counterfeits?

On the other hand . . . if they're more or less straight . . . why would they need an outfit like Parker Security Service, Inc.? Why would Lehman-Stone, an investment banker, need that bunch of thugs?

No Rasmussens at Lehman-Stone either.

He started on his second stack of documents.

An hour later, Doyle had finished his reading. He said, "I'll be damned" for perhaps the fifth time.

He reached for his telephone, thought better of it, then picked up the cellular phone instead. He tapped out Arnie Aaronson's number.

"Tell me," he said when Aaronson answered. "You brought

your briefcase when you came to my office. Were those FDA articles in it?''

"I gather you went and got your own."

"Yes, I did. Why didn't you save me the trouble?"

"Because I want no part of this."

"But it's public record, Arnie. It's a magazine. How could sharing it possibly harm you?"

A slow exhalation of breath.

"That list I gave you? Those people I called? The ones with a checkmark called me back at least twice. They wanted a face to face meeting. The ones with two checks hinted very strongly that we might make some arrangement."

"A payoff. You told me. But in return for what?"

"For telling them who's asking. And for helping to put a lid on it."

"Arnie . . . let me get this straight. Are you telling me that the entire pharmaceutical industry is engaged in a massive cover-up?"

"They're not felons, Brendan. Call it damage control."

"To protect their business at the expense of the public?"

"Wrong, Brendan. It is to protect it from a massive and *unwarranted* loss of public confidence. It is to prevent the panic selling of pharmaceutical and biotech stocks and the damage that would do to this same public you're talking about. If spending a few bucks will accomplish that, they'll spend."

It was Doyle's turn to be silent.

"Counterfeits are a fact of life, Brendan. I still don't think it's half but most of what's out there, by far, is probably just as good as the real thing. If you were the president of Merck or Pfizer, would you want to stand up and say that on television? Or at a congressional hearing?"

Doyle let him go.

He could understand Arnie's reluctance to be involved. It was not a matter of being afraid of the drug companies. Not at all. Nor was it anything like criminal complicity. It was more a fear that he'd never have a moment's peace once his name became associated with a subject so potentially explosive as this.

All those firms wondering what he's got. Badgering him, dangling carrots at him, offering him lucrative consulting contracts if he'll tell what he knows. If it's about a competitor, the deal still holds. Knowing that is worth money as well. On second thought, therefore, Arnie could indeed find himself exposed to charges of criminal conspiracy.

As if that were not enough, in Arnie's view, we now add Michael to the equation. Michael's involvement with AdChem means that the interest of Michael's lawyer is hardly academic. Add the knowledge that Jake Fallon was murdered. Add the killing of Bronwyn Kelsey, who was also involved in this industry. Might these not be related? And, finally, add in that the attorney of both Jake and Michael Fallon is also the attorney of the infamous Giordano brothers who control the Brooklyn docks and are therefore, prima facie, already involved in smuggling.

Arnie Aaronson is no coward. He's a good and decent man. Given the right thing to do, he'll do it. But he has no wish to be put on a witness stand and have a prosecutor say, "If you knew *this* and *this* and *this,* Mr. Aaronson, how are we to believe that you didn't know *that?* Or at least that you didn't see it coming?"

Back to the FDA papers.

What Doyle found in them was breathtaking.

Item:

Not long ago, in Nigeria, 109 young children died of kidney failure after ingesting a chemical solvent. The solvent was in a paracetamol syrup—sort of like Tylenol for children—which had been administered by several Nigerian hospitals. The product was counterfeit. A wholesale pharmacist had used the correct active ingredient, acetaminophen, and even in the right concentration.

But he had purchased an unmarked drum that supposedly contained propylene glycol, the preservative used in the genuine syrup. The drum actually held diethyelene glycol, which is used in antifreeze. The pharmacist bottled this poison, slapped on phony labels, and sold it to the hospitals.

What was Arnie's argument? That no wholesaler would take such a risk for such a small reward? Here's one who clearly did. Ah, but that's in Africa he'd say. In corrupt and chaotic Nigeria. Couldn't happen here.

Item:

An Iranian counterfeiter, now in prison, was arrested by the U.S. Customs Service. They had been laying for him because he had once approached a broker with an offer to sell eight million pharmacy-sized bottles of three major prescription drugs. The drugs were Tagamet, an ulcer medication, three million bottles at $32.15 each; Anspor, an antibiotic, three million bottles at $47.70 each; and Naprosyn, for arthritis, two million bottles at $237.75 each.

His samples of Naprosyn, the arthritis medicine, contained mainly aspirin. They might well have killed patients who had ulcers. But otherwise they looked perfectly legitimate. According to the FDA, the Iranian, a man named Naghdi, had manufactured the counterfeit drug by obtaining tableting machines, bulk acetaminophen, aspirin, lactose, and coloring agents.

He bought tableting machines to press the bogus Naprosyn. He commissioned artwork that duplicated the Naprosyn package. He had the tooling to imprint the company trademark on the bottles, bottle liners, bottle caps, and the tablets themselves. Even the identical bar code.

He supplied fraudulent shipping documents, a fake insurance policy, and all the necessary paper, on company letterhead, to show that he had bought this stuff directly from the legitimate manufacturer.

What blew the deal? What tipped the Customs Service?

That broker, in his innocence, called the manufacturer to ask them if he was getting a good deal at the quoted prices. The Customs Service and the FDA then set up a sting to catch Naghdi. They wanted to buy the lot. He announced that the eight million bottles were already gone but, if they had the cash and were ready to deal, he could get them a million bottles of Tagamet at the bargain price of twenty-seven dollars each. The Tagamet was warehoused in Tampico, Mexico, ready to be smuggled in. Shipping would be arranged via someone called Five Star Distributors of Puerto Rico.

Doyle, at this point, had gone to his calculator. That first deal, just three drugs, which someone in this country bought, amounted to more than seven hundred million dollars. That's one deal. One time. The second deal, which never went through, was peanuts by comparison. Only twenty-seven million dollars.

The Naprosyn alone, two million bottles, totaled more than $475 million if the Iranian got his asking price. Naprosyn's *legitimate sales* that year, to the domestic market, were roughly the same amount.

Arnie? Do you still say half is horseshit?

No, I don't suppose you do.

Do you still say that few distributors would knowingly take the chance? I mean . . . these distributors . . . one expects them to have names like Blue Cross Pharmaceuticals or Mount Sinai Medicines for the Afflicted. They don't. They have names like Five Star Distributors of Puerto Rico. Triple-A Cigars of Jersey City. Mucci & Son Sundries of Miami.

Doyle ran the numbers three times. He could scarcely believe them himself but there they were. One deal, one arrest. The Iranian, obviously, had not made this stuff in his garage and sure as hell wasn't in it alone. He was a broker, a salesman, for an immensely sophisticated operation. Just as clearly, that seven-hundred-million-dollar deal was only the tip of the iceberg.

Oh, and look at this.

There's a fairly new drug called Zantac, an ulcer drug that has pretty much replaced Tagamet. It doesn't cure ulcers; it just cuts down on the acid your stomach produces. Want to know what the annual sales are? Four billion dollars. Zantac is, right now, the biggest selling drug in the world. Four billion dollars on one fucking pill that's basically a Band-Aid.

What *does* cure ulcers? Antibiotics, it says here, because ulcers are caused by a viral infection. But they push drugs like Zantac because there's no money in antibiotics—their patents have all run out—and because if you cure a disease, where's the repeat business?

Okay, Zantac has the number one spot. Three out of the next four top sellers are for cardiovascular problems. Heart attacks. The number one killer. But you know what seems to ward off heart attacks best? Aspirin. Aspirin and garlic. Even the FDA says so. In fact, it says that popping an aspirin *during* a heart attack can save one in four lives. But no maker of aspirin has asked the FDA if they could market their own product for that purpose.

Why should they? If they did, people might not buy their other
patent-protected heart drugs that sell for a couple of hundred times
the price.

An interesting ethical question, right? Here's a better one.
When a drug like Tagamet hits paydirt, everyone else tries to
jump on the bandwagon. But Tagamet was still under patent. So
along comes a Zantac and about six other drugs, all of which
do precisely the same thing but they do it through a different
mechanism. This is how they get around the patent.

So here's the assignment for our next ethics class. Explain in
a hundred words or less, how that is *not* the moral equivalent of
counterfeiting.

No wonder Jake hated these clowns.

Do the drug lords of Colombia know about this? Wouldn't they
like to stop being shot at? Hunted down? If caught, wouldn't
they rather get fourteen years, which is what the Iranian got,
and of which he'll probably serve five, than life without parole?
Wouldn't they rather have a customer base that can't "just say
no"? And whose enforced addictions are paid for by health insurance and Medicaid? And are a better class of people to boot?

Item:

Only thirty-five criminal investigators in the whole Food and
Drug Administration. There are another twelve hundred field investigators but their tasks are more routine, such as trying to
keep drug labs from fudging on test results and nabbing pharmacists who sell prescription drug samples that are intended strictly
for doctors. Of the twelve hundred, a good many concentrate on
agricultural products, veterinary medicines, and the like.

Veterinary medicines, thought Doyle, frowning.

The library computer had kicked out a few items on the subject. He almost hadn't bothered to copy them because they
seemed no more than marginally related to the larger subject.
Until this moment.

Item:

One firm, Johnson & Johnson, sells a colon cancer drug called
Ergomisol. It was charging thirteen hundred dollars for a single
fifty-milligram dose. But another firm sells a veterinary drug that

has the same active ingredient—levamisole—for just fourteen dollars a dose.

It would seem tempting for a cancer clinic to buy the animal drug in bulk, grind it up, then press it into the fifty-milligram tablets that would otherwise cost them almost one thousand percent more.

Item:

Something like that seems to be happening. The Customs Service seized thirty-two tons of adulterated, misbranded, or smuggled animal drugs. The article doesn't say what was ultimately being done with them. Perhaps the writer didn't wish to give people ideas.

If the DEA's experience is any guide, seizures represent no more than two percent of the total that actually gets through. The bad news, therefore, is that another fifteen hundred tons or so would have actually reached the market, some of it reformulated for human consumption. The good news is that these are real drugs. They'll probably work as well as any.

One must learn, thought Doyle, to listen to one's inner voices.

Veterinary medicine.

That's the business Eagle Sales was in. The business that Michael's father was in. It's the business that Armin Rasmussen owned until Big Jake Fallon, baseball bat in hand, gave him twenty-four hours to leave the country or have every bone in his body broken. His office and plant were in flames at the time. And later his home. Moon had burned them to the ground.

Doyle suddenly remembered something.

In his mind he saw the thick brown envelope that Marty Hennessy had brought over to his office. In it were the contents of Jake's pockets on the night he died. It was still in the office safe.

The contents of his pockets had shed little light at the time. His billfold had been left intact, cash and credit cards still there. His keys, watch, and rings as well. The intruder had taken nothing. All he cared about, thought Hennessy, was getting away from there.

Jake's notebook was no help either. Doyle had gone through it page by page, with Hennessy, looking for any hint that Jake might have had cause to look over his shoulder. There was an entry here and there that might have raised an eyebrow if a reporter had gotten his hands on it . . . notes of meetings with certain public figures . . . but no reference whatever to Lehman-Stone or AdChem.

Also in his pocket, however, was an AdChem annual report. Doyle hadn't thought much about it because Michael said that Bronwyn had given it to Jake that evening. She'd been bragging about Michael and touting AdChem as a stock to watch.

All things considered, maybe it was worth another look.

Moon?

Could you be right after all?

Could Armin Rasmussen have found his way into AdChem?

Moon, where the hell have you gone?

18

It was a four-car garage. Moon entered it in darkness. He made no sound. The only light shone down from the apartment above it. It was enough.

He saw the white BMW. The initials "BH" were written on the door in script. An electric golf cart, also white, sat at the far end. It bore the same initials. The remaining two spaces were empty. The garage, he noted, had its own supply of gasoline. An electric pump had been mounted on the wall nearest the driveway.

As he drew near the stairs that led to the apartment, he caught the scent of cheap perfume. He tested the stairs. They were made of wood but had runners of outdoor carpet. He readied the baseball bat and climbed, praying that the man had found no companion for this night. There was no one. The apartment was empty.

An ashtray by the bed held cigarettes with lipstick on them but these were dry and stale to the touch. The bed was unmade. It smelled of chlorine from the pool, of sweat, and of that perfume. The smell of those sheets, for some reason, made Moon think of Michael. He did not know why. Michael would never use a prostitute.

Moon searched the apartment. Between the mattress and box

spring of the bed he found two automatic pistols and a spare clip for each. One was large caliber, the other small. He examined the small one, a Beretta, .22 caliber. This, more than the other, was an assassin's weapon. It was meant for close work, fired into the brain, several shots, little noise. The sound, if there was anyone to hear it, would resemble the popping of balloons. He placed both pistols in his belt and made his way back toward the pool.

The man was stretched out on a lounge chair. He was dressed in shorts and a flowered shirt. He lay, legs crossed, his hands clasped behind his neck, looking up as if enjoying the night sky. Moon had little doubt that this was the one called Walter. He would like to have been certain of that. But now he could not be. The man was dead.

Moon had not meant to kill him. He realized too late that he had.

Before he had lifted him into that chair, arranged his body in that pose, Moon had sat astride him, massaging his heart, trying to bring back a pulse. The only pulse he felt was his own, throbbing at his temple.

He was disgusted with himself.

The choke hold was meant only to put him to sleep, give Moon a few minutes to study the security system. That done, he would have carried this man into the main house and he would have strapped him to a chair. He would have waited for him to wake up and see a black man sitting across from him. See the baseball bat in the black man's hands.

Moon would not have spoken. There would have been no need. He would have watched the man's eyes as his head began to clear. First, he would have looked for recognition. And then he would have watched them as they focused on the polished Louisville Slugger, bought new that afternoon from a store three towns away. The man's eyes would have told him the answer he was looking for.

He would have talked. And then he would have died hard.

But Moon had not been sure of his strength. What the stroke had sapped of it, all that therapy had restored, but in different ways and in different muscles. He should have known that his touch and timing would be off. He had squeezed just a little too tight and held for five seconds too long. He had neglected to make sure the man was breathing before he left him to look for others who might be there.

Moon placed the Louisville Slugger on the lounge chair beside the dead man's legs and entered the main house through a set of French doors. He was reasonably certain that the alarms had been turned off because he had found the doors ajar and a light on in the kitchen. The man had left himself access to the liquor supply. Still, he was reluctant to explore further. A home such as this might well have more than one system. Motion detectors. Pressure plates on the carpeted staircase. He would limit his search to the downstairs rooms.

In the living room, he found what he was looking for. Atop a grand piano, there was an assortment of family photographs. The gray-haired man in several of these had to be Hobbs. Moon studied his face, mentally darkening the hair, smoothing out the skin. It was not a face that he had seen before. He was disappointed. Bart Hobbs was not Armin Rasmussen. He was far too small, at least a decade too young.

The photos showed that Bart Hobbs led an active life for a Wall Street big shot. Most men in that field are reluctant to take vacations. Yet here was Hobbs in golfing attire, sitting in his monogrammed golf cart. Hobbs in tennis whites being handed a trophy. Hobbs with a fishing rod posing next to a hoisted marlin. Hobbs with several other men, a snowy background this time, all dressed in ski clothing.

Moon studied that photograph. He knew none of those faces either. In the background stood a house that resembled a Swiss chalet. It had window boxes with fake red flowers in them and elaborate carved molding under the eaves and on the wooden balconies. The chimney had his monogram, a large BH, set into the stone. An estate sign in the foreground bore the name *Playing Hobbs*. The man likes puns, thought Moon.

He turned the photograph over. A card, taped to the back, gave a date and a list of names. None was familiar. Most were what he called rich man names. Men with first names that sounded like last names, half of them followed by numerals.

Gardner Lowell IV . . . Frampton Childress II . . . Avery Haverford Bellows.

This last had no numeral but had *three* last names plus a nickname written in parentheses. Nickname was "Dink." Even their nicknames are rich.

There was a fourth name, not like the rest. That name was Victor Turkel. It was a clunky kind of name, and Moon had no trouble guessing which one it belonged to. He had to be the fat one wearing steamed-up glasses, kind of hanging back as if he was not all that eager to be in the picture. The other three, besides Hobbs, were all thin and looked fit and had haircuts in the style of George Bush.

But no Armin Rasmussen. No one who even resembled him. That would have been too much to hope for.

The photograph made him think of Michael again. But this time he realized why. The house was a ski lodge in Maine. Michael had gone there once with the English girl, Bronwyn. Hobbs had invited them.

Moon set it back down, not bothering to wipe it clean of fingerprints. He eased himself back outside and, sensing no other presence but that of the dead man, walked to the garage. There, in a storage room, he found two plastic buckets and a half-gallon can of paint remover. He poured paint remover into two buckets, carried them to the gas pump, and added several gallons of gasoline to each. He left the pump running.

Moon carried these back to the house, where he tested the flow of air. He opened certain doors and closed others, creating baffles and chambers where the heat would build before it spread. That done, he began pouring the mixture.

He had a match in his hand, ready to strike it, when he thought of the man outside. The police and firemen will find him dead and soon they will realize that he'd been throttled. Better to leave some doubt of how he died. Or, more importantly, how long it took him to die.

He returned to the lounge chair and took the dead man's right hand. He wrapped the man's fingers around the Beretta, keeping the heavier weapon for himself. Next, he took the man's head in his hands. Moon tilted it back, exposing more of the throat.

He picked up the bat. He would begin with the throat. The ankles would be next. He would then work his way back up.

* * *

Moon stopped for the night near Cape Kennedy.

He found a motel in an all-black section where he would not be especially noticed. There was a late-night laundromat nearby. He washed the blood and the gas fumes from his clothing. He dozed off watching the dryer.

The next morning, he rose early and took a long quiet walk on the beach, then found a pay phone where he placed a call to the machine at Jake's condo. He tapped out the code to hear messages.

There were several; all but one were from Brendan Doyle.

"I fucking can't believe you," said the last from Doyle. He took that to mean Doyle had heard about the fire.

The one after that confirmed it. It was from Julie Giordano. It said, "You do nice work. But we really gotta talk, okay?"

He tapped another code that left the messages intact. That made it harder to know when he called. He returned to his motel room with a container of convenience store coffee. He would head north soon; he had already mapped his route. Before that, however, he would spend another hour with Michael's laptop computer.

He still had Michael's watch and jewelry, which he had taken from the apartment. It had to look like a burglary. These he kept wrapped in a sock against the day when he might think of a way to return them. These and Bronwyn's photograph in its boxy little frame. He had wondered, idly, why Michael chose a frame that was so deep-set that her face was hard to see. A face like hers, you'd think he'd want to show it off.

At the hour of her service, he had slipped out of Mount Sinai. Michael's building was directly across Central Park from the hospital, five minutes away by taxi. Moon went in through the garage; he worked quickly and quietly, and was back within twenty minutes more. He had Michael's computer and a pocketful of disks but he had no clear idea of what he hoped to find in them or even how to use the computer. He knew only what Jake had always said.

"Someone dies unexpected, go look for his books. Always look for the ledgers but do it quick. You're liable to be in a foot race."

When Jake was murdered, and Michael's fiancee soon after,

the coincidence was too much to ignore. The connection, if there was one, might be found in Michael's files.

A twelve-year-old boy showed him how to use the laptop. The boy, just down the hall at Mount Sinai, had come in with bad headaches and the doctors found a tumor. Tumor or not, it took him less than an hour to find a way past the code that Michael had used to keep his records private. What he found there was a disappointment in some ways, but a great relief in others.

Michael seemed to know nothing. One file, marked *Misc. Personal,* was filled with random musings. Michael would use his computer the way some people use diaries. He would talk things over with himself. Private matters. Most of the more recent entries had to do with Bronwyn.

Should he ask her to marry him? What might she say? If it's yes, then what? One of them would probably have to resign. Lehman-Stone has a rule against couples. Screw Lehman-Stone. How about Europe for a while? Or maybe she'd like to try San Francisco? Talk to Uncle Jake. Have Jake and Moon over.

The "Screw Lehman-Stone" was comforting. It meant that, to Michael, it was just another job.

Here and there, Michael would go on about how wonderful Bronwyn is. How perfect she is. No question he was crazy about her. He would write *Mrs. Michael Fallon* or *Bronwyn Kelsey Fallon* just to see how it looked.

Fair breast, was another notation. It was repeated several times.

Fair breast?

Moon had no idea what it meant.

A second file marked *Misc. Financial* showed that Michael was doing well, real well, but he was far from getting rich. His income was about right for his age, his education, and the kind of work he was doing. No suspiciously large bonuses. No big deposits. He wasn't blackmailing anyone. That, taken with Michael's willingness to leave Lehman-Stone for love, made Moon ashamed that he had even wondered.

The rest of the files were all homework. All Lehman-Stone and AdChem business, much of it routine. For the most part, Moon could penetrate enough of the Wall Street jargon to get the sense of it.

There were musings in these files as well. Judging by some of them, he liked the job well enough, he liked most of the people, but he did not seem to think much of Bart Hobbs. Michael wasn't so much hostile to him as he was mystified. Hobbs, he observed, made a great deal of money and Michael couldn't for the life of him see what Hobbs ever did to deserve it. He traveled a lot. Played golf a lot. And he jumped when AdChem said jump. And even when Security said jump.

Michael didn't write *Parker*. He wrote *Security*. Moon took that to mean that Michael didn't know much about Parker either.

His musings about AdChem were more respectful. He seemed almost in awe. They were not the biggest, he notes, in terms of research facilities but they certainly make the most of what they have. Largest number of new drug patents in the industry. And, lately, the fastest FDA approvals. They keep beating out competitors, often by a matter of days. But those few days, he says, are worth millions.

AdChem's not only good, it's lucky. Time after time, says Michael, a major competitor was poised for a launch but either had to recall its product, or the FDA changed the language of an approval, or their research was called into question.

Moon frowned. Thoughts of product tampering crossed his mind. So did thoughts of moles inside the FDA.

The company, Michael notes, has huge cash reserves. He says that's not unusual by itself. But he can't see where they came from and there's no way to find out. AdChem doesn't open its books for anyone. No, thought Moon. I guess I wouldn't either. Not if Julie Giordano is right.

What struck him about these musings, the ones about AdChem, was that Michael must have wondered. It's like, you wouldn't write down, *Gosh, Fat Julie sure has a lot of money for someone who doesn't work. And people who borrow some of that money and then stiff him sure seem to be accident prone.* You wouldn't write that without finishing the thought. Unless you just don't want to know. Or unless you're only beginning to catch on.

Moon had been through these files several times, every line of them, before Doyle called to say Michael was safe. He was looking for the name "Rasmussen." He could feel it there. He just couldn't see it.

But then Giordano called and gave him another name. Philip

Parker. Fat Julie had no home address for him. But Moon would find him.

He also had those other names, the ones from the back of that picture. Friends of Bart Hobbs. Guests at his house up in Maine. And now he knew who they were. He found them on memos in Michael's computer. Most were copied on almost every report he wrote. One was with Lehman-Stone, one with AdChem's New York office, one with their Washington law firm. And Moon had their home, business, and vacation home addresses from one of Michael's disks.

Except the fat one. Victor Turkel. Moon did not see that name anywhere. For all he knew, Turkel could have been the caretaker of the house in Maine.

But the rest would do for a start.

19

Michael now owned the Taylor House.

The closing was held on the tenth of May. It was all done in Boston through a young attorney who had been retained for that purpose by Brendan Doyle. The Daggetts were there but Michael was not. There was no need. The young lawyer, technically, held the deed to the inn but he held it in trust for Michael.

This was done, Doyle explained, to make the ownership harder to trace in the unlikely event that these shadows of Michael's actually existed. These hunters and killers. This man with no face from his dreams.

"Then why go to that trouble," Michael had asked him, "if you don't believe it?"

"Do *you?* Do you still?"

"I don't know. I suppose not."

"Well, when you make up your mind, we'll tell the world that you're now an Edgartown innkeeper."

"No," Michael said quietly. "No, let's not tell the world."

This was going to be his life. All the pain of the life he had before, all the crime and crud of New York City . . . these seemed more distant than ever, far to the west of an Edgartown sunset.

The Taylor House was heavily booked already.

It was booked to capacity, in fact, from Memorial Day weekend through the second week of August and there was even a waiting list for the Fourth of July weekend. Given the number of ghost groupies who had taken rooms, it struck Michael as dishonest to say nothing about the starlings. He told Harold what Megan had said.

"I'd keep that to myself," was Harold's advice. "They won't believe you nohow."

"But they're birds. They'll *sound* like birds."

"Michael . . . they sounded like birds right along. But what folks chose to hear was children."

He supposed.

People doubt or believe according to their needs. Megan said that as well and who was he to argue? If someone had told him just three months ago that he was going to be an innkeeper . . . and that next he'd fall in love with a loony psychic . . .

But it was all happening.

He had even made love to Megan.

That happened after three solid days of being together.

She had slept through the night on his sitting room floor. The next morning he fixed a breakfast so big that they both felt a need to walk it off. They walked the length of Lighthouse Beach. By the time they turned back she was holding his hand.

Later, she took him out for a sail. They didn't really talk much, at least not about themselves. It was mostly about boats and about movies they'd seen. With a bit of gentle urging, she stayed the next night in one of his guest rooms. It pleased him that she didn't bolt her door.

But he wouldn't have knocked. He wouldn't have pushed it at all. He wanted her, no question. He wanted her, he supposed, from the first time he saw her from the deck of the ferry. But he also wanted it to be good and right. Like Megan, he was afraid of what might happen if it wasn't.

It was Megan who picked the time and place.

The moment, when it came, was on her boat. He had asked her to have dinner with him on shore. She said she wanted to shower first. Megan seemed to shower at least three times a day. She told him to crack a beer and wait for her on deck.

It struck him after a while that she was using too much water.

Short showers are the rule on a boat. Wet down, suds up, rinse off. He asked her if she was all right. She came to the hatch, dripping wet, wrapped in a beach towel. She looked up at him, took a big deep breath, and said that she was ready to try if he was.

They never did get to dinner. And it was wonderful. In its way.

He might have guessed, he supposed, that when the moment came, she would want it to be in her own space. A boat can be like a womb. But a boat is also a place where sail bags have to be dragged off the berth and where you crack your head climbing in and where the wake of a passing power boat causes you to fall on your ass while you're trying to kick off your pants.

And of course she was terribly nervous. At least in the beginning. So he asked if they could just lie close, hold each other, without worrying too much about making things happen. She said that sounded like a good idea. At that, she jumped up, dragging a blanket with her and stuck a cassette of Pink Floyd's *Dark Side of the Moon* into her tape deck. If that was her idea of mood music, thought Fallon, he might have stumbled onto one source, at least, of her problem.

The blanket fell away while she was doing this. She felt his eyes on her and moved to cover herself. But she stopped in mid-reach. She let him look and he whispered, "Thank you." She really did have a marvelous body. And had worked at keeping it that way. He felt badly out of shape in comparison.

At last she climbed back in and warmed herself against him.

"I'm ready," she told him.

He grumbled.

She said, "Uh-oh. What did I do wrong?"

"Nothing. It's just so nice. Being here with you."

We say, "Dinner is ready." We ask the cleaner if our shirts are ready. When we're tacking our boat, we say "Ready about." But we don't jump under the covers and say, "I'm ready" unless we expect cash to be left on the end table. This was not the time, however, to offer a critique.

They did make love. It was actually more of a practice session. She was considerably tense but it was wonderful all the same because it was with Megan. He could not imagine a place in the world where he would rather be. Or anyone, not even Bronwyn, with whom he would rather be. They made love twice. The only thing was . . . she would still stop and *listen* at the damndest times.

But he'd learned that it's best not to bring up that subject. He'd asked, during one of their walks, how someone becomes a Megan. He wasn't prying. Just curious. Like, was she born with it? A head injury, maybe? Ah . . . a bad trip on drugs? At that she closed up like a vault. Not now, though. This was a whole new Megan.

"Michael?" She brushed her fingers across his chest.

"Um . . . ?"

"This is all for me so far. I mean, you're doing everything."

"Me? I thought you were."

She bit his shoulder.

"Megan . . . trust me. You have nothing to feel self-conscious about."

"Okay, but what do you like?"

"We're doing it."

"I mean . . . I know there are things men like. If you'll show me how, I'll try to do them for you."

"Are you serious?"

"I tried to tell you. This has never been my sport."

"I've got news. You're a natural."

"You're a liar but you're sweet."

"Okay, you want the truth?"

"Kind of."

"You're only good with me. With anyone else, you might as well be a haddock."

She laughed aloud. She laughed each time she thought of it.

"Back to your offer. You're saying you'll do my favorite thing. No matter how weird?"

"Ah . . . how weird is weird?"

"You holding my hand. Me falling asleep with you holding my hand. That's my favorite thing."

That made a tear well up. But she wasn't sad this time. This was going to be okay.

20

Fat Julie was getting worried.

He had still heard nothing from Moon. Nor, he thought, had Doyle. But Doyle was so pissed off at him—for setting Moon off—that he probably won't call if he does.

Julie had known about the fire within hours. Some friends of friends, from the docks at Port Everglades, had flown up to check out the house for him. That night, they faxed him the clippings from the morning paper. There, on page one, was a helicopter shot. The house was gutted. An inset showed the dead man, as yet unidentified. Just a smashed-up lump, framed by a metal lounge chair whose plastic had melted out from under him.

Two days later they faxed him the police report. The corpse had been tentatively identified as one Ayub Raspoor Ghentner, a.k.a. Walter Ghentner, a guard in the employ of a private security firm.

From the way Moon worked him over, Julie had to assume that Moon now knew everything that Walter could tell him. And that Moon now had a hit list.

This in itself troubled him. Moon was no killer. He might have no problem turning the guy who killed Jake into a pot roast, and then whomever gave the order. But, knowing Moon, Julie felt he would try not to hurt anyone else who might get in the way. That's a dangerous attitude.

Say a woman, for example, turned out to be involved in this. Moon might have a problem with doing a woman. But say it's a man, which it is. Moon will want to look him in the eye. He'll want to be sure the guy knows why he's dying. A real killer wouldn't give a fuck.

It gets worse. If Moon has a hit list, the Parker guy and Michael's old boss are at the top. And they'd realize that by now. Moon will turn up in New York before long and they'll be waiting for him. A real killer doesn't let you know he's coming.

What bothered Julie's conscience a little is that all this is what he'd been banking on. Setting Moon loose, waiting while he stirs up the nest, watching where the pieces fall. Which is what Doyle suspected. Which is why Doyle is so pissed.

But it was Moon's own fault. All Moon had to do was answer some questions. If he had, Julie would have made one phone call to his friends in Florida and Moon would have had all the shooters he needed.

Because there's money here. There's a mountain of it. The trick, however, is to find a way in. You don't just say, "Hey, this looks like a good business. Let's hire a few pharmacists and set up a factory, maybe on one of our ships." You have to know how to move what you've made and who you have to grease. You have to have either knocked off the competition or made some kind of deal with them. Having friends in the FDA couldn't hurt either but, even there, you have to know who to buy.

Yahya, on the other hand, says the selling part's easy.

"How easy?"

"Go to any distributor. Show him your sample. Tell him the price is one third off wholesale."

"Won't he know right away it's bogus?"

"Of course. At such a price, it is either bogus or stolen."

"Stolen happens too?"

"Of course."

"Okay . . . say the guy's honest."

Yahya knew what he was asking. "He will want no part of it. But he will not call the police."

"Why not?"

A shrug. "Why should he make enemies? It is enough to politely decline."

Fat Julie made a doubtful face. "Well . . . say he doesn't. Say he bites."

"He will ask for your documents."

"Yeah, but where do *I* get them? And how do I know what he wants?"

"He will show you. He will show you exactly."

To hear Yahya tell it, this distributor then goes to his files and pulls out samples of the documentation he needs. Invoices, bills of lading, licensing agreements, and letters on the maker's corporate letterhead certifying their point of origin and giving batch numbers and production dates. He's saying, "This is what I need to protect my ass," but not out loud in case this is a sting. He leaves them on his desk while he goes to take a piss. He's saying, "I'll lend you these. Take them when I'm not looking and make me a set just as nice."

Could it really be as simple as that?

Johnny G. had one good idea. He said let's send Yahya up to the Bronx, up around University Avenue, which was Mohammed Mizda's neighborhood and where half the Pakistanis in New York seem to live. Yahya must have friends up there, right? They know he did time for dealing pills and got early release on probation. Probation has expired so now he can bag his crummy job on the docks and start looking for a new connection. We get lucky, Yahya will get steered to AdChem, which will give us someone inside.

It seemed worth a shot. Johnny G. sat down with Mohammed Yahya and explained the job, dangled some very nice financial incentives, but he also outlined the new Giordano brothers termination policy—two Brooklyn rats under a heated pasta bowl—in case he should be tempted to fuck with them. Yahya jumped at the deal.

So we wait.

Waiting, thought Julie, was basically what Johnny had in mind because Johnny was beginning to have second thoughts about grabbing a piece of this bogus pill thing.

"We promised Pop," was what he said. "We swore to God we wouldn't."

"Yeah, but that was about drugs. This stuff is medicine."

"It's all medicine, Julie. That's where all the street shit started. When Pop was a kid, you could buy it off the shelves."

"Johnny . . . what's bothering you?"

But he only shrugged and looked away.

"Okay, I said it wrong. This isn't just medicine. This is health care for the masses."

"Say what?"

"Come on, Johnny. You can't turn on the TV without hearing about health care. You hear about old ladies going without food because they have to spend the money on medicine because, for years now, the big drug companies have been ripping them off."

His brother closed one eye. "We'd be doing this for old ladies? Is that what you're telling me, Julie?"

No, smart-ass, we wouldn't.

But they'd benefit, right? They'd benefit from managed competition which everyone says is good. And it's us who'd do the managing.

Julie had been reading up on this. Even if they passed national health insurance, all the drugs under patent will still be expensive. Of the others, maybe you need more than they'll give you. Or maybe it's a drug you can't get at all because it isn't approved in this country.

Even when patents run out and you can buy generic versions of drugs, you still need a prescription. There can also be a big difference between one batch of generics and the next. They said that on TV too. On "60 Minutes," he thought it was.

Quality control. That's what we'd give them. Any pill they want, from any country, guaranteed as good or better than the original and at a price they can live with. The only catch is it can't be too cheap, people have to need it every day, and they have to need it forever. As long as the pill works, how is this wrong? Would Pop say this is wrong?

"And very little risk, Johnny. You said so yourself."

"Tell that to Jake Fallon."

Goddamn it.

"Johnny . . . are you going to tell me what put a bug up your ass?"

"I'm not sure."

"Two weeks ago, I never seen you so excited. What's the matter, it's too big? Villanova didn't teach you to think big?"

"No. Big is what's good about it."

"Well, what? That it's a crime? Because I got news for you, Johnny. You've been a fucking criminal since—"

"I want to talk to Moon. Or at least to Michael."

"Wait a minute. What for?"

"Because if AdChem was doing this, and Jake or Michael found out, what if that's what got Jake killed?"

"It probably was."

"So? What'll you say to Moon? 'Sorry about Jake, Moon, but those guys had a good idea. Too bad about Bronwyn, Michael, but we see a way to score here.' "

"Johnny, it's not the same."

"I want Moon to tell me that. Moon or Michael."

Twice in the past several nights, Doyle's home phone had rung and there was silence when he answered. He had stayed up each time for a couple of hours, sitting in the dark with a gun at his side.

He suspected, however, that the caller was Moon. He felt that Moon had just wanted to hear his voice so he'd know there had been no reprisal for that business in Palm Beach. But Moon could also be dead for all he knew. Thanks to goddamned Julie.

He could be dead at the hands of Parker and his bunch or dead in some hotel room from another stroke. Or, God forbid, Parker might have him.

But the last did not seem likely.

He would have heard by now because someone would have approached him with a deal. The deal would be, "You want Moon back? More or less in one piece? Then drop Michael's lawsuit, withdraw the subpoena of Lehman-Stone's files, and we'll call it a draw."

But Doyle had heard nothing. Not even an offer from their lawyers to settle for a couple of hundred grand or so just to get rid of this thing. On the contrary, their lawyers were spending a lot of time in court trying to stonewall him on the discovery process. This struck Doyle as dumb. It's the same as admitting either that Michael has a case or that Lehman-Stone has something much bigger to hide.

Doyle had never intended to drop this suit. He'd made noises to Michael that it wasn't worth pursuing but that was to keep him away from it. If he'd found what he hoped to find, he didn't want Michael looking over his shoulder. But so far he'd come up empty. He had even dug out that AdChem annual report, the one Jake had in his pocket, and read it again word by word. If it held some clue to what they and Hobbs were up to, Doyle had failed to find it.

Hobbs, on the other hand, doesn't know that. Perhaps, therefore, it's time to get his attention. How does ten million dollars sound?

That, he decided, would be the new price tag for defaming Michael Fallon as part of an elaborate cover-up of a longstanding pattern of securities fraud that has recently been uncovered by our investigators.

What investigators?

None, unless you'd count Arnie, but they don't know that either.

What fraud?

We don't know but they do. Let them sweat it.

And, as long as we're tossing bombs, let's name AdChem in the complaint. We didn't do so at first because AdChem had no relevance to an action over wrongful dismissal and slander. It doesn't now either, not so far as we can prove, but what the hell.

And . . . if we really want to shake the bastards up, why not name Armin Rasmussen? If we're wrong, what's the worst that could happen? They'll say who the hell is Rasmussen, right?

Yeah, thought Doyle. What the hell.

First thing tomorrow, he would draw up an amended complaint. File it after lunch, ruin a few dinners. But on second thought, why wait?

Let's pick up the phone, call their lawyers, let them know it's coming.

Better idea.

Securities fraud is federal. Call whatzizname . . . Bellows. Their hotshot Washington lawyer. Professional courtesy, right?

21

Michael still knew almost nothing about her, not even her last name.

He had picked up a few things, of course. He gathered that she'd crewed once or twice on long expeditions out of the Woods Hole Oceanographic Institute, which was within walking distance of her slip. Whether she went as researcher, navigator, diver, or cook, or whether that was her means of support, he had no idea. Whenever his questions got too specific, or too personal, he would suddenly find himself alone. Megan's body might still be there but the rest of her might as well have beamed up to the mother ship for all that he'd get out of her.

But not all personal subjects were off-limits. She mentioned, for example, that she once did a solo sail around the world. Seven months. Mostly to be alone with herself . . . find out who she is . . . listen to herself. Had a long talk with a dolphin who stayed with her for three days.

"You can talk to dolphins?"

"Michael . . . get a grip."

"But you just said . . ."

"Have you ever talked to a dog?"

"Um . . . sure."

"Did that dog wag his tail or did he start quoting Chaucer?

Did he say now that we've broken the ice, let's discuss global warming?''

"Oh."

"See that? You talk to animals and no one gives it a thought. I do it and they start genuflecting."

Oh, and Megan loved to dance.

He wasn't sure why that surprised him but it did. She was graceful and fluid and she liked to cut loose. For his part, he loved to go dancing with her because that was the only time she ever wore a dress and put on serious makeup and wore jewelry. She was a beautiful woman when she wanted to be. And at most other times she was becoming a regular, happy, more or less normal girl.

Woman.

No . . . girl.

At times it was as if she had never grown up. She was still in the wonder years. She could be chatty, happy, wide-eyed, and spontaneous. See some kid walking a puppy and she'll cross a busy street to play with it. She likes pizza with the most revolting combinations. Anchovies and pineapple was one. She likes playground swings, maple walnut ice cream, and any movie with Robin Williams in it. One day, she got him to climb a tree with her. She promised she'd respect him in the morning.

It was barely two weeks since that night by his fireplace. Two weeks filled with a hundred small delights.

The psychic thing seldom came up anymore. The *listening* became less frequent. But he had come to accept that she really did have some sort of gift. If he misplaced something, for example, she would chew her lip like she does and then tell him where to look. Unless she caught him watching her, or decided that he was testing her. In that case, the thing would stay lost.

Okay, knowing where his car keys are is not so big a deal. But one time she touched a shirt that he was wearing and she knew that Bronwyn had bought it for him. And she knew that a pair of gaudy gold cuff links had belonged to Uncle Jake. Things like that.

Megan says, "Michael . . . half the women in the world can do that. It's called taste. It's called knowing what a man would buy for himself versus what someone must have given him."

Well, maybe. But so far she's batting a thousand.

As for the sex thing, the frigidity thing, it was getting better all the time. He didn't flatter himself that he had worked some kind of miracle. It was largely a matter of learning what she was comfortable with and helping her to feel okay about herself. For example, Megan did not especially like to make love at bedtime. At bedtime, she liked to get all warm and snug. By herself. In fact, she really didn't like to be touched at bedtime and she liked it even less after she'd fallen asleep. But she would reach to touch him, just to know he was there. Then she'd smile and drift off to sleep.

Mornings were another story. In the morning, she liked having him cuddle up with her, hold her. As long as he didn't rush it, she liked making love in the morning. But even then, she would want to take a shower first. She needed to feel clean for some reason. You would think, if anything, that she'd want to shower afterward.

She could also be spontaneous about sex, however. Especially during bad weather. They could be out in the middle of a squall, she'd be soaked to the skin, and suddenly she'd drop the sails, toss a sea anchor off the stern, and start peeling off her clothes right out there on deck. Whether this was related to her thing about showers, he didn't know. He was not about to look a gift horse in the mouth.

He had managed to convince her, he hoped, that there was nothing in the world wrong with any of this. He was a morning person himself. And she smelled so great fresh out of a shower. It was fine. Everything was fine. Except Pink Floyd. Next time she pulls out that tape it's going over the side.

The only problem was, and perhaps had always been, in this gift of hers. Imagine being a woman, having sex with some guy, and knowing, virtually on contact, things you'd just as soon not know. Who wouldn't freeze up? But with him, apparently, there wasn't that much left to learn.

He had asked her again about all that death she saw. She said it might not have been real. Psychics, she told him, have imaginations too. She was lying. Megan is good at a lot of things but lying isn't one of them. He pressed her. She listened for a long moment. She said whatever it is, whatever it meant, it was fading. It was getting farther away.

The relief on her face was no lie.

On the Wednesday before Memorial Day weekend, he came over on his whaler and they went sailing on Buzzards Bay. He'd given himself Wednesdays off. They docked at New Bedford for lunch, polished off a bucket of steamers.

Sailing back, Fallon at the helm, neither said much. Megan was playing the spinnaker sheet, trying to keep it filled in light air, and Fallon's mind was on his birthday, which was coming in two days. Or rather he was trying not to think about it. He certainly wouldn't mention it to Megan. She might get him a cake or some damned thing.

Megan seemed preoccupied as well. She glanced back at him once or twice, then turned away when he looked up. After a while, she said, "Cole."

"Beg pardon?"

"It's Cole."

"Um . . . you want me to get you a sweater?"

"No. *Cole.* You asked my name. It's Megan Cole."

"Oh."

Nice to know you, Megan Cole.

He knew that Megan would have understood about his birthday. She has her hang-ups, he's allowed to have his.

She would tell him that it's time to let that go and that what happened then, on his twelfth birthday, had nothing to do with any other.

Easy for you to say.

Year after year, Uncle Jake had done his best to blur the memory. He had planned some spectacular birthdays. There were parties, sports outings, even a three-day cruise to Bermuda when he turned sixteen. But nothing really worked. Fallon blamed himself for what happened that day and he probably always would. That he was only a kid didn't matter. He should have seen it coming.

His mother had been gone for a year by then and, in some ways, her going was a relief. Until about a year before that, his parents' marriage had seemed as solid, or as routine, as any other. His mother had a mouth and some strong opinions. She also had trouble cutting a little slack and letting boys be boys, or men be men, but she was never really mean about it. She could be kind, she could be funny, and she was totally devoted to her family. Family was everything to her. Well . . . family and the church.

You wouldn't know it to look at her, though. Anne Murray was black Irish. Spanish blood in her veins. Some ancestor had to have been a shipwrecked sailor from the Spanish Armada who washed up on the Irish coast and said the hell with it, I'm staying right here. She had very dark hair, flashing brown eyes, and a trim, lithe figure. Put her in the right kind of dress and she could easily have been a flamenco dancer. Maybe in a past life she was.

They had, by most standards, a pretty nice life. A six-room high-rise on Horatio Street in Greenwich Village. A little place on Fire Island. Boxing and the GI Bill had put his father through college—the first ever in the Fallon family—and through graduate school where he studied to become a certified public accountant.

Maybe that was at the root of it somewhere. Becoming an accountant. Michael understood that it was no mean accomplishment to become a CPA but, still, it must have been a come-down after such an adventurous young-manhood. His Bronze Star, his Purple Hearts, and his several campaign medals were kept framed on the wall of the room Pop used as an office. Around it were photographs of himself and his tank crew and one in which Eisenhower himself had stopped to shoot the breeze with them during a lull in the fighting.

There were other photos from his boxing days, most of them clipped from newspapers. In one, he stood in the ring, arms raised, over a prostrate fighter named Buddy Nash. The headline was "Nash Mashed." His father had seemed so full of life back then. Always that grin.

Working as a CPA wasn't exactly stultifying either. He did a good deal of traveling and much of it was glamorous. None of the other kids' fathers got to travel to Germany, Switzerland, even to India a few times. Working for Eagle Sales wasn't crossing the Rhine or mashing Nash, but then, few jobs are.

Michael came along late, in the sixth year of their marriage.

By that time, his father was doing pretty well. The Horatio Street building was one of the few in the whole Village with a full-time doorman.

The change, when it came, seemed almost overnight. Michael was eleven. The arguments suddenly became nasty. At one point, he thought it was because his father had stopped going to church. His mother would nag him for not going to Mass but, when he did go just to shut her up, she would ask how he dared show his face to God. She threatened, one time, to have her policeman cousins come over and slap some sense into him. Michael was never clear on what he'd done to deserve such contempt. But it hurt him that his father would just take it. He wanted him to say, "If your cousins come through that door, I will kick their asses all the way back to Queens."

And he could have. But he didn't say that.

Instead, he asked, "You didn't tell them, did you?"

Her answer was, "I'd die of shame."

Uncle Jake, those days, didn't seem to have much use for his younger brother either. His attitude, however, seemed to be more of a wistfulness, an unspoken sadness, than an active contempt. More than once, in the years since, Uncle Jake would begin to remark on the sort of man Tom Fallon might have been, and once was. But he would always stop himself.

"Don't judge him too harshly, lad," was all he'd say. That and, "We all lose our way sometimes. We have to find our own way back."

Nor would Moon shed much light on the subject.

"Moon? Was my father a crook?"

"That ain't the word, exactly."

"What *is* the word?"

"He . . . got caught up in something. I don't know the whole of it but I'll tell you this. There was never a time when he decided to do bad. It just kinda grew. It got away from him. You get older, you're gonna see how easy that can happen."

His mother had never approved of Uncle Jake. She was never all that crazy about Moon either—she considered him a thug—but she was never deliberately rude to him. She said that God might have mercy on Moon, he might consider what it's like to grow up black, but Uncle Jake would have no such excuse. Jake Fallon was an irredeemable rogue who should count himself lucky to get off with an eon or two in purgatory and was certainly no fit example for a growing boy.

"But I'll say this for him," he once heard her say to his father. "He's not a coward. Corrupt and a hypocrite, surely, but at least he's a man."

Michael did not let on that he heard. What made Uncle Jake a hypocrite in her eyes was that he was a grafter who had cops and judges in his pocket and yet still went to Mass. Mass wasn't the half of it. Uncle Jake marched in parades at the head of the Knights of Columbus. Uncle Jake boozed with bishops. Cardinal Spellman used to sit in Jake's box at the Polo Grounds. This made his mother crazy.

Michael did not understand, however, how she could call his father a coward. Cowards don't become prizefighters. They don't win the Bronze Star.

And then one day his mother was gone. No note. Not even to her parents. That letter came later. His father was never the same.

He didn't work. He rarely left the apartment. He bathed erratically. He spent his days, usually drunk, watching television in a ratty bathrobe. And yet there was plenty of money.

He would pay the rent, with cash, only when the building's agent came to the door, and he'd tip him for his trouble. He would pay for liquor deliveries the same way. It was Michael who saw that there was food in the apartment. The money came from various wads that his father kept in cereal boxes, coffee cans, and old shoes, and with the fifty-dollar bills that were pressed inside nearly every book his father owned. Years would pass before it struck Michael that not everyone kept that much money at home.

His mother being gone, Uncle Jake went out of his way to fill some of the void. He would take Michael to museums and bring him books to read. These were things that his mother had always done and that Uncle Jake learned to do by quietly consulting with Michael's grade school nuns.

But his mother, unlike Uncle Jake, never took him to the Friday night fights at St. Nicholas Arena and to Sunnyside Gardens where his father had once fought. His mother never took him to Mets and Yankee games. She never introduced him to the players, many of whom knew Uncle Jake, or got them to sign baseballs for him.

Jake would show up at the apartment every week or so with his own housekeeper in tow. They would stay until the place was in order. He never had much to say to his brother.

By his twelfth birthday, which fell on a Sunday, Michael knew better than to expect a gift from his father or even for him to remember what day it was. But his father had gotten up early, had showered and shaved, and was making breakfast with trembling hands when Michael emerged from his room. He said he thought they might go shopping together, buy some new clothes for school, and then maybe go to the Radio City Music Hall, see *Funny Girl* with Barbra Streisand.

Michael was embarrassed for him.

For one thing, *Funny Girl*'s run at Radio City had ended almost six months before. For another, he'd already seen it because everyone said the Nicky Arnstein character was so much like Uncle Jake. Fine figure of a man, great smile, an inveterate rascal, could charm the devil himself.

More to the point, Uncle Jake was coming by at noon to take him to a Yankee/Red Sox game followed by dinner at Toots Shor's, where Mickey Mantle had promised to stop by their table. This, Michael told his father, had been planned for weeks. His father said that he understood, poured himself a drink, turned on the TV, left Michael's breakfast in the pan.

When Uncle Jake arrived, his father, already well on his way, did not look up. Michael thought of asking him to join them. Uncle Jake saw it on his face.

"We'll stay if you wish, lad," he told Michael. "But let's not take him out until he's had a nap."

"Pop?"

"You go, Mike. Your uncle knows best. Your uncle *always* knows best."

He got up and went into his office.

"I've got something downstairs for you," Jake said to Michael. "Let's see if it'll cheer you up."

In the taxi, waiting at the curb, a genuine team-issue Yankees jacket was hanging from the coat hook. Michael gaped when he saw it. He wanted to try it on at once. As he did so, on the sidewalk, he happened to glance up. He saw his father looking down at him from their sixth floor window. His father raised a hand, gave him a little salute. It was the last time he saw his father alive. Tom Fallon, according to neighbors who heard him hit, must have jumped within minutes of that cab pulling away.

"Megan?"

"Um?"

"When is your birthday?"

"July fourth. It's very widely celebrated."

"How old are you, by the way? I mean, now that I know your last name and all . . ."

A small hesitation. Just a beat. "I'll be twenty-seven."

"Let's do something special."

"If you're there, it will be special."

Uncle Jake, himself a widower—Aunt Bess died young of breast cancer—took Michael into his home. The Brooklyn Heights town house was a handsome ivy-clad brownstone, four stories high, with twelve-foot ceilings on the first three floors. But by far its best feature was that collection of his. For a twelve-year-old kid, Jake's house was like Cooperstown and Massillon combined.

That stuff aside, Jake undertook to raise and educate Michael. He took the job seriously.

Jake Fallon loved the Jesuits. He especially believed in Jesuit discipline. Accordingly, Jake had him take the entrance exam for St. Francis Xavier High School, a military school for day students. Xavier always marched in New York's parades. Jake Fallon loved parades.

Michael was accepted. His uncle then hired tutors to assure top grades, and trainers to make sure that he could win a spot on any team he wished to try out for. Xavier didn't have a boxing team. That led to the great Golden Gloves debate and Moon becoming his newest trainer. He always wondered whether Uncle Jake really knew what sort of things Moon was teaching him. It was some pretty brutal shit.

"Doctors learn to cut off a leg," Moon pointed out. "That doesn't mean they'll jump at the chance to do it."

Michael lettered in three sports, made cadet major, and got to salute the cardinal with his saber as his battalion marched past St. Patrick's Cathedral. And to wink at Uncle Jake, who was usually up there with him.

While still a junior, Michael thought he might try to get into Yale or Harvard. He had the grades and his uncle had said that money was not a problem. But Jake hated the idea.

For openers, he said, those schools can be real snotty about whom they take and he might need to call in a marker here and there to get him admitted. Michael would then spend his next four years trying to live down not having gone to Andover or Choate and being frozen out by those who had. People go to those schools, he said, to make connections. They graduate, they spend the rest of their lives sitting in meetings and joining clubs that keep everyone else out. Go where you learn to *do* things. Go where a quick mind and a good set of balls counts for more than who your father is.

Unsaid, according to Moon, was the fear that Uncle Jake might lose his nephew to the cucumber-sandwich set. Fat chance.

In the end, his choices narrowed to Notre Dame and Villanova. As for Villanova, Rocco Giordano's son, Johnny, was in his second year there after failing to get accepted by Notre Dame. Johnny had aced their entrance exam and his SAT scores were in the top ten percent. Still, they passed on him. Michael learned, much later, that it was because of talk that his father was about to be indicted.

At the time, Jake didn't realize that either. So it became a sort of competition. Jake lobbied hard for Notre Dame.

"The only pain in the ass," he told Michael, "is that for the rest of your life everyone will ask if you played football there. Otherwise it's perfect. Everyone trusts a man who went to Notre Dame."

"Michael?"

Megan was staring at the horizon. She had an odd, dreamy look.

"Yes'm."

"Where did you go to college?"

"Um . . . what made you ask that? I mean, just now, out of the blue."

An innocent shrug. "Just wondered."

"Notre Dame. I went to Notre Dame."

Uncle Jake threw a party when the letter of acceptance came. It was an embarrassingly expensive affair at the River Club. Moon said don't worry about it. He said, "Your uncle won some bet with Rocco Giordano."

Jake's pleasure didn't last, however. During Michael's first two months in South Bend he was suspended over one incident, then arrested and nearly expelled over another.

He had barely moved into the freshman dormitory when, while he attended an orientation lecture, his new electric typewriter, his stereo and two new sport jackets were stolen from his room. Several freshmen had similar losses.

Two weeks later, he spotted one of his jackets. The student who was wearing it, upon learning that it was stolen, was as angry as he was. He said that he bought it from a senior, a scholarship hurdler on the track team, who told him that the jacket was a gift from an alumnus but the sleeves were too short for him.

The hurdler lived off campus. Michael went to his apartment complex and knocked on the door. No one answered. The door was locked. He went back outside, climbed in through a window, and found his typewriter, two TV sets, and several clock radios and pocket calculators. His stereo and his other jacket had apparently been sold. He waited for the athlete to return.

The thief opened the door, found Michael standing amid the loot, went pale for an instant, then proceeded to deny that any of that stuff has been stolen. Michael said fine, we'll call campus security. He stepped toward the phone on the kitchen wall but the hurdler blocked his path. He told Michael that he could have his typewriter back. But if he said one word, made one accusation, the player had friends who would beat him bloody every day that he was still at Notre Dame.

Michael ended the hurdler's career with two kicks to the knee. He was promptly suspended.

The suspension was soon lifted, however, after an inventory of the stolen goods and after other students came forward to claim items that had been stolen from them. The thief and his room-mate had made a specialty of robbing incoming freshmen because more of their possessions tended to be new and because freshmen were more easily intimidated.

Michael became something of a hero to his class. Stories about the episode, some wildly exaggerated, spread through the dorms. Michael would try to shrug them off. Moon had always said, "You put a man down, never crow about it. It comes back to haunt you." But his reluctance to speak only added to his reputation.

This led, indirectly, to a second incident several weeks later. On a Friday night in November, Michael had gone to an off-campus pizza parlor with two other freshmen and their dates. The place was patronized largely by factory workers, most of them under thirty. Friday was pay day. Several had been cele-brating.

Two men, early twenties, were staring at the girls at Michael's table. They wore work boots and jeans. Michael noticed but paid no attention. The two men began needling them, offering their opinions of Notre Dame football, then of Notre Dame in general, and then of Catholics in general. Nothing need have come of it. It must happen in college towns everywhere. But one of the freshmen made a reference to "hard hats, hard heads." The two came over, beers in hand, and asked him to repeat it.

The others at the table looked to Michael as if asking him to deal with this. Michael tried. He said his friend meant nothing by it and this is scaring the girls. Give us a break, let us finish our pizza and leave. He asked if he could buy them a beer. The drunker of the two jabbed a finger against Michael's chest and leaned close to his face.

"I live here, faggot," he said. "You don't come to my town and tell me what to do." The other spit beer on Michael's shoes.

The two other students kicked back their chairs. They asked Michael if he needed any help. He saw in their eyes that they hoped he'd say no. The owner stepped from behind the counter with a wooden mallet in his hand. "Sit down," he said, "or take it outside." Michael asked everyone to relax. He suggested that just he and the factory workers step into the parking lot and see if they can't settle this peacefully.

He had both men down, and unable to continue, within less than a minute. But the owner had called the police. All three were arrested, charged with disturbing the peace, and one had to be hospitalized for a possible ruptured spleen. Michael was also charged with battery.

He might well have been expelled had not his Uncle Jake called in a favor from a congressman who had close ties with Father Hesburgh, then president of Notre Dame. All charges were subsequently dropped.

Soon afterward, he flew home for the Thanksgiving holiday. Moon met his flight at La Guardia Airport. They took the shuttle bus to the far end of the long-term parking lot. The sun had set. Michael asked him why he parked so far away. Moon watched the bus drive off, then knocked him to the ground.

He waited for Michael's head to clear. He said that Big Jake had not asked him to do this. It was his own idea. He had decided that Michael was in need of a lesson.

Michael got up off the ground twice. The third time, he could not. As he tried to catch his breath—his face unmarked, however—Moon patiently repeated what he thought he'd made clear earlier.

"I taught you to handle yourself," he said, "so you wouldn't get hurt. It wasn't so you could bust up some klepto over a damned typewriter."

"Moon . . . he took more than that . . . from a lot of scared kids."

"Yeah, but you didn't know that then. I also didn't teach you so you could take out two pieces of redneck shit who hate you for gettin' what they'll never have. What's rule one, Michael?"

"Walk away. Try to walk away."

"Did you?"

"Moon, I tried."

"Not hard enough. What's rule two?"

"Never ask anyone to step outside."

"That's rule three. Rule two is no Lone Ranger crap if you can help it. Way I heard, there was people in the pizza place who would have backed you."

Michael hesitated, then nodded.

"But you wanted to show off. Wanted them coeds to see what a tough grown-up man Michael Fallon is."

Fallon grimaced. "It . . . wasn't that."

Moon ignored the denial. "So now the whole school knows. Is that good or bad, Michael?"

"Moon . . . I know. It was stupid."

"Next guy you cross," Moon told him, "he's gonna say, 'That Fallon's one tough son of a bitch. Got all these moves. Maybe I better get me a billy club, maybe a gun, come up behind him.' You want people thinkin' like that, Michael?"

"No."

"When you say to some dude, 'Let's step outside,' he knows you don't want to dance. He has any sense, he'll lay a bottle over your head right then and there."

Michael said nothing.

"Even if he don't, you just gave away your edge and, Mikey, you ain't good enough to do that. What you're good enough for is to push most people around. That one of your goals in life?"

"Moon . . . for Pete's sake. That's two fights since I was twelve years old. I'm not a bully."

"See you don't turn into one, Michael. See you don't start to like it."

He already didn't like it.

He wished Moon had never taught him all those things. Anyway, what was the point of learning them if he was going to get hammered by Moon every time he put them to use?

Still, he knew that Moon was right. "If you have to do it," Moon always said, "do it quick, do it private, and then walk away. Don't get a reputation. They take forever to shake. And the surest way to get dead, in jail, or hit from behind is to have a reputation."

It's also the surest way to have no close friends. He'd learned, over the past few months, that notoriety was one thing and popularity was another. It seemed as if every classmate he liked, or wanted to like, was suddenly keeping his or her distance. Those he did attract always seemed, well, damaged in some way.

Especially the girls. A couple of them, who had paid no special notice before, now found him exciting. They said so, straight out. He could have taken them to bed in a minute. He didn't for two reasons. First, they struck him as the kind of girls who would have joined the Manson family. The second reason was more honest. He was afraid to even try. They might have laughed at him.

To hear all his male classmates talk, Michael Fallon had to be the only virgin in the entire freshman class at Notre Dame. It was the one area of his education that both Moon and Uncle Jake had neglected. Growing up Catholic didn't make it any easier. When you grow up Catholic, with all that emphasis on impure thoughts and monkish morals, you end up feeling that robbery, arson, and even murder must be lesser mortal sins than sex before marriage. That, right there, he had often thought, probably explains the Mafia.

In time, his notoriety faded. But Moon was right. It never quite went away, even though he never had another fight during his four years at Notre Dame. Unless you'd count two bench-clearing brawls during football games. But those were fun and essentially harmless. You couldn't get hurt unless you were dumb enough to pull off your helmet or to throw a punch at a face mask.

Yes, he'd gone out for the team because Uncle Jake was right. Everyone always asked. He made it as a walk-on in his sophomore year. He was never a starter but he did make the traveling squad. Played in almost every game. Not for long, but he played.

He had also joined the karate club for just one semester. Long enough to know a few moves in case Moon decided he needed more humility. It was a waste of time. Moon would have clobbered the best of them. Not if they were ready for him, necessarily, but that was the point. They would not have been ready.

He was still a virgin until the beginning of his sophomore year. And then he met Mary Beth. She was a freshman at St. Mary's.

Mary Beth, as it turned out, was a virgin as well but she arrived in South Bend determined to get over that hurdle as quickly as possible. It was she, actually, who picked him to be her first partner. She knew none of that other stuff about him. She simply liked him at first meeting and assumed, after two or three dates, that he would probably know what he was doing.

He admitted the truth. She laughed, then quickly did the same. She suggested that they learn together. For the next several months, they did.

"When we break up . . ." she said to him one day.

"Who says we will?"

"Come on, Mike. I'm only a freshman."

"Well anyway, what?"

"After your next girl and my next guy, let's sneak off and do it once more, okay? I mean, just to swap notes."

You had to know Mary Beth.

To her, it made perfect sense to make this pact now because later you would have to call it two-timing. Doing it in advance made this a one-time prior commitment that would probably be of benefit to everyone concerned.

They did break up—when she thought it was time—and they did meet again. Just once at an airport motel before she flew back home to Tampa for the summer.

He wasn't sure how much he'd learned during their time apart. He'd been with one other freshman and one South Bend waitress. Enough to teach him that different women have very different needs and that not all of them see sex as a thing that should necessarily be enjoyed. Or that the enjoyment should be mutual.

Mary Beth certainly did. She didn't do quickies. She didn't do backseats or locked bathrooms. Mary Beth only made love. She did it slowly, considerately, and, above all, exuberantly. She did it in a way that could not be a sin. *Fucking* might be a sin. Making someone feel special was not.

She never came back to St. Mary's. She decided, over the summer, that she hated the cold weather and had forgotten how much she loved and missed her parents. She transferred to Florida State. They exchanged letters and phone calls for a while but he never saw her again. Still, she was, and would always be, a very special memory.

*   *   *

"You're falling off, Michael. Head up."

Megan's voice brought him back to the present. He realized that she'd been watching him. He eased the bow into the wind.

"Tell me you were thinking about me," she said.

She said it with a smile. But he thought he heard a hint of jealousy.

"I hardly *stop* thinking about you."

"Except just then."

"I was . . . remembering an old friend. From years ago."

"Will you ever tell me about her?"

He had to laugh. "You're something else, you know that, Megan?"

"What do you mean?"

"I only just learned your name, for Pete's sake. When do I find out about you?"

"I told you. You will over time."

He made a face.

"Well?"

"Well, what?"

"Will you tell me about her?"

"I might. I might over time."

She curled a lip, then stuck out her tongue at him.

Gotcha, Megan Cole. Gotcha.

22

It took Mohammed Yahya just one afternoon, one visit to the Bronx, to make three new connections. Two of them were wholesale distributors. One was only a discount pharmacy.

The pharmacy, however, had the most interesting products and seemed to have them in good supply. It also, as a sideline, rented wheelchairs to convalescents and had an exclusive contract to service other wheelchairs that were owned by the several hospitals in the area. An exclusive contract, nearly always, meant that bribes had been paid and that hospital personnel, therefore, had been compromised. This was another good sign.

Best of all, on the window of this pharmacy was a bright orange decal with blue lettering. The decal said, "These premises protected by Parker Security Services, Inc."

Mohammed Yahya smiled all the way back to Brooklyn and Villardi's Seafood Palace. Mr. Johnny, he thought, will be very pleased.

"Johnny had things to do," said his brother. "Tell me."

Yahya would have preferred to speak to the younger Giordano. Of the two, Mr. Johnny was the more respectful. Nonetheless, Yahya told him of the afternoon's events.

"Just like that?" Fat Julie asked. "You walked in off the street and they hired you?"

Best proof, thought the Pakistani, wounded. "I did not always drive a crane, sir."

"Even so . . ."

"All three tested my knowledge of pharmacology. They were most impressed. Mr. Giordano . . . this is not standing on street corners selling little bags of crack to drivers of cars from New Jersey."

"Um . . . no offense, Mohammed."

"I am not without credentials. I am an educated man."

Christ.

"Mohammed . . . have some orange juice." He signaled the waiter.

As Julie had suspected, there was more to Yahya's getting hired than he wanted to admit. A couple of Yahya's paisans—who *did* sell little bags—had vouched for him. But his ace-in-the-hole reference had been the Giordano brothers.

Yahya's problem was that everyone knew that he'd been running a crane. This was a blue-collar job. It hurt his pride. All this time, therefore, he'd been telling those Bronx Pakistanis that the job on the docks was only a cover for the benefit of his parole officer. His real job had been more in the nature of a disciplinarian for the Giordano brothers.

Yahya, no doubt, had flicked a thumb across his throat as he said this. But he also said that the job was distasteful to a man of his entrepreneurial bent. It was time to strike out on his own again.

Fat Julie had no problem with the embroidery. It's good that Yahya admitted it because someone might check. But he was much more interested in what Yahya would be selling for this drugstore that was protected by the people who killed Jake.

"I will be selling these," Yahya told him.

Yahya reached into the gym bag that he had brought with him. He produced two pharmacy-sized bottles, one of white pills and one of capsules.

"The capsules are Prozac. They are certainly counterfeit. The white pills are Vicodin. These may or may not be genuine."

"Prozac." Fat Julie had heard of it. "Isn't that the stuff that makes you crazy?"

"A canard. No doubt spread by competitors."

"Bullshit. I seen it on TV. They said how some users get violent and a bunch of them killed themselves."

"Not a bunch, Mr. Giordano. A handful out of perhaps five million. This should surprise anyone? The drug, after all, is taken for depression."

"All the same . . ."

"Even your Food and Drug Administration has declined to take action. They said you don't throw out the baby for a few bad apples."

Fat Julie doubted, somehow, that these were their exact words. But let's move along here. "These are both from AdChem?"

"So one would infer."

Julie nodded. That decal on the window, "Protected by Parker," did not suggest a tolerance of competitive lines.

"The Prozac. How can you tell it's bogus?"

The Pakistani opened one bottle and took out one capsule. It was half white, half pale green. The green half showed the maker's logo. The white half showed the brand name and dosage.

"Here." Yahya pointed. "You see twenty milligrams? The abbreviation, 'mg,' is followed by a period. Some pills put a period after 'mg' but not Prozac. The typesetter made a mistake."

"So they go cut rate or what?"

Yahya shook his head. "Full price, but only through street dealers. No hospitals. A doctor would not notice the error but a med nurse probably would."

Fat Julie raised an eyebrow. "You said five million users?"

"Worldwide, more like ten."

"And you think they're all hooked?"

"Hooked is not the right word. They simply want to feel the way it makes them feel."

"Prozac's still fairly new. What's the potential?"

Yahya pointed to the sky.

"There are that many depressed?"

The Pakistani smiled.

Once again he was the teacher and that made him feel good. In this country, to see dark skin is to see an inferior. But that dark-skinned inferior might speak five languages. Most Americans can barely speak their own.

"Prozac," he explained, "is for subclinical depression. That means you feel a little bit bad. For fifty cents, Prozac makes you feel much better. You are more confident, more aggressive, and you can have more fun at parties."

"Sounds like cocaine," Fat Julie noted, frowning.

"Better," said the Pakistani.

Mohammed Yahya had gone back to work, a bonus of twenty crisp new fifties in his pocket. Fat Julie reviewed what he had scribbled on his cocktail napkin. Johnny was right. Notes do help you collect your thoughts. You just want to be sure you don't leave them in your pocket.

Vicodin, which Yahya had to spell for him, did not seem all that interesting. You take it for pain but it also numbs the mind. No high, no rush, you just get this cozy, warm glow all over. There's money in it, Yahya says, because you keep needing more. Before long, you need a fix of a hundred pills a day to get the same feeling you got from four when you started. To get prescriptions for that many, you'd have to spend all day going to different doctors and that gets expensive. Or you forge prescriptions or you break into drugstores, both of which put you in jail. Better to buy them on the street.

But the street dealer can't make a living selling Vicodin alone. He needs to find people who are seriously hooked and there aren't that many of them out there. The distributor had made Yahya take it on because, like distributors anywhere, they won't let you sell their top-of-the-line products unless you agree to take a dog or two as part of the package.

What makes Prozac top of the line, better even than Xanax, is that *everybody's* going to want it. Yahya says it's already very hot in all the big cities and on all the college campuses. He says forget about people who are looking to get high. He says Prozac is for people who are just a little bummed out—which is basically every teenager, every college kid, every adult who's ever been shit on, and anyone who's a fan of the Chicago Cubs. He says go to a cocktail party and ask around. He says try to find a salesman or a stockbroker or a guy in advertising who isn't on Prozac already.

Doctors and shrinks write a ton of prescriptions for it because it works, it's not addictive, and it's cheap. The biggest side effect is weight loss, and even that is good. It doesn't zone you out like, say, heroin or Quaaludes. It's not a supercharger like cocaine or crystal meth but you don't come crashing down from it either and you don't get holes in your nasal passage. All it does is let you be at your best.

This, says Yahya, is what makes it too good to last. Guaranteed, he says, that whenever that many people are having a nice time, someone will rain on their parade. Maybe the Fed, the AMA, or even the religious right. They'll say hold it. Life is a vale of tears, right? You're *supposed* to have ups and downs. What's all this *up* shit all the time?

It's already happening, says Yahya. More and more doctors are getting nervous. They say maybe this is too good to be true. They say screwing around with the brain's chemistry too long has got to be bad so they start weaning their patients off it. What does the patient say? He says fuck you, Doc. Next party I go to, I'm damned if I'll be the only wallflower there. Next time I have to speak before an audience, or I have a job interview lined up, or I want to strike up a conversation with the lady down the bar, I don't want to freeze up anymore. You won't renew the prescription? Okay. I'll ask some high school kid to point me to his pusher. I'll load up with a year's supply.

The more Julie thought about this, the less wrong it seemed.

There are drugs that do bad and drugs that do good. Even Pop wouldn't argue with that. Offer him heroin, he'd slap your face. But the morphine he took for the pain that last month, that was just liquid heroin, right? Did he care where it came from? If his doctor wouldn't give him enough, and his sons said don't worry, we'll go pick up some more on the street, would he have said no?

Yeah.

Yeah, maybe he would have.

The bartender was waving at him. The one who was wired.

Wired or not, he seemed a nice kid. The customers all like him and he doesn't dip into the till. Julie had no idea what agency he worked for but it had to be federal. Local cops don't have the patience to plant a guy full-time. They don't have the budget, either.

"Call for you, Mr. Giordano." He's holding up the bar phone.

"Who is it, Jimmy?"

"Man named Parker. Says he wants to check a reference."

No shit?

"Get a number. Say I'll call him right back."

"You can take it right here, Mr. G. I'll give you some privacy."

Kid . . . don't push it, okay?

"Five minutes, Jimmy. I'll call him from back in the office."

Privacy, huh?

Christ! That means the kid has the whole fucking bar wired.

23

Megan knew, somehow, that it wasn't Bronwyn he'd been thinking about.

You must have a different look in your eyes, thought Fallon, a different kind of smile, when the memory is an old one. And Megan was definitely jealous. Jealous and a little sad.

He had a sense that, in her life, relationships never lasted very long. It wasn't the frigidity thing. They would last until the guy found out whatever it is in her background that she's in no big hurry to reveal. Like her father was the commandant of Auschwitz or she used to drink the blood of sleeping children.

It was hard to imagine what she could possibly tell him that would make him want to back off. She was such a terrific woman in so many ways that it was hard even to feel the need to reassure her. Or explain about Mary Beth. About how there's nothing wrong with leaving room in your heart for special people.

On that subject, come to think of it, he was feeling a little guilty himself about how quickly he was getting over Bronwyn. Another remarkable woman. One in a million. He would never forget her. But Megan was . . . he didn't know . . .

Fresher.

Softer.

And if she likes you, she lets it all hang out. That's how some women get hurt. But he would never hurt Megan.

She took the helm as they approached the Woods Hole Race. The race was a narrow channel with very strong and tricky currents. Most sailboats powered through. Needless to say, not Megan.

He stood behind her, his arms around her chest and shoulders, smelling her hair. Getting through the tidal rip took all her concentration. That was good. It was nice, for a change, to be able to think about other days without feeling like he was on a party line.

He never became a bully.

But he did, he supposed, become something of a snob. It happened very gradually.

He learned to play tennis and golf because Uncle Jake insisted and paid for the lessons. He would tell the instructors, "Keep on him until he's good." He joined a sailing club and learned the basics because his uncle thought yachting was classy. His yacht was a Sunfish but you have to start somewhere. And he liked it.

He learned to play bridge but drew the line at joining a classical music appreciation club that Jake had spotted in the Notre Dame catalog.

"You don't want to know about opera? Ballet?"

"Uncle Jake, have you ever been to either one?"

"I was deprived. You aren't."

"Well, I'm sorry. There are only so many hours in the day."

"How about Rugby? Nothing like a good scrum to get your juices flowing."

A good scrum?

It's not always easy to know when Jake is pulling your leg.

But over all, he'd been a pretty good student, top ten percent, a well-rounded if not stand-out jock, and people thought he was good-looking, especially in his ROTC uniform.

Add to this that dumb reputation. It was more than just those two episodes during his freshman year. His subsequent disdain for the karate club could only mean that he was far more advanced than anything they could teach him. He was rumored to

be an expert in several disciplines of the martial arts. Denying it
had no effect.

There was more. Add four years of whispers about certain powerful and mysterious New York connections, add being orphaned
by some equally mysterious tragedy, and you had a young guy
who was almost irresistible to the more vacuous young ladies of
the country club set. Their fathers, oddly, seemed to like him just
as much. He'd get invitations to their clubs whether he was actively seeing their daughters or not. It went to his head for a
while.

One of the fathers actually proposed to him. Told him he could
do a lot worse than marrying into the Johnson family. The Win-
netka, Illinois, Johnsons. Princes of the automotive aftermarket
industry. He and Tracey would make a beautiful couple. Or he
and Kimberly. Michael couldn't remember. They were *all* named
Tracey or Kimberly.

He majored in international marketing and minored in finance.
This had been Uncle Jake's suggestion.

"International's the future, Mike. You remember when it was
a big deal to say a thing you bought was 'imported'?"

"Uh . . . no."

"Trust me. But now *everything's* imported. Moving goods in
and out and moving money. Those are two things you should
know about."

He graduated with honors, won a prize or two, lettered in
football, and was commissioned a lieutenant in the U.S. Army
Reserves. After stateside training, he would be joining an armored unit in Germany. Michael's first choice had been flight
training in attack helicopters. Too dangerous, said his uncle. Stay
on the ground. Michael applied anyway and was promptly re-
jected. He wondered aloud whether the army chief of staff, per
chance, owed Big Jake Fallon a favor.

"Count your blessings," was all his uncle would say. "If you're
going to crash something, crash a tank."

Both Uncle Jake and Moon came out for the graduation cere-
mony. Brendan Doyle had to beg off. He was tied up in court

but he sent a nice watch that Michael promptly lost. He never did have much luck with watches.

Jake and Moon didn't look much like the other parents. Moon had worn a good suit for the occasion but on Moon, suits always had a sort of secondhand look. Suits on cops tend to have the same look for the same reason. Baggy. A full cut to hide a weapon and to allow free movement.

The other thing about Moon was that he rarely looked anyone in the eye except when he knew everyone in sight. He would always be looking past them at what else was going on, at whomever was coming up next. Here again, it's the same with cops. But it's also the same with thieves.

Uncle Jake was another story. He looked right at you. And right into you. Even during small talk. In consequence of the many stories about Moon and Uncle Jake, most of them wildly untrue, quite a few people wanted introductions. A few of these were people with whom Michael had not been especially close, and some he actively disliked. There were smirks behind their smiles. He had already overheard a sampling of their remarks.

"Mike Fallon's uncle . . . politician from Noo Yawk . . . so you *know* he has his hand out . . . fixes boxing matches . . . fight game is where Mike gets it . . . nigger's the bodyguard . . . ex-con, I hear . . . doesn't look so tough . . . looks more like a wino."

If Mike was getting angry, and more than a little embarrassed, his uncle seemed to be having the time of his life. He kept bragging about his nephew, told New York stories, fight game and mob stories. Some were true, some invented on the spot, all while he was chewing on a cigar.

Actually, most of the parents seemed to enjoy him. But one man, dressed in a club-crested blazer, walked away saying to his wife, "Do you believe that Irish clown?"

Michael wanted to go after him. He didn't. He looked over at his uncle and saw his uncle looking back. Looking deep. With a touch of disappointment. Jake then turned and ambled after the man who had made the remark. He put an arm around his shoulder and whispered into his ear. The man didn't move for a long moment. When he did, he had his wife by the arm and was dragging her, head down, toward the parking lot.

*   *   *

They went to dinner that night. Moon was more than usually quiet. Over coffee, his uncle handed him an envelope.

"A graduation present. It's from your father."

Michael didn't understand.

"Open it."

He did. There were several documents on Merrill-Lynch letterhead. They were the earnings statements of a group of mutual funds. The account was in his uncle's name but it was held in trust for Michael Fallon. The amount was just under two hundred thousand dollars. Michael could only stare.

"I took the cash from the apartment, same day he died. You knew it was there, right?"

Michael nodded. "But this much?"

"It grew. How come you never asked what happened to it?"

"I . . . assumed you've been spending it on me."

"Some, maybe. The rest is for when you get married, maybe need to buy a house or something. Meantime, it stays put."

Again, Michael stared. In his mind he saw himself, back in that apartment on Horatio Street, peeling off bills to buy groceries. He took only what he needed because he realized, even then, that it would have to last. He knew that his father might never hold a job again.

As for its source, he had tried not to think about it. Certainly it had crossed his mind that his father might have embezzled it, or had been paid off for cooking someone's books, or perhaps had simply accumulated it over the years. Cash payments for services rendered. Under the table. Tax-free.

He had tried not to think about it because then he'd also have to think about his mother, who also must have known, who had lost all respect for his father, who had walked out of their lives without taking a dime of this money. Most of all, he would have to remember that his father had killed himself on the one day when he managed to stay sober until noon, and after his son had shamed him by going off with his Uncle Jake. "You go, Mike. Your uncle knows best." Then, bitterly, "Your uncle *always* knows best."

"Uncle Jake . . . how bad was it?"

"How bad was what?"

"How dirty is that money?"

His uncle looked at him through hooded eyes.

"Is it drug money?" Michael asked.

The question seemed to startle him. Even Moon. "Drugs like what?" Jake asked him.

"You know. Heroin. Cocaine."

And now he seemed relieved. "No. Nothing like that."

Moon looked away.

"The money," his uncle said at last, "was severance pay. The deal he had with the Eagle outfit, it had what they call a non-compete clause. That's why he didn't work after that. Anyway, he didn't have to."

"But . . . this much severance . . . for a bookkeeper?"

"Lump sum. They were closing up shop anyway."

"Then why a noncompete clause?"

Jake Fallon grunted. "Mike . . . do you trust your uncle?"

"You know I do."

"Then here's all you have to know. Anything that needed to be fixed is fixed. What's past is past and money is money. Go live your life."

"Think you can take me yet, Michael?"

Moon asked this question after Uncle Jake rose to find the men's room.

"Ah . . . what brings that up?"

"Just askin'."

Michael thought for a moment. "It would be . . . closer."

"Maybe. But not if you got your nose so high in the air you wouldn't see me comin'."

Michael grimaced. "Am I doing that, Moon?"

"Don't you ever again let anyone mock your uncle and then walk away. He waited, Michael. He gave you time to step in."

A deep sigh. "I know he did."

"Just don't forget who you are. And don't make me remind you."

Don't forget who you are?

Okay, who *am* I?

Am I Tom Fallon's son or Jake Fallon's nephew? Am I the son of a drunken dropout who was probably a criminal or am I what

Uncle Jake has been working so hard to turn me into? Do I look for another Mary Beth or do I keep scouting out the country club Kimberlys?

Dean's list grad from Notre Dame. An officer and a gentleman. Don't forget who you are? Don't change?

What *hasn't* changed?

After four months' training in Texas, he was shipped to Germany, where he joined the 2nd Armored Cavalry, based in Nuremberg. While there, he studied the language and, because of a compulsion he could not resist, spent a week's leave following the route along which his father fought more than thirty years earlier. It took him through half of Austria and well up into Czechoslovakia. Patton would have taken Prague if Eisenhower hadn't stopped him. Hell, Patton would have taken Moscow. And Tom Fallon would have followed him.

He spent his third year of active duty in England where, he was pleased to tell Uncle Jake, he finally got to play Rugby. The army promoted him to captain in the hope that he'd extend his tour but Michael had other plans. He was taking courses toward a graduate degree at the London School of Economics. If Uncle Jake would advance him the money from his trust, he would stay to complete it.

Uncle Jake liked the sound of it. The London School of Economics. Very classy. A clear step up for a former stickball player from Horatio Street.

Two years later he was on Wall Street, still in his twenties and making more than ninety thousand dollars a year. He had a nice apartment and an active social life.

Moon would drop by every now and then.

Now . . . this was not snobbishness. It really wasn't. But he would have preferred to meet Moon elsewhere because, from the looks the other tenants gave him afterward, Moon was presumed to be his dealer making a delivery.

Moon, of course, knew this as well as he did. Moon was no doubt waiting to dump all over him if he should suggest an alternative arrangement. Once a young woman, in whom Michael was interested, was there for one of Moon's visits. He introduced himself as "Mike's Uncle Moon." The young woman's interest cooled before his eyes. She suddenly remembered a hair appointment.

"Count your blessings, Michael," said Moon when she left.

After four years with Shearson, he was recruited by Lehman-Stone. They had learned that he had a good working knowledge of business German and they needed a specialist in West German offerings, primarily in the area of chemicals and pharmaceuticals. The job would involve considerable travel. That was a welcome change from Shearson where he stared at a computer screen all day with a phone at each ear. And the money was double.

At Lehman-Stone, he worked with three West German clients but, eventually, the needs of the business forced him to concentrate on one firm in particular. AdlerChemiker AG. Or AdChem. It was a fast-growing pharmaceutical company based in Munich with branches in the Far East. Lehman-Stone held a major position in the company's stock and had raised much of AdChem's start-up and expansion capital.

He was now thirty-five, doing quite well, but getting increasing heat from his Uncle Jake about not having started a family.

"Michael . . . not that I'd think any the less of you . . ."

"I'm not gay, Uncle Jake."

"Who said gay? Did I say gay?"

Groan. "Come on. Let's have it."

"Why is your bathroom pink?"

"Because the *tile* is pink, Uncle Jake. It was that way when I moved in."

He picked up a magazine that was on the coffee table.

"*Art & Antiques?*"

Michael lapsed into Brooklynese. "You wanted I should get refined."

"Not *that* fucking refined."

"I'll run out and get *Playboy*."

"That bathroom . . . why don't I send over some Italians? They'll rip it out and make you something nice."

"I'll handle it, Uncle Jake."

"You got a girlfriend? Someone special?"

"I'm working on it."

* * *

"Michael . . ."

Megan had dropped one hand to his thigh. She kept the other on the wheel. He snapped out of it.

Her slip was just ahead. He released her and turned to get a stern line ready.

"No, no," she said quickly. "You feel good where you are."

"So do you. But aren't we going to dock?"

"Let's stay out awhile longer."

Michael wasn't sure what Megan had picked up on. Or why she wanted to stay out. Maybe girlfriends. Maybe marriage.

He shouted in his head, *Hey, Megan. Want to get married? Raise a couple of nice warlocks? . . . Just kidding . . . Or what the hell. Maybe I'm not.*

"Could you hear that?" he asked her.

"Hear what?"

"Nothing. I thought we ticked the bottom back there."

"Michael?"

"Um?"

"Say some of it out loud."

"You *did* hear me. Didn't you?"

"No. Not the way you think."

Oh, well. Where was he?

Oh, yeah. Marriage.

First there was Uncle Jake, nagging that it was time. Then there was Bart Hobbs, that prick, going out of his way to make it happen. He wasn't sure how much of this he was inclined to tell Megan.

Hobbs, for some reason, had taken a sudden interest in him. Checking his work. Asking questions about him, particularly of the executive who had recruited him to Lehman-Stone. Michael wasn't concerned, especially. He assumed, in fact, that he was being considered for a promotion.

Early one evening, Hobbs called him into his office. As he entered, Hobbs covered up a blue vinyl folder that was on his desk. Michael recognized it as a personnel folder, presumably his own.

Hobbs stood and switched on that permanent half-smile of his. He extended a hand. Michael shook it.

He just wanted to chew the fat, he said. Get caught up on how things are going generally. Michael doubted that there was much he didn't know but he briefed him anyway. He could see, however, that Hobbs was not really listening. Whatever was actually on his mind, he was dancing around it. That was not unusual. Bart Hobbs, as a rule, was not one who would attack a subject head-on if he could help it. He did ask, however, what Michael found so uniquely fascinating about AdChem.

It seemed an odd question. It was not as if he had begged for the assignment. AdChem, however, was a huge, far-flung operation, it was minting money, and Michael was helping it to make even more. The work was interesting, even important, but he was hardly manic on the subject. Still, when your boss wants to hear enthusiasm, that's what you give him. He spoke of how rewarding it was to work with a company that did well while doing good.

"Excellent," Hobbs said when he finished. "Keep up the good work, Michael."

He offered his hand again. Fallon pumped it and turned to leave. Hobbs said "Hmmph."

Michael stopped. "Was there something else, Mr. Hobbs?"

"Fallon." Hobbs said the name as if to himself. He cocked his head. "Michael, did I hear somewhere that you're related to Big Jake Fallon?"

"He's my uncle. Do you know him?"

Hobbs shook his head quickly as if to say, "A different set entirely, dear boy." Aloud, he said, "He's quite a character, though, from what I've heard. Did your uncle . . . steer you into this, um, line of work?"

"Far from it. But he did say go where the money is."

"Well, the old scoundrel was right." Still the half-smile. "Ah, when I say scoundrel, I don't mean to impugn . . ."

"I know you don't, Mr. Hobbs."

"Good job, Michael. Go enjoy your evening."

A week later, Michael had a new assistant. It was Bronwyn. She had transferred in from the London office and she was absolutely breathtaking. By the end of another week, Michael knew that either of two things would happen. He would marry this girl or he would make a total ass of himself in the attempt.

Part of it was the voice. Everyone knew that he'd always been a sucker for an upper-class British accent. He had one himself when he came home from England but only until Jake said, "Nice accent, Michael. Goes with your pretty pink bathroom."

Beyond the voice, she had those amazing violet eyes and a wonderfully open smile. And smart? Talented?

"Quite an accomplished young lady," Hobbs had told him. "It seems that she'd trained since childhood to become a concert pianist. But when her parents lost two homes to the Lloyd's of London debacle, she decided she'd try her hand at making money instead. Headed straight for the London Exchange where she soon made a name for herself. That's where we found her."

A part of him wondered whether it was really Uncle Jake who found her. That was silly, of course. It was just that Hobbs had suddenly brought up Jake's name and now, out of nowhere, here's the kind of woman who, except that she's a Brit, Uncle Jake would have *bought* for him if he could.

As an inflexible rule, Michael avoided relationships with female employees of the firm for all the usual reasons. He avoided them within the industry at large because such relationships tended to become exploitative or competitive very quickly. A good rule. But to hell with it. They were lovers before the second week was out. Bronwyn had already moved in with him.

Hobbs had mentioned that they'd had trouble finding an apartment for her and that she hated living in a hotel. Too many hookers coming and going, too many male guests hitting on her every time she takes a meal in the dining room. Michael had a spare bedroom; he asked her if she'd consider using it. She thought it over and said yes. He couldn't believe his luck. But, she insisted, it was to be strictly temporary. He had his own life and she would not dream of interfering with it. She'll be out like a shot at the first sign that she's a bother. Fair enough, he told her. Strictly temporary.

But that day, he rented a Steinway for her and ordered a new mattress for himself. By the end of the weekend, she was sharing it with him. Bronwyn, incidentally, thought the bathroom was just fine as it was.

Bronwyn.

It's Welsh. He looked it up.

It means "Fair breast."

But he would gargle with Drano before he'd share that little tidbit with Moon or his Uncle Jake.

When Jake came by that night to meet her, it was Bronwyn who did most of the pumping. She wanted to hear all about his nephew. What was he like as a boy? How did someone raised in Manhattan grow up to be such a gentleman? His parents must have been very special people indeed.

Big Jake hit a few of the high spots and passed over the lows. Bronwyn seemed enthralled. She told him how lucky she felt to have been assigned to Michael. He's so very generous. Gives her every chance to learn by doing. Especially on the AdChem account. Splendid company. Forever breaking new ground through research.

Jake Fallon's eyes began to glaze over. Michael understood why. She seems great, Jake would have said, but anyone who gets that excited about a drug company needs to get out more. Michael tried to change the subject but Bronwyn was on a roll. She began rattling off figures, projections, earnings. She said the stock was still a good buy, especially longer term, and Uncle Jake would do well to consider it.

She went to his desk and returned with a copy of the new annual report, which she opened and handed to him.

"Ah, Bronwyn . . . " Michael signaled time out. "He already has some."

"Do you really?" she asked Jake Fallon.

"A few bucks' worth." He smiled up at her. "But you tell it better than Mike did."

Bronwyn blushed winningly. "Well, read up on it all the same. You'll see how clever you were to buy it."

She sat watching him to see that he did. At this, Michael drew the line. He reached to take the brochure from him. His uncle raised a hand.

"Wait a second," he said distantly.

"You're actually going to sit here and read that?"

Big Jake reached for a pen, then stopped himself. He folded the report in half and put it in his pocket. As he did so, he looked up at Michael. A curious stare. Those intelligent eyes. Looking right through him.

"What?" Michael asked.

Jake shook his head. "Nothing," he said. "Nothing at all." He looked at Bronwyn and smiled. "How about some more of that Chopin?"

There were times, such as that one, when Michael would wonder how well he really knew his uncle. He would not have bet a nickel that Big Jake Fallon would know Chopin when he heard it. But it was mostly the eyes. In that instant, Jake had changed into someone he hardly recognized. Perhaps he'd read something that reminded him of what his younger brother was into. Or that reminded him of why he didn't like drug companies. He would not return to the subject.

They walked him to the street where Bronwyn spotted a taxi and flagged it down. She offered her cheek to Uncle Jake, then hugged him. He seemed his old self again. Jake climbed into the taxi. He blew them a kiss. It was the last time Michael saw him alive.

"You really loved him," said Megan quietly.

She stroked the arm that he held across her chest.

"Yes," he whispered.

"And Bronwyn."

He hesitated, not sure quite how to answer.

It had nothing to do with telling Megan that he had loved another woman. Just as Megan had nothing to do with Bronwyn. It was more that what he felt for Uncle Jake and what he felt for Bronwyn did not seem to belong in the same conversation. Jake was one of a kind. So was Bronwyn in her way but who knows how long that would have lasted. People do break up. Jake, however, will be with him until the day he dies. And, if there's a heaven, for a long time after that.

"It wasn't the same," was all he said.

A lot of the people he knew, growing up, going through school, had expressed a degree of envy over his relationship with Uncle

Jake. They envied the respect, the trust, and maybe most of all, the fun. Some had none of that at home. For others, their own relationships with their fathers might have been perfectly healthy but there always seemed to be a constant low-level tension between them as one tried to steer and the other tried to take some time to browse.

God knows Uncle Jake did a lot of steering. But the path he would point you down was very wide. Plenty of room to browse. You wouldn't see much of him because he was always back there behind you. Unless you got too close to the edge or had one foot over. Then you'd suddenly notice him standing there. Not saying anything. Maybe not even looking at you. Maybe shooting the breeze with Moon, both of them strolling along in the same direction. And you'd say maybe I should pay some attention to what I'm doing here.

"Megan?"

"Yes."

"Fair is fair. I want to know what your folks were like."

She said nothing.

"Do you ever see them? Do you miss them?"

His arm, where it crossed her heart, felt an odd extra beat. It might have meant yes. He didn't think so.

"Tell me about Bronwyn, Michael."

"I have."

He felt her muscles go tense. She was concentrating hard for some reason. "I mean . . . on the night she died. What happened that night?"

He let out a breath. "You read the papers."

"Please. It would help me to . . ."

"Yeah, but it wouldn't help me. Let's leave it alone, okay?"

"If that's what you want."

She didn't push it. And yet Michael knew . . . that she knew . . . that now he couldn't help but think about it. He was tempted to back away from her. Not touch her. Make it harder for her to *listen* if that was what she was trying to do. But he didn't. The ache seemed not as deep while he could feel the warmth of her body.

*   *   *

On that night, last November, the store was just closing. But the Korean counterman knew Michael by sight and had read about his Uncle Jake in the newspapers he sold. He let them in and told Michael how sorry he was.

Bronwyn had drifted away, over to the magazine rack, where she picked up a copy of *Newsweek* and began idly browsing through it. They had that issue at home but Bronwyn, he assumed, had heard all the condolences she could handle.

Michael had moved toward her to say let's buy your pack and go, when he heard a voice mutter, "Your money. Give me your money."

He turned toward the sound. He saw a man with a ski mask pulled crookedly over his face, an ugly sawed-off shotgun in his hands. He heard Bronwyn's magazine fall to the floor. He glanced back. She was crouching, trying to make herself small, her eyes locked on that shotgun. She seemed more wary than frightened.

When Michael turned again—this was all in the space of a second—the man in the ski mask was looking straight at him. The shotgun was swinging in an arc toward his face. He wanted to dive over the counter, away from Bronwyn. That or lunge *at* Bronwyn, protect her with his body. He did neither. He stood frozen to the spot as he saw another blur of motion. Then flashes of light and a deafening echoing roar. All together. All in the same instant.

Blood and black wool sprayed from the ski mask. White flame spewed from the shotgun but the man who was holding it was already dead. The Korean had fired twice at point-blank range. The bullets expanded as they entered at his cheek, fragmented, and exploded upward. The man in the mask seemed to rise up on his toes, standing rigid. Then, as straight as a falling tree, he pitched forward on his face.

The Korean raced around the counter, ready to shoot again if the man who came to rob him moved. There was no need. He groped for the telephone. As he did so, he looked at Michael, then past him. A low wail came from his throat. Michael was afraid to turn but he did.

The rest would remain a jumble in his mind. Shouts and running feet, flashing lights and sirens. It seemed real one moment and a dream the next.

The blast had caught Bronwyn high in the chest. It was a terrible, bubbling wound. A mangled silver necklace had been driven into her flesh. And yet she was alive, floating in and out of shock. One hand reached for his face. Her eyes found his. They stared hard. He saw not fear or pain in them but disbelief. And then blame. She seemed to be asking why he had not protected her. Her fingernails raked his cheek. The hand fell away. He looked once more into her eyes. The light in them had faded. One had changed color.

He was sure of that now.

It was not his imagination nor was it some trick of the fluorescent lights. But he had not imagined that she died hating him.

He said all this to Megan. It was the first time he'd told anyone, not counting Dr. Greenberg. And except Moon. Moon had made him relive that whole afternoon and evening, what everyone said and did, who was where, practically minute by minute. The doctors were making him do the same thing himself, he said, to get his brain using all its cylinders again. It was good therapy, he said.

It wasn't for Fallon. But maybe telling Megan was. He must have said that as well because she told him she was glad that he did.

She squeezed his arm. "But now you wish you hadn't."

"Will you cut that out?"

"Be honest, Michael."

A sigh. "I guess I wish you'd never seen those newspaper stories. I was trying to leave this in New York."

"Maybe now you can. When we dock, I'll show you a way to do that."

Megan thought that Bronwyn must have worn cosmetic contact lenses. The tinted kind. One had simply slipped off under the impact of the blast. He didn't think so. He told her he'd never seen Bronwyn take them out, nor had he seen, among her toiletries, any of the paraphernalia that goes with wearing contacts.

Megan said that doesn't mean much necessarily. Women have their private vanities. She might have been wondering when and how to tell him that those striking eyes he fell for came from a color chart. After all, said Megan, a man who's had a hair replacement or has had a tattoo scraped off—such as one that says "Mary Beth Forever"—might not rush to volunteer that information either.

Mary Beth forever.

Had he mentioned that name out loud?

Cute, Megan. Very cute.

But her theory about contacts sounds reasonable enough, he thought. Except that her heart did a drum roll as she finished saying it. The same, come to think of it, as when she saw that shirt Bronwyn gave him.

Michael . . . forget it.

You'll just make yourself crazy again.

24

He was called the Baron. Sometimes the Chairman.

Properly, he was the Baron Franz Gerhardt Rast von Scharnhorst. Baron Franz Rast would do. The Baron von Scharnhorst was preferred. In dealing with Americans, he knew that he must tolerate Herr Rast or even Mr. Rast. But certainly not Franz.

He was chairman and chief executive officer of AdlerChemiker AG, headquartered in Munich and with subsidiaries, wholly owned or controlled, in twenty countries around the globe. All these were on the books. Off the books were "understandings" with over one hundred distributors, shipping companies, health ministries, and well-placed executives of rival firms.

The Baron was a tall man, fashionably thin and gracefully slow of movement. His English had only the barest trace of accent. Among his many vanities was a dueling scar from his student days at Leipzig. It split his left eyebrow and ran, straight and deep, down across the corner of his eye.

The general manager of New York's Pierre Hotel, where the Baron kept an apartment, was aware that the fifth anniversary of his stay at the Pierre fell on the day after tomorrow. But the Baron, alas, had let it be known that he would be leaving in the morning for the White Mountains of Maine. A well-earned holiday before returning to Munich. Do a bit of fly-casting. Outwit a few trout.

The manager had asked, therefore, whether he might honor the Pierre by partaking of an evening meal created by Marcel, his favorite chef. For days now, Marcel had been planning a special menu—it was to be a surprise—and he was crushed to learn that his efforts were to be for naught.

The Baron answered that it's he who would be honored. He would have preferred to take the meal in the comfort and security of his apartment but he knew that to suggest such a thing would disappoint his host. The theatrics of presentation demand an audience of other diners. Further, Marcel would sooner open a vein than permit his creation to be trundled about on a room service cart.

The Baron would take it in the restaurant but he would dine alone. Such a meal deserves one's full attention. He would post his bodyguards, all of them German, at the entrance and at a table nearby in case that Fallon boy should come calling prematurely.

The meal was indeed splendid. The leek soup caused him to moan with pleasure. The milk-fed veal, flown in—smuggled in was more like it—nearly caused him to weep. The wines . . . the desserts . . . were a fantasy. Perhaps two other times in his memory had he enjoyed such a meal.

Trust Hobbs to ruin it.

"Well, we can forget about Maine," said Hobbs, pulling out a chair unbidden. His breath smelled of alcohol. "Would you care to see what's left of my chalet?"

From his pocket, Hobbs produced a group of photographs. He spread them before Franz Rast. The chalet, Playing Hobbs, was a pile of smoldering timbers. It would not have been recognizable but for the three stone chimneys rising out of the rubble. One of them showed the letters "BH" set in green ceramic tile.

The Baron was not greatly surprised. "When did this happen?"

"Last night. Right under the noses of two armed guards."

Hobbs produced a second and thicker group of photographs. "Look," he said bitterly. "Just look at what the son of a bitch has done."

He slapped them down, one by one, as if they were playing cards.

"Dink Bellows's Rolls-Royce," Hobbs said of the first. "Taken from his garage as his family slept. Set ablaze in the middle of his street."

The Baron scowled, more at the use of that insipid schoolboy nickname than at the sight of this charred pile of scrap. *Avery* Bellows is the managing partner of their Washington law firm. A *Dink* Bellows is a boy who sits in malt shops strumming on a ukelele.

Hobbs pushed another toward him. This one a photo of a residence.

"Gardner Lowell's Scarsdale home. The firemen managed to save most of it but the whole west wing is in ruins. Fram Childress wasn't so lucky."

Lowell was a partner at Lehman-Stone. Childress was executive VP/sales for AdChem, North America. His house in Glen Cove, a fine old Victorian, was a total loss.

"Victor Turkel's house was spared. But now we can't find Victor. He seems to have gone into hiding."

The Baron could only sigh. "Mr. Hobbs . . . please put those away."

"How could Michael have known about Victor? He's never laid eyes on Victor. He didn't torture it out of the taxi driver. That man knew none of our names, least of all Victor's."

Hobbs pushed two more forward.

Finally, Hobbs laid out the oldest of the set. Those of his home in Palm Beach. Another grimace from the older man.

Truth be told, thought the Baron, he was genuinely saddened by the destruction of the Palm Beach house. It had been a showplace, really, even by Palm Beach standards. Italian Renaissance style, patterned after Vizcaya. At least a million dollars' worth of art on the walls. Now it was a blackened shell. Only the pool house was spared.

Nor could he resist lingering on the photo of the man in the melted lounge chair. What remained of him. Smashed into pulp with a baseball bat and then baked to a turn by the heat that radiated from the house. The bat, broken in two, had been washed clean in the swimming pool and left on his chest. As if that were not symbolism enough, his pistol had been left in his hand to demonstrate, one must imagine, the impotence of weaponry against an avenging angel.

"He knew," Hobbs repeated. His eyes returned to the photo of the house in Maine. He seemed about to cry.

The Baron sniffed. He was far less sympathetic to the loss of Hobbs's mountain retreat. The builder, some local rustic, thought that if he did enough doodling with a jigsaw, he could call that *barracks* a chalet.

It did have one advantage, however. Michael Fallon, clearly, was working his way north and this house had seemed the best place to trap him. It sits in its own private valley and is reached by a single dirt road. Two men at each end could easily seal it. Two more, chosen for their resemblance to him and Hobbs, dressed in fishing gear, would serve as bait while he and Hobbs concealed themselves.

This was Parker's idea. Mr. Fallon, however, had unsportingly jumped the gun. No great surprise in that. The Baron had never thought much of the plan. Fallon did not *know* that they were laying a trap. He is simply not stupid.

"Suggestions, Mr. Hobbs?"

Hobbs, his eyes on the photo, could only shake his head.

"We could always try this again in France," said the Baron, dryly. "You have one house left, don't you? In Cap d'Antibes?"

"I don't own that one. I lease it."

"He'll take that into account, I'm sure."

Hobbs smiled unpleasantly. "If Fallon makes it to Europe, the von Scharnhorsts have a lot more to burn than I do."

The Baron sucked his cheek. "I suppose you have a point."

Several drinks had emboldened Hobbs. "He might even decide to drop in on the Countess," he added. "He might tell her it's time she paid attention to business."

For an instant, Hobbs thought that the Baron might strike him. His knuckles became white. A tic began at his temple. But the older man only closed his eyes. "How will we end this, Mr. Hobbs?" he asked quietly.

End it? Hobbs wanted to shout out that it would never have happened, *need* never have happened, if the good Baron had kept his head. But part of the blame was his own. He had seriously underestimated Michael.

"Were you aware, incidentally, that he's some kind of martial arts expert?"

"An impressive young man."

"Those two he crippled . . . Parker's men. Parker doubted their story at first but according to some of Michael's college classmates . . ."

The Baron had raised an eyebrow. "You've been interviewing these people yourself?"

"I'm not a fool, Franz. I only speak to—"

"*Franz,*" the older man said icily, "is one of my chauffeurs. I am the Baron Franz Rast. The distinction is considerable."

Again, Hobbs held his tongue with difficulty. The Baron sipped his capuccino, now gone cold. He put it down. "You were saying, Mr. Hobbs?"

"That . . . I only speak to Parker. Parker speaks to them. He wants more money for this, by the way."

"He is well paid as it is. If he thinks he can blackmail me . . ."

Hobbs curled his lip. "Blackmailing *us*, my dear Baron, is how he got his job in the first place. The money, as it happens, is to hire better people."

A grunt. "Who speak English, I trust."

"And who know the city better. He says he would have done so at the outset if he'd had decent information on Michael Fallon. He's now lost two dead, the Jamaican is back in prison, and the Pakistani is still missing."

"Two dead? Who are the two?"

Hobbs tapped his photographs. "The taxi driver, remember? Palm Beach?"

"I know about that one. Who is the other?"

"The idiot who managed to shoot Bronwyn."

The Baron pursed his lips. "That was hardly the Fallon boy's doing. But the taxi driver . . ." His expression turned thoughtful. "To be skilled in the martial arts is one thing. But that business by your pool was an act of cruel and calculated savagery."

You should know, you old bastard, thought Hobbs.

"Is that boy really capable of such an act?"

Hobbs raised an eyebrow. "You can ask? After what he did to

two armed attackers? And now he's armed as well. He took that Jamaican's—''

The Baron gestured dismissively. "I should think he would be. Karate or the like is not a magic shirt. I'm sure its practitioners are shot with great regularity by people with lesser skills and greater sense. Will Parker find him, Mr. Hobbs?"

"He says he will. He's sure he will."

"How comforting."

"We've had some bad luck. But Parker says—''

"Bad luck?" Franz Rast felt the veal rising. "Three failed attempts plus one botched burglary and you call that bad luck? And this latest absurdity. Did we really expect a man born and raised in New York City to stalk us through the Maine woods in the hope that he might catch us sloshing about in hip-waders?"

"You agreed, as I recall, that it was worth a try."

"*Absent* a less desperate idea, Mr. Hobbs. And I'll say again. The way to find that boy is through that lawyer."

Hobbs rubbed his chin nervously. He took a breath to prepare himself. "I've . . . just had a call from Bellows. I'm afraid there's more bad news."

Blood drained from the Baron's cheeks as he heard the details of Doyle's amended suit. Slowly, his color rose again. Two thin fists crashed down upon the table. His bodyguards straightened. Other diners turned their heads. Franz Rast brought his napkin to his lips.

"End this, Mr. Hobbs," he hissed.

He rose to his feet.

"For the sake of my digestion, to say nothing of your future, put an end to this once and for all."

Hobbs bit his lip. "I will . . . speak to Parker."

The Baron closed his eyes. He shook his head slowly. "Mr. Hobbs, I will teach you the German word for 'incompetent.' The word is *unbefugt*. Chew on it. Let it roll on your tongue. One would have to summon gutter language to find a word more apt than *unbefugt*."

He threw his napkin at Hobbs's array of photographs.

"I will speak to Mr. Parker myself."

*   *   *

Hobbs, seething, watched the Baron go.

They had been through this before. And it *was* bad luck.

Bronwyn. Such a terrible loss. Steering Michael into that convenience store at the precise moment when its owner, who had only that morning bought a pistol on the street, must have been praying to his Buddha that some hooded addict would try to rob him again. What else was that but damnable luck?

The shotgun going off not into Michael, not even into a display of beef jerky, but into Bronwyn, who had moved well away from the line of fire.

It goes on and on.

A professional burglar who arrives at Michael's building to find the police already there and the apartment already burgled. The one suspect, a building resident who swore on his life, which it nearly cost him, that he knew nothing about it.

Add the reflexes of a fat black woman who didn't know Michael Fallon from Bull Connor and would have cared even less if she'd had a chance to stop and think.

Add two inept muggers to whom it never occurred that if a white man fails to cross the street when he sees them approaching, he's probably as ready for them as that Korean was.

And of course that was it, thought Hobbs. By that time, Michael knew. Somehow he knew, or at least suspected, and he was ready. He disabled those two, disarmed them, and then he asked them for names.

The Jamaican, the only one who spoke English, swears that he told him nothing. That Michael asked them nothing. The Pakistani confirmed it. Not a word, they say, was spoken by anyone. Not even by Michael.

Perhaps.

But Michael did have that pistol aimed at the Jamaican's knee and he did choose not to shoot. Why such generosity? Was it in payment, after all, for a satisfactory answer? Did the Jamaican, in fact, tell Michael that it was the taxi driver, not they, who beat his uncle to death?

Parker says no.

To begin with, says Parker, the only way they'd know that Walter did that job would be if Walter told them. And Walter, by all accounts, was none too popular with his third world brethren, who thought he was a patronizing shit and a snob about being half Belgian. He would hardly admit to capital murder just to be one of the guys.

But say he did, says Parker. And say the Jamaican gave his name to Michael. Why then did Michael not wait for the police and tell them, "These two just tried to kill me. They say they work for a man named Philip Parker who is chief of security at Lehman-Stone. Parker's boss is a man named Bart Hobbs. Hobbs ordered the death of my uncle but these two say they didn't do it. They say that a certain taxi driver did."

Why, instead, did Michael walk away?

Why did he then vanish for all these months?

Very well. Parker makes a valid point. Those two told Michael nothing. And he knew nothing, at least that he could prove. This is all well and good until we get to the question of why he would resurface after several months, beat that taxi driver to death, and then start burning down the homes of everyone who's been involved in this.

Parker was just full of answers to that one.

"In the first place," says Parker, "you never should have fired him. That just pissed him off. It made you the enemy."

Hobbs snorted. "So he went off for three months and sulked about it? Then he decided that a suitable revenge was to burn my house in Florida?"

"I would have."

Hobbs closed one eye.

"Come on," said Parker. "At the uncle's funeral, you tell the guy, take Bronwyn, go use the Palm Beach house, take a couple weeks' R&R."

"At your suggestion."

Parker's eyes became hooded. "Mine. Yours. The Pope's. Don't start that shit, Mr. Hobbs."

"I only meant . . ." Hobbs had to look away.

Parker stared for another beat. "Anyway . . . *we* had Walter down there housesitting. Did you hear anyone tell him to do more than that?"

Hobbs winced at the mention of the taxi driver's name. He disliked using or even knowing their actual names and Parker was fully aware of that. Parker was getting a bit too fresh lately.

The man, in any case, had left the city immediately after the Jake Fallon business was finished. Parker posted him to the Palm Beach house. It's true that he, Hobbs, had heard no order given. And yet he knew. If Michael had gone down there, Walter and Bronwyn would have arranged an understandably despondent suicide.

Some security guard. Some suicide.

"What's your point?" he asked Parker.

"I don't know. Could be Fallon smelled a rat but I doubt it. Maybe after he thinks about it he just says, 'This hypocritical prick'—no offense—'offers me this house he's so proud of and then he fires me. You want me to use your house? Okay. I'll go grill some steaks on your living room floor.' "

How he detested this man, thought Hobbs. With his foul mouth and crooked teeth. The hooded eyes and perpetual sneer of a bully. He probably has a tattoo. Hobbs took a breath and waited.

"But then," Parker went on, "you have to believe that this kid ran into Walter, who is no pussy himself, kicked the piss out of him, and then killed him. From what we hear, the kid can handle himself but there's a big jump between fighting and killing."

"Even if he found out somehow that this man had—"

"Whacked his uncle? We've been through that. The only people who could finger him are you, me, the Baron, and Bronwyn. It sure as hell wasn't us and Bronwyn was in no shape to make a deathbed confession. It wasn't Walter because how would that leave him better off? They went there to burn the house, he was there, and they took him out. It's that simple."

"They? You're saying that it wasn't Michael?"

"Not alone, it wasn't."

"The black man? The one called Moon?"

A shrug. "No one's seen him since he walked out of Mount Sinai."

"But the same questions apply. How would he know? And why would he have waited this long?"

"Mr. Hobbs . . . think about it."

"Enlighten me."

Smug son of a bitch. His theories change with the wind.

"All it is," insisted Parker, "somewhere, somehow, they got a few names. But other than that, they don't have shit."

Hobbs *had* thought about it. He'd been trying to believe just that. But the call from Bellows, if nothing else, had put an end to any such self-delusion.

Michael hadn't run, exactly. And he certainly did not go off to sulk. He had merely gone underground.

Witness the fact that he laid a false trail to Cape Cod. An elaborate trail. Even down to his gas receipts. Witness the *probability* that he had two or more men positioned to cover his departure. Parker's people had seen them. They said they had hard faces and they wore their clothing loosely.

So Michael clearly had allies. Probably those "investigators" of Doyle's. He went underground when it dawned on him that nearly everyone he saw seemed to want to kill him. And he spent those three months digging. Digging and planning.

What is it he wants? Revenge, certainly, but with a new wrinkle. He now wants ten million dollars' worth.

But then why all the arson? Why the campaign of terror?

"To spook you," says Parker, as if the answer were obvious. "To me, that means they still can't prove a thing."

Perhaps.

But at least Parker, swine that he is, is *doing* something. He has people out looking. For Michael, for Jake Fallon's shadow whom the Baron wants dead just as much, and now for Victor Turkel. And for the missing Pakistani whom Parker seems to think he'll find hiding from the INS in some Muslim sanctuary such as Jersey City or the Bronx.

Hobbs left the dining room.

He made his way through the lobby, toward Fifth Avenue, then thought better of it. He opted for the side entrance opening onto 61st Street. This is what it's come to, he thought bitterly. Bartholomew Harriman Hobbs III, chewing Maalox by the handful, sneaking out through side doors while that vindictive old bastard hides away in his tower.

Unraveling. It's all unraveling.

Parker was right about one thing. The mistake, if there was one, was firing Michael. Better the devil you can see.

But it had been just too nerve-wracking, waiting to see whether he would come back to work as if nothing had happened. Wondering whether he really did know or whether—as Bronwyn seemed to think—he knew nothing at all. There's an irony for you. Bronwyn arguing that there was no need to kill him. But Rast would have none of it and Bronwyn, as always, was a good and willing soldier.

Of what the uncle knew, at least, she had little doubt. Bronwyn saw in Jake Fallon's eyes that he had recognized Franz Rast in that copy of the annual report. From twenty-five years earlier. Before he was a baron. Before he was a corporate giant.

Before he was even Franz Rast.

25

They sat in the cockpit of Megan's ketch, watching the sunset. The dinner dishes had been washed and stowed. He would have to head back soon. Tomorrow would be a long and busy day because his first guests would be arriving on Friday. But there was always tomorrow night. Michael squeezed her hand.

"What was that thing you were going to show me?"

"What thing was that?"

"You know. How to leave all the bad stuff in New York."

"Oh." She smiled as if at a private joke. "I don't think you need that now."

Never mind, again.

"Yeah, but now I'm curious. Is it something that we, ah, do together?"

The smile spread into a grin. "It doesn't require undressing, Michael."

"I wasn't thinking that."

"The heck you weren't."

"Megan . . ."

"Okay. Okay, give me a minute."

What it turned out to be was a mental exercise that she said she learned from an old Hindu fakir. They've used it for centuries, she told him, to clear their minds of excess baggage. It's how they make ropes climb up by themselves and it's how they stick big steel pins through their tongues without apparent pain or injury. He told her he'd settle for a couple of beers but she sat him down and made him try it. It turned out to be pretty interesting. More than that, it really seemed to work.

All you do is sit quietly, close your eyes, and focus on any bad memory, any old hurt, any recent personal stupidity. You take that one thing, whatever it is, and you isolate it right in the middle of your brain and let it float there like a single rain cloud. You try to go blank on everything else. If other thoughts intrude, you pluck them away like you'd pluck Kleenex out of a box. That done, you start to ease the hurtful part forward. What you want to do is push it, using steady pressure, through the center of your forehead.

Now comes the fun part.

It's floating a foot in front of your forehead now. You bring up both hands, cup them, and gradually compress it into a ball. Tennis-ball size is about right. As you're shaping it, you get so you can actually feel it. It gives off heat, just a little, and it has weight. You can heft it in one hand. You can toss it back and forth and feel it when you catch it.

This, according to Megan, is because thought waves are matter. An idea is matter. A memory is matter. This is because all brain activity is electrical and electrons themselves are matter. They give off heat and they have weight.

You now have this bad memory, this ball, right where you want it. You rear back your head and send that sucker flying straight over the horizon. In this case, straight toward New York. As it disappears from sight, you start counting down from ten. The instant you hit zero, there's this distant flash of light where it made impact. Follow that, if you wish, with a mushroom cloud.

Megan appeared at the hatch. She handed him a beer.

"Feel better?"

"I'll be darned. Yes."

"Told you so."

"I even nuked New York."

"Whatever works for you."

"Is this what you do?"

"Um . . . not exactly."

"Well, where do you send your bad memories?"

An odd little smile. Suddenly, it broke wide open.

"Come on, Megan. Where?"

"Nowhere. I've never tried that exercise."

"How come?"

She backed away from the hatch.

"I'm not as gullible as you are."

Megan ran for her life. She locked herself in the head and called, "Gotcha, Michael Fallon."

Damn.

"Dr. Greenberg?"

"Yes?"

"She just said her 'gotcha' out loud. Did I say mine out loud?"

"You're on your own, Michael."

Later, they sat quietly, listening to frogs and crickets.

Okay, thought Fallon. That round went to Megan. She said she wouldn't know a Hindu fakir from an L.A. Laker. She just thought she'd try some power of suggestion on him but then he was so enthusiastic about his magic cure that she couldn't keep a straight face.

He refused to believe, however, that she made all that up on the spot. That business about electrons having weight did not have the sound of coming off the top of her head. Anyway, they do have weight. An electron is an atomic particle. Smaller than a proton but bigger than nothing. He remembered that much from sophomore physics.

She said she might have heard it somewhere. She couldn't recall. And then when he pressed her, the grin went away and she started to get quiet. So he dropped it. Anyway, it was time to start back to Edgartown.

But hey, it worked.

The memory of Bronwyn, and especially the guilt, were already so far gone that it seemed almost indecent. And he could think of Uncle Jake as he was in life instead of always seeing him inside a medical examiner's chalk outline. But he still missed him desperately. And he wished he'd hear something from Moon. He was getting to the point, however, where he was almost beginning to agree with Mr. Doyle. Forget the Bart Hobbs thing. You just vaporized him anyway. Lehman-Stone along with him. Go on with your life. He didn't even hate New York anymore.

Life was getting sweeter by the day. He loved owning the Taylor House, he loved Martha's Vineyard and, most of all, he loved being with Megan. Her own demons, whatever their source, seemed to be keeping their distance as well.

There was a wonderful old movie called *Bell, Book & Candle.* Kim Novak played a witch who lost all her powers by falling in love with Jimmy Stewart. Maybe that, he thought, is what's happening to Megan. Maybe psychics have to be miserable or at least psychologically damaged for their powers to work. Nothing would please Megan more, he felt sure, than to wake up in the morning and find them gone.

Off to the west, Fallon could still see the mushroom cloud. What he was looking at, actually, was just a stratocumulus backlit by the retreating sun but he was beginning to feel sorry he did that anyway. He had realized for some time, of course, that blaming a whole city for what a handful of crummy people did was dumb. It had just been so hard to accept that a man like Big Jake Fallon and a girl like Bronwyn could be dead because some miserable piece of shit needed money for a fix.

New Yorkers, most of them, were as decent as any. Most are just people trying to get by, trying not to become victims of the predators you'll find in any large city. And they're stuck there. They can't just pick up and leave the way he did.

He thought about Mrs. Mayfield, the woman who had saved his life and whom he never thanked properly. He wondered how she'd feel about a week, all expenses, at an inn on Martha's Vineyard.

Good idea. Should have thought of it before.

Brendan Doyle must have her address.

He'll call him tonight from the Taylor House.

26

Hobbs stood, watching for a taxi, inside the 61st Street entrance to the Pierre Hotel. Out of long habit, he patted the pocket where he once carried cigarettes. He reached instead for his pill box, hoping to find a Xanax.

There were none. Only antibiotics for his ulcer and two Dexedrine tablets. Damn. He needed to go down, not up. And it was not a good idea to take speed on top of vodka. But he swallowed one of each, then chewed two more Maalox.

Five minutes passed. He had still not seen an unoccupied cab. His apartment building was on Fifth at 77th. Too far to walk. Fifth Avenue ran one-way south but Madison ran north. He would have more luck finding a cab at the corner of Madison. He stepped through the doors and turned, head down, in that direction.

He hated being frightened. He hated it all the more because it had been so unnecessary. Yes, Big Jake Fallon had reacted to that photograph of Rast. He saw past twenty-five years of aging and the loss of some eighty pounds of weight. He saw past jowls that had been tucked and one protruding ear that had been reduced. And yes, he saw that so-called dueling scar that was made by no Leipzig saber. It had been made by a ring on Jake Fallon's right fist.

THE SHADOW BOX ■

But the very fact that he reacted argues that Rast's portrait looking back at him must have come as a total surprise. And he *still* could not have been certain. The moment he got home, however, he went straight to that dictionary. A large one, they say. One of those monsters that have foreign language sections in the back. French-English dictionaries. Spanish-English. German-English. What will we bet that he was looking up "Adler" to see if it meant what he thought it meant.

The Baron certainly hoped so. He prayed so. It would be all the more poetic if just as his eye found "Adler," just as it moved a fraction to the right and he saw that the word meant "Eagle," the first blow of that bat came down across his shoulders.

But Parker's man—this Walter—could not be sure of that. All he could swear to, and the autopsy seemed to bear him out, was that Big Jake Fallon knew why he was going to die and had ample time to think about it. He knew on whose orders. He knew why the means was to be a baseball bat. Rast's orders, through Parker, were very specific. The arms first, then the legs. Smash every joint. Stay away from the head. He is to be conscious throughout. Revive him if necessary. Make him beg you to end it. When he does, however, first go to work on his face.

The taxi driver followed his instructions. Or claimed that he had.

"Do you believe him?" Hobbs had asked Parker.

Parker shrugged. "As long as the old man's happy."

"What did Fallon really say, if anything?"

"When my guy asked him to beg?"

"Yes."

"What I would have said. Go fuck yourself."

Parker's man had been waiting, behind the wheel of a stolen cab, a few doors down from Michael's building. Bronwyn was to flag him. She was to give him one signal if the elder Fallon had seemed to recognize Franz Rast from that photo. Another if he had not.

If the former, or even if he showed an undue interest in the AdChem annual report, Parker's man was to finish him that night. He was to take him home, say how glad he was to have a fare to Brooklyn because his wife was due to give birth at

Brooklyn General, then gain entrance by claiming that his dispatcher would not relay personal messages and ask if he might call the hospital on Fallon's phone. Should Fallon refuse, but only then, and only after Fallon unlocked his door, he was permitted to gain entrance at gunpoint.

Just inside, if Parker's information was correct, he would see an umbrella stand that usually had at least one baseball bat in it. This would do. Much preferred, however, would be one of Fallon's more treasured bats which the taxi driver would find, first door on the right, in Jake Fallon's library.

If, vis-a-vis Bronwyn's signal, he had shown neither recognition nor interest, Jake Fallon was to be spared but only for the time being. Long enough for Bronwyn to satisfy herself that young Michael's coming to Lehman-Stone was simply a coincidence. If it was not, he would confide in her soon enough. He was, after all, infatuated with her. He would want to protect her against being involved in an organization that he knew to be criminal. At the very least, he would give himself away by the sort of questions he asked her.

Ridiculous. Every bit of it.

This, thought Bart Hobbs, is the sort of micro-management that is typical of Franz Rast. Everything done just so. His way. No room for individual initiative.

Granted, the stakes were enormous. And Rast was the ultimate wellspring of the millions they'd all made. What Jake Fallon knew would have ruined him. AdChem's stock might have lost tens of millions and would have dragged an entire industry down with it. Trading would have been suspended. The Baron Franz Gerhard Rast von Scharnhorst would have lost every friend his money ever bought him and would likely end up in a federal prison. Minus his testicles. The Countess would have sliced them off.

And this was just Rast. The tip of the iceberg. Once the SEC got its hooks into this, and the Justice Department, and about ten other jurisdictions both here and abroad, that prison would need to build a new wing.

Hobbs reached Madison Avenue. There were cabs. But the thought of climbing into one suddenly gave him pause. Silly, of course. A brisk walk, however, might do him good after all. Madison Avenue was lined with shops, plenty of pedestrians, perfectly safe.

This was all so unnecessary. It should not have happened.

Michael had never *penetrated* Lehman-Stone. He had not spent his life training for the moment when he could unmask the chairman of AdChem and bring his whole empire down around his ears. Why go to all that trouble when a single phone call to the *Wall Street Journal* might have done the trick.

The answer? Bronwyn had been right. He knew nothing. His uncle had never told him.

"Naive," Rast had thundered. "This is childishly naive. This is whistling past the graveyard."

Rast's point, which had modest merit, was that even if one believes in coincidence, even if Michael knows nothing, would Jake Fallon not have wondered why the young man would end up in pharmaceuticals of all things? Would it not have struck him as odd?

Perhaps. But it's quite a leap to think that Jake would zero in on AdChem, which was, after all, just one of many clients with whom Michael was involved. Why would he? Simply because it's German? Nonsense. Until Bronwyn stuck that report in Jake Fallon's face, he had no reason to think that Armin Rasmussen was still in that business. Or that he was even still alive.

Totally stupid.

It grew out of one routine meeting, one of several that both Michael and Rast had attended. Rast had known him, worked with him, for two years. The name had certainly rung a troubling bell but even Rast admits that he dismissed the possibility as too farfetched. It was only then, during this one meeting, that he began to notice the family resemblance and told Parker to look, quickly but quietly, into Michael's past. What he learned gave him nightmares. The nightmares made him crazy.

Lost in these thoughts, Hobbs turned west onto 77th Street.

His poor chalet.

Jocelyn, his wife, will be devastated. She was so fond of the place. She could name every variety of tree, every wildflower. Every summer weekend she would have a houseful of guests, friends from school or from her charities, and she would take them on her famous nature walks. In winter, she'd take them cross-country skiing the length of the valley or for a few downhill runs from the top of Black Mountain.

It was Jocelyn who had that sign made up. *Playing Hobbs.* She surprised him with it last summer. Now he didn't know what he'd tell her. She had no trouble believing that drug dealers had broken into the Palm Beach house, killed the guard who tried to stop them, and set the place ablaze. But how would he explain that it's happened to them twice?

Damn.

Damn Rast for all of it. Damn him for—

Hobbs noticed the two men.

They were black. Young, by the look of them. They were dressed in hooded sweatshirts, baggy trousers, high-topped sneakers. They were walking in his direction, probably coming from Central Park. Must have filled their quota for the day, their pockets filled with cash and credit cards from women's purses and from the Velcro wallets of joggers. Going home now to spend it on their crack habits.

Hobbs started to cross to the other side of the street.

But no. Damned if he would. Michael Fallon didn't.

Oh, my.

That taller one, the lighter one, could almost be Michael. Hard to tell with the hood. The other one, darker, could be Jake Fallon's bodyguard, the one they call Moon.

Hobbs slowed. He stared. They kept on coming.

By day, Marvis Shockley worked for the Parks Department. By night he took courses at NYU toward a degree in education. The smaller man was Ahmad Shabaz. He was a plainclothes officer with the Transit Authority Police.

If this were a subway, he might have given chase to the middle-aged white man who, just ahead, just now, suddenly turned and ran. Back toward Madison Avenue. Shouting. Coat flying. Losing one of his shoes.

"He seen a ghost?" asked Marvis Shockley.

"He seen two spooks," said Officer Shabaz.

"What's that he yelled?"

" 'Wasn't me.' "

"Wasn't him who what?"

"Just keep walkin'."

"Think he made you for a cop?"

"No."

"Then why he run?"

"Keep walkin'."

Marvis smiled. "White men can't *run*, either."

Officer Ahmad Shabaz didn't know what was worse. Being white and scared of any black man who's not in some uniform. Or being black and seeing how scared they get. Both ways are bad.

Army uniform, cop uniform, hospital whites . . . all those say we're housebroke. Tuxedo says we're musicians or waiters. A good business suit will ease their minds as long as we don't wear shades with it 'cause then they think we're Muslims. Found Allah in prison. Hate whitey. Hate Jews even more.

But wear your sweathoods and high-tops, be out walkin' at night, white folks run into white stores or dive down a subway where they hope there's a cop. But in your own neighborhood you *have* to wear them or you stand out. Wear anything else and you get dissed by your brothers for dressin' too white.

Every way is bad. No way to win.

One time, upstate, he stopped in this little store. Woman didn't know whether to scream or hold her breath or ease over toward the gun she most likely had under the counter. He had to tell her, "Lady, all I want is some toothpaste. See here? Here's my money." Damned if he'd tell her he's a cop.

That never stops. And it always feels bad even when it feels good. The goodfeel part is why Marvis is smilin'.

Feels good watchin' the white man run.

Lena Mayfield said thank you but no.

The lawyer had called her first thing Thursday morning. She was dressed in her bathrobe, busy frying up breakfast.

Yes, she remembered the little wavy-haired lawyer, she appreciated what he'd done for her back then and it was nice of the Fallon boy to offer. But she just had no time for such foolishness.

First off, she couldn't hardly afford one sick day, never mind a whole week with no money coming in. Time was, she had four part-time jobs but in March she got laid off from two of them because one lady she cleaned for moved to Florida and the man who owned the video store had to give that job to kin. Second, Mr. Doyle wouldn't tell her where this vacation-with-all-expenses place is. He said he'd tell her when she's packed and ready to go. All he'd say is the place is real pretty.

Heck. Selma, Alabama, was *pretty*.

Anyhow, the lawyer sounded just as glad that she declined.

"Mr. Doyle . . . try her one more time. Tell her I'll—"

"She said no, Michael."

"How about if I make up any pay she misses?"

"She thanks you for the offer but she can't."

"Okay, I'll ask her myself."

"No. Don't do that."

A beat on Michael's end. "Are you sure that you even called her?"

"Fuck you for asking."

"Come on, Mr. Doyle. You're a persuasive guy. Persuade her."

A weary breath. "You going to be home?"

"I'm here all day."

Again, Lena Mayfield said no. But the lawyer sounded like he meant it this time. He wouldn't let up. He told her it was Martha's Vineyard. It's where the president goes on vacation, he said. It's where Jimmy Cagney used to live. Man was runnin' short on arguments.

In the end, what made her say yes was not the limousine—one of those block-long suckers—which would come right up her street where everyone could see and the chauffeur would hold the door open for her. It wasn't being driven way up to Westchester Airport and then put on a bitty little plane. And it wasn't Mr. Doyle's whopper about how it's a mortal sin for Catholics if they don't do a good deed back.

That boy had looked after her, even busted up like he was. Lookin' in on him was the least she could do. And with Memorial Day weekend coming, people going away, the folks she still cleans for don't need her then anyhow. She'd go up first thing tomorrow, stay till Monday lunch if that suits Michael. But she won't take his money and he's got to let her pitch in with the chores.

Three days is enough idleness for anyone.

27

Parker too was sorely tempted to think about a change of scenery.

For some weeks now, an inner voice had been telling him that it was time to pick up his marbles and vanish. That voice had never been louder than this morning, sitting in the old man's suite, watching him eat breakfast—the man eats cold cuts and yogurt—listening to his rantings and knowing that meanwhile, that piss-ant Hobbs was getting dangerously close to a breakdown.

Twice now, the Baron had postponed going back to Munich. Twice, he'd ducked board meetings until he could get this settled. Parker had no idea what the board knew or didn't know or what set of books he was showing them. But AdChem's earnings had been taking a bath for more than a year now and the Baron was under pressure to show some turnaround. The last thing he needed was Doyle's new lawsuit. If the von Scharnhorsts are clean, they'll vote him out in a second. The Baron is family, but only by marriage. If they're dirty, and if they're smart, they'll let him take the fall.

"Who is Armin Rasmussen, by the way?" asked Parker.

The Baron's eyes went cold.

"Someone on the board, or what?"

The old man's scar was twitching. "He doesn't concern you," he answered distantly. "He's someone who died . . . a long time ago."

Sure he did, thought Parker. That's why the name scares the shit out of you. But screw it. Parker had his own problems.

Turkel might have been the smart one. He's probably down on Grand Cayman right now stuffing cash in a suitcase. That's unless they have him. And the Baron's afraid that they might. In which case, he says, we'll need a hostage of our own.

"Like who? Like Doyle?"

"Who *else* but Doyle? He's the only one we can get our hands on."

Oh, boy. "Look . . . let's think about this."

"And it must be done quickly. I want him before he can file that lawsuit."

Parker felt a headache coming on. "Doyle calls Bellows to say he's upping the ante. He says he's naming AdChem this time and he claims he's got evidence of fraud and then, one day later, he gets snatched. You think no one will make the connection?"

"The man is a lawyer. Lawyers have enemies."

Oh, Christ, thought Parker. He's talking about killing him.

"That's what you'll tell Bellows when he turns up dead? It wasn't us? Must have been some divorce case he handled where he fucked some guy over?"

"A street crime, then. Or a hit-run accident. You might, for example . . ."

Parker stopped listening. This is where the Baron tells you how to do your job. He lays out detailed scenarios of exactly how it should happen. It's like he's never heard of Murphy's Law.

This is all Bellows needs, thought Parker. He's still in shock over his goddamned Rolls and he knows they could just as easily have torched the whole town house with him and his family trapped up in their bedrooms. It would take him about two stiff vodkas before he's on the phone to a federal prosecutor looking to cut himself a deal.

The Baron's now saying that just the other day a businessman from Cleveland was stabbed to death by a transvestite prostitute. He'd seen it on the news. Arrange something like that, he's saying. Something so sordid that his family will want to keep it quiet.

Parker signaled for time out. He shared his thoughts about how Bellows might react. The old man didn't want to hear it but in the end he knew it was right because he'd been having the same thoughts about Hobbs.

"Is anyone keeping an eye on him, by the way?"

"Hobbs? Where's he going to go?"

"Where do cockroaches go when you turn on the light?"

"Hobbs couldn't flip us. He's—"

"See to it, Mr. Parker."

Parker said he'd watch him just to keep the old man happy. But no way. Bellows might flip and then walk because the most he'd be facing is two years anyway, which, worst case, he'd spend playing tennis at Allenwood. Hobbs could sing himself hoarse and he'd still do life without.

The Baron was pacing. He stopped at a window, stared out at the city.

"*Does* Doyle have Turkel?" he asked.

"No."

"What has you so sure?"

"Because if Doyle had the first clue that you were wired into the FDA, and could prove it, how could he resist dropping a bomb like that on Bellows? He's got nothing, Mr. Rast."

The Baron nodded slowly. He tended to agree but he said it didn't matter. Doyle had told Bellows that he'd be filing this afternoon. The mere act of filing that suit, which would then be public record, would be enough to throw AdChem's stock into free fall.

"Do you understand what that would mean?"

"Yeah." It means I lose a lot of money, thought Parker. "Yeah, I do."

"Silence him."

"Um . . . let's slow down here, okay?"

"Did I just give you an order?"

"Instead, what if we—"

"Damn you . . . DO IT!!"

The scream was a vein popper. It made two of his Germans rush in. The Baron cocked his head toward him and then toward the door. The bigger of the two Germans nodded, then crossed the room reaching for him.

"Come," said the bodyguard. "For you it's time to go."

Parker's shoe caught him full in the crotch. As he folded in two, Parker snatched his Beretta from the small of his back and chopped at the big German's ear. The man yelped. Parker hit him again as he went down. He raised the pistol to the second man's face and then dropped its sights to his knee. The second bodyguard froze.

Parker backed away toward the Baron. With his free hand, he made a calming gesture toward the second German. Now, with that hand, he reached for the Baron's shoulder and turned his lips to the Baron's ear.

"Don't fuck with me, Mr. Rasmussen," he whispered.

28

Moon could not put it off much longer.

He would have to face Doyle and get it over with. But first he'd go visit with Jake.

He had not lingered in Maine. He stayed just long enough to make sure that the blaze was out of control and to watch two security guards running around like Chinamen. They were yelling in what could have *been* Chinese for all he knew. For sure, it wasn't English. They were shooting at shadows, not even trying to turn on a hose. But a hose would not have helped. He had shut off all the water before he lit the match.

They had automatic weapons this time. And they weren't sitting by some pool. These two, he realized, had been waiting for him in the woods. Real quiet, had the road covered, had the house in a crossfire. Thing is, one was smoking hashish that he smelled from a quarter mile away and the other wore a big yellow slicker that squeaked like cheap shoes every time he moved. You'd think they'd have hired better help by now.

It had taken him an hour to circle back to his car. He headed due west, over the New Hampshire state line and on through Vermont until he reached the New York State Thruway. It was not the fastest way back to Brooklyn but he was in no big hurry. The fastest way would be straight down I-95. But that road is

too easy to watch. It funnels all the traffic from six New England
states into one narrow stretch way down in the corner of Connecticut. Men drive up from the Bronx all the time to do bur-
glaries in Greenwich or shoplift in Stamford and they wonder
why the state police keep pulling them over on their way back
down.

Moon had stayed the night at a Yonkers motel in another
mostly black area. This morning, he had poked along with the
rush hour traffic, reaching midtown Manhattan before nine. He
found a meter on Madison Avenue and walked two blocks back
to a florist he'd passed. He made two purchases. The first was a
spray of bluebells and heather because these were Jake's favor-
ites. The other was a box of long-stemmed lilies.

He left the lilies, no card, with the doorman at Bart Hobbs's
apartment house up Fifth Avenue near the museum. There was
no need for a card because he'd packed a new Louisville Slugger
with the lilies. From there, he drove out to Holy Cross Cemetery,
where he tidied Jake's grave, put the floral spray in place, and
spent the next hour bringing Jake up to date.

Jake, as he expected, wasn't all that happy with him either.

"Lilies?" Jake asked him. *"You actually sent lilies?"*

Well . . . all he'd *meant* to do was buy a long box for the bat.
But, Easter being over, all the lilies were on sale at half price
and . . .

*"Moon . . . do yourself a favor. Don't tell Brendan or Julie you did
that. Ten years from now, they'll still be giving you crap about it."*

Doyle, maybe. But Julie, thought Moon, would have sent him
Walter's ears.

As for the rest of what he'd been up to—torching houses and
cars—putting the fear of God into Hobbs and all those other
suits—Jake could see how this was personally satisfying but he
thought it wasn't really what you'd call a plan. A plan, Jake
reminded him, is suckering your opponent into making a mistake
and being ready to hammer him when he does.

*"Say the torching works. Say one or more of them panics. Do you
have anything set up?"*

"No."

"What, by the way, do you have against Rolls-Royces?"

"House was a town house," Moon told him. "It had two others

flush up against it. Might have burned the whole block down so
I settled for the car."

He could feel Jake shaking his head, thinking, *"That's something
else I wouldn't mention to Julie."*

But the fact is, thought Moon, Fat Julie would understand. Not
the part about being so considerate, maybe, but he knows that
nothing scares a man like knowing he's being hunted.

Plan or no plan, the thing is to *do* something. That way, the
man you're doing it to sets to wondering what your plan is and
so he comes up with one of his own. His won't work either
because it's built on what he only *thinks* you're doing.

Big Jake heard that. He's thinking, *"Moon, I heard some loony
logic in my day but . . ."* He thought it but he didn't say it.

"Fine," he said instead. *"But, suppose one of them wants to make
a deal. Say it's Hobbs. Can he even get a message to you?"*

"Won't be no deal."

*"Okay, look . . . you remember back in Mike's freshman year? You
remember that thumping you gave him? You remember why?"*

"Yeah. I know." It was for playing Lone Ranger.

*"It's why you have friends, Moon. I want you to stop this and go
talk to your friends."*

Moon knew that this was only his own heart talking. That,
and knowing what Jake would have said if he was still alive. He
would also have said that having friends is a two-way street. He'd
say maybe Parker and that bunch can't find you but they can
damned well find Doyle. You should be watching Brendan's back.

That had bothered Moon some. He didn't think they'd risk
hurting Doyle, not with him on the loose. Still, Jake was right.
The least he could have done was ask Julie Giordano to keep an
eye on him. But he did call Doyle's home and office a few times
just to see he was alive and hear how he sounded. Didn't talk
to him, though. Hung up when he answered.

He had also called Michael one time. He called him at that inn
he bought in Edgartown and Michael answered the phone himself. Moon had figured that a desk clerk would answer. But it
was Michael and he sounded real upbeat. He said, "Taylor House,
Michael speaking." He said it in a glad-to-meet-you kind of way.
Except when he got no answer he sort of sucked in his breath

like he wondered if trouble had found him again. Moon wished he hadn't made that call. Doyle, on the other hand, knew it was him. "Moon? It's you, right? Moon, you dumb fuck, talk to me." Nice to know he's still his old self.

"He's liable to belt you one when you see him," said Jake.

Moon grumbled. "Doyle swings on me," he answered, "he better be ready to hit on them too."

He wanted to ask Jake if that man in Palm Beach, that Walter, was the one who murdered him. But he didn't. That would have been crossing the line into crazy. If Jake was to say yes, Moon knew it would just be his own heart again telling him to stop feeling bad about that choke hold.

But if it *was* Walter, he liked to think that Jake was standing there waiting for him when Walter went to his judgment. Jake would have worked out a deal with God. *"Tell you what,"* he would have said. *"Give me ten minutes alone with this son of a bitch and I'll do an extra year in purgatory."*

If God's any kind of a mensch, he'd have gone for it.

Might not care for the cussin', though.

Moon's watch said half past twelve. He knew he was stalling because he was not looking forward to facing Doyle. Going over to see Julie wasn't much better. You got one who says, "Let's wait," and one who says, "Let's go blow their fucking heads off."

What he'd do, he decided, was sort of take the middle road. He'd go find Johnny G.

Today's Thursday? Johnny would be down the docks. On the way, he'd find a drugstore, see about getting his prescriptions refilled.

29

"Rasmussen" turned out to be the magic word.

Whatever it meant, whoever was who, it had worked for Parker just as well as it had worked for Doyle. It made the old man tell his Germans to get out. Made him shut up and listen for a change. Best of all, thought Parker, he had bought himself some time. Until he and the Baron had that little talk, he couldn't really afford to blow this burg anyway. But now, one way or another, give him three or four days and he just might be rich enough to do it.

By most standards, he was rich already. What Parker had, if he added it all up, came to about four million. Not bad for an ex-cop. Time was, he'd have been in pig heaven to have even a tenth of that put away. But economics aren't what they used to be.

Out of the four, about a million is in real estate which the Baron and Hobbs know nothing about. There's the house in Seattle, a restored Victorian, great view, looks out on Puget Sound. There's also a condo in Italy, up by Lake Como, and the place in Guatemala that is on a nice beach but the neighborhood otherwise sucks because everyone down there is either a retired drug dealer, or under indictment somewhere else, or some old-fart Nazi left over from Hitler.

He's got all new paper to go with each address. Like, in Seattle he'll be Granville "Granny" Futterman, originally from Pittsburgh where he owned a couple of Auto-Lubes. He picked that name himself. No one ever wonders if a name like that is an alias and there are only so many questions they can ask about the Auto-Lube game. He might even get new teeth.

There's another half million or so divided between those three houses. All under the floorboards except in Guatemala where it's in gold instead of cash because the rats there tend to make nests out of currency. Guatemala is his last choice anyway. He's seen enough spics and Germans for a lifetime.

The point is, these are not what you'd call liquid assets. Italy and Guatemala have to stay intact in case, for example, he runs into someone he knows in some Seattle gin mill and he can't be Granny Futterman anymore. Plus, the Seattle real estate market is still in the shithouse. It could take him two years to get his money back out of that house.

A third million, give or take, is what Parker Security Services, Inc., would bring if he could sell it. But that's a total write-off if he splits. The revenues dry up the day he goes and it's not like Burns or Pinkerton will be lining up to bid on what's left. There's also maybe a half-million bucks worth of chemicals back at his office, sitting in drums and on pallets, which he wished he'd lined up a buyer for but now he didn't think he'd have time.

There's a small stash here in the city but that's traveling money. All the rest, like a jerk, he took in AdChem stock, which, along with most of the industry, will be even deeper in the toilet than West Coast real estate. He could sell it but he'd have to do that, like, in five-thousand-share lots and over a year's time so the sale wouldn't raise any eyebrows or get back to the Baron. He didn't have a year. The way things were going, he'd be lucky to have two weeks.

So what's the bottom line?

He could bag this thing now and have three houses plus about six hundred thousand in cash. Spend it living halfway decently, and it's gone in five years. He could invest it, live on the interest, but if interest rates don't shoot up a lot more than they have, we're talking maybe forty grand a year. He did better than that as a cop. He'd have almost that much if he'd stayed on and gotten his pension. Fat chance, though. He was one step ahead of an indictment. But at least he stayed long enough to catch old Bart Hobbs, that pillar of the financial community, bankrolling a drug buy.

A lot of them did that. Hobbs just got greedier than most and he got stupid.

The way it usually would happen, word would get around that so and so, some lawyer, some accountant, can turn a hundred grand into two hundred grand, tax free, within five days. It's to make a buy and everyone knows it but no one ever says that out loud. All you're doing is lending this guy some money. If he even *mentions* the word "drugs," you say, "How dare you suggest such a thing" and you get up and walk away because you know he's wearing a wire. To be on the safe side, go back to your office and call the cops on him.

There's a risk you can lose your hundred but it's no worse than one chance in fifty that you will because ninety-eight percent of these deals go through. So, even if a shipment gets seized, you just put up more money on another deal because the law of averages says you can't lose. The dealers won't screw you because they're not about to rob their own bank. The middleman won't because the dealer would cut his balls off.

But Hobbs, would you believe, decides to cut out the middleman. Two to one isn't good enough. He wants three to one. Half the people he knows are doing cocaine so he tells one of them he wants to meet a dealer. The guy he asks has a possession rap pending so he flips Hobbs in return for a free ride and sets him up with an undercover cop.

Guess who?

All this, mind you, while Hobbs is already making very big money by driving down the value of a bunch of little companies so that AdChem can pick them up for a song. He's also AdChem's bag man for buying secrets from rival companies and for paying off certain government insiders, one of whom turned out to be Turkel.

Turkel's basically a shlub. But he ran a print shop in the basement of the FDA where they circulate confidential reports on what the big drug companies are developing, what's about to get approved, what isn't, and what drugs are about to be recalled.

He knows who the FDA is investigating on suspicion of fudging test results. No company fakes them entirely but sometimes, for example, their lab animals die when they shouldn't and no one knows why. Rather than go back to square one, they'll replace those dead animals with new live ones. All rats look alike, right?

Turkel's not supposed to be reading this stuff. He's supposed to print up, say, fifteen copies and assign a number to each one, then seal each in a special envelope for distribution to the people on a special list. They are then individually responsible for the security of their numbered copies. This is supposed to ensure confidentiality but everyone but the FDA knows that confidentiality went out with the invention of the Xerox.

He knows that this knowledge is worth money. The big money would be in tipping the drug companies but Turkel has no idea how to make the approach. You don't just call up and ask for the president. What if he's honest? What if he pretends to go along but sets up a sting? There's Turkel, in a public crapper, passing copies of documents under the stall and the FBI kicks in the door just as he's taking the cash. Seen it a hundred times on TV.

Being too nervous to steal, Turkel plays the market instead. He knows when a stock is likely to shoot up and when it's likely to drop like a stone. He knows what new issues can't lose and which ones will be a disaster. He's doing okay but he's trading in hundred-share lots because he doesn't have much money. So he takes out a loan and now he feels like a player. Being a schmuck, he plays in his own name. Luckily, he's still not playing for serious money, otherwise the SEC would have spotted him in a minute. But he's scoring just enough, and often enough, to make his name pop up on the Lehman-Stone computer. Hobbs tracks him to the FDA basement and knows he has a live one. He flies down to Washington, finds Turkel driving a new BMW, and explains the facts of life to him.

The deal is that Hobbs will front for Turkel while, of course, he's making himself and AdChem rich on what Turkel feeds him. They tell Turkel what else to look for and who else might need to make some money. Turkel steers them to a toxicologist who's been with the FDA for twenty years, is on the approvals committee, is seriously in hock to a Maryland bookie, and thinks the FDA has fucked him over on promotions.

To Hobbs, this is the mother lode. If you want to stall a competitor's new drug, it only takes one person on the committee to question the research and want it sent back for more testing. And, meantime, to slip you the formula.

Hobbs bought Turkel and the toxicologist for himself and Lehman-Stone, and of course for the Baron who had already bought Hobbs. Everyone's getting rich but human nature is funny. You'll take the money but you hate whoever bought you. Hobbs, who is a world-class snob, hates the Baron for being an even bigger snob and because the Baron treats him like shit. This was good for Detective Lieutenant Philip Parker because it made Hobbs look for ways to become *independently* wealthy. This was also good because when Hobbs tried doing one drug deal too many, and got caught, he tried to save his own ass by offering to flip Ad-Chem who he says is doing a whole new kind of dealing.

On the one hand, this had the makings of a very nice bust. Internal Affairs might have been so impressed that they'd be willing to forgive and forget. But his commander would have had to bring in the Feds and the Feds, as usual, would end up with all the headlines. He'd be lucky to get a citation out of it.

On the other hand, this also had the makings of a new career opportunity. Lehman-Stone and AdChem were in serious need of a security consultant who could keep such misunderstandings from arising in the future.

This was ten years ago. The job had made him a multimillionaire, but only on paper.

Three good things, however, had come out of Parker's breakfast with the Baron.

The first thing . . . Rast or Rasmussen or whoever the fuck he is backed off on whacking Doyle or even snatching him. And he said he was sorry for losing his temper, no hard feelings about decking his German or about the blood on the rug. But Rast still needs a hole card because he has to stop Doyle from filing that suit, so he asks why don't we snatch Doyle's wife.

Parker was in semi-agreement about the wisdom of a snatch. But not of Doyle and not of his wife either. Who we'll grab, he told the Baron, is the "investigator" Doyle bragged about to Bellows.

Yeah, I know who he is.

Yeah, I can bag him in time.

This put the Baron in such a generous mood that he not only agreed to an immediate bonus—a quarter-million if he pulls it off— but he also upped the ante on the karate kid and the jig, of whom he is basically scared shitless. One million cash for Michael Fallon dead. One million cash for Moon. That's two eighty-pound suitcases filled with fifties and twenties. They'll be ready and waiting the day he produces.

Talk about traveling money.

The third good thing was an idea on how to play this both ways. But first things first.

Doyle had said "investigators." Plural.

But as far as Parker could tell, they were all one guy. At least that's the word around the pharmaceutical industry. An investment counselor named Aaronson who's been making lots of phone calls to people in the business, asking lots of funny questions and who, lo and behold, happens to live not five minutes away from Doyle.

Parker had already put a tail on Aaronson and, sure enough, he was seen entering the building where Doyle has his office. His first thought was to go talk to him, lean on him hard. But how do you do that and then let him go?

"Just get him," says the Baron. "Let Doyle know you have him. Then question him. I need to know what Doyle knows."

"And if he doesn't want to tell me?"

"I leave that to you."

Yeah. I thought you would.

"If you're right," says the Baron, "and Doyle has nothing, you can release this Aaronson in due course."

Oh! I can? After tickling his balls with a live lamp cord wire? After he's seen my face? Release him, my ass.

In the end, and for his own peace of mind, he would have to give this guy to the camel drivers.

Parker returned to his office. It took him less than an hour to set up and rehearse the snatch.

They would steal a car, preferably a taxi, take Aaronson on his way to lunch. The tail says he eats at the same place every day, same greasy spoon diner on Flatbush Avenue where he always orders the same lunch. A Western or a Spanish omelet, home fries, buttered rye toast, and a Diet Pepsi. Always brings the *Wall Street Journal,* reads only the front page, then pulls out the *New York Times* and does the crossword.

Aaronson is a creature of habit. That's good, thought Parker. It should make this easy. That's if that shit he eats doesn't stop his heart while they're dragging him into a car.

That done, he would place another call to Mr. Julie Giordano. This was that third thing, the other good idea.

In one way, it had surprised him that Fat Julie Giordano took his call about the Pakistani . . . whatzizname . . . Yahya . . . after Yahya named him as a reference. Wise guys don't like to talk on the phone. The most Parker had expected was for one of Giordano's minions to put him on hold, then come back with something short and unspecific such as "Boss says he's okay."

But Giordano came on the line with a glowing recommendation. He said, "This person in question has been reliable on at least two occasions." This, Parker assumed, had to mean that he'd done two hits. "Many persons, however, are thusly reliable." Giordano had actually said "thusly." He said, "But this one is special. I am letting him move on because to hold him would be like keeping a brain surgeon around in case someone gets a headache."

The Brooklyn hood gave his blessing.

"But there's a condition," said Fat Julie Giordano. "If we ever decide to get into this health care thing, maybe start our own HMO, we're going to need the right people and we'll want this guy back."

You can't get much clearer than that.

Giordano as much as admitted that he was planting this guy. Getting him into the organization, finding out how it works, and eventually grabbing a piece of it. And he knew Parker heard him. It wasn't a warning because those guys don't warn. It was more of an invitation. He was saying, "Think about it and let's talk. I'll tell you what we can bring to the party, you tell me what's in it for us."

That's what you want?

Then how's this?

I will tell you exactly how it works, how the stuff comes in and how it's distributed. I'll draw up an organization chart. Names and addresses of all the key people. Names of everyone we've bought and how we keep them bought.

This will take me about a day to lay out. At the start of that day, I want to see another one of those million-dollar suitcases. That's my consultation fee. At the end of that day, I'm gone. Think it over. You've got till morning.

Parker was sure that Giordano would go for it. All that remained was to work out how he, Parker, leaves there with that suitcase alive.

What's that old saying?

The devil is in the details.

30

Michael had asked Doyle to be persuasive.

He didn't mean *that* persuasive.

"She's coming for Memorial Day weekend? We're totally booked for this weekend."

An exasperated snarl. "Listen, dickhead . . ."

Michael held the phone away from his ear. He waited until the lawyer paused to take a breath.

"Okay, wait," he said. "That will be fine. She can have my room."

In fact, it's better. It's the biggest room in the house and it's the least he can do, especially since she's only staying through Monday.

Mrs. Mayfield will fly in tomorrow. He'll meet her, he told Doyle, show her around the island, and then he and Megan can take her out to dinner. He can sack out on a cot in the office.

"Who's Megan?"

"Megan Cole. She's . . . a special friend."

A troubled pause. "From where? From New York?"

"No. She's more or less local."

Doyle softened. "I'm glad, Michael. I'm glad for you."

Fallon wrote down the flight information. The lawyer wished him a nice weekend and broke the connection.

They have one extra cot, thought Michael. But better yet, maybe Megan will bring her boat over, tie up for the weekend in Edgartown. She's not crazy about crowds but she might. He'll ask her tonight when he sees her.

Doyle, alone in his office, glanced at the notepad where he had scribbled *Megan Cole.*

"Megan, huh?" A good Irish name. And tomorrow, Friday, is Michael's birthday. It's nice he has someone on his birthday. And it's good that she's not some old friend from New York who might tell other friends where Michael is living.

Still, thought Doyle, it wouldn't hurt to know a little more about her. He had to call Boston anyway, the young lawyer who had handled Michael's closing. He would ask him to see what he could find.

Doyle made that call, then worked through a small stack of message slips, returning those calls as well. He returned all but two.

The two calls he had not returned were from Avery Bellows in Washington. Both were marked urgent. On the second one, his secretary had drawn two lines under the word. This did not seem to suggest that Bellows knew he was bluffing.

"Shame on you, counselor," Doyle muttered aloud. "Never let 'em see you sweat."

He dropped the slips in his wastebasket.

He would return them, but later. Maureen, his secretary, is out to lunch now, he'll go when she gets back, and then he'll call Bellows on the Priva-Fone. It ought to be very interest . . .

Doyle froze.

He had sensed, rather than heard, a presence in his outer office. His first thought was that it was Moon. The ghost who walks. Dumb black bastard. But just in case, he quietly opened the drawer in which he kept his Smith & Wesson. He placed his right hand over it. With his left, he took the phone off its cradle and pretended to tap out a number. From outside, he heard a shuddering sigh. Wasn't Moon. Doyle raised the revolver and aimed it.

Bart Hobbs stepped into his line of sight. Doyle knew him from Jake's funeral and from Bronwyn's. But the Bart Hobbs of those two occasions had been well groomed, well dressed, and composed. This one looked like a drunk.

And this time he had a gun in his hand.

Moon saw the commotion outside the diner.

A few blocks back, on Flatbush, he had driven past a fender bender. No police there yet but two women, screaming at each other, had attracted a crowd. One had her hair up in curlers. They must have been the drivers.

Now he saw what had kept the police. Three squad cars, lights flashing, were gathered outside the diner. One cop was taking statements from a man in an apron and from another who carried a briefcase. The two men were arguing about who saw what and who was right. There were newspapers all over the sidewalk and Moon thought he saw a single shoe.

Just a typical Brooklyn morning.

Doyle's office was only a few blocks down but Moon kept going. He'd called Johnny G. from a drugstore outside the cemetery. Johnny sounded real anxious to see him but he said don't come down to the docks. Meet him halfway, outside Blockbuster Video, the one just up Prospect from Villardi's Seafood Palace.

Johnny wouldn't say why on the phone. But whatever this was about, Moon realized, he didn't want his brother to hear it.

Aaronson was more confused than afraid. One moment he's trying to give directions to a cab driver who barely speaks English and the next he's punched in the kidneys from behind, or stabbed, or shot, it's hard to tell, and two men are throwing him into the cab.

They had him in the well of the backseat now. The two men had their feet on him while the cab driver drove. One of them kicked him in the head every time he tried to struggle or yell and then jabbed him in the neck with something sharp. But yelling didn't seem so urgent now.

He was starting to feel all warm and dreamy.

Could he be dreaming this?

There are times when he feels like he's not in a taxi at all. He has a funny taste in his mouth. Maybe he's just lying down.

What did he do with his other shoe? And where are his glasses?

If he doesn't have his glasses he must be lying down. He always takes his glasses off first but where did he put them?

He'll find them later, he decided. Right now he has to sleep.

Hobbs's gun was a tiny automatic, chromed, small caliber. He never raised it all the way. But he wouldn't put it down either.

"It wasn't me," was all he said. He repeated it three times. He said it through a fog.

A part of Brendan Doyle was thinking, *Just kill the son of a bitch.*

He knew he couldn't ask for a cleaner shoot than this. The man walks into his office with a gun, pupils are dilated, he's incoherent, and best of all, he's holding this dumb-ass little thing that he must have lifted from his mother's purse. He's holding it at his hip, pointing more or less forward but angled downward. It's like they held guns in the early Cagney movies until some director explained about lining up the sights. If Hobbs pulls that trigger, he'll be lucky to hit the desk.

"Doyle?" Hobbs said it again. "It wasn't me."

It wasn't you who what? Killed Jake, you fucking weeny? No shit. Doyle decided to risk lowering his revolver. He eased the hammer back down.

"You want some coffee?"

Hobbs blinked a few times. A flicker of relief. A hesitant nod.

"Over there." Doyle gestured toward the machine on his credenza. "You want a drink instead, the liquor's in the cabinet underneath."

Hobbs went for the booze. It took him a while and it was all in slow motion but he found a fifth of Popov back behind a bottle of Jameson's. He poured the vodka into a coffee mug, spilling almost an equal amount. Doyle was glad he bought cheap vodka.

"Me too," said Doyle. "The Jameson's."

Drinking with him seemed a good idea. But it flustered Hobbs because it reminded him that he had forgotten his manners. He muttered an apology as he groped for the Irish whiskey. Then he muttered other things as he poured.

From what Doyle could make out of it, Moon was back in town. But so was Michael. Hobbs had seen them both yesterday. Over in Manhattan on the street near his building. And they came back this morning. They brought him a bat and some lilies.

It wasn't Michael. Doyle knew for a fact that Michael had never left the island. Moon, maybe, but then who was he with? A bat, maybe, but lilies? There's no way in hell that Moon would send lilies and therefore it couldn't have been Moon either.

Why ruin a good thing, however.

"Sit down, Mr. Hobbs. Tell me all about it."

He could see that Hobbs was right on the edge. Hobbs patted his pocket, reached in for what looked like a bunch of snapshots. Of what, Doyle couldn't see. Now he's trying to figure out how to pick up two mugs while holding both the snapshots and his mother's pea-shooter.

"Mr. Hobbs . . . you don't need the gun. Come sit."

Hobbs actually giggled. Half-giggle, half-sob.

"What you came here for is help. Sit. Let's see if we can help each other."

Doyle set his Smith & Wesson down but he kept his hand near it. With his left hand he made a calming gesture toward Hobbs and then, slowly, he reached to open the middle drawer of his desk. From it, he took out the plastic bag that contained the items from Jake's pockets, including the copy of the annual report. Hobbs recognized it. He sagged even more.

Doyle slid it from the bag and opened it to the inside front cover. That page contained a photograph that was typical of all such publications—a bunch of suits sitting around a conference table. He knew that to ask was not terribly smart because if he was wrong that would weaken his hand. But he didn't think he was wrong.

"This one." He touched his finger to the tall, thin man in the middle, the one with the scar. "Jake recognized this one."

He saw the truth in Bart Hobbs's eyes. He also saw hatred and fear.

"I didn't . . . I didn't know him back then."

Hobbs was talking, Doyle realized, about what happened twenty-five years ago.

"That's good," Doyle lied. "Because then is all I care about."

"I'm not to blame, you know. I'm as much a victim as—"

"Sit down, Mr. Hobbs. Let's talk about how to fix it."

*   *   *

It was not that Moon mistrusted Johnny G.

But he knew that you could fill a graveyard with all the men who were found dead in their cars after a real good friend called and said let's meet at such and such a place.

He did two fly-bys of the Blockbuster Video store, one with the traffic, one going slow. A more thorough look would be on foot but he was reasonably satisfied that the place Johnny named had not been staked out. Too many people around. There was a bus stop right across the street, saloons on each corner, a busy Exxon station on one side and an A&P supermarket on the other. It was not a good place for a hit.

Still, he waited until Johnny G. drove up, by himself, and stepped out of his car to look around for him. Moon caught his attention. That he came without bodyguards might still mean only that he wants to look harmless. He signaled Johnny G. to move his car into that gas station and park it. Johnny understood. That done, Moon waved him over, all the time watching the street. Johnny G. gave him a dirty look.

"You satisfied?" he asked as he climbed into the passenger side. "I mean, shouldn't I get out again so you can pat me down?"

But his feelings weren't hurt that badly. He would have done the same thing. Moon pulled out and made his first right turn onto a residential street. He watched his mirror. No one followed. Johnny G. could not resist a little sulking.

"Moon . . . how long have you known me?"

Since his first communion, was the answer. But this was now. Those people Michael worked for want him dead and they're all very rich. If he knows Julie, Julie's been scheming up ways to get some of their money. Anyone can get tempted. Maybe not Johnny so much. But anyone, Johnny included, can be used.

"Screw it," said the younger man. "Stop and let me out."

A sigh. "You want I'm sorry? I'm sorry."

"It's not even that. Let me out, Moon. This is a bad idea."

Moon slowed but he kept the car moving. "I visited with your father," he said. "I went to see Jake but I stopped off to see your father before I left."

Johnny G. was silent for a long moment.

"Hang a right," he said abruptly. "Let's both of us go see him."

*   *   *

Ten minutes into listening to Hobbs, and pouring him another shot of Popov, Doyle agreed to call Moon and Michael off. He said he would need to get on his Priva-Fone. He would get the word out to all his people that we're declaring a one-day truce.

"Never mind all *what* people," he told the increasingly slopped Bart Hobbs. "We have a network. You'd be surprised how many want a piece of those bastards."

This last had the hoped-for effect. It told Hobbs that he'd done the right thing and that he'd done it just in time. Doyle, of course, could only pretend to make the call because Moon might be anywhere and the closest thing he had to a network was Aaronson who didn't want to talk to him and the Giordanos who weren't so crazy about him either.

But he had to step into the outer office and make a show of playing with his phone. A temptation came over him. He tapped out the number of his broker. What he was going to do now is what he pays Aaronson for but Aaronson would give him an argument.

"What I want you to do," he told Vincent Keating, his Merrill-Lynch broker, "is sell all my Upjohn and Pfizer and go short on AdChem."

Keating asked him why he was whispering. Doyle said he had a cold. Keating asked him how short. Doyle picked a number. Keating said this is stupid because if Doyle had heard certain rumors about AdChem they've been around a long time and the market has already shrugged them off. Doyle said do it anyway.

Keating said that with the time difference the German exchange won't open for another twelve hours and Doyle has that long to come to his senses before he loses his ass. Doyle said put the order in now. Also sell the Coca-Cola, the GM, and the Microsoft. Put it all on AdChem to fold.

He'd make seven hundred thousand minimum.

What the hell, he thought. He hit the memory code for Villardi's Seafood Palace. A voice answered, he asked for Julie Giordano, Giordano came on.

"You wanted to make money on this? Here's what you do."

Giordano said, "Hold it. Let me go to the office."

Doyle said, "I don't have all day. What you do, you take every dime you don't have on the street and you put it on AdChem to go down."

"Brendan . . . in my office."

"Here's the price you want." Doyle told him. He started to explain what going short meant but Julie yelled something about the bar and abruptly hung up on him.

Oh, yeah. Shit. The kid with the wire.

But since when was a stock tip an indictable offense? Insider trading? Hey, this is the German exchange. If that kid is smart, he'll put down a few bucks himself.

If Johnny's impulse to visit old Rocco sounded strange to Moon, he didn't feel that he was one to talk. His hunch was that if Johnny felt the need to be with family, then family is what this is about.

"Julie been busy?" he asked.

No answer. Johnny changed the subject.

"You worked for my father once. Is that true?"

Moon nodded. "Some. For a while."

"Collecting?"

"Some."

"Would he have dealt pills? I'm talking medicine now."

"No."

He went quiet again.

But that answered one question, thought Moon. Julie wants to deal pills and Johnny doesn't. The cemetery gate was just ahead.

The Giordano family plot was smaller than Vatican Square but only because the popes had a little more money.

Cemeteries, Moon had noticed, are laid out a lot like cities. First there's the tenements. Thousands of them, all with just one little stone marker and where caskets get piled one on top of the other because that's the cheapest way to die. Next there's the row house section where the monuments are bigger but they butt right up against one another. And then a high-rise section where the caskets and urns are cemented into walls, some of which have terraces so you have a place to put flowers.

After that, there's the suburbs. Those graves, like where Jake was buried, have a little more grass around them and a nicer view. Finally there's the country estates like Rocco Giordano had. They have columns, marble benches, and statues of angels and saints. Rocco's had a life-sized Saint Anthony with a little stone bird lighting on his hand. From the look of it, it gave a lot of real life birds the same idea.

Rocco himself would not have spent the money. It was Julie who did. Rocco lived his whole married life in the same frame house on Newkirk Avenue with a yard just big enough to grow zucchini and plum tomatoes. Here he could have grown wheat except that the ground had to be kept clear for when his wife and sons would need their plots. Moon could never understand buying graves in advance. He'd feel funny looking at ground that he's going to be under.

Moon had time to reflect on all this because there wasn't much conversation from Johnny. Johnny, at the moment, was kneeling on a marble prie-dieu saying a prayer to Saint Anthony. He seemed about through. That was good because Moon could use a little updating.

"Moon . . ." Johnny G. blessed himself as he rose. He paused to brush soot from his knees. "I might have to go against my brother."

Moon nodded. He waited.

"The pill thing. You know he wants a piece, right?"

"I figured."

"Will you fight him?"

"Depends."

"On whether he goes in?"

"Depends on with who."

"On whether he goes in with the people who killed Jake?"

Moon could hear Jake calling from three rows back. Saying, *"Moon . . . never threaten. Never warn."* But a warning to a friend is part of being friends.

"First way, I'll talk to him," he told Johnny G. "Second way I'll stop him."

"This is my brother, Moon."

"I know."

"This is hard for me."

"I know that too."

"If I'm going to go against family, I need to know I'm right."

"Johnny . . . what is it you want?"

"I need to know why Jake died. I need to know all of it."

31

Parker was furious.

The good news of the day was that Julie Giordano was *extremely* interested in talking a deal. The meet is set for noon tomorrow. The bad news is that Doyle's bird dog, Aaronson, was barely conscious because he'd been pumped full of Nembutal. At the rate he was breathing, they'd be lucky to get three words out of him.

"But Meester Parker. It was only to quiet him. Meester Parker, please don't hit me for this."

"Hit you? No, I won't hit you. I'll just shove that syringe right up your ass."

At least the new man, Yahya, knew what to try. D-amphetamines. Stimulants. The only bad thing about Yahya is you can't give him an order without getting a science lecture. "This man is obese. He might be hypertensive. Give him too much, too fast, and his heart will—"

"Hey! You want to get paid? Shut the fuck up and give it. I need him awake. Today, Yahya. Today."

But Yahya turned out to be right.

Aaronson came around but he went right from coma to spasm. His heart sounded like an Uzi and he was starting to hallucinate. It's that shit that he eats. It's all that grease and cholesterol.

Parker tried slapping him. "Talk to me, Arnold. Say words. What does Doyle have on AdChem?"

Aaronson took a flaccid swipe at him, tried to slap him back. Parker brushed the arm away but the porker tried to grab him in a headlock while yelling something about Doyle. His first reaction was that this guy has more guts than he expected, that this might take a while, but then he realized that Aaronson thought he was Doyle. So Parker tried playing the part.

He said, come on, wake up, we have to be in court. Did you bring all the stuff about Lehman-Stone? Did you bring all the stuff about AdChem? Aaronson said, "You go to . . ." and "Leave me . . ." and other part sentences that sounded very much like he was blowing Doyle off. He seemed to want no part of this.

Okay, then how about the Baron?

Nothing.

Rast? The Baron Franz Rast von Scharnhorst?

A blank.

Same when he tried Rasmussen. Aaronson's eyes said he didn't know and didn't care. He leaned over to one side and threw up.

"Nausea," said the Pakistani, Yahya. "Nausea, disorientation, aggressiveness. All these are symptoms of overdose."

Parker ignored him. "Arnold? Where's Moon? The bad guys are looking for him because he burned down their houses. Let's go get Moon. We have to find him and hide him."

As far as Parker could tell, all this meant absolutely nothing to Aaronson. Doyle's friend seemed more interested in picking half-digested bacon off his pants. Parker repeated the name and the part about burning. There was no sign, not a glimmer, that Aaronson had the first clue about the torchings or that he'd ever heard of anyone named Moon.

Let's try the Fallons.

"Arnold . . . these guys murdered Jake. And now they want to hurt Michael. We really should go find him and tell him."

A spark appeared.

"You know what else? They killed Bronwyn. They were trying to get him but they got Bronwyn by accident. Poor Michael. He was going to marry her."

The spark became angry. "Lehman . . . Stone? Pills?"

"Yeah. Good boy, Arnold. Michael found out about Lehman-Stone and the pills. We can't let them hurt him anymore."

"Scumbags . . ."

"They certainly are. Shouldn't we tell Michael?"

"Safe. Michael's safe."

"Yeah, but you can't be too careful. Safe where, Arnold?"

"Hotel. Dums . . . dummas hotel."

"Dummas Hotel? Where's the Dummas Hotel?"

Aaronson gave him a look as if he was an idiot. He pronounced it more clearly. "Dumb-ass hotel. Martha's dumb-ass hotel."

Ah, shit.

Okay, let's work on Martha.

"Martha who, Arnold?"

"Martha Vin-yer."

Parker blinked. Cape Cod had popped into his mind. The Fallon kid left a trail to Cape Cod. Could Arnold be saying Martha's Vineyard? Would Fallon go to all that trouble and then hide out right next door? Maybe. Maybe it's even smart.

"Enunciate, Arnold. You confuse me when you don't enunciate. Say Martha's . . ."

Aaronson said it with him. "Martha's . . . Vin . . . yard."

"Good, Arnold." That's a one-suitcase answer. "Now let's see if we can pin it down a little better."

But Parker had to wait because a call had come in from the Mexican, Hector, who was one of the two men tailing Hobbs. He would take it in the other room.

Once there, he put the phone to his ear and looked back out through the door at Aaronson. Doyle's snoop had slid from his chair and was down on all fours in front of it. His arms were trembling. They had trouble holding his weight. And now they collapsed. He hit face-first but it didn't seem to hurt him. He rolled off his belly and onto his side where he curled himself up in a fetal position. One leg kept twitching but the rest of him was still. Good. Let him sleep some of it off.

"Yeah, Hector."

"We are in Brooklyn," said the voice. "Mr. Hobbs came by taxi. He went into a little office building. It's more than two hours and we don't see him come out. Do you want that we wait because Haroun thinks he maybe sneaked out the back."

A look of pain.

"Hector . . . you didn't cover the back?"

"Yes, but in back there is a fence with barbed wire. I said to Haroun, Mr. Hobbs is too rich to climb fences but Haroun said—"

"Wait a minute. Brooklyn? Where's this office?"

"Also in Brooklyn."

"The *address*, fuckhead. Is that a glass-front building on Flatbush?"

"Brown glass. Yes."

Jesus Christ, thought Parker. He's in with Doyle.

"Hector, which Haroun is with you?"

"The one who is from Ankara."

The Turk, nodded Parker. Claims he killed fifty Kurds for the bounty. Says he still has a necklace made out of their fingers.

"Get back here, Hector. Tell Haroun to stay."

"Haroun thinks Mr. Hobbs is no longer our friend."

"Yeah, well, tell him . . ." Got to be careful on the phone. "Tell him we don't like Mr. Hobbs either. He's worse than the Kurds. Do you hear what I'm saying, Hector?"

"I will tell Haroun."

Parker broke the connection.

He looked up to see Mohammed Yahya standing in the doorway, his eyes on the floor. He could have done without Yahya hearing that. But he would need this one, at least until he made his deal with the dagos.

"Something on your mind?" he asked him.

"I said it was too much. It was too much."

Yahya stepped aside and cocked his head toward Aaronson. Aaronson's eyes were partially open. He was no longer twitching.

32

Why Jake died was vengeance, pure and simple.

It wasn't money, it wasn't greed and it wasn't that Jake got into something he shouldn't.

Johnny G. said, "I understand that, I believe it, but I still have to know what we've got here."

Moon nodded. He would tell him what he could. Parts of it, Johnny knew already because he was going on fifteen back when Tom Fallon died and had heard a lot of the talk.

The "family problem" Jake needed him for had started long before. Tom Fallon came home from the army, went to college, and got his degree in accounting because he had a head for figures and Jake said he'd throw him lots of business. Jake, it should be understood, never took a dime in graft. What he'd do, you'd come to him for a favor and if he helped you he'd pull out someone's business card. He might tell you, for example, that you ought to have more insurance or who you might use when you need a lawyer or, in Tom's case, who you should get to do your taxes.

Johnny G. is making faces. He understands one hand washing the other and he's asking could we speed this up a little.

Well, the long and the short, Tom didn't want handouts and

242

THE SHADOW BOX ■

he especially didn't want to be under his brother's shadow, which he was even when he was in the ring and winning. He didn't want to work in New York either because everybody there knew Jake. He went to work in Bayonne, New Jersey. Company was the American Eagle Import-Export Company. Back then, lots of companies had patriotic names but this was laying it on a bit thick considering that the founder had been in the Nazi navy before that.

Armin Rasmussen. He was pharmacist's mate on a German U-boat that got depth charged by a destroyer off Cape May and had to surface. Officers got sent out west but the enlisted men got put in a camp just outside Uniontown, New Jersey. Some were put to work on farms, some on road gangs, and some worked in factories that were left short-handed by the war as long as they weren't in war-related industries. The Geneva Convention said you couldn't make them do that.

The war ended, the crew got sent home, saw what was left of Germany, and some of them turned around and went back to the only country that was still in one piece. The pharmacist's mate went back to work for this little drug and chemical company he'd been working for as a prisoner. He showed them how they could get a lot bigger selling certain products to Germany because Germany didn't have anything except money. They had money because the Marshall Plan was helping them buy what they needed. Within four or five years, Rasmussen owned the company.

Like Moon said, too many companies had "American" in their names and it got confusing when you went to the yellow pages. He changed the name to the Eagle Chemical Company and had an offshoot called Eagle Sales and also a printing company for making labels and such, a shipping firm, a couple of warehouses, and they bought a maker of veterinary products over near Philadelphia. Drugs meant for livestock didn't get the same scrutiny as drugs meant for people so, before long, they were regrinding those medicines to stamp out counterfeit pills.

Tom Fallon knew it. Maybe not from the start but he knew it and he found a way to justify it.

"How?" asked Johnny G. He looked away when he asked.

"The pills were good, they were doing good, and the company

was making money. Add to that, the bigger companies were trying to drive Eagle out of business by low-balling their prices and claiming Eagle's goods were tainted. That wasn't right either because Tom says they weren't."

"Up to a point."

"Yeah. Up to a point."

To back up just a bit, Annie Fallon worked at Eagle, too. It's where Tom met her. She married Tom, stayed for another five or six years, and quit when she was pregnant with Michael. Another ten years went by. Then one day, Annie took some pain-killers made by Eagle and gave them to one of her aunts who had sciatica. The aunt went into convulsions and died. She told Tom. Until that minute, she might not have suspected the pills but she saw how stunned and sweaty he got and she knew that something was wrong. The same night, Tom says she must have been listening in when he called his boss to ask what they put in those pills. Long story short, they were only supposed to be for export and Tom had no business taking a bottle home.

Moon couldn't recall what was in them. And no one put poison in them on purpose. Tom said they were just cutting corners and someone got careless with this one batch and they used a kind of solvent that was meant for cleaning machinery. Rasmussen said they'd caught the whole shipment and dumped it in the New Jersey marshes but Tom knew better from the shipping records.

Annie, meanwhile, with her husband not able to look her in the eye, decided to do some detective work. On a hunch, she went out to the New Jersey printing plant and bluffed her way in because they knew her. She spotted printing proofs of labels for drugs that she knew were made by other companies. She swiped some. Then she saw cases of animal drugs, all made by Eagle, but they were being relabeled for humans.

Right then, she got caught. The security chief back then was another German named Brunner. He came down, ripped her coat off, began searching her. When she fought him, he slapped her. Being Annie Fallon, she slapped him back. He knocked her cold.

Rasmussen, of course, called Tom Fallon in. Brunner was there. Rasmussen reminded Tom that if his wife ever opens her mouth, his son will have a jailbird for a father. He pointed to a photograph of his own wife and children which he kept on his desk.

We all have families, he said, and all of them are innocent. We will not let them suffer just because one woman can't keep her nose out where it doesn't belong. Control your wife or this man—he's pointing to Brunner—will do it for you.

He made it clear that going to the authorities in hopes of getting favorable treatment would be a serious mistake. Brunner would not stop with his wife. The boy would also pay.

"So Mike's mother never ran off," said Johnny G., frowning. "Brunner killed her?"

Moon was silent for a long moment. That was a reasonable suspicion. He was tempted to let it stand. But he decided to try not to lie. He shook his head no.

"She . . . lost all respect for Tom," Moon told him. "Shouldn't surprise you that she'd want to leave him."

"It doesn't. But she would have taken Michael."

Moon shrugged. "When love turns to hate," he said, "who knows what a woman will do?"

Part of the hate was that her husband, who fought in the ring, was in the same room with the man who broke three of her teeth, threatened her life and that of her kid, and did nothing about it. She told him that she'd be no wife to him. She said he was no husband, no Catholic, not even a man. That's when Tom took real hard to the bottle. But it was a good while after that before Annie was gone. They lived together, for Michael's sake, though it didn't do any of them much good. And, after a time, Annie started to crack.

She wasn't a drinker herself. Just wine on holidays. But all this time she was pretty sure that other people, somewhere, had to be dying from the pills that killed her aunt and from God knows what else Eagle was making. By her lights, knowing that and not stopping it was the same as murder or at least it was a mortal sin. But she couldn't tell anyone except her priest and all he was telling her was to pray for guidance. She got close to a breakdown, went to her doctor, her doctor prescribed Valium.

A while after that, she and Tom took Michael out to the house on Fire Island. They were hardly speaking except to fight but they went out for Michael's sake. After they came back home she got this feeling that someone had been in the apartment. Tom said it's just her nerves. Nothing was missing or out of place.

Well, her nerves were certainly part of it and she needed another Valium to settle down.

She went to the medicine cabinet and again she sensed something was wrong. Even her Valium didn't smell quite right. She checked those in the cabinet against those she had packed and brought with her to Fire Island. They did smell different and they even felt different. She was sure that someone, maybe Tom, was trying to poison her.

She waited until the next morning, until Michael went off to school, to confront him about the bogus Valium. Tom was working at home now, partly to keep an eye on his wife so she didn't go blabbing to her cousins. She told him she's had enough. She was going to call her mother and ask if she and Michael could move in for a while. She'd give him twenty-four hours to make this right or she'd tell her mother everything. And then her cousins. The chips can fall where they may.

"It *was* poison this time?"

"Yup."

"Brunner?"

"Yup."

"And Mike's father still didn't do anything?"

Moon hesitated. "He finally went to see Jake. Jake called me."

Johnny G. waited.

"We listened. Heard all of it. Then me and Jake went back to get Annie. She was packed and gone and she wasn't at her mother's."

Johnny G. made a face.

"What?" Moon asked him.

"She ran off with her boyfriend. That's the story, right? Some guy who used to be a priest."

"That's the story."

"Came out of nowhere, didn't he?"

"Johnny . . . who else would an Annie Fallon run away with? Me?"

The younger man didn't press it.

"Jake picked up Michael at school, told him his mother got a little crazy and took off. Michael couldn't believe it either but I'm not sure he was real surprised. Jake took him home, left him with Jake's housekeeper, said he and his father would go out looking for her."

"Where were you?"

"I had Tom stashed at Brendan Doyle's place—it's just up the street—until Jake could come over and ask him more questions."

Jake, he explained, had supposed right along that Tom had some kind of sweetheart deal at Eagle. He was living too good to be a Boy Scout. But Jake figured it was just a bookkeeping crime like helping the owners do a little skimming. Counterfeiting drugs never crossed his mind.

Anyhow . . . that evening, with Tom passed out at Doyle's, he and Jake drove over to New Jersey to pay a call on Rasmussen. Jake caught him just as he was leaving his office, walking to his car. No mistaking him. Big man, bigger than Jake, and his license plate says, "Eagle I."

Jake says, "Mr. Rasmussen. A moment of your time."

Rasmussen looks down his nose. Says, "Tomorrow." Figures he's a salesman.

Jake says, "The name is Jake Fallon, you fat tub of shit." Jake threw a right hand that near to popped his eye out.

Jake went at his kidneys, whaled on him a few more times. Hit a man's kidneys just right and there's no need to tie and gag him for a while. Moon brought up Jake's car and they stuffed him in the trunk. Drove him back across the bridge and up near Westchester County Airport. Took an hour. Jake aimed at every pothole he saw.

The woods are thick up around that airport. And there's plenty of noise from planes taking off and landing, noise from cars on the parkways. He, Moon, began digging a grave. They left Rasmussen in the trunk where he could hear the digging and hear them discussing what was deep enough.

By the time Jake opened the trunk, dragged him out, Rasmussen was a gibbering idiot. He saw the grave and squealed. Jake says, "That's right, pal. You're going to die." Then Jake reaches into the backseat and pulls out a Louisville Slugger. He says, "But it's not going to be quick."

Jake tells him he's going to start at the ankles and work up from there. But not the head because after he gets done busting everything below it, they're going to bury him alive. He's going to be lying down the bottom of that grave, he's going to be conscious, and he's going to watch the dirt come in one scoop at a time.

Rasmussen had already fouled his pants. He starts whimpering and begging, blurts out that the Valium was none of his doing, says this Brunner did it on his own. Jake had never mentioned the Valium.

Rasmussen tried offering them money. He started at ten thousand. Jake wasn't offended, exactly, but he spends that much on a single congressman. He stood over Rasmussen and took aim. Now the German screamed that he had over a hundred thousand dollars in his office safe and another hundred at home. Jake said this was more like it.

Jake had figured on at least two safes because he said there'd be two sets of books. The combinations to those safes were what he really wanted. The German blurted them out. Jake waited ten minutes and asked him again, just to make sure he wasn't making them up. Jake took his keys and told him to go sit in the grave and shut up. Jake would keep him company while he, Moon, drove back to New Jersey.

"You were never going to kill him?" asked Johnny G.

"Only if I never got back."

"I would have. Either way."

"No, you wouldn't. Julie maybe, but not you."

Johnny G. glared at him. "Let's hear the rest," he said.

Megan was at Woods Hole, alone on her boat. Michael was in Edgartown. But she could feel him all the same.

She felt that now, at this moment, he was whistling. That he was happy. And that he was thinking about her. She did not feel that he was wondering. Only thinking.

She had made a promise to herself. She would not spend another minute of another day worrying about how long this might last. It will end when it ends.

The day will come, she realized, when being mysterious starts to get a little old. He'll want to know more about her. Her choice will be to lie or to tell him.

He would probably believe the lie. She felt sure that she could concoct a plausible past history, and then rehearse it, load it with details such as places and dates. She could even, if she concentrated, make it true in her mind. There's a technique for it. It's sort of like that trick she showed Michael. But she knew that in the end she would blow it because she can't stand herself when she lies. She would tell him the truth. And then he'll be gone.

Not right away, perhaps, but it will never be the same. He's such a gentle man; he'll tell her that what's past is past, and that it doesn't matter. But it does and it will. Michael will start to back away, he'll stop wanting to stay over quite so much, he'll find that running an inn takes more and more of his time. But she won't let that hurt her. As long as she knows it will happen, as long as she expects it and is ready for it, she should be able to handle it. It shouldn't break her heart.

With luck, however, they'll have the summer. Three months, maybe four, of being with him and of feeling him up against her. And inside her. She blushed and grinned at the thought. She could scarcely believe how brazen she had become.

The grin faded when a picture of Bronwyn flitted through her mind. She didn't let it stay. She didn't want to see them together or even think about her anymore because one day she might blurt out to Michael what she felt about her. That Bronwyn had never loved him. Michael won't want to know that. He'll think that it's jealousy talking. He might even be right.

She had also begun to worry about making love with Michael. It was okay for now. Much more than okay. But she couldn't be sure how she might react to it after the weather turns warmer—in August, for example—and she feels his skin getting sweaty.

What if it takes her back?

What if she starts thinking of those men who would come into her room at night. And cover her mouth so she couldn't scream. And hold her down. What if she suddenly panics and starts clawing at Michael? She knew that he wouldn't start beating her. Not Michael. He's not like them at all. But what if it just gets him more excited? She would hate it if he liked it when she gets that way.

September, in any case, will be time to move on. She thought she would sail down to the Yucatan, stay there for a year or two. The Oceanographic Institute will be doing studies for at least that long of the area where the big comet struck. The one that wiped out all the dinosaurs. The ocean floor there is unlike any in the world. It should be very interesting. It should help her forget.

Megan blinked her eyes. She brought her fingers to her temples.

Right now, suddenly, she was seeing graves.

A lot of them.

She wondered why she was seeing graves.

Moon got back, he told Johnny G., almost four hours later.

Rasmussen, he said, was near out of his mind because every crawly thing in those woods must have stopped to visit that hole and try to lap at the blood where Jake had ripped his eyebrow open.

Moon had the money. He had one set of books from the office and two more from Rasmussen's house. He had Rasmussen's bankbooks, checkbooks, and passport. He also had the personnel file of a man named Reinhardt Brunner. He told Jake that he had set fire to the office after searching it, then waited a few blocks away until he could see flames coming through the roof.

Jake asked, "That took you four hours?"

"Had some other business. And I burned his house down, too."

Jake's eyes went wide. "Tom said he had a wife and kids."

"I looked. No kid ever lived in that house. Only pictures of kids."

It turned out later that he'd married some divorced woman just so he could stay in the country. As far as anyone knew, he never saw her again once he got his papers. And it turned out that Brunner had an SS tattoo under his armpit. He'd tried to get it scraped off but they could still make it out.

"What was that other business?" asked Johnny G.

"I left Brunner on Rasmussen's front lawn."

"Oh."

There wasn't much more to tell. After going through the ledgers, the ones from his house in particular, Jake told Rasmussen that if he wasn't out over the Atlantic by ten the next morning, he wouldn't be leaving at all. Told him Westchester Airport was a good place to start. He could walk there in half an hour. Jake handed him his passport. They left him in the woods.

Jake got home, waited until nine the next morning, and made a few phone calls. Before noon, the two warehouses had been raided and everything in them seized. The print shop was pad-locked and Eagle's bank accounts were frozen. Jake told them it was Tom they had to thank for shutting that whole operation down but, all the same, the deal was he didn't want to see the name Fallon—not *any* Fallon—in any newspapers, court papers, or even on a thank-you note.

Jake had waited, as opposed to calling in the middle of the night, because he wanted to give Rasmussen time to get away. Jake didn't want a trial either.

Those ledgers, come to think on it, are probably still in Jake's basement. He and Doyle spent a few days going over them. He said one of these days he'd get around to burning them. For now, however, he had a brother and a nephew to take care of.

"Did Rasmussen leave the country?"

"Guess so."

"He went back to Germany. Where you think he worked his way into AdChem?"

Moon shrugged, then nodded.

"Does Michael know all this?"

"No."

"And yet he ends up working for them."

"John . . . we've been through this." His tone carried a warning.

Johnny G. raised both hands. "Look," he said quietly. "People do things and they don't know why they do them."

He got up from the bench, started pacing. In part to be out of Moon's reach.

"There was this house I saw once," said the younger man. "Just a plain everyday house over in Bayside but I couldn't get it out of my mind. This ever happen to you? I kept driving past it. I didn't know why and I still don't."

Moon saw where he was headed. Michael might not have known—except for bits and pieces—but maybe he *felt*. Maybe AdChem pulled at Michael without him ever realizing it. It was possible. But it also didn't matter.

"Moon . . . why don't you just tell him?"

Because there's more.

"I mean . . . Mike and I used to talk about this. He knew back in high school that his father was no saint."

"I know he did."
"You're afraid he'll think less of you and Jake?"
Moon didn't answer.
"Or you're scared he'll go looking for Rasmussen."
Moon shook his head.
"What, then?"
"Scared he'll find him before I do."

A grave again. Just one.
Megan was showering and she saw it in her mind.
She dismissed it at first because she thought that she knew what it was. It had happened before. She'd had flashbacks to that grave up in Braintree where that man buried two of his victims. She had seen him dig it and she had watched as he filled it. She saw him go back to his car and sit, his shoulders hunched forward, for several minutes before he drove away. She knew that he was masturbating. And there were birds. She kept hearing the sounds of birds.

She saw him again, or that part of her mind did, when he reached the street where he lived and stopped in the driveway of his house. A woman, a neighbor, had gone out to her mailbox. She greeted the man by name and wished him a happy Thanksgiving. The woman called him Andy. He preferred to be called Andrew. He smiled and waved at the woman. But he called her a cunt in his mind.

His house was a saltbox, she thought, painted Williamsburg blue with red or maroon shutters. She never quite saw the interior but she knew that he kept it very neat. He lived alone. An older woman had lived there, until not long ago, perhaps his mother. She was dead now, thought Megan, but Megan had no particular sense that this man had harmed her.

Megan did have one odd notion. She had a sense that this man, this Andrew, became invisible once he stepped through his door. The police asked her what that meant. She had no idea.

But she saw a little bit more of the neighbor's house, she told them. Perhaps that would help them find this man. The neighbor's mailbox had lavender mums planted at its base. On her door she'd hung a pretty arrangement of autumn leaves and three ears of indian corn. Just inside, on a little table, she kept a silver bowl that still had Halloween candies in it.

Within hours, the police arrested Andrew Birdsong. They knew him and they didn't. They had questioned him almost a year before this but only as a possible witness to an earlier murder. They'd never had a reason to suspect him.

There was semen on the front seat of his car. By the end of that day, he confessed to the murders of six women. The murders began after his mother died. Or, as Andrew had put it, after she was taken from him.

And he had no mirrors in that house. Not one, not even on the bathroom cabinets. That, she supposed, is why he felt invisible.

The strange thing was that he needn't have confessed. Her visions were useless as evidence. Nothing tied him to the gravesite except a few fibers and the mud on his shoes. He didn't bat an eye when the police said they had a witness who had seen him digging that grave. He only began to fidget when they said that the witness was a woman. The woman, they lied, had been walking her dog in those woods. She had seen everything he did that day. What made Andrew Birdsong fall apart, what humiliated him, was learning that a woman, a hated woman, had caught him jacking off.

Megan felt a sudden chill.

This grave, she realized, was different. She had thought they were the same because both were in a forest but the trees around this one still had leaves. This could not be Thanksgiving. This was spring or summer. The chill swept over her. The warmth of the shower could not defeat it.

33

The snooper, Aaronson, was dead.

Parker had stood over Yahya, making him try everything he could, made him do mouth to mouth and pump all kinds of crap into Aaronson's veins. Yahya said it won't help and it didn't. But he'd learned one thing . . . maybe . . . so it wasn't a total loss. And Aaronson could still be useful.

The best way to do this, Parker decided, might be through Doyle's wife. What's her name? Sheila.

He placed the call from a pay phone at the Vanderbilt entrance to Grand Central. He had to go over to that side of town anyway. There was a bookstore just down the ramp and he needed to do some research.

"Here's a message for your husband," he said when she answered. "We have his friend, Arnold. Fuck with us and he's dead. You got that? If he goes near a courthouse, his friend is dead."

He thought that she'd gasp and hang up. She just gasped. What the hell, he decided. Might as well use the whole quarter.

"And Sheila? You're going to be next. We know everything you do, every place you go. Look out your window, Sheila. There's a blue car with a man in it. You know what he likes to do to women? First he fucks them in the—"

254

This time she used bad words. She slammed the phone down in his ear.

Right now, he felt sure, she'll be peeking through the drapes. There's no blue car, no man, but her imagination will supply one. Ten seconds of that and she'll be dialing her husband. The first message was the main thing. Get Doyle to sit on that lawsuit at least until after the weekend. That might be all the time he needs.

The second message should get Doyle tear-assing back to Brooklyn Heights. He wouldn't bring Hobbs. He'd tell Hobbs to sit tight. It's expecting a lot to think that Haroun might recognize this as an opportunity but we can always hope.

Parker walked down to the Arcade Book Store, which, he seemed to recall, had a fairly good-sized section on travel. It did. It had nothing on Martha's Vineyard alone but it had six different guides to Cape Cod, all of which talked about the Vineyard and Nantucket. Parker bought two of them plus a *Fodor's Guide* to Massachusetts. And he bought a good map. The map even said when the ferries ran.

Back at his office, he started with the town of Vineyard Haven. Aaronson had said it was "some dumb-ass hotel" and almost every listing seemed to fit that description. Names like the Captain Dexter Inn, the Ocean Side Inn, the Lothrop Merry House. No big chains. No Hiltons or Hyatts. Not even a Howard Johnson's.

He called each one and asked for Michael Fallon. They had no such guest. He might be using a different name so Parker described him, mentioning that his right arm would have been in a cast up until March or April. They had no one who looked like him either.

Parker kept dialing. With the map in front of him he worked his way around the island counter-clockwise because the towns in that direction seemed more remote. It's why, according to one book, most of the island's celebrities have bought houses down that way.

Tisbury, West Tisbury, Chilmark, Gay Head. Same result. No Michael Fallon. Parker was getting discouraged. On an island this size, you'd think everyone knows everyone else's business. If he's there, remember, it was winter when he got there. The island's basically shut down when a stranger shows up, arm in a cast, driving a Mercedes with New York plates, possibly traveling with an older black male. How could no one have noticed him?

About all that was left was Edgartown and it didn't seem promising. Edgartown was apparently the tourist capitol of the island. It seemed to Parker that if you're going to lie low, you lie low. But he started calling. If he came up empty, he'd go back to square one and start calling bartenders.

But bingo!!

Lady at the Harborview said, "Michael? Oh, he's not here. He bought the Taylor House."

Bought?

Parker checked one of his books. There it was. North Water Street. Sea captain's house, antique furnishings, charming legend of laughing children, listed in *Haunted Houses of New England.*

He buys a haunted house? What the hell is this? He's looking to commune with Big Jake Fallon?

Parker called, just to make sure, and sure enough Michael Fallon answered. There was no mistaking the voice. He'd heard it on tape often enough. Parker almost broke the connection but he doubted that Michael would know his voice. He'd know the face, had seen him around Lehman-Stone and at Bronwyn's service. But he wouldn't know the voice.

"Realize it's a long shot," said Parker with a twang, "but might you have a vacancy this weekend?" He said he and the wife are from Chicago, wife just loves haunted houses, have been on the road two weeks now touring them all up and down the New England coast. Calling from New Bedford at the moment.

"I'm afraid we're booked solid," Fallon told him.

"Figured as much. I told Betsy—Betsy's the wife—but she had her heart set."

"Well . . ." Fallon tried to ease her disappointment. "You know it's not really all *that* haunted."

"Comes and goes, you're saying."

"That's a good way to put it. Listen, the whole island's pretty well booked but if you do find something, you're welcome to stop by."

"Why, that's real friendly of you. The name's Peabody, by the way. Wally Peabody." Nice harmless name. Almost as good as Granny Futterman.

"Michael Fallon, Wally. And it would be my pleasure to show you the house."

In fact, he suggested, if you're in town, you might also look up a man named Parnel Minter who is on a first-name basis with half the ghosts in Massachusetts. Parker thanked him. He and Betsy might just do that, he said.

Parker said goodbye and sat staring at the phone.

Michael Fallon, he thought.

No hesitation when he gave his name. Not a care in the world in his voice. And yet there's no question that when he left New York last February, he knew he was running for his life.

What changed? All Parker could imagine was that Fallon must think it's over. But why? Because Doyle has the evidence? It didn't sound that recent. It sounded like, for some time now, Fallon's biggest problem was whether he had enough towels for his weekend guests. No way that he's been out burning down houses.

He's not hiding. He's been stashed. He's being kept out of this while Doyle and the jig play their games. But a million bucks is still a million bucks.

"Hector?"

Let's see. They'll need a boat for this. You don't kill a man on an island and then sit around waiting for a ferry. He'd use Hector. Hector knows how to drive one and Fram Childress has one. Keeps it up in Oyster Bay. He'd use Haroun and Yahya. Haroun's a good knife and Yahya's done this before. He's made hits for Giordano.

Hector came in.

"You're going to make some money," Parker told him. "And you get another shot at Fallon. Here's what I need by tomorrow."

Bart Hobbs had begged Doyle not to leave.

"Lock yourself in," was all Doyle said. It was the same thing he said to his wife when she called. He grabbed the gun from his desk and ran out. Hobbs tried to stop him. He grabbed his arm. Doyle would have hit him if he hadn't let go.

Then Doyle yelled back from the hallway.

"Hobbs? My secretary's back. Maureen, don't let anyone go in there."

Hobbs heard the sound of running feet as Doyle sprinted down the fire stairs. He sank into a chair.

This is how he helps me? This is how he protects me?

But at least he had his pistol. The double doors to Doyle's office seemed solid and they had two locks plus a bolt that slid into the floor. He locked them in every way he could.

"Um . . . Mr. Hobbs?" The secretary's voice. "Are you all right in there?"

He tried to say yes but no sound came out.

He went to the windows behind Doyle's desk and looked down. They were only on the second floor. He could get out that way if Michael came. Michael and the black man.

But the windows were the kind that didn't open. He could smash one with a chair but, even then, even if he jumped to the alley below, he could see no other way to get out. There was a chain link fence, topped with wire, and beyond it an apartment building. He could climb that fence, he supposed. He was still athletic enough. But if he hung himself up at the top, he'd be right at the level of this window and ten feet away from whomever he was trying to escape.

There was a bathroom. That door had a lock as well. He would sit in the bathroom and wait in there.

Haroun, the Turk, did not like this so much.

He stood on the sidewalk watching the building that was made of brown glass. He watched for several minutes after the lawyer came running out and jumped up and down until a taxi stopped for him. And so he is gone. But how does one know what to do?

Every time Mr. Parker says a thing to Hector, Hector says, "Here is what he means, Haroun."

English is very difficult. There is no such confusion in Turkish. In Turkish, "We don't like him" means "We don't like him," and "Go cut his throat" means "Go cut his throat."

Mr. Parker says many things which are equally imprecise. One time, his use of the phrase "Fuck him" very nearly caused great embarrassment. Since then, Hector always translates.

And yet, thought Haroun, he cannot do nothing. Hector says, "If you see the chance, Mr. Parker wants you to take it."

Easy for Hector but what if it's he who misunderstood? Will Hector take the blame? Haroun did not think so. Not after the thing in the subway last winter when all Hector had to do was give a little push to a tired man with a full belly.

Haroun made a decision. Between killing and nothing there is room for other choices. He will go into that building and he will look for Mr. Hobbs. If he is no longer our friend, it is right that he be punished.

Haroun would just cut him a little.

Moon had parked a block away. On his one slow pass of Doyle's building, he saw a Con Ed crew that had chalked off a strip of pavement and was about to tear it up with jackhammers. And he saw the man who was watching. Neither had alarmed him greatly. Neither had the look of a surveillance. The Con Ed men were busy watching women and the dark-skinned man seemed in a dither.

He was talking to himself, he was wringing his hands. Any decent surveillance takes two men at least. From what Moon could see, this man was alone and he wasn't really watching the entrance. It was more the whole building. He wasn't staring up at Doyle's window either because Doyle's office was on the second floor rear.

There were other lawyers in Doyle's building. The man's wife, for all Moon knew, might be in there talking divorce. That would account for a certain wildness in his eyes. At one point, Moon thought he saw him mouth "Fuck him." Or "Fuck her." One of those.

Moon drove on and parked. When he came back on foot, the man was gone.

Hobbs, sitting on the lid of Doyle's toilet, heard the commotion in the outer office.

The sounds were muffled by the thickness of two sets of doors and by the chatter of a distant jackhammer. But he had heard a third door open and close and he heard Doyle's secretary ask,

"What do you want?" She asked, "What do you think you're doing?" And then she tried to scream. It ended with a squawk.

Hobbs put his vodka glass down and felt for his pistol. But it could not be them, he told himself. The woman would surely know them both. He pressed his ear against the bathroom door. He heard the sound of the knob of the double doors being turned this way and that and the duller sound of a shoulder testing its strength. The next sounds shocked him. A booted foot, stomping against wood. And now of wood splitting.

Hobbs backed away. His legs became rubber. They threatened to desert him. One hand struck the glass which he had drained of vodka and sent it clattering into the sink. He lunged for it, seized it, caressed it as if he were silencing a dog. The shattered door, its hinges bent, creaked open. And suddenly, he heard a cry of pain. Then, with a sickening, splintering crash, the doors exploded inward.

Moon had kicked him low, aiming for the spine. But the man from the sidewalk had twisted as the double doors gave way and the kick caught his hip instead. The man slashed at him, blindly, with a long curved knife which Moon had not seen. Moon caught the man's wrist in passing. He bunched the fingers of his free hand and jabbed with their tips at the killer's eye. He felt only soft tissue. This blow was clean.

The man yelped and tried too late to cover it. For an instant, he probed with his fingers, searching for an eye that had been flattened and displaced. With an anguished roar, he spat at Moon and whipped his foot at Moon's crotch. But Moon was too close. Moon jabbed at his throat with a rigid thumb and then at the remaining eye. The man let out a choking wail. He wrenched himself free of Moon's grip and stumbled, limping, through the shattered double doors. Moon saw no sign of Doyle inside.

"Moo . . . Moon?"

He glanced toward Maureen who was behind her desk, trying to pull herself up. Her mouth was bloodied. One side of her face had begun to swell. The glance took the smallest part of a second but in that time the man had whipped his knife, blindly, at the place where he thought Moon was standing. Moon ducked and covered. The spinning knife caught the top of his skull. The handle, not the blade, took skin. Now the man was clawing at his waist for a pistol. He found it. Hands slippery with blood, he fumbled for the safety.

Moon knew the weapon. It was the same Beretta, an assassin's gun, that the man in Palm Beach had carried. Moon could only imagine that this man preferred a knife. Knife men like to see your eyes. This one wouldn't, not after today. The man could not see but that gun still made him dangerous.

"Moon?"

Maureen again. The man fired toward the sound of her voice. Three pops like a hammer tapping wood, barely louder than the noise from the jackhammer outside. Maureen was safe. She was shielded by the door frame and the .22 slugs could not punch through the wall. The man got quiet. He was listening for more movement.

Doyle must be under the desk, thought Moon, although that would be unlike him. Hiding. Leaving Maureen to get beat up or cut.

"Where's Doyle?" he asked her. The man snapped a shot. Moon ignored it.

Still dazed, she shook her head. She said, "B-bathroom."

Inside, the man was moving by feel, trying to hobble. Moon's kick, he knew, should have broken his hip. He watched as the man fell across Doyle's desk, righted himself, and fired two more shots toward the sound inside the bathroom. The wood of that door was thin. Those did penetrate. Moon listened. He heard a scrambling inside and the sound of a dropped glass or bottle smashing against the tile. But he heard no sound of a body falling. The bullets must have missed.

Moon had his own pistol. He had the .45 Browning he had taken from Walter and could have blown this man across the room. But he wanted to take him, talk to him, snap his fingers one by one until the killer gave him the answers he wanted. The main thing, though, was the noise. He had closed the hallway door behind him. The smashing of the double doors had not caused a stir in the corridors, nor had all the hollering or the pop of that .22. One shot from Moon's weapon, however, inside a closed room, would vibrate through half the building.

"You got nowhere to go," Moon told him from the cover of

the doorway. He worked the slide of his pistol so that the man could hear it. "Put it down, we'll see about a doctor for you."

The man moved, Moon couldn't see where, but he heard him breathing, feeling his way. Moon heard his own heart thumping as well and his head had begun to feel floaty. Better end this, he thought. He hit the floor with a roll, aiming his body toward the cover of the desk. But as he readied himself to rise, he heard three more shots, duller than the others. He heard a bubbly kind of whistle that he'd heard once before in a man who'd been lung-shot. Moon looked.

The man was sliding down the bathroom door, very slowly, his jaw slack. Moon saw three new holes in the door. The wood around these was splintered out. Doyle must have seen him through the first two holes and fired when his shadow crossed the door.

Moon made no sound. He didn't speak or say, "Come on out" or the like because he was busy saying, "Damn it" to himself. He didn't want that one dead just yet.

The lock on the bathroom door clicked. It opened a crack. And Moon thought he heard giggling. It didn't sound like Doyle.

It wasn't.

"It's a Mr. Hobbs," whispered Maureen, thickly. It was hard for her to talk with that mouth. A shrug said she didn't know much more. "Mr. Doyle had to . . . he told Mr. Hobbs to wait here."

Moon recognized him, at last, from those photographs in Florida. But if Hobbs saw him or heard Maureen, he gave no sign. He was poking the man he'd just shot. Prodding him with his shoe. Holding one hand to his mouth. That hand had a little silver gun in it.

This worked out after all, thought Moon. Doyle or no Doyle, he'd rather question Hobbs.

"You can put the gun down now," said Moon. He rose cautiously, showing himself. "He can't hurt you no more."

Hobbs had to have known, Moon felt sure, there was another man out here. He'd heard sounds and words from both of them. Who he thought the second man was, maybe police, maybe building security, maybe even Brendan Doyle come back, Moon couldn't say. But what he did not expect was a black man, breathing hard, blood trickling down his forehead, who he knew was the man called Moon.

Hobbs's eyes went strangely flat. His jaw went slack. He looked down at Moon's hand. Not the one with the gun. The empty one. Moon knew that he must be looking for a Louisville Slugger.

Moon tried to calm him. He showed that the hand was empty. He glanced down at it himself. But there, on the desk, just beneath his open palm, was another face that he knew. It was in a brochure, glossy paper, bunch of men, a big AdChem logo on the wall behind them. Right about here, he must have said the wrong thing. Hobbs, too, saw where he was looking.

"I can see you talked to Doyle," is what Moon said. "Now you can talk to me."

Hobbs, very slowly, took the gun from where it touched his lips. He lowered it. But just a little. The flat eyes took a shine. For a moment, he seemed to be hugging the little pistol. Against his chest. Just under his chin.

But then Bart Hobbs pulled the trigger.

34

Parker looked at his watch.

Three hours had passed and still nothing from Haroun. He might still be standing on Flatbush Avenue, waiting for Hobbs to come out.

Parker tried a call to Doyle's office. He got a machine. He tried Doyle's home. No answer there either. There was no telling, therefore, whether Doyle ran home or not. If he didn't, Hobbs has to still be in there spilling his guts. But Parker wasn't sure it was that big a problem.

He'll be claiming that he knew nothing of Jake Fallon, had never laid eyes on him, and was horrified to learn that those other bad people had killed him. Doyle will know that half of what Hobbs tells him is self-serving bullshit and the rest is only hearsay. And Hobbs isn't so dumb or so scared that he'll sign his name to anything. Not until he's cut a deal—which only the Fed can make with him—and that can take weeks to negotiate because Hobbs will try to hold out for a pass.

Lots of luck.

Before any of that, however, Doyle has to think about Aaronson, to say nothing of Doyle's wife, so he's going to take this real slow. Which brings up Hobbs's wife, Jocelyn. The socialite. The tree-hugger. Hobbs will need to think long and hard about how she'll look after acid gets tossed in her face.

Parker still had time.

His immediate problem was personnel. He wouldn't be surprised if Haroun has split and is off somewhere doing hashish and sulking about being left alone. Hector claims he made it real clear that he was to ice Hobbs but some of these clowns, Hector included, have the IQ of a mothball. The only smart one is the new one, Yahya, and even he keeps looking like he'd rather be somewhere else. Like back with Fat Julie Giordano.

Hey! You wanted a career move? You made one. And no one leaves this building except Hector, no one even makes a phone call.

Parker was sorely tempted to call Giordano himself. Ask him to lend him some shooters. Those bozos tend not to be geniuses either but at least they'd blend in better up in Edgartown which sounds like a very white-bread kind of place. But best to keep this in the family. And he needs Hector anyway to drive Childress's boat—which comes with rods and reels and twin engines that sound like two Harleys—and which Childress bitched about lending but he was not in a position to say no.

He'd sent Hector out to Bloomingdale's with some money, told him to buy enough outfits for four men. He sent him to Bloomingdale's because left to Hector's own taste, they would all look like Tijuana pimps. He's to buy warm-up suits like the joggers wear but get nice quiet colors. Buy sneakers but no high tops. Buy a dozen or so pairs of Bermuda shorts, T-shirts, a few golf jackets. Also some fanny packs. That's where we'll carry our weapons. On your way back, go down to Peerless and buy a couple of camera bags. Same purpose.

He would decide tonight who all was going. See if Haroun turns up. He wished he still had Walter who at least had blue eyes. But that gave him another thought. First thing in the morning, he'll send all of them out together to get short haircuts and get shaved. Most of them look like armpits.

Parker's telephone rang. He hoped it was Haroun. But, speaking of bozos, it was Paulie something or other from Villardi's Seafood Palace. He said, "Hold on, okay? Mr. Johnny Giordano would like a *woid*."

*   *   *

"My brother," said the younger Giordano, "has outlined your proposal for me. I had questions he couldn't answer."

Parker knew about this one. Been to college.

"Yeah, well, we can all talk more tomorrow."

"That's at twelve. My brother and I have another meeting at two. Some serious people will be flying in to attend it."

"For this?"

"You have aroused considerable interest."

"How . . . serious are they?"

"Think global, Mr. Parker. To prepare for that meeting, I will need a detailed briefing by you *before* we have lunch with my brother."

"Detailed? It's the details I get paid for, Mr. Giordano."

"Just an overview, Mr. Parker. If it's sound, you'll get your money."

"Sure. Eleven okay?"

"Eleven's fine, same place. You may bring an escort. Position them as you see fit but not within earshot of our meeting."

He's reading my mind, thought Parker. "Your brother won't care I'm bringing shooters?"

A small laugh.

"What's funny?"

"He'll think you're a fool if you don't. You're a former policeman, Mr. Parker?"

"Twenty years."

"Then, speaking of bodyguards, you'll probably notice very heavy security in and around the restaurant. It's not for you. Don't let it spook you. It's for the people who are coming at two."

Parker hung up his phone and smiled. No question they're hot for this. More wise guys flying in, Vegas, Miami, maybe even from Palermo from the way Giordano talks. This is looking very good.

What's also good is he's out of there by two without having to sit through some ritual dago lunch while his boys are waiting outside for him. They're in Oyster Bay by three and in Edgartown by dark.

This could be a *most* profitable weekend.

35

Megan was showering for the third time that day.

She knew that she was borderline compulsive about washing but this time she had an excuse. She'd cleaned out her bilge which had begun to smell of oil and, while down there, had replaced a gasket on her auxiliary engine.

Besides, she would be with Michael tonight.

It was almost six, time to get dressed. It would take her an hour to motor to Edgartown where he'd asked her to tie up for the weekend. They would have dinner on board and then go back to the Taylor House and watch a couple of movies in his room. She'd rented two Robin Williams films from the video store in Falmouth. She'd seen them before but Michael had not.

They would watch *Aladdin* first because it's wonderful and because she loved to see Michael laugh. Then intermission . . . during which she planned to screw his brains out . . . and then she'd fall asleep watching *Awakenings*.

This would be their last quiet evening before the weekend crowd arrives in force . . . many were here already . . . and before Michael loses his room to that woman who saved his life. She was looking forward to meeting her.

Megan's ketch trembled slightly. She heard the groan of nearby pilings as the incoming ferry crushed against them. It would be almost empty but not for long. There were hundreds of people waiting to board. Cars lined up all the way to—

Graves again. She was seeing a grave in her mind. Only one this time. And it was freshly dug.

Megan shut off the tap and grabbed a towel. She stepped from the shower. The image quickly faded. Patting herself dry, she climbed forward to the galley where she pulled two swordfish steaks from the refrigerator. She'd meant to marinate them before this. Perhaps it's not too late.

Damn. The image of that grave was coming back.

She'd hoped, she supposed, that the shower stall was doing it. It's about the right size for a coffin. But this one was coming from outside. It was not like the other graves. This one was in a densely wooded area and there were sounds of airplanes going overhead. It was very dark. She was seeing it late at night.

Come on, Megan. Stop it. Ball it up and get rid of it.

She tried. But it wouldn't go.

And now she saw the man. And the body he was carrying. He was little more than a shadow but she knew that he was young and strong because he carried the body in his arms. It was wrapped in blankets. He lowered it into the grave. He seemed to do it very tenderly.

"Michael?"

She did not know why she called his name. She had no feeling that the man was Michael Fallon. This man was younger, darker, very powerful shoulders. His hands seemed unusually large. It was *not* Michael. And yet she felt his presence there.

Megan felt that chill again. It began to swell into panic. She squeezed her eyes tight and tried to see Michael, hear him whistling, anything, but there were too many faces and voices.

Clutching her towel, more nude than covered, she climbed the hatchway stairs. Perhaps if she got higher. Faces on the ferry, others in the parking lot, turned in her direction. She heard the buzzing of their voices. She ignored them. She climbed higher, onto the foredeck. Her eyes, her mind, that part of it, were locked in the direction of Edgartown. Her temples throbbed, her heart was pounding. She listened hard.

The last of the cars clanked onto the ferry. Its engine growled as it climbed the ramp. As that sound faded, so did the image of that wooded grave. The man, the shadow, lingered but he too was beginning to fade. Like Andrew, the man up in Braintree, he was driving away.

At last, minutes later, she felt Michael.

He was alive. He seemed vaguely troubled, that was her sense, but Michael was definitely alive. He was not the man who dug that grave. He was not the figure she saw buried there. She allowed herself to breathe again.

Megan pulled at the towel to cover a bit more of herself. But what was Michael doing? She knew that he was well because she could feel him tugging at his face. Contorting it as if in anguish. And yet she felt no great distress. At last, she realized why.

Michael, damn him, was shaving.

She's standing here naked, half crazy with worry, and Michael Fallon is shaving.

Moon had no idea what that boat girl was doing.

Except trying to cause rear end collisions.

"Hey look! Hey look! That blond's bare-ass naked."

The young man who yelled that was driving a Chevy Blazer. He nearly climbed right up Moon's tail.

Moon parked in the line the crewman waved him into, locked up, and made his way to the upper deck. A sign said there were refreshments up that way. He thought he'd earned himself a beer.

Hobbs wasn't dead. At least not when he left. The bullet had punched a hole up through his tongue and the roof of his mouth and on up into his brain. Must have scrambled it some but he was still alive. The other one sure wasn't. He died on the spot and all he had were belly wounds. You never know about gunshots.

After Moon had calmed Maureen down, put a wet cloth on her cheek and a hanky to his bleeding head, he called Doyle at home and told him what happened. Doyle didn't yell at him for once. He was glad to hear his voice. He told him of the threat against Sheila and wanted him to call an ambulance, take Maureen and come right over. Doyle would handle the police.

Moon knew that he would not have been arrested but he wouldn't have been let go either. Captain Hennessy might have helped sneak him in and out, might have kept the cameras away, but he wouldn't have had much freedom. It was as good a time as any to go look in on Michael. He dropped Maureen off, visited just a few minutes with Doyle, got hugged by Sheila, then headed on north.

This might, he'd decided, be a *real* good time to look in on Michael. Arnie Aaronson has been snatched. Doyle said Arnie had asked him where Michael is and the answer had almost slipped out. He said he's pretty sure he caught himself in time. Not dead sure. Just pretty sure.

It was almost a four-hour drive. He wanted to get going because he wouldn't feel easy until he got past Greenwich. It's like in cowboy movies where the soldiers ride through this narrow pass and you know damned well there's going to be an ambush. But there wasn't and he had three more hours to think.

Doyle knew that Rasmussen had cocooned himself. That he'd lost all his flab, got a tuck here and there, made himself a Baron. But he'd only just found that out. Doyle had that AdChem brochure all along but he never thought to open it before today. Can't fault him for that, though. Doyle had never laid eyes on Rasmussen so it wouldn't have mattered. But if he, Moon, had seen it back last November, and if he hadn't got sick, he would have saved everyone a lot of grief. Rasmussen would not have lived to see December.

Spilt milk.

He'll find Rasmussen in the end. Hobbs never got to say where he is right now but he mostly lives in Munich.

Munich, Timbuktu, the North Pole. It doesn't matter.

The world isn't big enough for Rasmussen to hide. A man can turn himself into a baron a lot easier than he can turn himself back into . . . whatever Joe Blow is in German. He'll want to live rich. But he'll also want to live restful so he'll be sending shooters after this dumb old nigger who's hunting him. Trouble with that is most shooters are what they call dysfunctional.

Dysfunctional, hell. They're morons. That's how come they're shooters. Hiring them is like laying bread crumbs right back to your door.

That Parker might be harder. A man like that knows how to disappear. If he's smart, he will, now that he knows Hobbs rolled over on him. And he'll see that grabbing Arnie Aaronson won't slow Doyle down for more than a day. It might have if he hadn't talked so trashy to Sheila. Doyle's sure it was him. Doyle says, "Moon, that one's mine. You leave that fucker for me."

Moon paid for his beer, along with two hot dogs, and took them out on the deck. It was a pretty big ship, the biggest he'd ever been on unless you'd count the Staten Island Ferry. It calmed him, being out on the water, everything smelling so clean, troubles left behind for a bit. He could see why people went on cruises. Didn't seem to do much for that boat girl, though.

He saved half the roll from his second hot dog and tossed pieces of it to the gulls. They would catch it on the wing. The last piece, he held up high until the boldest of them sort of hovered in and nipped it from his fingers. Boldness always takes the prize. He checked his watch, found a bench, and unfolded the map he got with his ticket.

From the schedule, he should still have a good hour of daylight left by the time this thing docked and he drove on to Edgartown. Time to find this Taylor House, check out the town, get the lay of the land. He wasn't sure whether he'd go ring the bell just yet. Michael would get all emotional, drag him inside, want to know where he's been. He'd ask too many questions, get told a few lies. But like he said to Doyle, he didn't raise Michael stupid.

What he'd really like to do, truth be told, is find someplace quiet and lie down for a while. Those hot dogs were disputin' him, as Satchel Paige used to say. He was feeling a little dizzy.

That boat girl. She kept popping into his head.

He'd push her out and back she'd come. It wasn't like he was lusting for her. It's a good twenty years since a young girl's body made him foolish. A white girl in particular. It's more like . . . back there . . . for just a second, he had this flickery little feeling that it's him she was looking for.

Sure, Moon. Sure she was. So is Whitney Houston.

Must be he's just tired. Tired and lonesome.

Doyle had spent an hour with Marty Hennessy.

Captain Hennessy then talked to his boss, who talked to the district attorney, who talked to the precinct commander where the shootings had occurred. He wanted Hobbs kept under wraps, his identity withheld from the press, at least until after the weekend, or at least until Aaronson is found. Mostly, he wanted time.

"Sorry," he reported back to Doyle. "I couldn't get you a deal."

Hennessy was a great rumply bear of a man who smoked foul cigars, the best that thirteen cents can buy. He had come to Doyle's town house because the office was roped off as a crime scene. It was just as well, thought Doyle. In the office, his cigar would have set off the sprinklers.

"For one thing," Hennessy told him, "you won't get anything more out of Hobbs. You might as well talk to a cauliflower. Second, if you're right that this Parker snatched Arnie, we have to at least try to find him. We're going to pick up Parker and sweat him. You knew he was a cop once?"

"No."

"He was. He went dirty."

"I'm shocked." Doyle curled his lip.

"Don't get smart, Brendan. I'm trying to be your friend here."

"Can you at least keep this out of the papers?"

"That I can do. We're also going to hit Parker's company. He's got three floors in a loft building, 48th and Ninth. If he doesn't know he's a suspect, maybe that's where he has Arnie. Meantime, you have to give up Moon."

"You heard Maureen. Moon's clean."

"Yeah, well . . . we need to have a talk about excessive force. The stiff in your office looked like birds were eating him."

"Marty . . . I don't know where he is."

A weary sigh. "Those names I gave you a few weeks back. You remember I asked you if this was about Jake?"

Doyle only shrugged.

"Those two worked for Parker. So did the stiff in your office. Parker works for Hobbs. Michael also worked for Hobbs. Is Michael alive, by the way?"

"Michael's out of this."

Hennessy grunted. "Meanwhile," he continued, "there's an arson epidemic all up and down the East Coast. There's another stiff, who someone rotisseried, at Hobbs's place in Florida. Guess who all these arson victims work for."

Doyle shouldn't have said it but he did. "Victims, my ass."

A pained expression. "Brendan . . . the word 'vendetta' comes to mind."

Doyle said nothing.

"Now . . . stay with me on this. I think vendetta and I say, 'This is an Italian word.' I think Italian and I say, 'The Giordano brothers are Italian.' Not to jump to conclusions or anything but then I say, 'Gee. I wonder if they're in this. I wonder if my friend, Brendan Doyle, has been conferring with Julie and Johnny Giordano.' "

Fucking bartender, thought Doyle.

"Last time I saw them," said Hennessy, "was at Jake's funeral. I told Johnny we were looking for a cab driver. Was one of those stiffs a cab driver, Brendan?"

"I don't know, Marty. That's the truth."

The policeman didn't seem to care that much. He made a gesture, as if to erase that question and get back to his train of thought.

"I think Giordano and I think money. I think Hobbs, who is this big investment banker, and again I think money. How do these two thoughts connect, Brendan?"

The lawyer in him wanted to say, "Who says they do?" But you don't tapdance with friends. "It's privileged, Marty. I'll tell you when I can."

"Michael's the client?"

A nod.

"Is Michael rich?"

"Jake left him a few bucks. He's clean, Marty."

"I believe you. But I'm just me."

"Who else is there?"

"The D.A. He smells money too. More than that, he smells headlines."

Doyle held his gaze. "What would they say?"

"You remember how Rudy Giuliani got famous? He nailed Ivan Boesky, Michael Milken, and—who's the fat one?—Levine. He nailed that whole Jewish mafia down on Wall Street and now all of a sudden he's our mayor. The D.A. is mindful of this."

Doyle waited.

"He's thinking, if the papers liked that one, they might like a bunch of Harvards and Yalies who are suddenly homeless even better. Especially when one is a former U.S. senator. Added to the mix we have some Brooklyn wise guys who, if he can nail them, lets him say that he cleaned up the Brooklyn docks. Fuck the mayor's office, Brendan. This has governor written all over it."

Doyle still said nothing. Hennessy studied him.

"It's bigger, isn't it, Brendan. It's even bigger than that."

Doyle rubbed his chin and stared ahead. "Tell him no press, Marty. Tell him to go real slow."

"He'll want a reason. I'll ask you again. Is this why Jake died?"

"I think it's why a lot of people died."

It was late Thursday evening.

Megan, with Michael, had watched her tape of *Aladdin*. It pleased her that he enjoyed it so much.

And they did make love afterward. It wasn't quite the rip-snorter Megan had in mind because while she was trying to vamp him he was sneaking a hit on the rewind button to go back to his favorite parts. There were things about men that would take some getting used to.

His very favorite part was the "Whole New World" duet—a whole new world for you and me. On the replay, he began to sing along with it. He was singing it to her. She had to get up and go sit in the bathroom. Otherwise he'd have noticed that she was starting to cry.

While there, other feelings began to pull at her. The damned grave was one. For a moment, back at Woods Hole, she'd almost seen the man. She almost could have reached out and touched him but he was moving away too quickly.

The other was that Michael's troubles . . . the ones that brought him here . . . didn't feel so distant anymore. Some felt nearer than others. But it's all mixed up. It's as if . . .

Oh, Megan. She sighed. You stop this right now.

If you were anyone else, she told herself, you'd know an anxiety attack when you see it. You're becoming a drag, a downer, a mope. As in, if Michael makes you happy, it follows that heartbreak must be just around the corner. Enough, already.

Here's what you do. Have you noticed that you have a body?

And that Michael thinks it's beautiful? Even your boobs? Even though you think they're a little boyish?

Go back in there, put *Awakenings* on, then sit way down at the foot of the bed watching it. Sit up on your heels, naked, but just out of his reach. You want to play psychic? Predict how long he can stand it. Predict how long you'll feel his eyes moving up and down your back before he lunges at you.

"Be right out," she called through the door.

She did fall asleep during *Awakenings*.

She slept curled up against Michael, which was a first, but only after two more intermissions. There were also a few more tears but these were over scenes in the movie. One time was over the part when the hospital nurses and orderlies handed back their paychecks so that Robin Williams could buy more L-Dopa for his patients so that he could wake them from their comas the way he woke Robert De Niro. Even Michael had to wipe his eye. She liked that. And that he didn't try to hide it.

Megan had seen that movie a dozen times. She would never have been able to watch it if anyone but Robin Williams had played the lead. It was just too close to home. Her shrink, no doubt, would have an opinion as to why she chose to watch it with Michael. He'd think she's saying, "You wanted to know about me? Just watch this. It's not the whole picture but this is a start."

She slept soundly for most of the night. But as dawn approached she began to dream. There were several. Or a jumble of many. The first was a mixture of her own recurring dream—men in white standing over her, in the dark, touching her, she could smell their sweat—and of Michael's dream. The one he told her about.

In her dream, Michael was in bed with her when the men in white came. But another man came for Michael. He had no face. He had a baseball bat in his hand and he had dug a grave, right there in the ward. Next to it was a gasoline can. Sometimes where they were was a hospital and sometimes it was Michael's inn. Outside, sometimes it was New York and sometimes it was Edgartown. When it was Edgartown, the man she had seen at that wooded grave was standing outside the inn, just watching. But in his arms he was carrying that bundle wrapped in blankets. The one she had seen him bury.

Megan shook herself awake. She almost panicked when she saw a man in bed with her but the fog lifted quickly and she realized it was Michael. She didn't want to dream again. Carefully, not to wake him, she eased out of the bed and took the coverlet that was gathered at its foot. She wrapped herself in it and walked to the window where the first light of dawn had made the water a silver-gray. She looked down on North Water Street where the dark man of her dream had been standing. He was gone. There was no one.

She wanted to believe that it was just a dream, that she'd had no vision, no intuition. But she could feel him there. She backed away from the window, toward Michael's side of the bed. He was on his stomach, snoring softly. She reached for the drawer of his night table and opened it soundlessly. The big chrome revolver was still there, way in the back. Toward the front, partially concealing it, there was an operating manual for the VCR and a copy of the TV listings. The revolver looked forgotten. She reached for it, and quietly slid it out. She returned to the window where she held it against her chest.

The man this gun was taken from ... Michael said he was dark. She'd felt that man when she first touched his weapon but not now. He wasn't near. He wasn't anywhere. She didn't seem to feel him at all.

As she stood looking out, the certainty that *anyone* had been out there faded. It was, after all, only a dream. Dreams don't reveal, they don't foretell, and most mean absolutely nothing.

She had explained that to Michael when he told her of his dream. When she sees a thing, when she's awake, what she sees is always real. She might not interpret it correctly, and it's not even necessarily significant. People, she told him, think psychics only see really dramatic stuff, like telegrams coming from the war department but the truth is that most of it's more like junk mail. Still, it's always real.

Dreams aren't real, not even for psychics. Her shrink had taught her that. He said they can't be interpreted because all they are are random memories—fantasies and fears and self-doubts included—popping off like sparks as you sleep. The subconscious mind doesn't like disorder. So it tries to organize them, interpret them. The result is a dream that now seems to have a plot.

You say, yes but in my dream there was this person, a woman, for example. I can still see her in my mind and I'm absolutely certain that I've never laid eyes on her before so she must be someone in my future. Don't hold your breath. You dreamed about a woman, true. You didn't know her, also true. That's why your subconscious had to give her a face. And because it likes order, it throws in the details. It gives her a hairdo, clothing, freckled shoulders, even an accent sometimes.

A dream can scare you, sure. It can evoke any emotion that your mind decides on while it's piecing this mess together. It can amuse you just as easily. It can also piss you off.

Michael agreed that this seemed to make sense. And talking it out had seemed to help him. He no longer had that same recurring dream and he'd gotten so he could enjoy his regular dreams again. He did enjoy some of them, he told her. Always had. He loved having sex dreams where he finds himself in bed with a naked lady because you wake up with a smile and no regrets. And you're right, Megan, he said. Those women were never anyone he'd ever seen before.

He rushed to say that he didn't do that anymore either. The only naked lady he dreamed about now, both asleep and awake, was Mysterious Megan and she was all the woman he could handle.

Silver-tongued devil.

And she was right, he said, about dreams that piss you off. There was one in particular. He was in a bed somewhere, not his own, but he was by himself. But suddenly this girl climbed in with him. She walked into the room, said a sexy "Hi," pulled off her dress, unhooked her bra, tossed it, and climbed in. He's still half asleep so he didn't argue. He's not sure he was even that interested.

She starts tickling his back. She runs her fingers, soft and slow, from his neck all the way down to his bun. Back and forth, back and forth. Naturally, he starts to get, um, unsleepy. He rolls over a bit and begins touching her in return. He moves closer. He feels the warmth of her body up against his. He leans forward to kiss her. But she backs away. She says, "Maybe we better not," gets up, grabs her clothes, and leaves the room.

He could have killed her. "I mean," he told Megan, "this is my *dream*, right? Did I invite her? Did I so much as make room in the bed for her? I get blown off enough in real life without getting it in my own goddamned sex dream."

Megan thought this was hilarious. But it served him right. Dream or no dream, he should have jumped up and run out of the room saying, "What do you take me for, you minx? I'm saving myself for Megan Cole."

"Good morning, gorgeous."

She heard his sleepy voice. She didn't turn.

"Hi, sailor," she answered huskily. She hid the Colt in the folds of the coverlet. The bed creaked and he was up. A few groggy steps and she felt warm hands on her shoulders, his lips against her hair. They stood for several moments, looking out at the gathering light, at the sailboats dozing at anchor.

"How about some coffee?" he asked her. "I'll go make some coffee."

"I'll be here," she told him.

He picked up his robe and left the room. She heard him on the stairs. She turned back toward his night table, intending to put the gun away. But that wouldn't do. Michael's friend, Mrs. Mayfield, would be here in a few hours. Can't leave it for her to find.

She went to the canvas tote she'd brought her things in, placed the heavy Colt inside, and covered it over with her toiletries kit. This way she won't forget it. She'll tell him it's there when they get back to her boat.

In the meantime, a cup of coffee sounds good. This lovely room feels good. Her body feels good. And she had a pretty strong hunch that in about fifteen minutes it would feel even better.

God, listen to her.

He's done what all the shrinks couldn't do. Or all the showers.

She was grinning.

Move it, Michael. Get your ass back up here.

36

On Friday morning, the day before Memorial
Day weekend, Parker's taxi reached Villardi's Seafood Palace with
fifteen minutes to spare.

Hector drove, Yahya rode shotgun, Parker sat in the rear with
a Sri Lankan named Tami who, while hardly WASP in appear-
ance, could probably pass for a Japanese tourist. Japs, Parker
reasoned, could not be that rare on Martha's Vineyard. Japs go
everywhere they sell film.

Parker had enlisted Tami because there was still no word from
Haroun. Tami was a distinctly second choice. What's good about
Tami, Parker decided, is that he moves very quietly and is into
that ninja shit. What's bad is he's a schmuck. He liked to prowl
around at night in this black outfit he has, with this Jap knife
he has, and show the Pakis how easily he could have cut their
throats. He doesn't do that anymore and he only has half a
pecker because one night he tried that on Haroun.

Don't get me started, Parker muttered to himself. On personnel, don't get me started.

Parker told Hector to make two passes. He was most impressed.
If Johnny G. had not thought to warn him of all the security he
would have kept on going. He noted two parked vans that probably held spotters with radios, at least one man on a rooftop sig-

naling another on the sidewalk, and several cars with men sitting low in them spread out along the avenue. The man being signaled walked over to a delivery truck and ordered the driver to move. It was blocking the view from one of the vans.

All this seemed a little early for a two o'clock meeting but the out-of-town bosses, he reasoned, might be planning to grab some lunch first.

"Pull up in front," he told Hector. "Yahya, you know these guys. You come in with me. If it all looks kosher, go back outside and wait."

Johnny G. was at the bar, dressed in a dark suit and tie.

The maitre d'—Paulie—the one who called—pointed him out but Parker already knew him from the papers. He nodded a greeting, took a slow look around, but Yahya walked straight over to Giordano. Johnny gave him a smile, offered his hand. Yahya took it and kissed it.

This seemed a little bit much. Now Johnny Giordano has his hands on the Paki's head like he's giving benediction. Yahya backed away, bowing.

"Hey," Parker hissed at him. "Who do you work for? Go wait in the car."

Johnny G. beckoned him, saluting with his glass, pulling out the stool next to his own. The bar was otherwise empty.

"This is Diet Pepsi," he said. "What can I offer you."

"I don't know. Same thing." He gestured vaguely toward the street but hesitated at the presence of the bartender.

"He's okay." Johnny G. flicked a hand. "He's my cousin."

The bartender blinked.

"Yeah, well . . ." Parker cocked his head toward the street again. "I spotted your so-called security in about five seconds. I mean, maybe that's the idea, a show of force, but it looks more like a parade out there."

Johnny G. turned to the bartender. "You hear that?"

The bartender blinked again.

"Go tell them to be more discreet."

He didn't move. Not much upstairs, Parker decided.

"Jimmy . . ." Giordano repeated himself, more slowly this time. "Go out, find whoever's in charge, tell him to get his act together.

Then come right back. I need you to take some notes for me here.''

The bartender hesitated, looked a little flustered. It was like, thought Parker, "Why me? Those are scary people out there.'' But he took a deep breath and nodded.

"Sure, Johnny.'' He stepped from behind the bar.

Hennessy had found Arnie Aaronson.

It had taken him until half past ten that morning to get a warrant. This was because the Manhattan D.A. had requested it, and because it was an election year, and because the issuing judge had become very tired of issuing warrants just so the candidates could showboat.

In the meantime, however, the detectives on stakeout near Parker Security Services, Inc., had no authority to detain anyone leaving. They could only record the plate number of the taxi that picked up three men at 10:17 A.M., one of whom could have been Parker. The other two were dark-skinned, carried camera bags, and were dressed like tourists from Ohio.

Aaronson's body had been forced into a plastic drum marked *Acetic Anhydride, Bhatpara Chemical Company Ltd., Akra, India.*

There were dozens of such drums filled with all different chemicals. Some were labeled *French Chalk* which one cop said was like a talc. He said he thinks it's what you make pills out of, not counting the active ingredients. He was more sure about acetic anhydride which he said is not illegal but which you need to make heroin.

The stuff looked like dirty sugar. There were several plastic buckets of it, sitting open, and some of it had spilled on the floor near one of the drums. It looked as if someone had emptied that drum because he had another use for it. This was how they found Aaronson's body.

Down by the loading dock, another cop found a pallet stacked with plastic bags full of Halite. Halite was like rock salt, used for melting ice on sidewalks. Hennessy wondered why anyone would stock up on Halite in May and also why a whole pallet of it had been shipped in from Tampico, Mexico, when the stuff was available at any local hardware store. He cut a bag open and tasted some. It turned out to be crystal meth, smokable metham-phetamines, worse than crack.

Another interesting find was a bunch of empty shopping bags from Bloomingdale's and one from Peerless Camera. They still had the sales slips in them for about a thousand bucks worth of "cruise wear and casuals." Hennessy noted the report of the three who left the building earlier. What the hell is this he wondered? They're going to skip town on the *QE2?*

They made forty-two arrests. The department of corrections had to send a bus. And interpreters. There was not one green card in the place.

He would have to call Doyle. Break the news about Arnie. It was time they had another talk anyway.

Fat Julie, riding with Frankie, his driver, was heading back to Villardi's Seafood Palace. His mood was unsettled. He did not feel at peace betting so much money that a stock would go in the tank.

He had bet large sums before—although not this large—and only on fighters and a couple of jockeys. And only when some-one reliable, like someone who owed him, had given him the word that a certain horse would pull up lame in the stretch or that a certain middleweight would walk into a hook in the sixth. There was no suspense. At least not for long. And if it didn't go right, like the fighter clocks the other guy instead, you always knew where to find the guy who sucked you in.

But he had taken Doyle's advice because if it worked, he could earn back in a week what he said he'd pay Parker and have some seed money left over besides. If it didn't, he knew where to find Doyle.

And he did need Parker. Some people he'd talked to, last night and this morning, all say they might want in but not if it's just an idea. They want factories already in place, already pumping out pills. And they had trouble grasping how we'd all make money just by making knockoffs and selling them cheap.

"Sounds too much like K mart," one of them said. "K mart is not first class."

"You want class, go watch a ballet. I'm talking money here."

"Yeah, but K mart is a good simile," said another. "Give us

like a Johnson & Johnson. You know, where they already got all the pill-making stuff and they already got customers. Get it like that and maybe we buy in."

Simile, yet. Fucking morons.

What happened to the can-do attitude we used to have in this country? Where's the entrepreneurial spirit?

The hell with them. He'd do this himself.

Frankie spotted the vans outside Villardi's. The windows were darkly tinted, including glass panels on their sides. "Taking pictures, it looks like," said Frankie.

Julie nodded. They do this every so often. They videotape who comes and goes but mostly nothing ever comes of it.

Frankie pointed to a taxi parked at the curb. "Three guys," he said. "They're watching the door."

"Drive past," Julie told him.

He looked in at the three men. Minorities. From the haircuts, they looked like Feds. He read where the Fed was hiring more minorities so maybe . . . Oh, for Christ's sake . . . that's Yahya in behind the driver. Almost didn't recognize him.

"They're okay," he told Frankie.

Parker must be in there already. Julie was afraid those vans might have spooked him. It's not real polite to bring backup, however. He made a mental note to mention that to Parker.

"Drive around," he said to Frankie. "I'll go in through the back."

I can't be seeing this, thought Julie Giordano.

There's Johnny, the guy he's with must be Parker, and they're sitting at the bar. Parker's drawing something on a napkin. Right there with them, elbows on the bar, is fucking Jimmy the bartender who is hanging on their every word.

Julie gave his brother the high sign as in "What the hell are you doing?" Johnny just looks at him like, "Oh, Hi."

Julie mouthed, "Can we talk? Like over here?"

His brother calls, "Julie, come say hello to Phil Parker," which dashed all hopes that Parker was maybe in the crapper and nowhere near Jimmy's wire.

Now having no choice, Julie crossed and shook hands with

him. He asked him how long he's been there. Parker says about
an hour. He asked Parker if he would care to go sit at his private
table, over there by the fish tank. Julie would be with him in five
minutes. First he needs to have a little talk with his brother here.

Parker says yeah, sure. He goes over and sits.

"That was just getting interesting," said Johnny G. "He was
explaining how the FDA works."

"Hey, can we cool it here?" This is still in front of Jimmy.
Johnny doesn't seem to notice.

"They got moles inside," he says. "You know, like spies? They
know everything the FDA's going to do before they do it."

"Johnny . . . will you shut your fucking mouth."

"You want to know something else? The FDA kills more people
than bad drugs ever did. You know how many people die because
the FDA—"

He grabbed his brother by the arm, gestured toward the men's
room. "In there," he said.

Johnny G. resisted. "I know what you're going to tell me. I
think Jimmy should hear it, too."

Julie looked at him. He looked at Jimmy. "He's jerking me off,
right? You're both jerking me off."

"Um . . ." A helpless shrug from the young bartender. "Mr.
Giordano, I'm not real sure myself."

"What you're going to tell me," said Johnny G., "is that our
family has never dealt drugs and that you wouldn't touch this
shit with gloves on."

Dumbfounded, he again looked at Jimmy. Jimmy is mouthing,
"Good idea. Say it." He's practically pleading.

Julie's eye was drawn to the bar at Jimmy's elbow. On it was
a pad of bar checks, several sheets of which were filled with notes
and Jimmy's still holding a pencil. He's taking notes? thought
Julie. What, he had technical difficulties? His microphone went
on the blink?

Julie pulled his brother off the stool. He dragged him ten feet
away to the big potted fern by the entrance. The entrance reminded him of something else.

"Those vans outside," he said. "What's the story with them?"

"Not just the vans," said Johnny G. pleasantly. "They're up on
the roof, they have chase cars both ends, and they also have two

THE SHADOW BOX ■

in here." He hooked a thumb toward two men at a window table. They had ordered iced tea and were nursing it.

Julie didn't bother to look. "And Parker walked into this?"

"He thinks they're ours."

He told his brother about the two o'clock meeting, which he invented—although he had a hunch that Julie had just come from a real one—and which he told Parker about from the bar phone. He did that, he said, to make sure he got their attention.

"Johnny . . . whose attention?"

"Whoever's been listening," he said patiently. "My guess is it's strictly FBI. If there were any Brooklyn cops outside, someone we know would have called us."

Julie could see what his brother had done. Believing it was another story.

"What about the cab? Parker brought shooters in a cab."

"I suggested it."

"So the Fed would know what they look like?"

"So I'd know."

"Yeah, well, Yahya's out there. You even set up Yahya?"

Johnny grimaced. It was like, "Oops. Forgot." But no problem, he says. We'll handle that with Jimmy.

An exasperated sigh. "You know I'm going to kill you for this, right?"

"Behave yourself. You're going to thank me. Moon will kill *you*, you get into this shit."

Fat Julie stared. "You heard from him?"

"Yesterday. We sat by Pop's grave."

Julie was silent for a long moment.

"Which is near Jake's grave," his brother reminded him.

A deep breath. Julie blew it out slowly.

"So what now?" he asked quietly.

"Go have your lunch with Parker. Show him some money. Take it out of mine if it'll make you feel better."

"You're damned right it will. But what's the point?"

"Just find out all you can about how this works."

"Johnny . . . you've blown this. It's gone."

"We need to know. Trust me."

Julie shook his head slowly. "Jesus, Johnny."

"Hey . . ." His brother touched his chest. "I said trust me. This isn't all bad."

"What's good? Tell me one thing good."

"For openers? The FBI will owe us."

A pained expression. "You're serious, right?"

"They will. Wait and see."

"How? We're now FBI approved? We're going to put that on business cards like the fucking Good Housekeeping seal?"

Johnny ignored the sarcasm. "I have an idea. But I need to talk to Mike first."

At this point, Julie didn't even want to hear it. He peered over the fern toward the table by the fish tank. Parker wasn't looking. He was busy annoying a flounder. Julie glanced back toward the bar. Jimmy's looking at him like, "No hard feelings, okay?"

"Does he leave with the Feds now? Or will he at least finish the weekend?"

"Who? You mean Jimmy?"

"It's a holiday weekend. If they owe us so much, the least they can do is not leave us short."

37

Michael and Megan stowed their things on the ketch, which was tied up at the Edgartown dock. That done, they made the ten-minute drive to the airport where they waited for Lena Mayfield's flight.

Megan's ketch had no name on the transom. It had tax and registration stamps and a Coast Guard serial number but no name. Michael passed the time suggesting a few. He thought *Wraith* might be good. It had just the right touch of mystery.

No reaction from Megan. She said, "Here comes her plane."

"Okay . . . How about *Sorceress?* Tell me that's not a perfect name for—"

She asked him if he wanted a Tic-Tac.

"Something more classic, then. How about *Sibyl?* Sibyls were these women in ancient Rome who—"

"I know what a Sibyl is, Michael."

"Maybe Sibyls had boats named Megan."

"Michael . . ."

"Get off it, right?"

"You know how some people have unlisted numbers? I have an unlisted boat."

Oh, yeah. Too bad. *Sorceress* would be a gas but she's right. It would be like hanging out a sign. So *Great Lay,* he supposed, was probably out of the question.

She laughed aloud. She gave him an elbow.

"Okay." He stepped out of range. "Tell me you didn't hear that. Tell me you can't read minds."

"You mumbled it."

"The heck I did." Did I?

"You mumble all the time, Michael. You talk to yourself all the time. Do you want to hear an imitation of you?"

He didn't, but she launched into one anyway. First there was Michael sailing. "Um . . . we're pinching . . . fall off, fall off . . . wind line over there . . . look out, lobster pot . . . come on, baby, you can go faster . . ." Next, there was Michael driving out here. "Ah . . . which way? . . . oh . . . says Airport Road . . . do we need gas? . . . nuts, I meant to get fresh flowers . . ."

"I get the picture," he said. Enough. Before we get into Michael making love.

"And in bed, you . . ."

He clapped his hands to his ears and screamed. People looked. Megan reached for him, grinning, and threw her arms around his neck.

"Here's how you stop mumbling," she told him. She kissed him. He kissed her back. They were still in an embrace when Lena Mayfield's plane taxied to a stop.

"Saw you two," said Lena. She pointed to the sky, indicating where from. "You sure you want company just now?"

Megan liked her from the start. And she liked Megan. She didn't seem so sure about Edgartown, though. They gave her a tour in the Mercedes.

"Pretty," she said. "No argument there."

"It's, um, fairly multicultural, I think."

"That mean you got darkies who ain't maids?"

Megan guffawed from the backseat.

Lena smiled with Megan and punched Michael's arm. He could only grin. She had told him to call her Lena. "Hasn't been a Mr. Mayfield since '83. The Lord took him. Emphysema."

She waved off their sympathy and reached into the canvas shopping bag which she'd carried on the plane. "Happy birthday," she said to Michael. "Got you some presents here."

Megan blinked and leaned forward. "When is your birthday?"
she demanded.

Settles that, thought Fallon. She can't read minds after all.

"Beg pardon, Michael?" asked Lena.

"Um . . . what?"

"You said, 'Settles that.' "

"No, I didn't."

"You did plain as day. Settles what?"

He glanced at Megan in the mirror. She was looking out the
side window, biting her fist to keep from laughing. She got a
grip, decided to be stern again.

"Michael . . . damn it . . . is today your birthday?"

"Now that you mention it."

"And you never told me?"

He shrugged. "Loved your presents, though."

"What presents?"

"Last night and this morning."

"Maybe I should go for a walk," said Lena.

"No, no. We're almost there."

She produced a small package. "This is from Mr. Doyle. He said
give you a kiss with it. Think I'll leave that chore for Megan."

"Forget it," she sulked. "He's been a creep."

"Megan . . ."

"What did you get?" she asked.

I'm a creep, he thought, but she's peering over the seat like a
six-year-old wondering what's in the box. He made her wait until
they were back at the Taylor House.

Doyle had sent him three watches, all Seikos, nice but not
expensive. The card said, "With care, these might last you
through June."

Mrs. Mayfield—Lena—had baked him some Toll House cookies
which she said don't eat now because she's going to fix a special
birthday brunch so everyone go wash up and sit. *Everyone* included Harold and Myra Lovelace, who had stocked up on what
she needed because she'd called them and said she planned to
do some cooking this weekend. Harold and Myra, made aware
of his birthday by Lena, gave him a Gary Larson birthday card

and an antique brass telescope with tripod that had belonged to Myra's grandfather.

"Doesn't do much good in a trailer," she told him. "Here you got a widow's walk. Meant to set it up there anyhow."

The Taylor House had never served meals, only continental breakfast and afternoon tea, but it had a well-equipped kitchen and the captain's original dining room furniture, which Michael thought was a crime not to use. Maybe next year. Myra, meantime, produced a pitcher of Bloody Marys and poured them as Lena went to work.

He was not sure what he expected from her, ham and eggs with grits, maybe, but she was back in half an hour with a classic New England brunch, some of which she'd brought with her in her big canvas bag. On a platter in the shape of a fish, she brought out kippers, smoked finnan haddie in cream, pan-fried potatoes with onions, scrambled eggs with sun-dried tomatoes and chives, and a basket of fresh-baked blueberry muffins.

Two other guests, following the smell, looked into the dining room on their way out the door. Lena snapped her fingers and pointed to two chairs. "Plenty to go around," she said. It was an order. They sat.

Megan's pout did not affect her appetite, she went nuts over the finnan haddie, but it didn't stop her from making cracks.

"He's a Gemini . . . might have known . . . two-faced."

She wanted Lena to tell everyone how they met, what happened in that New York subway. Lena declined. "Over and done with," she said. "Boy does need lookin' after, though."

The phone rang. Harold rose to answer it. Megan started gathering the dishes. She paused and cocked an ear toward Harold, who was only listening, but she shook it off and turned toward the kitchen.

"Michael," Harold waved a finger. "It's a doctor at the hospital."

"What hospital?"

"Ain't but one, over to Oak Bluffs. Doctor's asking do you know a Montague Mullens."

"Me? I don't think so."

"Says the police found him staggerin' around up by Lighthouse Beach. Said your name and address was in his pocket."

The man who called about the ghosts came to mind. But no, his name was Peabody. "Did he say what's wrong with him?"

"This Mullens thinks he's having a stroke. Doctor's not so sure."

Stroke. Michael felt as if slapped. "A black man? Late fifties?"

Harold asked the doctor. "Says that's him," he said.

Fallon's chair toppled backward as he rose. Megan set her dishes down.

"I'll drive you," she said.

"You never knew his real name?" asked Megan. She turned onto Beach Road. The sign said three miles to the hospital.

"Not Montague. I never heard Montague."

In fact, the last time he heard Mullen—not Mullens, *Mullen*— was when he asked what room he was in at Mount Sinai and Michael had to stop and think that he had a name besides Moon.

"Michael? When did he come here?"

"Last night, I guess."

"Last evening? On the ferry from Woods Hole?"

"I don't know. Why?"

"Nothing." She reached for his hand and squeezed it. "I'll have you there in five minutes."

38

Special Agents Mowbray and Phipps, driving separate cars, had followed the taxi to Oyster Bay. The order to tail it had been a disappointment. They would rather have stayed at the restaurant for when all the top dagos showed up.

The taxi proceeded toward Long Island Sound where it entered the grounds of the Corinthian Yacht Club. The sign outside said *Members Only.*

No amount of wardrobe advice, thought Agent Phipps, would pass this bunch off as members or even as acceptable guests. Agent Mowbray shared this view. He thought that they were obviously here for a meeting but with whom? Who would want to meet them at a chi-chi club like Corinthian? They realized, too late, that such a meeting would only be held on a boat, preferably out on the water, possibly a rendezvous with a second boat, possibly a pickup of smuggled contraband.

The four men, two of them carrying camera bags, one with a price tag still hanging from his warm-up suit, were seen to board a Grady-White sport fisherman named *Child's Play.* They cast off the lines immediately. It bumped its way out of the slip.

Agent Phipps radioed a request for a helicopter although he knew that it was probably useless. From where he stood, it seemed that every boat ever made was already out on Long Island Sound. Agent Mowbray, who had noted the registration number through binoculars, radioed the Coast Guard. The Coast Guard quickly identified the owner as a Mr. Frampton Childress of Oyster Bay, New York.

Childress . . . *Child's Play.* Cute, thought Mowbray.

The name rang a bell. He'd heard it before. He'd heard it, he was fairly sure, in connection with that Iranian a few years back who was peddling all those bogus pills. His memory was vague on the subject because either it never amounted to anything or . . . no . . . now he remembered. He had been ordered not to pursue it. But that was then.

Mowbray placed another call. He asked that a file be pulled on one Frampton Childress II.

39

The hospital was good-sized but no Mount Sinai. Fallon found Moon right away.

He was still in ER, in a small treatment room. A nurse showed them in. She said that his signs were stable, he's in no immediate danger, but that Michael must not leave without speaking to the doctor who called him.

Moon's eyes cracked open at the sound of their voices. He was propped up in a bed, an oxygen tube at his nose and a glucose drip in his arm. The arm was bandaged where they had taken blood. It was badly discolored as well.

The eyes, when they recognized Michael, showed a flicker of displeasure. They had not yet focused on Megan. She stayed back by the door where she made no sound. Moon forced a smile. He reached out with his free hand and Michael took it. But then he felt Megan's cold stare. He looked at her past Michael's shoulder. He blinked twice as if confused, then suddenly his eyes opened wide. Moon wet his lips.

"Friend of yours?" he asked Michael.

Megan had moved. She had stepped to a rack where Moon's clothing had been hung. She was fingering his shirt.

"This is Megan Cole," said Michael. "She's more than a friend. She's—"

''I'll wait outside,'' said Megan. Her voice seemed flat and hard.

Michael had no idea what caused Megan's behavior. Or, for that matter, why Moon was staring so hard at the door she'd gone out of.

''Pretty woman,'' he said. ''She local?''

''From Woods Hole. How are you feeling?''

''Been better. How long you known her?''

''Moon . . . will you stop about Megan?''

''Just glad you found a friend, that's all. You look real good, by the way.''

''Thank you. Where the hell have you been?''

''Just wandering . . . healing.''

''But not a whole lot of calling.''

Moon cleared his throat. ''Listen, Michael. I need you to do an errand for me.''

He told Michael that he had Jake's car. It's a maroon Buick, Florida plates. Being on the road so much, he also had a gun. When he got sick, over near Lighthouse Beach, and feared he might pass out, he thought he'd better not get found with a gun on him. He buried it at the base of a *No Clamming* sign along with his car keys and wallet. Didn't want the car impounded while they checked to see if he stole it.

''I'll take care of it,'' Michael told him. ''Moon, why didn't you tell me you were here?''

''Doc did it for me. I was too woozy.''

''The doctor said he found my name. He didn't say you gave it to him.''

Moon rubbed his face. ''Hard to think. Guess I'm still in a fog.''

Michael wanted to say, ''Bullshit.'' He'd seen Moon's eyes when they narrowed at Megan. He'd heard the crispness with which he said go get his keys and gun. Now all of a sudden he's a sick old man. It didn't fly. If Moon showed up here, armed, and wasn't going to tell him he was on this island, that could only mean . . .

''Moon . . . is someone after me?''

''You? Why should anyone—''

''Okay, after you.''

''Michael . . . I just missed you, that's all.''

"Screw this. I'll go call Doyle."

The eyes again. The eyes didn't like that idea.

"If I tell Doyle you're here"—Fallon folded his arms—"and that you told me *everything,* what will he say, Moon? Will he ask me what the hell I'm talking about?"

Moon chewed his lip.

"It's Jake, isn't it? You found who killed Jake."

Moon let out a breath. It was more of a sigh. "Sit down, Michael. Tell me more about Megan."

He threw up his hands. "I'm calling Doyle."

"I said sit."

"For the last time, Moon. Who killed him?"

"Hobbs was part of it. Now sit."

For the first ten minutes, he only felt rage. He saw the Baron, Franz Rast, in his mind. Michael had sat with him in meetings, and in private dining rooms, and had shaken his hand.

He'd had, in his grip, the evil old bastard who had broken his father's spirit, torn his parents apart, and made his mother so crazy that all she could think to do was run. He'd had his hands on the man who would soon order Jake Fallon's murder. And Moon's. And his own. He was also the man who had caused poor Bronwyn's death.

And that was still not all of it. Hobbs . . . Childress . . . Bellows . . . Parker. They had played him like a harp. He had been part of a criminal organization and he'd been too blind or stupid to see it. Or he didn't want to see it.

Moon was still talking. He was asking again about Megan. Fallon, at first, couldn't answer. It was all so much, so overwhelming, that a numbness had begun to set in. But he told Moon some part of what little he knew. He spoke as if he were sleepwalking. At last, he excused himself and stepped out into the corridor where Megan had been waiting. She sat on a bench, her knees drawn up to her chin. She too seemed off in a world of her own.

"Megan . . . listen," he said, approaching her. He felt for his car keys, remembered that she had them. "Moon and I . . . have a lot to catch up on. I want you to go back. I'll call a cab when I—"

"I'm staying, Michael." She stared straight ahead.

A weary breath. How much she'd picked up of what Moon had just told him, or sensed, or intuited, or simply heard with her ear to the door, he really didn't care right now.

He gestured toward the nurses station. "I have a call to make and I need to talk to the doctor. Please take my car. Let me call you later."

"Michael . . . I'll *wait*," she said firmly.

The doctor was an internist named Berman. The duty nurse paged him. Fallon waited by her station. He came along in about five minutes, tall and thin, about Michael's age, wore glasses low on his nose. The nurse waved a folder at him.

"Just came in," she said.

Berman raised a staying hand to Michael. "His records from Florida," he said. "Give me a second." He leafed quickly through several curled-up fax pages while sucking on his lip. He nodded a few times, then closed the folder.

"He's a friend of yours?"

"He's family."

"Family what? Employee? Bodyguard?"

The question angered Fallon. "You're asking can he pay his bill? Black man in a wrinkled suit?"

The doctor peered over his glasses. A hard stare. "I'm a doctor, Fallon. I don't give a shit if he's Magic Johnson. But two scars from bullet wounds make me wonder about his medical history."

Michael blinked. "He's been shot?"

"Not lately. They're old or I'd have called the cops."

Fallon was surprised and he wasn't. The wonder, if anything, was that Moon lived this long getting shot only twice.

"Either way," he told Berman, "I want him to have the best. Believe me, he can afford it."

The doctor tossed a hand. "You want to talk money? Cashier's one flight up. You want to talk about the patient, call me when you're ready."

"I'm . . . a little upset."

"As it happens, so am I. It's not a stroke. Not this time."

"What, then?"

"If I had to put money? I'd say he's been poisoned."

                    *   *   *

Moon heard her enter.

He opened his eyes. It took them a moment to focus. She had closed the door behind her but did not approach the bed. From the look on her face, thought Moon, she was not here to comfort the sick. The boat girl didn't like him one bit.

"Last night," he said, "back by that ferry. That was you."

She did not respond.

"Been talking to Michael. He says you're special. How special are you, Miss Cole?"

Still nothing.

Moon wasn't sure she was afraid of him, exactly. Some, maybe, when she first walked in with Michael. But now, right here, it was more like she hated that he'd come back into Michael's life.

"My grandma . . . back home . . . she was special, too," he told her. "Women with the gift . . . they called them granny women back then."

Her little chest rose and fell.

"Speak your mind, miss," he said gently.

She ran her tongue across her lips. "I want to touch you. Will you let me?"

Moon grunted. He wanted to say he'd been asked that friendlier. But his grandma wasn't much on small talk either.

"Will you?"

"Yes, Miss Cole. If that will ease you."

He offered his left hand, the one free of tubes. She moved closer to the bed and took it. Then she cocked one ear like his grandma did except Grandma Lucy would hum and rock. What Grandma did *not* do, and this one did, was to take the hand and hold it flush against her heart.

Whatever she heard, it seemed to confuse her. She tried harder. She took to massaging the back of his hand, running fingertips up and down his arm unmindful, it seemed, that he was still attached to it. Moon wanted to pull away lest Michael walk in. But suddenly she broke off, took two steps back. In that second, the door slapped open and a nurse, not Michael, came in. Moon hadn't heard her coming. This girl had, though.

The nurse said, "How we doing?" She replaced the glucose with a plasma bottle, checked the drip rate, then the tube in

Moon's arm. The bruise around the needle, he saw, was still spreading. The nurse studied it for a moment, then she patted his thigh and left. The boat girl stood feeling her throat on the spot where his hand had touched her. She took another step back.

"You're not his friend," she said quietly, glaring.

He took a breath. "I think you know better."

"I know you've lied to him. You've kept things from him."

He nodded. "A friend will do that sometimes."

"And you've taken things from him. You took Bron—" She stopped herself.

Moon squinted. "Did you start to say Bronwyn?"

Her face showed confusion again. Whatever she was seeing, she seemed unsure of what it meant. Moon tried to regain the advantage.

"My turn, Miss Cole. You been in prison?"

A beat. Some color drained. She shook her head.

"People who've done time . . . there's a look. You have that look."

"The answer is no, Mr. Mullen."

He shrugged and gave a nod as if satisfied. He wasn't. There's a yes, a no, and there's an in between. Of the three, the no seemed farthest from the truth. But now her chin was coming up. She knew that he had broken her rhythm and she's about to come charging right back.

"You murder people, don't you, Mr. Mullen?"

Moon wasn't quite ready for that one. Did she think, for some reason, he killed Bronwyn? Or had she been listening to stories.

"Something Michael told you?" he asked.

A small shrug. Defiant. He knew then that it hadn't come from Michael but she had him off balance. Pictures were coming into his head that he didn't want there now or ever.

The first was of the grave, the grave in Westchester that he'd dug for Rasmussen. He saw himself coming back to it, not that night but the next. He could smell a woman's hair through the bundle he was carrying. He could hear himself talking to her, saying he's sorry, saying everyone's so sorry, as he lowered Annie Fallon down.

He tried to wash the scene away before Megan could see it

too. In its place he put other scenes, other dead men. The man in Doyle's office, the man in Palm Beach and the German, years ago, named Brunner. He showed her Brunner, sprawled out on a lawn, his eyes swollen shut, his jaw hanging crooked, his head half twisted off. Yes, I did that, he said in his mind. Yes, you could say I'm a murderer.

But the girl, he realized, was seeing none of what he tried to show her. Her eyes, like his grandma's when she saw deep inside, were shiny and full of pain. In that instant, he knew that she knew.

"Miss Cole . . . sometimes . . ." He began but couldn't finish.

She nodded, near to tears. The nod said he needn't explain.

Moon tried to say it all the same. He said, "Sometimes there's . . ."

She finished for him.

"There's an in-between. I know."

"He's got blood in his urine," said the internist named Berman, "some in his stomach and he's bruising badly. I think it's these."

He produced an amber-colored prescription bottle from his pocket. Michael read the label. The drug was Warfarin, a blood-thinner. It came from a pharmacy in Brooklyn.

"This is dated yesterday," said Michael.

"Lucky him," the doctor replied. "Warfarin's an anticoagulant. In stroke patients, it keeps the—"

"I know what it is. I was in the business."

Berman raised an eyebrow. He thumbed the bottle open and sprinkled a few on his palm. "Do you know it when you see it?"

Michael looked. "You're saying those are fake?"

"I didn't. But it's interesting you'd ask."

"I've just been hearing about fakes. What's wrong with these?"

"Color's off, for one. In this particular brand, a seven-and-a-half-milligram pill should be beige. These are closer to yellow. I'm having them analyzed but I know what we'll find because I've seen these before."

Michael only half listened as Berman told him about Warfarin in general. That even well made, it's tricky stuff. That there are more ways for this drug to interact with other drugs, other physical conditions, with fatal hemorrhage a result, than almost any other drug on the market. Michael knew all that.

He was more attentive when Berman spoke of the last bad batch he had analyzed.

"In a given tablet," he told Michael, "the amount of actual Warfarin was found to range from zero, which lets the clots happen, to twenty milligrams, which can kill you in another way. Worse, the pills in that batch were contaminated. Whoever made them ground up a lot of other cheap drugs, almost all of which interact badly with Warfarin. For a binder, they must have run out of French chalk. That batch used plaster of Paris. Whoever made it didn't even pretend to try."

Michael stared at the bottle. He now understood what Megan had meant when she said she saw many people dead. People who were poisoned.

"Were they ever traced?" he asked Berman.

"Not so anyone could prove. Who'd you say you were with?"

"*Was* with. I . . . did some work for AdChem."

Berman almost sneered. "Small world, Mr. Fallon," he said.

Michael still needed to call Doyle. But seeing the empty bench, he walked back to the treatment room to see whether Megan had left after all. She was in there with Moon. He saw odd looks on their faces and that Megan had been crying.

He asked Moon, with his eyes, how much he'd told her.

Moon shook his head. "Just getting acquainted."

Megan shrugged in agreement.

Fine, thought Michael. Whatever that initial hostility was about, they seemed to have smoothed it over. He reached a hand to Megan's cheek. He wiped moisture away with the tips of his fingers. He told her that he's glad she stayed. He would go make his call and he'd try to make it quick.

Megan watched through the small glass window as Fallon disappeared down the corridor. She felt the spot where he touched her.

"How good a friend is this Doyle?" she asked.

Moon smiled. He was beginning to appreciate this girl.

"Real good. In his way."

"What way is that?"

Moon considered how to answer. "Lawyers . . . the bottom-feeding kind . . . run these ads on TV. They say, you got injured, you might be entitled to money damages."

She didn't understand.

"Money damages," he repeated. "That's Brendan Doyle's way. He's a friend in all the ways that count. But money damages is how he thinks."

"And you don't?"

"No."

"Will Michael?"

Moon shook his head. "It's why I'm glad we're talking. Can you keep him on this island?"

"I think so."

"Keep him indoors until I'm on my feet?"

"How long after that?"

"Until I've finished it."

"Yes."

"Miss Cole . . . now tell me about you."

She looked away.

"I know, don't I?" he said softly.

Her eyes flashed. "I have not, damn it, been in prison."

"No offense meant by that." He wanted to say that there's all kinds of prisons. All kinds of injuries. But there was no need. He had a pretty good idea what kind.

"I need a favor from you," he said. "Will you take my word that there's no harm to Michael in it?"

"Yes."

"Just like that? Yes?"

"I'm wrong sometimes. I was wrong before. You'd never hurt Michael."

"Thank you. And it's Moon."

"Megan."

He thanked her for that as well.

"When you two leave here, Megan, he's going to go pick up my car. In the trunk, there's an old sock with some cuff links, a watch, and a picture in a boxy little frame stuffed into it. Gettin' sick, I forgot it was there."

"The picture's of Bronwyn?"

Moon closed one eye. "You knew that from me or from Michael?"

"He told me. He said a burglar took his only photograph of her."

"But a while ago, you knew that burglar was me."

"I'm . . . not sure what I knew. I don't always know why I say things."

And that's a comfort, thought Moon.

"I took those things when I doubted him. I'd as soon he didn't find that sock. I wish I'd dropped it off the ferry."

"He doesn't need that picture."

"I'm grateful to you."

"He doesn't need another watch, either."

Michael had started to dial when he heard his name paged.

He walked back to the nurses station where he was handed a message from Harold Lovelace. It said, "Man named John Giordano called, says he's a friend, says he's arriving by air, early evening. Where do we put him? Hope your other friend is okay."

Moon should be fine, thought Michael. Berman says so. As long as he doesn't get cut. As for Johnny G., Michael knew that this visit wasn't social. Moon had told him that Doyle cut them in, that they had snatched one of those two who weren't muggers after all and, once he talked, steered Moon to the man who very likely killed Jake.

If it was Julie coming up, it would be to present his bill. Julie, being Julie, would want a piece of whatever AdChem has going. Not Johnny, though. Moon says he wants no part of it.

So why is he coming? Maybe Doyle knows.

He went back to the pay phone and tried his call again. A man answered, not Doyle. He sounded like a goon. He said, "Mr. Doyle ain't available. Who's this?" Alarmed, Michael gave his first name, which the goon repeated aloud. Sheila Doyle picked up an extension.

"Michael? Oh, Michael, it's so good to—"

"Aunt Sheila, who was that?"

"His name is Emil. Julie sent two more just like him to look after me and Maureen. Did you hear what happened here?"

"Moon told me," he said.

"Moon's there?"

"He called me," Michael lied. "He wouldn't say from where. Are you and Maureen all right?"

"I guess. Thanks to Julie."

"Is Brendan there?"

"He's on his way to you. He said he's flying up with Johnny. Did Moon know about Arnie Aaronson?"

"Aaronson? The money manager?"

"They murdered him, Michael. He was asking questions for Brendan and they killed him. Marty Hennessy found him. He said he knows who did it. He's looking for a man named Parker."

Michael's head seemed to swell. The rage that had been building now pounded against his skull.

"So am I, Sheila," he said softly. "So am I."

He replaced the phone. He stood for a moment, once again seeing faces in his mind. Parker . . . Hobbs . . . and the Baron Franz Gerhardt Rast. He might not find Parker before Hennessy does but he'll damned well start looking for Rast. Moon says sit tight. Moon says promise me, let me take care of Rast.

Sorry, Moon. Rast is mine.

"Michael?"

He hadn't seen Megan standing there. He had asked her, nicely, to leave. This time he would tell her. Get away from here, Megan. I want you to climb on your boat and sail back to Woods Hole. Better yet, go sail it around the world again. I want you to stay far away from me until—

"Forget it, Michael. No chance."

Moon looked for his clothing, saw it still on the chair. He scanned the shelves of the treatment room. He saw a box of gauze pads. Satisfied, he leaned his head back on the pillow.

He would need a supply of those pads, he feared, for when he pulled these tubes out. But they could wait. He would rest a while longer until Michael was gone.

Megan.

The boat girl did remind him of his Grandma Lucy. But Megan was different in two ways. One was that, given the choice, she'd rather not know the things she knew. The second was that Megan would fret over what she saw, not sure whether it was fact or fancy or even what it meant. Old Lucy, being not as bright, never troubled herself too much. She knew what she knew and that was the end of it.

Both of them could read a man's heart, though. They could see a thing, and the thing could look bad, and yet they could know that the man doing that thing had no bad in his heart.

Annie Fallon. That was a *real* bad thing.

How much Megan saw of it, how much she understood of how Annie died, he didn't know. She never asked a single question. He almost wanted to tell her all the same, just so she'd know there was no meanness in it. But she put a hand on him, shook her head as if to say there was no need. He knew, right there, that she'd never speak of that grave again.

He, Moon, had only buried Annie. It was Tom, Michael's father, who killed her.

Annie, that day, the day she found that poisoned Valium, had had enough. She tried to call her mother, say that she and Michael were moving in with her, but Tom kept her from dialing the phone. She started packing bags; Tom tried to stop that as well. He said he'd handle Brunner and Rasmussen. He begged her to give him the chance but she wouldn't have it. She said she was going to go to the police, starting with her cousins, and she tried to use the phone again. Tom ripped it from the wall.

She said if he tried to stop her from leaving she'd scream until the neighbors called the cops. He let her go but he was frantic. He chased after her, caught her in the building's garage just as she was slamming the trunk and tried to wrest the car keys from her. She did scream. She kicked and clawed at him. He dragged her into the car, held her tight, tried to quiet her. He held her until she stopped fighting him.

It was never clear what killed her. There were no marks on her throat, no blood except from Tom's cut lip, no sign he'd used his fists. Likely, she suffocated. Not that it matters.

He sat with her two hours in that lonesome garage. He thought about Michael and what this would do to him. He thought about prison. He thought about taking the car out, onto a highway, and driving it into a bridge abutment so it would look like they died in an accident. But he didn't. Instead he drove over to Jake's house. He needed Jake to tell him what to do. And he needed Jake to know he never meant to kill Annie.

Life turns on little things. If Jake's housekeeper hadn't gone to the dentist about then, if Sheila Doyle hadn't been up in Boston visiting kin, Jake wouldn't have had much choice but to call the police. As it was, he checked to see if Annie was dead, saw she was, then called Doyle over and they listened to Tom's story. It was Doyle who asked if anyone had seen or heard them fighting, if anyone had walked through that garage and saw him sitting there. Tom said he didn't think so.

Jake saw where Doyle was headed. It was taking an awful chance because there was no telling whether Tom would be able to handle his part. But he just couldn't see the gain in having Tom go to prison, having Michael grow up knowing that his father killed his mother. They drove Annie down the street to Doyle's house. This wasn't exactly what Doyle had in mind but he had a garage and Jake didn't. This is when Jake called him, Moon, and asked him to come stay with Tom while he, Jake, went to straighten up the apartment and pick Michael up at school.

That afternoon, they thought out what they'd do. Moon had to give Doyle credit. He never would have thought that Doyle would stand up like he did. He could have ended up disbarred. Anyhow, that night, they went and finished their business with Rasmussen. Or thought they had.

That grave they dug for Rasmussen . . . Jake never really intended to bury him in it. He had it in mind all along that they'd use it for Annie. After they made it look like she ran off. They took her up there the next night. They buried her with the crucifix she kept over her bed. That crucifix had been a gift from Jake, blessed by Cardinal Spellman himself. To Jake, that seemed the next best thing to consecrated ground.

Jake burned her luggage, purse, jewelry in his furnace. He kept samples of her handwriting. That was Doyle's idea, that letter from Chicago. Doyle forged it, even flew out there to mail it after some time went by. Tom knew it was coming. He knew he was to read it to Michael, let him look but not too closely, then let Michael see him destroy it.

Jake wasn't sure about that part. He thought it would be too hard on Michael. Doyle said it won't be as hard as the truth.

Moon looked up at the clock. It was going on four.

He knew that Michael would be sticking his head in one more time. He closed his eyes. Let Michael see him sleeping. The fact is, he could do with a few hours' rest before he unplugged himself and headed back over to Edgartown.

He moved best at night anyway.

40

The next flight to Munich was not until six. The London Concorde left at three. Rast had booked himself on that one. He could make a connection from London and still be safely in Munich by morning. He made this decision within minutes of learning that Parker's office had been raided. And that a dead man had been found.

He took only a briefcase. He told the front desk that he'd be out attending meetings. Within the hour, he checked in with British Airways. An hour after that, he was sipping a glass of Beaujolais, looking out at the coast of Massachusetts.

The wine did not calm him. He was seething inside.

Twice now they have done this, he thought. Twice now they have forced him to run. This time, however, the damage could be infinitely greater.

Hobbs unaccounted for. No doubt in a drunken stupor somewhere. Turkel missing, no doubt flown the coop. Parker very probably in custody. The dead man can only be that investigator of Doyle's. And Avery Bellows not taking his calls. He's in conference, they say. No doubt with a good criminal lawyer.

He drained his glass, snapped his fingers for another.

His welcome in Munich might not be the warmest, global communications being what they are, but it would surely be an improvement over anything he might have faced in New York. The German authorities, however, would not dare detain him. He would have to have been accused of spying for the East before they would even ask to question him. A civilized country, Germany.

Once there, he would sequester himself at Schloss Scharnhorst. The Countess won't be there. Tomorrow through Wednesday she'll be at her hospital. Wiping the noses of puling children. He'll have those three days to sit down at his computer, have a number of factories dismantled, move some inventories around, and perhaps arrange a few fires of his own.

This will die down. The authorities, once reasoned with, will see that it does. The industry, for that matter, will insist that it does.

But it won't be over for him. Not while that Fallon boy lives. Fallon and that lawyer. Fallon and everyone dear to him. Fallon and that black bastard, Moon.

Johnny G. met Doyle at La Guardia.

Doyle wanted to talk. Johnny said "Not now" because the air taxi to Bridgeport was being held for them and because an FBI tail was about twenty feet behind him. Once aboard, they couldn't talk either, at least not about Lehman-Stone and Ad-Chem, because the plane was packed with Wall Street types who were getting an early start on the holiday weekend.

Johnny knew they were Wall Street because here it was Friday afternoon and they're all still playing with their laptops. They're talking to themselves. They're muttering, "Shit!" or "Way to go!" depending on what chart they called up on their screens. Most of them also had these little microcassette recorders for recording their thoughts and for spying on each others' conversations. Some of those were interesting.

On two occasions during the flight, Johnny heard references to the FDA. The first was in connection with a new lotion, a cure for male impotence, which the Israelis had developed. The second was about a powerful anti-emetic, developed by the Japanese, that prevents nausea in chemotherapy patients. These led to some jokes about limp dicks and barfing but also to the observation that the whole world is beating the shit out of us on R&D, thanks to, as one said, "the fucking FDA and its bullshit rules."

After the first such comment, Johnny G. leaned to Doyle's ear and said, "Don't get me started on the FDA." After the second, he said, "Just don't get me started."

"On my life," said Doyle. "I won't."

Doyle had too much else on his mind. Low on the list but troubling all the same was a call that had come in from that young Boston lawyer. Doyle almost hadn't taken it, being busy at the time with Marty Hennessy. But he did and he learned that Michael's new friend, this Megan Cole, was semi-famous. The lawyer said he hadn't found out much about her personal history yet but she's known to the Massachussetts State Police. It seems she's worked with them on some murders.

She works with the cops? As a *psychic*, yet? What the hell is she doing with Michael?

They changed planes at Bridgeport.

"Do you know what else stops nausea?" Johnny asked this as they took their seats.

"Marijuana," Doyle answered distractedly.

Johnny G. nodded. "Family down the street from us," he said, "has a fifteen-year-old kid with cancer. He's getting chemo. But he's barely back home from the doctor's before he starts heaving his guts out."

This is as the stewardess served a snack.

"Johnny . . ."

"Just listen to me. So someone tells his father about grass. He figures it's worth a shot so he gets some for his kid. Kid puffs a joint before his next chemo session and this time, right after, the kid's not only not sick but he wants to go to Burger King. True story, Brendan."

"It has a point?"

"Every doctor knows what grass does for chemo patients. But do you think the FDA would let any of them prescribe it?"

Doyle shrugged.

"They claim other drugs work as well, but the fact is they don't. They also say grass has carcinogens in it. Can you believe that? They're saying don't take it for cancer because you might get cancer."

Another shrug. "So? The father gets it on the street."

"The point is why should he have to? The point is why won't they let a doctor give this poor kid a break? You want to hear worse stories?"

"No. You said don't get you started."

Johnny ignored the reminder. "All over the world, there are good new drugs that work, that keep people from suffering the way my father did." He turned in his seat for emphasis. "Not only can't you get them here, your doctor isn't even allowed to tell you that they *exist*. If he does, he gets hammered by the FDA. You didn't know that, did you?"

"Johnny . . ."

"You want to hear a statistic? Eighty percent of all new drugs that are available in this country—and I'm talking miracle drugs now—were available in other countries an average of six years earlier. How many people died waiting, Brendan? How many died not knowing about a drug that could have kept them alive?"

This went on for most of the flight.

The part about how the FDA kills people took ten minutes by itself. Boiled down, Johnny says that the FDA has become a polit-ical rats' nest, self-perpetuating, secretive, a powerful bully with standards that are considered absurdly rigorous by every other developed country. We'd be nowhere on AIDS if it wasn't for the French, nowhere on the cancer that killed Rocco if it wasn't for the Japs.

"That Jap drug was there all the time, Brendan, and no one would tell me. Do you hear what I'm saying?"

Doyle began to understand the dynamic here.

The FDA, Johnny went on, does not protect consumers. It pro-tects its own turf. The drug companies don't complain out loud, he says, because the FDA, which is famously vindictive, can shut them down with a word. Or they'll say, "You been talking to reporters? You been bitching about us? Fine. You just bought another two years before we let you sell that new Alzheimer's drug you're so proud of."

This, he says, is why the drug companies are moving as much of their R&D as possible to Europe and lately to China. The small biotechs have no choice but to do that because they can no longer attract venture capital in this country. They can't afford the hun-

dred grand that the FDA charges everyone, big or small, just to
make an application.

All of this, clearly, had come as a recent revelation to Johnny
G. But it was hardly a surprise to Doyle. The FDA is, after all, a
government agency. It has absolute power over a very rich industry. Regulators, by their nature, cling to such power because once
it's gone, they're virtually unemployable in an industry that has
grown to detest them. The smart ones know that. They make it
while they can and park it in accounts on Grand Cayman.

"Enough," said Doyle at last. "I want to know why we're talking about this."

"Because it makes me crazy. If you saw my father . . ."

"Johnny, I did see your father. Cut to the chase here."

He was silent for a moment.

Then, "You're looking to bring down AdChem. Find another
way, Brendan."

"Another way than what?"

"You shorting their stock?"

"Yeah. Isn't Julie?"

"Big time. Now let me guess. You're going to sit down with a
congressman or two, cut them in, and when the time is right
they'll blow the whistle, call in the FDA who will then shut down
all of AdChem's North American operations and then lean on
Germany to shut them down over there. The stock drops like a
stone and you get rich."

Doyle made a face. "You're way ahead of me, Johnny."

A snort. "Bullshit."

"Hey! Fuck you, kid. It happens that I'm still on Jake Fallon.
I'm on who pays for Jake and after that I'm on who pays for
Arnie Aaronson."

Johnny G. rubbed his chin. He sat back in his seat. After a
moment, he gave Doyle's arm a light punch. The punch was a
limited apology.

"Anyway," said Johnny, "Michael won't like doing it that
way."

"What way?"

"Starting a run on their stock. Too many people get burned."

"You know another way?"

"No."

"You know a way to keep the FDA out? How do they stay out?"

"I don't know. But there's something I want to try. Just to see if I can do it."

"Like what?"

"Parker did some bragging. Said he's got some FDA people in his pocket. He named a few names."

"And you want to take them down?"

"I want to take the whole thing down."

41

Michael found the car keys and the pistol near the sign that said *No Clamming*. Moon had wrapped them in a potato chips bag from the trash and buried them in the sand. Jake's Buick was in the Lighthouse Beach lot. It was the only car still parked there. Michael thought that was as good a place for it as any but Megan insisted on moving it. She said there's been some vandalism lately.

She traded keys with him, told him she needed to stop at the pharmacy first but then she'd park the Buick in back of the Taylor House. Michael said he'd see her there. He wanted to check in with Harold and Myra and make sure all the guests were comfortable, especially Mrs. Mayfield.

Afterward, he would drive back out to the airport and pick up Doyle and Giordano. If Megan wouldn't mind, he'd like to talk to them alone. Later, perhaps, they could all grab some dinner together.

"He's really a gangster?" Megan asked him. "You grew up with gangsters?"

"It's . . . more of a family business."

"But the kids. Don't they ever, you know, decide they'd rather go straight?"

A shrug. "I think Johnny's pretty straight."

"In his way?"
He nodded. "In his way."

Megan did stop at the pharmacy, but only so she hadn't lied.
She bought a magazine in case she had to do more waiting.
After that, she opened the Buick's trunk and found Moon's sock.
It was tucked in the well of the spare tire. She had to move four
gasoline cans, three of them empty, to get at the well. The touch
of the gas cans caused a montage of fires to flash through her
mind. She closed the trunk and, sock in hand, walked the short
block down to the waterfront.

There were quite a few tourists there, some sipping cocktails,
enjoying the early evening. She found a fairly private spot and
sat on the edge of the jetty, her feet dangling over the water, the
sock held hidden between her knees. She shook the cuff links
out first. They barely made a splash. The watch followed. The
frame stayed wedged in the sock.

She had promised herself that she would simply let it go, sock
and all, without looking at the photograph. She knew all that
she wanted to know about Bronwyn. That Bronwyn was more
talented than she is. More educated, more worldly, more beautiful. But also that she never loved Michael. And that the color of
her eyes and her hair were as false as she was.

Megan was sure of that. She felt it when she touched the
shirt that Bronwyn had bought for him and again when she felt
Bronwyn herself through Michael's body.

She was *almost* sure.

What she didn't need now was to let her skin touch that photograph. Even without that, even just holding the sock, she was
beginning to see visions of Michael making love to Bronwyn, the
two of them pumping up and down, moaning and gasping, Bronwyn doing things to him that she, Megan, couldn't bring herself
to do quite yet and doing them better than she ever would.

Megan . . . stop it, she scolded herself.

She knew that this was no psychic gift talking. It's just herself.
All she is, right now, is an ordinary, everyday woman, jealous
and insecure.

So act the part.

Drown the bitch, Megan. Let go of the sock.

She did.

She heard the splash and listened as a long line of bubbles came belching to the surface. She almost smiled. She stopped herself. A smile, all things considered, would be unattractively smug. She smiled all the same.

Megan sat for a while, enjoying the evening panorama and the parade of big yachts, both sail and power, coming in from all over. Out in the harbor, several were circling, looking for a place to drop anchor. On board, some were already having cocktails. Others were hailing the town launch to come ferry them ashore. Smaller boats sat in line, their engines coughing, waiting for a space at the public landing.

On one of them, a glitzy sport fisherman, a dark-skinned man in a green jogging suit looked woefully seasick. He was retching over the side. The others seemed disgusted by him. Megan watched as the skipper of that boat finally bumped his way into a space just aft of her ketch. It was about to hit her transom when a tall, thin figure in a hooded black slicker dashed forward to fend it off. Megan recognized Parnel Minter. She groaned aloud.

Parnel, she realized, had spotted her boat and was hanging around it, hoping to talk to her. It was always the same. She had found no way to convince him that she doesn't do spirits. They exist, or they don't, suit yourself. But they could be having a convention here and she wouldn't know it. Nor does she do readings for ghost-freak tourists even when they offer Parnel fifty bucks for an introduction.

She would sit here for a while, wait for him to leave. Michael won't miss her. He'll have left for the airport by now. She would go get Moon's Buick, drive it back to the inn.

But before that, she decided, hanging a few extra fenders from her railing seemed a good idea. Some of those power boaters were already a little drunk and the evening was only beginning.

The best plans, thought Parker, are improvised plans.

Of all the police raids he'd been on, he could think of maybe two that had gone as rehearsed. Cops never seem to learn that the bad guys weren't there at the rehearsal.

It did not greatly trouble him, therefore, that they were playing this by ear. The trick, he told Hector, was to keep this simple, use the element of surprise. We do a fast reconnoiter, hit quick, and get out.

What did trouble him a little was Tami. At the mention of a reconnoiter, Tami, like an asshole, starts to strip out of his jogging suit. He's wearing his dumb ninja suit underneath, complete with a belt full of knives and stars and other ninja shit. Parker had to smack him.

"Look around you, numb-nuts. Does this look like fucking Hong Kong?"

Thank God he's almost done with these clowns.

The good news, however, was that reconnoitering could be easy. With luck, he could do that by phone. He climbed to the dock, Childress's cellular phone in his hand, and extended the antenna. He practiced what he would say.

Hey, Mr. Fallon? Wally Peabody again. Yup, made it after all. Me and Betsy won't be staying because you're right, the whole island's booked solid, but we'd sure like to take you up on your offer. What might be a good time to look at the house?

Parker would suggest after dinner. That way, chances are, the other guests would be out walking it off. He'd go there with Tami, knock on the door, and by the time Fallon recognized him it would be too late. He pops Fallon in the mouth, Tami cuts his throat, they take a Polaroid to show Rast and they're gone. Hector would be watching the street. Yahya, who is so fucking seasick he's useless, would stay and watch the boat to make sure no one boxed it in.

Parker punched out the number.

But wouldn't you know it, Fallon was out. A hick named Harold answered. He said Fallon had gone to the airport to pick up some visitors.

Parker took visitors to mean guests.

"Then what?" he asked. "You all sit down and eat?"

The hick didn't understand the question.

"You know. Dinner. What's a good time to call after that?"

Now Harold got it. He said, no, they don't serve evening meals but there are many fine restaurants right here in Edgartown. This launches him into a commercial.

He says the Taylor House serves a continental breakfast and an afternoon tea with real English scones and Devonshire cream and there'll be a nice brunch this Sunday because one of the guests wants to fix it but no, no evening meals.

For tonight, he says, they're all having dinner at Square Rigger restaurant over on Main Street—Harold knows this because he and Myra, that's his wife, got them all a table together—it's sort of a tradition—and Myra reads them a ghost story over dessert.

"This is what time?" Parker asked.

"Reservation's at seven. It'll run till nine or so."

"And Mike will be there or what?"

"He'll be right here, most likely. Michael's not much on ghost stories."

"Oh, great. Would you tell him Wally Peabody called? Tell him I'll call again later. Hey, Harold?"

"Yessir."

"It's been a few years since I been there. Michael didn't make too many changes, did he? I mean, he didn't make it too modern."

"Now bathrooms is all, but that was Mrs. Daggett. Michael never changed a thing."

"Glad to hear it. What room did he take for himself?"

"Room the Daggetts had. Third floor front."

This was good information, thought Parker. He snapped the phone shut, digesting it. On a wall nearby, he saw a bank of public phones.

Here's what we'll do, thought Parker. We'll send Hector and Tami up to the Taylor House now. They'll keep an eye on that house and on that third floor bedroom in particular. Hector will take the cellular phone and the number of one of these pay phones. He, Parker, will sit tight and wait for Hector to call him with the comings and goings. This is also a very good spot because from here he can see the whole waterfront and also all the foot and vehicular traffic that is now going up and down Water Street.

Around eight, he'll call Fallon again. Invite himself over. Same game plan from there. Don't forget to bring a camera. If everyone's out eating, it could be well after nine before anyone finds Fallon's body. By then, Parker would be halfway back to Oyster

Bay and a million dollars richer. Or he will be by tomorrow once he calls Rast and says have that suitcase ready. Says he got a snapshot the Baron's going to like.

And then another million on Sunday from the Giordano brothers, less the fifty grand Julie paid him today. He had told that hood, and especially his brother, more than he wanted to. Especially their connections in the FDA. He should not have named names just yet. But when someone lays fifty thousand in cash on the table it's hard to leave it sitting there.

Screw it.

That's two million by Sunday. Sunday night, he's on his way to Seattle.

Out there, maybe, he'll buy a boat of his own. Not just for fishing. Something classy. Maybe like the one parked in front of theirs. The one that girl is on. Must be the owner's squeeze. Too good looking to be a deckhand.

That's what he'd do. Get a boat just like that, two masts, lots of shiny brass, dark wood all polished up like furniture, and get a young blond hard-body just like her to teach him how to work it.

How about it, honey?

Want to come to Seattle?

Old Granny Futterman will treat you real good.

Baggage claim, at the Martha's Vineyard airport, is a section of sidewalk outside the little terminal. Johnny G. saw Michael waiting for them. He was not surprised. The look on Michael's face said he'd talked to Moon. It figured that he would then have called Doyle, got Sheila instead. Sheila would have told him they were coming.

Michael stood, arms folded, leaning against his car as they collected their overnight bags, all the time glaring at Doyle. His expression softened only slightly when Johnny G. approached him and embraced him.

"Mike . . ." said Johnny G. quietly, "Doyle wasn't sure who killed Jake. Not before today."

"Like hell he wasn't."

"Michael . . . listen to me."

"If he didn't know, he should have. When he saw they used a bat on Jake, he should have known."

"Hey." Doyle threw down his bag. "I didn't come up here to—"

Johnny G. took Michael's arm.

"Come on," he said. "Let's take a walk."

He steered him toward a sign that said *Rental Car Returns*. They left Doyle with the black Mercedes, fuming.

"In the first place," Johnny G. told him, "don't fold your arms when you have a gun in your belt. It pulls your jacket, makes an outline. In the second place, we're your friends. Let's stop all this other shit right now."

"Doyle's no friend of mine."

"Michael . . . you've had no fucking clue who your friends are. It was Bronwyn who set up Jake."

The next few minutes would remain a blur. Fallon remembered getting angry, more at Doyle than at Johnny, furious that Doyle would try to lay this on Bronwyn. He remembered Johnny, reaching into his pocket, pulling out a creased and wrinkled copy of the AdChem annual report, saying it was in Jake's pocket when he died.

"Who gave this to him, Mike? Who opened it to Franz Rast's picture and made sure Jake Fallon looked at it?"

Michael tried to get away from him. He remembered pushing him when he tried to follow and the sharp sting on his cheek when Johnny slapped him. Michael threw a punch. It was a reflex, mostly. But Johnny stepped inside it and they grappled. The next thing he knew, Doyle was running toward them. And Johnny was waving him off. But he, Michael, was looking up at them.

Fallon realized, dimly that he was sitting on the ground, his back against the door of someone's car. He saw Doyle, walking away, back to the Mercedes. He saw Johnny come back over, ease himself down, sit next to him on the pavement.

"You settled down now?" he asked.

Fallon's left temple felt thick and swollen. The nerves there were coming back to life. "Did you hit me?" he asked.

"Damned right I did." He raised his right hand to show the pistol that had been in Michael's belt.

Fallon understood. He felt, with his fingertips, the welt that was already rising. But he was also seeing Bronwyn. He was seeing, at last, that what Johnny told him was true. That everything about her was a lie. The pain of that was greater. He buried his face in his hands.

They sat in silence a while longer.

"Let's get clear about the bat," said the younger Giordano at last.

Fallon tried to get up. Johnny pulled him back.

"If I was a burglar," Johnny said quietly, "and Jake had walked in on me, I would have grabbed the first thing handy. In Jake Fallon's house, the first thing handy was a bat. This was twenty-five years after that other bat, Mike. Don't tell me Doyle should have known."

Fallon's eyes were still glazed.

"You listening to me?"

Fallon wet his lips and nodded.

"You want someone to blame? How about Jake and Moon? If they finished Rast back when this started, none of this would have happened."

Michael said nothing. He was still seeing Bronwyn. Even those violet eyes were a lie.

"And then of course there's your father. If he'd listened to Jake in the first place, if he'd gone to him, up front, when he saw what he was into . . ."

Johnny G. didn't bother to finish. He waved the AdChem report at Michael.

"You don't get a pass on this either," he said. "You go to work for a company and they pay you some nice bucks. You see they're on a hot streak that never seems to end but you never wonder how it is that they never pick a loser. Why sniff the hand that feeds you, right?"

Michael's color rose. But he knew he had that coming.

"And you even speak German. Adler—eagle, eagle—Adler. That never crossed your mind?"

It had and it hadn't. Any more than he'd think "star" when he heard the name Stern, or "small" when he heard the name Klein.

"And *then*," Johnny smacked him with the brochure for emphasis, "there's running the way you did. That's how Jake and Moon raised you? Someone's trying to hurt you, you couldn't have at least called *me*?"

A sheet of paper, torn from a notebook, fell out of the annual report. Michael picked it up.

"What turned the corner here," Johnny G. reminded him, "was when you finally called in and told Doyle about the two who tried to ice you. It was Doyle who got their names. It's thanks to him that we know what's been happening here."

The sheet of paper was a list of names and telephone numbers. Michael recognized some of the names.

"Doyle got us where we are," said Johnny G., "but we could have been there months ago if only you trusted him back then. Doyle is family, Mike. He's not blood, neither is Moon, but they're family all the same."

Michael took a breath. "How long has Doyle known about Bronwyn?"

"Just since today. Since Hobbs spilled his guts."

"So Moon knew too?"

"I guess."

"And he never told me."

"He probably didn't have the heart."

"What else didn't he tell me, Johnny?"

"Mike . . . don't do that. For your own good, don't start."

"Yeah." Fallon nodded slowly. "Yeah, okay."

"Where's Moon, by the way?"

Michael told him. He told him about the bad Warfarin that had caused internal bleeding and had almost killed him.

Johnny G. grimaced. "You heard about Arnie Aaronson?"

"I heard he's dead. Sheila told me."

"Same way, Mike. They fed him drugs. Good, bad, I don't know, but Parker overdosed him and he died."

"Where's Parker? Do you know?"

"He'll keep. Trust me."

Michael looked at the list he'd picked up. "Johnny, what are these names?"

"Drug company execs. Aaronson called them for Doyle. We think that's why Parker snatched him."

Johnny got to his feet. He pulled Michael up with him and steered him back toward Doyle. Doyle had been watching them. His chin was up and his hands were balled into fists.

"That," said Johnny G., "is his I've-taken-enough-of-your-crap look. Go tell him you're sorry or go duke it out. Either way, put this behind you, Mike. The three of us have work to do."

"What work? Except nailing Rast."

"We're going to bring this down. You're going to help us figure how."

Michael folded the list.

"I already know how," he said.

Moon had finally been unplugged.

He was given a bed in a four-room ward and served cod cakes and Jell-o for dinner. Only one other bed was occupied, a man with a bleeding ulcer who seemed less than pleased at having him for a roommate.

Moon waited until his tray was collected. He gathered his clothing and went into the bathroom to dress. The puncture in his arm began to seep from the effort. He packed it with another gauze pad and taped it.

He told his roommate that he thought he'd scout the day rooms, find a good jigsaw puzzle to work on. The ulcer patient ignored him. Moon said then he'd drop by the office, see about getting a different room. Wouldn't want to aggravate an ulcer, he said. The man still ignored him. But he looked up at the ceiling as if to say, "Thank you, God."

For his sake, God'd better be white.

He was out of the hospital five minutes later. He saw a bus stop nearby but decided he'd better walk a while, get his legs back, give those cod cakes a chance to settle. He walked down into Oak Bluffs where he found a taxi. He was back in Edgartown before dark.

43

Lena Mayfield was loving it.

She had this whole big room to herself. A four-poster bed with a goosedown comforter. Oriental rugs. An upholstered rocker. Thick velvet drapes and chintz curtains. All this and a bathroom to die for.

In fact, with everyone gone to dinner she had this whole big house to herself. Except, just now, for Megan. Megan had stopped by to leave that sick man's car and was downstairs gathering up some extra pillows and blankets. Two more friends of Michael's, she said, would be sleeping on her boat.

Lena, meanwhile, had undressed down to her slip, put on a big soft terry robe, and started filling the tub. She had brought up a tray from the kitchen with a bottle of wine, some crackers, and three kinds of cheese and set them on a chair next to the Jacuzzi. She had wheeled the TV in, lit a scented candle, and turned off all the lights. In about ten minutes, she would be in heaven.

"Mrs. Mayfield?" Megan's voice from below. "Are you sure you're okay here alone?"

"It's Lena, child. And you just scoot."

"We'll go sailing tomorrow. How's that?"

"Sounds pretty. Now git."

She heard the front door slam. Lena crossed to her window

and saw Megan, a bundle of linens flung over her shoulder, starting down the hill. The bundle was bigger than she was. But suddenly Megan slowed in the middle of the street. She looked around. She seemed puzzled by something, cocked her head like a dog. Lena saw no one else. After a moment, she looked up at the window and waved. That must have been it, thought Lena. Megan must have felt a pair of eyes on her. But now, satisfied, she hitched up her bundle and went on.

A sail might be nice, thought Lena. She'd never been on a real sailboat. Been on a cruise ship though. Cruised to Nassau with her husband the year before he died. Right now, though, the only water she's interested in is what she's going to soak in once she figures out how to get that Jacuzzi swirling.

Candlelight and wine, she thought. And a big bubbly tub. The only thing missing is a man. And isn't it just her luck that the only black man her age on this whole island is laid up over in that hospital.

Megan says it's not true he's the only one. She says Myra knows a bunch more. One runs the hardware store in Tisbury—he's a bachelor—and another is a retired State Trooper—he's a widower. She says Myra's already offered to fix her up with either one.

But this Moon sounds more interesting, mostly because when Megan talks about him she gets all smiley and girly. She says he's sweet and kind. She says he's loyal and true. Lena teased her some about that.

"You got your cap set for him, white girl?"

"I could do worse."

"Old buck like him? What's he got over Michael?"

She thought for a second. She said, "Michael makes me feel good. Moon makes me feel safe."

She wasn't done yet either. She went through about six more adjectives, all with her head cocked the way she does, as if someone's calling them in to her from another part of the house. Like "strong." Like "rugged." Like hands that could crush a full beer can. She didn't mention a thick head of hair but she said he's "sort of rich" which made up for that failing real nicely.

Lena noticed Michael's big brass telescope, the one Myra gave him. It was propped up in a corner doing no earthly good. Michael hadn't had a chance to try it out. Maybe the bath would keep. Maybe she'd set it up in that window and watch the other rich folks cavort on their yachts.

Lena set up the tripod.

It was mostly dark out now. Lena tried the telescope first on a lighted window across the street. She could see a bedside table with books underneath and, turning the eyepiece, she could read the titles on the books clear as day. But she didn't feel right snooping on a bedroom. Lena turned it to the harbor.

She focused in on a big motor yacht that had a living room in the back. A real, regular living room with a rug and couches and a TV. It seemed to her that a boat should be a boat and not a floating apartment but the man had paid his money and she supposed he had a right. A steward in a white coat was serving drinks. She couldn't quite see who to because a tree across the street blocked that part of the view. A blurry shadow moved. The shadow seemed to be within that tree.

She adjusted the eyepiece. Sure enough, she realized, someone had climbed it. The shadow was sharper but it was still a shadow. The man—or a boy maybe—had no features at all. And something was covering his face. A cat burglar? She didn't think so. No house could be reached from the limbs of that tree. A peeping Tom? Maybe. But from where he sat, there didn't seem much to peep at except this house over here.

Lena stepped around the telescope and peeked through the edge of the drapes. She glanced up and down the street. She was hoping, she supposed, to see a policeman but there was only a man riding up on a bike. A tall skinny man in a black hooded slicker.

She looked back at the tree and noticed, for the first time, still another man standing at its base. He was in deep shadow. The man on the bike slowed. Now *he's* looking up at this house. He stopped and stood straddling his bike.

What is it, she wondered that's so interesting about this house? But now his head snapped back toward that tree like he heard a noise. The man at the base of the tree was moving. He was tugging at his trouser leg as if it got caught in some brambles. Now he sees the man on the bike watching him. The man on the bike's getting off. He put down his kickstand; he's walking over. Man by the tree tries to wave him off. He jerks his thumb as if to say, "Keep moving."

Skinny man is pointing back over his shoulder, pointing at this house, acts like he's asking a question. Tree man tries again to get rid of him. Skinny man's in no hurry. He looks like he wants to chat and the subject, from his gestures, is this here Taylor House. This goes on for a while. Finally, the tree man moves out of the shadows.

He's dressed in a jogging suit and a white floppy hat. He steps forward, looks back down the street, then up, then down again. Lena could only see part of his face. He's got one hand on the bike man's shoulder. Bike man's trying to show him what looks like a business card. Tree man takes it, crumples it, throws it away.

He raised his free hand like you do to say, "Wait," but he's looking down toward the waterfront. He waves that hand slow-like to say, "Not yet . . . not yet" and the skinny man's wondering what he's doing. But suddenly, the hand came down. It came down sharply like when you say, "Now."

That other shadow dropped down from the tree. The peeping Tom darted straight out. He's wearing all black and has a cloth wrapped around his face. They both grab the bike man, they drag him toward the tree. Now there's just one big tossing shadow back by the trunk of that tree. It goes kind of stiff. The tossing stops.

Lena knew that she'd just watched a mugging. She was about to back away, get to the phone and call 911, when the tree man came back out for that bike. He had lost his hat in the tussle.

Something about that man. Something familiar.

He reached to grab the bike but he was watching down the street. He bumped it, knocked it over. It fell with a crash. Lena tried to open the window. It was stuck. She yelled, "Hey" through the glass as loud as she could. He heard her. He looked up and around, wondering where it came from. Lena got her first good look at his face.

"Wha . . . well, I'll be damned," she sputtered. "I know that little worm."

*   *   *

The bus from Oak Bluffs let Moon off on Kelly Street, a short block from Edgartown's waterfront. He made his way to the main landing, a long gray concrete structure with an observation deck on top. It offered clear views of the entire waterfront area and of the harbor beyond. The three-block length of Dock Street was brightly lit, every shop was open and busy, the side streets were thick with strolling tourists.

One of them, Moon knew, just might be a man named Parker. And here he was without a weapon. He had considered asking Michael to leave his gun where he could find it but that would have been foolish. It would have been the same as telling him that he wasn't going to stay in that hospital. Michael would have gone straight to that doctor and, next thing Moon knew, a nurse would have been pumping his butt full of sedatives.

He climbed the stairs to the promenade level where several coin-operated viewers were mounted on swivels. He fed a dime into one of them and scanned the harbor area. He found Megan's boat where she told him it would be. It was one of perhaps two dozen pleasure boats tied up at slips. Some were dark, their owners ashore. Others were aswarm with partying sailors.

He saw Megan through the viewer. She was rigging a blue canopy over the cockpit and she seemed to be alone on her boat. Just beyond those slips and a few yards inland was a white wooden building. The signs on it offered facilities for boaters. Toilets, showers, and such. There was a laundry and a chandlery, and two public phones on the outside wall. Young girls, dressed for the evening, were talking on both of them. He saw a man there, pacing, glancing at his watch as if impatient to use one of the phones. Moon swung the viewer back to Megan's boat.

He was disappointed not to see Michael. Michael, he thought, should be long since back from the airport by now. Likely he's sitting on a roadside somewhere getting an earful from Johnny and Doyle. Things they didn't want to say in front of Megan.

Still, Moon had been hoping they'd come straight to that boat. Michael would be safest there. No one would look for him on a boat. They would look for him, wait for him, up at the Taylor House. Moon, meanwhile, could watch him from here.

The viewer clicked off. Moon fed it another coin. He swung it toward Dock Street and began scanning the crowds of tourists, looking for anyone who doesn't quite fit.

Moon realized that this could be a waste of time. Doyle might or might not have told Aaronson where Michael is. If he did, Parker might or might not have gotten it out of him. The assumption, however, has to be that Parker knows. That he'd track him to the Taylor House. If so, Moon felt sure, Parker would be coming himself. Not alone, but he'd come. After three blown attempts at Michael, this time he'd want to make sure.

The trouble was that Moon had never seen Parker or heard him described. Even Parker's age was just a guess. All Moon knew was that Parker, if he's here, would check the Taylor House first. Finding that Michael's not there, he might wait outside but more likely he'll start looking through the town. He'll be peering at faces just like this, looking through restaurant windows, keeping an eye out for Michael's car. That's how Moon hoped to spot him.

Moon did not know what he looked like but he knew enough about him to pick out likely candidates. Parker, and anyone he brought, would not show up here in pin-striped suits and fedoras. They would know to blend in but they can't keep themselves from looking watchful.

They'll be armed. That would rule out anyone in shorts and a T-shirt unless he's carrying a shopping bag. They won't be with women, or with kids, or college age or getting drunk. So far, that ruled out just about everyone.

Cab drivers, thought Moon.

Parker likes to use cabs and that might be smart. Parker could keep cruising around with his shooters, they'd look like passengers. The thing was, he'd have to steal one of those island minivans, do so in a way that the theft would not be reported too soon—like killing the driver—and then later he'd have to get away with it. But get away where? How, Moon wondered, do you make a hit on an island where one phone call from the police would stop the ferries from running?

Damn, he thought. They'll come by boat is how.

They'll come in, hit fast, and get back out before the harbor gets too quiet.

Another thought stabbed at Moon. If Michael's not here, and

he's back from the airport, they might have gone to that house after all.

Moon swung the viewer in that direction. It was useless. Too many big trees in the way. But he could be up there inside a minute. Steeling himself to walk, not run, Moon turned back to the stairs.

Parker saw the middle-aged black man crossing Dock Street at an angle, taking long measured strides toward North Water Street. He reached for the pay phone but stopped.

He could not ring Hector's cellular, giving his position away, every time he saw a spade who might be Moon. Hector would call if that one, or anyone, goes into the Taylor House.

Moon, if Parker had to guess, was probably in New York hanging around the Pierre. Or maybe he got Hobbs by now. If he's here, however, it would be lovely to catch Moon and Fallon together. Two Polaroids. A million each. He'd pour gasoline over Moon. Light him and let him run through the Taylor House, setting the whole place on fire. That would be a nice touch. Rast would probably—

Parker saw the black Mercedes creeping down through the crowd. It did not have New York plates but that could still be Fallon's car. He's a resident here now. He'd have Massachusetts plates. Parker couldn't see the driver clearly but he could very well be Fallon. One . . . no . . . two other heads in there with him. It's Fallon all right, with his guests from the airport. But the car wasn't turning. It was heading this way.

Oh . . .

Oh, God damn them.

The low moan that started in Parker's chest came when the Mercedes stopped at the dock. His first thought was that they'd made him. There they were, it was definitely Fallon, and his headlights are aimed straight at Childress's boat. Somehow Fallon knows. And there's Yahya, totally oblivious, his head still down between his knees.

Parker froze. His instinct was to wait, let Fallon make his move, then come in behind him, put a bullet through his ear. Then he could pop a few caps at the crowd, get them yelling and screaming, get away in the confusion.

He sucked in a breath because now, climbing out the other side, was a small man with wavy red hair. From the photographs he'd seen, it could only be Doyle. He left his wife to fly up here? What for? Doyle's no shooter and he's damned sure not here to serve papers. The third man in the car must be their muscle, maybe even a cop.

Parker realized that he couldn't get them all. He needed a plan that had some chance of working. His brain was so busy groping for options, try to sort smart from stupid, he almost didn't notice that the girl on that sailboat was waving a greeting at Fallon.

Parker forced himself to breathe slowly. The girl, the young blond he'd admired, is being introduced to Doyle. She's reaching down to shake his hand . . . no, to help him climb on board. But suddenly she freezes. She lets go of his hand and backs away from him as if she just found out he has AIDS.

Doyle doesn't want to board anyway. He's gesturing back toward the car where the third man, the muscle, is out and has popped the trunk. Parker couldn't see him yet. But now Doyle is pointing this way. Right at me, thought Parker. He's turning and walking right at me.

Parker had nowhere to hide. He could only wait. He watched as the girl hopped down from the boat and put both her hands against Fallon's chest. Her expression is . . . he didn't know . . . sympathetic? How're you doing? I missed you? Whatever it was, it was not, "Glad you're back. Let's start blasting the fuckers in the boat behind mine." Maybe they don't know after all.

Parker lit a cigarette. It's good for looking casual. Doyle glanced toward the glow of his lighter but no more than that. No hesitation, no recognition, no interest. He seemed to be heading toward one of the phones. Parker fished for a quarter. He would take one of the phones, fake a call of his own, listen to whatever Doyle was saying.

Dropping his coin, he punched out a random set of numbers and listened to a recording say his call could not be completed as dialed. By that time the lawyer had dialed as well. Parker turned his back to the phone so that his free ear was on Doyle and his eyes could be on Fallon.

It was then he saw Johnny G. He could barely believe it but there he was. Parker knew that he'd been had.

* * *

On the sidewalk, just across from Michael's inn, Moon saw what looked like a domestic dispute. A big woman, dressed in robe and slippers, had a smaller man by the hair and was whaling on him, cussing him, trying to kick him. The man broke away but tripped over a bike. She got him again.

Moon slowed to a crawl, unwilling to get caught up in this. But the woman, he realized, was black. The smaller man was not. They seemed an unlikely couple. A prowler, maybe? She caught him looking through her window?

The man tried to kick her and got wrenched off his feet. Now he's yelling for help. And help must be coming, thought Moon, because she suddenly let out a yip and swung to face whatever else was moving in on her. The violence of her move tore the little man free and sent him toppling over a fence into someone's front garden. The man hollered in pain. Branches were sticking to his back and shoulders. He must have landed in thorns.

Moon saw no one else at first. Then he saw the shadow. The shadow stepped out, almost to the sidewalk, and did a nervous little dance between her and the man she'd just flung to the brambles. He wasn't so sure how to handle her either. Moon saw that his face was masked by a scarf. Round his waist he wore some sort of tool belt. Moon's thought was that they might be burglars working the Water Street inns.

But burglars don't like to go armed because it's twice as much time if they're caught. This one was armed. He was pulling a knife from that tool belt. Knife, hell. He was pulling a short Jap sword.

Moon wanted to shout, try to scare him off. But just then the woman reached down for that bike. She lifted it by the handle bars and seat and commenced to swing it at the man all in black. The man dodged her, tried to slash at her, but he couldn't reach past the wheels.

Crouched low, Moon broke into a silent run.

Parker said, "Take the call, Mom. I'll hold."

He said this into his own dead phone and tried to look bored as Doyle, not a foot away, punched out a credit card number. But a cold, calm fury had enveloped him.

Those lying wop bastards had suckered him. Yeah, well, let them enjoy the moment because tonight, one way or the other, Fat Julie's little brother is going to die.

With that thought, he glanced back at the Mercedes, half expecting to see Julie climbing out of it as well. Half wishing that he would. But it's better this way. This way he'd have the satisfaction of calling him tomorrow or the next day, saying, "Yeah, fuckface, it was me killed your little brother. Next I'm coming after your kids."

Not that he'd bother to make good the threat. He'd be in his new life. But that dago would never have another day's peace.

Parker listened as Doyle called his wife. "You're okay? . . . We're okay, we're with Michael now . . . No . . . No, Moon's still in the hospital here, we'll go see him in the morning . . . Yeah, he's fine. Michael says he's out of danger."

Hospital? Here? Parker had no idea what that was about but the words "out of danger" means it must have been serious. Maybe he got burned trying to touch another house, maybe another stroke. Either way, though, he's out of the picture. That's too bad in one way. This could have been a sweep.

Doyle finished with his wife. He made a second call to someone named Eddie and said, "I'm glad I caught you. Look, I need a sheet on someone."

He said the name "Megan Cole" and spelled it. He looked back toward her as he spoke. "Middle to late twenties, lives on a boat in Woods Hole, Mass. Here's the registration number."

Parker saw that he was reading a set of numbers and letters off the front end of her boat. All the boats had them.

"Start with the Coast Guard," Doyle was saying, "see if the boat's in that name. I want credit history, priors, if any, and she's had some press so check that, too. Oh, and she's supposed to have worked with the Massachusetts State Police . . . never mind how . . . see what they say. Also check with—"

He stopped short, gave a tired nod. Eddie must have said, "Brendan, don't tell me my job."

Eddie, Parker realized, must be a skip-tracer. All lawyers use them.

Why the girl was so important, why Doyle didn't seem to trust her, Parker didn't know. All he cared about at the moment was that she had this boat, they were all going to meet on it, and they had no clue that he was parked just behind it.

But just now, for a second or two, he almost thought the girl had spotted him. She had climbed up into the cockpit, handed two beers to Fallon who is huddled with Johnny G., who is flipping through the pages of that notebook he carries.

Johnny G. stopped reading when he saw her approach. He covered the notebook with his hand. Parker took that to mean that the girl is not in this. She turned and started back down the hatch but suddenly she stopped. She seemed confused. Now her eyes were darting all over the waterfront as if she hears someone calling her but can't place the source. Now she's looking up at these phones. She seemed to be looking right at him.

But no. Who she's looking at is Doyle. Looking daggers at him. She must have somehow figured why he's up here making calls. She brings both hands to her face, gives what looks like a sigh. Fallon's asking her what's wrong. She shakes her head, waves him off, climbs back down below.

Good, thought Parker. One less pair of eyes. Now if those two would just go down after her, he could take Doyle right here. March him into the shower room, leave him dead in one of the stalls, leave the water running on him so no one would look in. Then call Hector and Tami, get them down here, finish this and go.

Doyle hung up his phone. He started back, but stopped and turned toward a door marked *Men*. A toilet stall would do. Parker was about to follow when a couple of college kids walked in after Doyle. Parker waited, lit another cigarette, and an inspiration struck him.

Fire. Fire was the way to do it. We burn them, boat and all.

He tapped out the number of Hector's cellular.

Come on, schmuck. Answer.

We have two extra gas cans on board. We have empties of Snapple Iced Tea, thin glass, good for Molotov cocktails. Nothing panics a crowd like explosions and fire. Lots of running and screaming and yelling. Hey, Baron? What do you think? Is this worth a bonus or not?

Hector's not picking up. Or he's shut off the ring.

Parker broke the connection. He'll go pour the gas himself,

have it ready. Let Doyle take his piss and go back. It's no good to kill him and have Fallon come looking for him before they have a chance to set this up.

Okay, thought Parker, let's think this out.

Fire is noisy. People scream and run. If we have to use guns that will cover the sound. But no automatic weapons, no blasting away with 9 millimeters. We use strictly the .22s. Against all that racket they'll sound like Rice Krispies.

Tami will toss the bombs. He can light them in the parking lot and throw them from there. One into the cockpit, then one down the hatch, and a couple more into the crowd. He, Parker, will wait on the dock to pop anyone who makes it off.

Parker nodded, satisfied.

You guys like fires? You like burning houses? I'll show you a fucking fire.

He flicked his butt and started back down toward the dock.

Dear lord, here's another one, thought Lena Mayfield.

A black man, loping up the street. She raised the bike high, still fending off the shadow man, but ready to swing it when the black man got in range. The subway man was back on his feet but he was thrashing around in that garden as if he dropped something in the bushes. He found it. Looks like a ditty bag on a belt. Oh, my, thought Lena. He's pulling a gun out. The gun got stuck on the zipper. He tugged at it, cussing. Just then a beeper in his belt went off.

The black man heard it, saw the gun. He veered in just a hair, snatched at that gun, ditty bag and all. The subway man never saw him coming. But he saw that gun leave his hands, float up, then smash back down across his nose. Now he's falling back into that bush and the black man hardly broke his stride. He's no friend to these two, she realized.

"Throw it," he said. "Throw the bike."

Lena hesitated. She knew he meant throw it at the shadow man, that he meant to go in behind it, but the bike was her only protection. Too late now. Shadow man backed away, shifted his knife to his other hand, and whizzed something shiny at the black man. The black man tried to spin from it but it caught him high on the shoulder. It stuck there. The black man pulled it free, tossed it away, kept coming. Lena saw what it was when it bounced. It was one of those throwing stars from kung fu movies.

The beeper in the bush was still beeping.

Shadow man is dancing now, flicking his knife. He's making squealy Chinese noises like from those same movies. Black man slows and stops. He doesn't look afraid. It's more like he's thinking this over. He has that gun, still mostly in the ditty bag, but he doesn't seem to want to use it. Shadow man tries two of those karate kicks, the ones where you spin, but all the black man did was sort of turn his cheek and they missed.

It was then that Lena saw the plastic bracelet on his wrist, the kind they give hospital patients.

"You'd be Moon," she blurted.

He glanced at her, startled. Shadow man froze where he stood.

Lena knew, full well, that this was no time to visit. But with nobody moving for a second just now, she might as well say who's who.

"I'm Lena. Friend of Michael's. Man you just hit? He's the one, last winter, tried to push Michael in the path of a—"

That's all she got out because shadow man's eyes, peering out from that cloth, had gone real wide and crazy. He backed up two steps, reached to his belt, and pulled out one of those sticks-on-a-chain things. He shook the sticks loose, whirled them over his head, and yelled, "Ay-yee-yah." Must be Chinese for "Charge" because, yelling it, he launched himself through the air, feet-first, at the face of the black man called Moon.

Lena had always wondered about kung fu and the like. It seemed to depend an awful lot on the other man standing still. She did not dwell on that now, however, because she had launched her own body into a grunting hammer-throw pivot and hurled the bike into shadow man's flight path.

The bike caught him flush between the legs. Worse, the gear assembly did. He gave a yip only dogs could hear, did a full mid-air flip, and came down on his head with a splat. The bike flipped with him like it was welded to him. Moon was on him before he could bounce. He snatched those sticks and wrapped the chain around his throat. He crossed the two sticks, using one as a lever, and was about to snap his neck when Lena gasped aloud.

Moon hesitated. He glanced up the street. A block distant, he saw people on foot and they were watching, afraid to approach. Down the street, just behind him, he heard the sound of feet on pavement. The man from the bush was running away, stumbling blindly, both hands to the nose Moon had smashed. Moon cursed himself. He gestured toward the Taylor House.

"Are there any more inside?" he asked quietly.

"House is empty. Just these. Man who came on this bike, they left him over by that tree."

Moon eased his grip on the sticks. Lena saw that it didn't matter. Shadow man's eyes were rolled up in his head. His last breath on earth came bubbling up from his chest. Moon picked up the ditty, tore the gun free, and walked quickly to the lump at the base of the tree. She watched as he felt the man's throat. There was no life there either. He looked up at her.

"Lena? Where might Michael be?"

For the first time, she noticed the blood. It had spread down Moon's shirt and was starting to soak through his jacket where the star had hit him. There seemed far too much for a simple puncture.

"That thing stuck you good, Moon."

"Lena . . . where is he?"

She gripped his lapel. "First we'll see to that cut."

He was gone a minute later, slipping down through backyards. "Megan's sailboat, by now," is what she finally told him.

But at least she had packed his wound. The bleeding had slowed some. She made him promise he'd find Michael, get right back to that hospital, have it stitched up proper. She'd wanted to ask him what kind of a man carries gauze pads and tape in his pocket on the chance he runs into a ninja assassin on Martha's Vineyard. Even New York's not that crazy.

Lena's toe touched the business card that the subway man had crumpled. The card the bike man tried to give him. She picked it up, opened it, read it. It said, "Parnel Minter. Medium, Spiritualist, Ghost Hunter."

Poor man. He wouldn't have to hunt very far now. But what am I doing reading this damned thing?

Lena ran to the Taylor House. From the phone at the desk, she dialed 911.

44

Parker eased his way back to his boat.

He moved slowly, carefully, keeping his eyes on Johnny G. and Fallon, praying that they wouldn't glance up from that notebook. They didn't, not even when Doyle climbed back aboard. Fallon, however, had stopped listening. He seemed more concerned with the girl who'd gone below. Parker couldn't see why but he didn't care. Just as long as they all keep busy.

Parker's immediate problem was Yahya. If the Giordano brothers had set him up, then Yahya must be a plant. But did Yahya know Johnny was here? Not twenty feet away? Parker didn't think so.

Yahya's chin was on his chest, he had fallen asleep. He had never so much as looked up at the people in the boat next to theirs. Parker intended to keep it that way.

He stepped onto the boat, shook Yahya awake, and pulled him into the small forward cabin. He put him to work filling empties of Snapple with gas.

Yahya was spilling as much as he poured but at least he was getting it done and he was down where he couldn't see out. Parker laid low as well. He grabbed a hat and a pair of sunglasses, put them on. He would sit here, tearing towels into strips, and wait for Hector and Tami. When they got here, same plan, minus Yahya. Tami's first job will be to cut Yahya's throat.

Suddenly he saw Hector coming.

Hector had rounded the corner running. He had both hands to his face, there was blood on his jacket, and he was dragging a twig from one sneaker. There was no sign of Tami. Heads were already turning, looking at him. Parker had to take the chance. He stood up in the boat, waved his arms at Hector, made a palms-down gesture that said, "Get down. Down. Now go slow."

Hector saw him. He understood. He crouched and pretended to be tying his laces. For the tourists who were near him, this made him stand out even more because his nose, Parker saw, was all over his face. But at least he could no longer be seen from the sailboat.

Parker spread his hands as in "What's wrong? What happened?"

Hector's hands flew helplessly. He pointed up the hill. He drew a hand across his throat to say that someone's dead up there. Then he jabbed his finger at the sky.

Parker groaned inwardly. We're playing fucking charades here. Worse, Hector's crouching there all bloody, about six people staring at him, and his clues are telling every one of them that there's probably just been a murder.

New clue. Eyes. He's holding his fingers to his eyes . . . pushing up at the corners . . . slant eyes? . . . you mean Tami? . . . Tami what? . . . and now the throat again . . . no, not cut . . . new clue . . . twisted . . . Someone twisted Tami's neck? . . . Who? . . . the sky? . . . something round in the sky? . . . flying saucers? . . . aliens? . . . Hector, what the fuck are you talking about?

The Mexican, desperate, stood up like a signpost and pointed one arm at the eastern sky.

The moon. At last Parker got it. The moon is what's round.

"Megan? . . ."

Michael had stepped away from Johnny G. and leaned into the hatch. For some minutes now, he had seen that she was acting strangely. It began, he thought, after Doyle went ashore to make his call. More so since he returned. She was pacing the walkway from cabin to galley, hugging herself, her eyes glazed and distant.

"Megan . . . sweetheart . . ."

Her eyes flashed at him. Or rather, it seemed, at his use of an endearment. She turned away. He stepped through the hatch and began to climb down. She raised one hand. The gesture and the look said, "Don't! Don't come near me."

Now, what?

"Look . . . I'm sorry," he told her. "I haven't been very attentive, but . . ."

"Get off my boat. All of you."

A silent groan. Just once in his life, when a woman gets . . . this way, he would like to have some idea of why and some clue as to how he should deal with it. Johnny G. heard her as well. He tried to help.

"This is my fault," he said over Michael's shoulder. "We had no right laying all this on you."

She didn't answer. She gave no sign that she heard. She was moving about the cabin, touching things again, the way she did that first night at the Taylor House. Her head kept twitching, this way and that, as if voices were calling from five different directions.

Johnny G. tried again. "Megan . . . Miss Cole . . . suppose Doyle and I take a walk, maybe get some dinner. That would give you two some time alone."

Her eyes met his and, for only a moment, she was herself again. The look seemed to say, "It's not you but thank you." She dropped her eyes. They fell on his overnight bag. "You'll need this," she told him. She passed it up through the hatch.

Next, she found Doyle's thick briefcase. She reached for it, but hesitated, as if reluctant to touch it. But she did. She passed it up as well.

Michael took it, frowning darkly. He ran his hands over the leather as if trying to feel what had made her react to it.

"It's Doyle?" he asked her. "Megan, what has he done?"

"Go, Michael. Just go."

Johnny G. touched Fallon's shoulder. "Let's give her a break," he said gently. "You can come see her later."

"Megan? Will you be here?"

She lowered her eyes, then nodded. He knew that she was lying.

Johnny tugged at him. "Let's go," he said.

*   *   *

Megan closed the hatch and locked it.

She turned, slowly, and lingered for a moment in the galley. She reached to touch a bottle of Chablis, now almost empty, whose contents she had shared with Michael. She moved on through the main cabin, running her fingers along the bed they had shared.

It had a set of drawers underneath. She opened one of them. Her eyes fell, sadly, on the birthday-wrapped package that she'd rushed out to buy while he was at the airport. It was only a sweater. But it would have looked good on him. It was a knit of Irish wool and part of the label was in Gaelic. He liked Irish things. She moved the package aside.

Beneath it, she found the Colt Python that she had taken from his bedside table. She picked it up, brought it to her lips. The gun was silent now. All the same, she would have waited before giving it back to Michael. She would have done it the next time they went out sailing. She would have asked him to drop it over the side.

She thought of the man named Hobbs. He had not killed his "*whole* self"—as Moon had put it—he killed "just the part where his fear was." For Hobbs, a gun had brought relief.

Megan knew that she would soon lose Michael. She had thought that she'd be able to deal with it. But here, already, she was falling apart. Hearing voices. Seeing flashes of visions. Seeing that lawyer, her file in his hands, reading aloud to a stunned and sickened Michael.

And she was seeing fires again. People screaming and running this time. People dying. She was hearing, all around her, other men who want to kill her, kill Michael, kill everyone. Even Moon. And Moon's not even here.

Even Parnel. That's how crazy she was getting. When the voices tell her that they've come to kill poor, simple, Parnel Minter, who is probably down at the A&P right now, munching grapes from Helen's produce section, it's time to try to make them shut up.

Her lips closed over the Python's muzzle.

Was there one single part of the brain, she wondered, where

the visions came from and where the voices lived? That's where she would aim if she knew.

But she won't shoot herself.

Not here. Not yet.

She'll do it the way she had meant to once before. Far out at sea. Nothing but horizon in either direction. She'll turn into the wind, sit out over the railing, and do it that way. No note, no blood on the deck, no sign that it was anything more than a sailor who went out alone and got knocked in the head by the boom.

This time, she wouldn't let some dolphin talk her out of it.

"Oh, Christ," muttered Parker.

He saw, through the wheelhouse window, that all three of them were leaving the boat. They were carrying their bags. Just once, before this day is out, he would like to have one thing go right.

But the girl, he realized, had stayed on board. Could be they're just stashing their bags in the car. He heard police sirens off in the distance. The way to bet, he thought, is they're heading for Tami.

Hector was still calming down, he's trying to straighten his nose, but he should still be able to drive this thing. Parker nudged him.

"Time to haul ass," he said quietly. "You're clear on what to do?"

Hector wet his lips. "Maybe you're wrong about Yahya."

Parker hissed. "Hector . . . we've been set up. How much clearer can it be?"

"But Yahya . . . look at him . . . does he look as if he's had instructions? All he cares about now is to stop being sick."

"Hector . . . when the noise starts, kill him."

Parker pulled out his lighter, made sure it still flicked. He handed it to Hector. At his feet was a bucket containing six bottles, each primed with a three-inch wick. He felt for the pistols he wore at his waist. Both safeties were off. He pulled the brim of his hat down over his eyes.

"Start counting," he told Hector. "At ten, you start the stampede. At sixty, we're heading home rich."

Parker stepped onto the dock.

*   *   *

"Brendan . . ." Fallon stopped at the trunk of his car. He looked up toward the bank of public phones. "Who did you call from up there?"

A shrug. "I told you. I checked with Sheila."

"You're sure?"

"As opposed to some tootsie? Michael . . . give me the key." He took it and opened the trunk.

"Did you say anything to her about Megan?"

"Will you stop? No. Sheila doesn't know she exists."

Johnny G. understood what Michael was asking. Something had set Megan off. One minute she's hospitable, the next she's throwing them out and she treats Doyle's briefcase like it's been laying in shit. His thought at the time was that she must have gone through it, found something she didn't like. Michael's thought was a little more weird but a hell of a lot more interesting.

"Brendan," said Johnny. "I saw you make two calls." It's a lie, but let's see.

No reaction from Doyle.

But no indignation reflex either. Johnny held up two fingers.

"The second was about Megan Cole. You asked for a make on her, didn't you."

Doyle looked away. "A good lawyer checks," he said lamely.

Michael turned red. He was, thought Johnny, about two seconds from liftoff and then would have wrung Doyle's neck. He had a right to be pissed but to Johnny this was missing the point. This girl *knew* that? She really *did*? When this is over, he thought, let's fly her to Vegas.

"Understand me, Brendan . . ." Michael spoke through his teeth, his voice like escaping steam. "Megan has told me all that she cares for me to know. When she's ready, she might give me more. If you learn one fucking fact more, I'm finished with you. If you . . ."

But Johnny was no longer listening. He was watching the strobe lights of two police cars picking their way through pedestrian traffic and now he turned toward the sound of a young girl's voice, off to his right, because he heard her say someone is bleeding.

He saw her now, up by the toilets. She was pointing and back-

ing away. He followed her finger to what looked like some drunk
who was staggering back down to his boat. It was Moon. Johnny
slapped Michael's arm and took off at a run.

Michael, confused, only watched him go. But he followed
Johnny G.'s line of sight until he, too, disbelieving, saw Moon.
Brushing Doyle aside, he pushed off in pursuit. A flickering flame
arched high overhead.

Michael saw it. It seemed, impossibly, to come from Megan's
boat. Still moving toward Moon, he followed its path through
the night sky. It came down on Dock Street, amid a cluster of
tourists. It exploded, spitting tongues of flame. The tourists
screamed and ran. A young woman's hair was on fire. She didn't
seem to know it. Two college boys chased her down, one beating
at her head with his jacket. A second bomb hit. It burst amid the
row of parked cars, missing but searing the Mercedes. Doyle ran
from it, covering his head.

Fallon was frozen. He turned his head, once again, to their
apparent source. Two more bursts came in quick succession. Megan's boat was ablaze. The blue cockpit cover became wisps of ash.
The main sail, furled on her boom, was melting. It was dripping
hot globules of dacron. Flames lapped at the main hatch, sucking
air from the cabin below.

He screamed Megan's name. Another voice, Johnny's or
Moon's, screamed his own. It said, "No, Michael. *Don't!*" He
heard gunshots over the screams. He ignored them all. His only
thought was of Megan.

"Hector, don't do this," a horrified Yahya had pleaded.

"Hold it steady," barked Hector.

He had moved the boat out, abeam of the sailboat, he told
Yahya to come hold the wheel. "This is only to help us get away
from here," he said.

Yahya watched, stricken, as the first two bottles soared high
overhead. He could only pray that they would land harmlessly,
that they would frighten, not burn. That Parker would jump back
on his boat and then they could all be gone.

"Fifteen," muttered Hector who was counting aloud. He lit two
more bottles and on "Eighteen" he threw them. But these were
not arched high over the sailboat. These were thrown like the

dunking of basketballs. They exploded in the boat not six feet away. Hector's hair was smoking from the heat they gave off. The force of the blast caused his nose to start bleeding again.

"Are you crazy?" cried Yahya.

So many screams. From all over. And now the crack of gunshots.

"I'll take the wheel," said Hector. "Get below."

Hector was lighting two more. But these he set down on the deck. He left them sitting as if they were lamps.

"I said get below," Hector told him. "You need to hide."

Yahya looked into his eyes. He saw, in an instant, what was now in the Mexican's heart. He saw Hector lean down and reach into a camera bag. That bag contained nothing but pistols. Hector knew that he knew. "I'm sorry to do this," said Hector.

A gun in one hand, Hector came forward. He reached out with the other to pull Yahya away from the wheel. Yahya wanted to scream, to demand to know why, but fear had taken his voice. He could only grip the throttle with all his strength so that Hector could not yet shoot him. Hector saw this. He moved to strike at Yahya's gripping hand. Yahya tried to kick him but he missed and he fell. The throttle came with him, back and down. The boat underneath them roared. It bucked and then charged in reverse. Hector went tumbling. The bottles came tumbling. Behind them was a row of small launches. This boat was going to smash into them.

Yahya let out a yelp. He threw himself over the side.

Parker heard the grinding crash. It came from down near the ferry.

He turned to see a fireball rising and at least two more followed as other fuel tanks ruptured. He saw what must have been a man, totally ablaze, staggering through the flames of one burning hulk.

Panic everywhere in sight. Sailors shouting, trying to cut their lines. Good man, Hector. Too bad I have to kill you once we're clear of this island.

He could no longer see Childress's boat but it's now forty seconds. It should be heading toward that big concrete landing by now.

His own luck was holding but not as he'd hoped. Giordano was down, not moving. Parker had snapped off three shots when he saw him running to the jig. At least one had hit him, hit him square. The jig is definitely Moon. He has a gun out, is creeping toward Giordano, carefully, because he still doesn't know where the shots came from. Too much going on all at once.

And now a woman, another jig, was coming down around the corner on a bicycle. The bike wobbled badly, the front wheel was bent. The woman, Parker realized, had to be the one who belted Hector. He says she was the one from the subway. God knows how she figures in this. She sees Moon. She's yelling his name. He tries to get up. She reaches him, drags him back down.

Parker *could* run over there. Yell out he's a cop. He could blow Moon away before he knows any different. But the real cops, goddamn it, were already here. There was one not fifty feet from Moon, his gun drawn but still in shock, trying to understand what was happening to his town. And there were fire engines coming. He could hear them wailing just a few blocks away.

Okay, he decided. Forget Moon. He looks like he's half dead already. Tami must have got a piece. Go take what you can get, which is Fallon.

Fallon was the only one who followed the script. When the boat flew, all three of them were supposed to run back to help. Parker would pop all three when they did. But the jig had shown up out of nowhere and the three of them split in three directions. No sign of the lawyer. He's probably looking for burn victims, handing them his fucking card. But Fallon's right on that boat, lit up like Christmas, trying to kick through the hatch.

Parker eased the .22 from his belt.

Say goodbye, Mr. Fallon.

Megan had crawled forward, away from the flames and smoke, into the V-bunks, and slammed the wooden bulkhead door behind her. She tried the forward hatch. The heat had warped it. It was stuck.

Her shower was forward as well. She turned it on, snatched up some of the bedding, began to wet it down. White smoke from burning teak, black smoke from melting fiberglass were pouring through the grating of the bulkhead door. She tried to pack it, keep it out, but she knew that she had only a minute or two. The smoke she'd inhaled had already made her dizzy. The door was hot to the touch.

Through it, she heard a furious pounding aft, the sound of splintering wood. She heard Michael's voice, he was screaming her name. She yelled, "Michael, get off. Get off!" The propane in the galley would go soon.

She saw no way out. The two forward portholes were far too small. Through them, port and starboard, she could see the glow of more fires. She had the big Colt Python. It was in her hands when her cockpit exploded into flame and when a second sheet of flame spread across her foredeck. That one, she knew, had made a bonfire of the sail bags she had stacked up there to make room for Michael's guests. The stack trapped noxious gases that now seeped down through melted seals.

She still heard Michael. She heard him kicking. But her main hatch was solid teak and she'd bolted it. He would need an axe to get through.

The gun was a comfort. She need not burn to death.

Parker had fired twice at Fallon. Hit, miss, he didn't know. But the din had made the gun almost silent. Get up close, he told himself. Make like you're coming to help. He'll recognize you, maybe, but not in time.

Parker approached from the bow end, out of Fallon's line of sight. He held the .22 close against his leg, his left hand on the butt of the nine in his belt. Good. Now get him to stand up.

He shouted to Michael, "Hey! Let me give you a ha—"

An explosion deafened him. Something stung at his face, cut into his arm. The .22 fell from his fingers, bounced, and tumbled off the edge of the dock. Now Fallon was leaping off the boat. Straight at him. Knocking him backward. Parker tugged at the nine but before he could raise it, two more quick explosions. Pieces flew off the side of the boat. He had to cover up his face.

If the gun was a comfort, it was also a tool.

Megan had snatched up a pillow, held it against the starboard porthole, and fired at its frame. If she could shoot out the frame, she just might squeeze through. The blast set the pillow on fire but a part of the frame and six inches of hull blew outward. Still not enough. She moved the pistol to the part still intact. She fired twice more.

Suddenly, she could see Michael's face. It was pocked and bleeding from shards of the frame. But he was helping her. He was tearing at the frame that still clung to the hull. He used his left hand. His right arm seemed to hang limp. Even the left hand was nearly useless because the jagged metal had torn at his fingers. With a desperate curse, he vanished to one side. She heard him on deck, and in seconds he was back again. He had gone for a coil of line. The line itself was smoldering.

He looped the coil on one end of the frame. She reached through to help him attach it. Above her, the forward hatch had melted through. Burning sail bags tumbled down. She kicked them away but now she was suffocating. Michael twisted the loop over one shoulder. He braced himself and heaved. The frame began to come free. She pushed at it from the inside, her face crowding the hole as she tried to find breathable air. Through the smoke pouring out, she saw the man. He wore a slouch hat, dark glasses. He was raising a pistol, aiming it at the back of Michael's head.

"Michael! Down!"

He ducked and wheeled. The man in the slouch hat fired. His bullet punched a hole in the hull near her face. A fragment struck her eye. She could no longer see.

And yet she *did* see. She knew that Michael had torn the coil of line free and was lashing the man who was trying to shoot him. She saw the burning coil strike at his hand, once, twice, a third time as the man tried to aim his gun again. Michael must have knocked it away because she heard the man snarl "Fuck!" and she knew that he was scrambling back to his feet. She knew that Michael was reaching for a weapon of his own but the right arm he tried with could not grip it.

The man almost smiled. He raised both his hands to show that they held nothing. He said, "Come on, tough guy. Let's dance."

Michael lunged, not at him, but at the porthole. He cried, "Push, Megan. Push!" She could not. She was groping blindly for the Python. She felt Michael gag and go rigid as the other man's fist slammed into his kidney. Still, he held on. The man kicked at Michael's knee.

"You like karate, tough guy? How was that for karate?"

Michael's whole body sagged. The frame sagged with him. It tore free. Michael fell. Megan heard him thump against the outside hull and she heard the splash as he slipped between hull and pilings.

The man said, "Shit!" as if with disgust. In her mind, she saw him looking around, eyes down, searching for his weapon. He found it. She saw him look up. Through his eyes, she saw Moon still struggling to rise but he could not. She saw Johnny Giordano, not moving. A man she did not know, dark skin, soaking wet, was kneeling at Johnny G.'s side. He was wringing his hands and wailing. He was tearing at his hair.

"Oh, for Christ's sake," the man muttered. He dropped to his knee, peered down through the pilings, and listened for sounds of splashing. He heard and saw Michael. He fit the muzzle of his gun between two planks.

Megan fired through the hull.

45

There are days, thought Parker, when you just can't win for losing.

He sat at the edge of the public landing, picking at one of the splinters that were lodged in his scalp. The girl had damned near killed him.

Little bitch.

She's stuck in a burning boat—the thing's melting all around her—so what's the first thing she should do? Get out, right?

She doesn't even try. She starts shooting. Everywhere he moves she starts blasting through the hull like she has fucking X-ray vision.

What's that Kenny Rogers song? You gotta know when to walk away, know when to run. The question was what to do now.

Whether the girl got out or not, he didn't wait around to see. Fallon drowned or he didn't. But Johnny G. and Moon, at least, were both probables. Moon might still be worth some money. The ambulance that took him didn't seem in much of a hurry.

Hector figured to be dead. If Yahya's alive, Hector must be toast. That first boat, the one that exploded, had to be theirs. So how does he get off this island?

Shouldn't be hard. The ferries are out of the question but there's about a thousand other boats to choose from. Some of these houses have their own docks. Pick one, knock on the door, say take me where I want to go and I won't kill your wife.

"Don't move a hair," said the voice.

Parker tried not to stiffen. His fingers crept toward the butt of the nine. He turned his head slightly. He saw an odd smallish shape in the shadows not ten feet behind him.

"Um . . . You talkin' to me, pal?"

"Hands where I can see them, asshole. Stand up. Back up slow."

"Hey, look. Long day. You want my wallet, take it. Here, I'll give you my watch." Parker held out his wrist. His other hand gripped the pistol.

A bullet slammed into his elbow. He could not believe, at first, that he'd been shot because he saw no muzzle flash. But he saw the blood, his arm was broken, and he knew he was as good as in prison. He had to go for it. He spun in a crouch and brought up the nine, searching for the shape behind him. It had moved. All he saw was the shoe coming up at his face.

"You can walk?" the voice asked.

Parker shook his head. He felt with his tongue where a row of teeth were missing.

"You can walk," the voice decided for him. "Just over to that car."

Parker could see him now. All but the face. What was odd about the shape was that he held a briefcase against his ribs. One arm was inside the briefcase, the other underneath it with a little charred hole in between. Gun's in the briefcase. That was why he never saw a flash or heard much of a noise. This guy wanted him alive. But he didn't want a crowd.

The voice moved closer, into the light. "I have to tell you again?"

Oh, Christ. It's the lawyer.

It's Brendan fucking Doyle.

46

Dr. Berman, the internist, had been called in from home.

So had every doctor on the island who was not then on duty. So had a vacationing cardiologist from New Jersey and a resident from a Boston trauma center who had hoped to get in some fishing.

Berman saw to Moon first. Moon's puncture wound had been cleaned and stitched and he'd been treated for shock. He was getting whole blood. He should have been responding. He was not. Berman suspected an embolism.

Moon was also under arrest; a police guard had been posted. The least of the charges was a weapons charge. There was also the matter of those two DOAs whom they found on North Water Street.

His friend, Lena Mayfield, had also been arrested. She assaulted the Edgartown policeman who had tried to hold up the ambulance so that he could read Moon his rights.

Berman found Michael in pre-op, barely recognized him. Most of his clothing had been cut away and he was strapped to a gurney. Both hands and one shoulder were packed with gauze, his burned and pocked face had been greased, much of his hair was gone. Michael begged him to find out about Megan. Megan

Cole. The girl who was in here last night. And Giordano. Find out about Johnny Giordano.

Berman made a call to the nurses station. He relayed the details as he heard them.

"Giordano's in surgery," he said. "Head wound. That's all she knows."

"Megan?"

"She's here."

Michael allowed himself to breathe.

"She was sutured in ER," said Berman. "Got a few lacerations when the fireman dragged her out of that boat . . . treated for smoke inhalation . . . right now she's down in ophthalmology. They say they're hopeful about the eye."

"What eye? What's wrong with her eye?"

Berman asked the nurse. "Bullet fragments," he told Michael.

Michael strained to get up. He asked Berman to unstrap him.

"You kidding?" Berman hung up the phone.

"I'm fine. This is just cuts and bruises."

Berman flipped his chart open. He snorted.

"You've got one bullet here." He touched Michael's shoulder. "It went in through the arm. Your shoulder is fractured. A second bullet entered here." He touched Michael's bicep. "It passed through. It's now down around your right kidney. You've got blood in your urine—make that urine in your blood—a possible ruptured spleen, and you'll probably need knee surgery. You've got first- and second-degree burns. Add to that a little sea water in your lungs but, hey, let's all go roller skating."

Michael couldn't believe it. The knee, maybe. And some blood from Parker's kidney punch. He'd been hurt worse than that playing sports. Hell, he'd been hurt worse than that by Moon. But he had no recollection at all of being shot.

"The good news," Berman told him, "is they're small caliber, copper jacket. Anything bigger, we wouldn't be having this chat."

Two orderlies came in. "Surgery. Right now," one said to Berman. The other covered Michael and turned the gurney toward the door.

"Wait. There was a man named Parker. Did they catch a man named Parker?"

Berman didn't know.

"And what happened to Doyle? Brendan Doyle, he's got wavy red hair."

Berman hadn't seen him. He told Michael he'd ask.

"Look, Doc . . . would you go see Megan? Tell her . . ."

Michael couldn't finish. Tell her what? That he tried?

"Mike . . . go get fixed," said Berman.

Fallon woke in the recovery room.

He felt at peace but he knew that it was only the narcotics. It bothered him that nothing bothered him. In another few hours, the drug would wear off. He knew that he would feel just as useless as he was. His eyes grew heavy.

When they opened again, it was early morning. He was in a four-bed ward. The three other beds were occupied. Burn victims. He had hoped that they'd put him with Moon.

The corridor outside seemed full of policemen. And men in dark suits. Some of them looked familiar. One looked in, then spoke to another. The other turned and walked away. Michael recognized Frankie Rizzo, who was Julie Giordano's driver. The man who left was named Emil, the maitre d' at Villardi's. Michael drifted off. He dreamed of Megan. She was holding his hand. She was saying it's okay. You did okay, Michael.

". . . you're gonna be okay."

That wasn't Megan. He opened one eye to see Julie Giordano at his bedside. It was Julie who was squeezing his hand.

"Johnny?" Michael had to wet his lips. "How's Johnny?"

"Not good. Say a prayer."

"His head?"

Julie touched his own to show where the bullet had struck his younger brother. It was above and behind the right ear. It had bounced off, said Julie. Thank God. But it had smashed in the side of his skull.

"It was Parker," said Michael.

"I know."

"Julie . . . I never even saw him. All I could think of was Megan in that . . ."

The gangster stopped Michael with a wave of his hand. He had tears in his eyes. Michael saw that he blamed no one but himself. He looked so very tired.

"You've been here all night?"

"Most of it. Got here before midnight. Hired a plane soon as Brendan called."

Fallon felt his own anger rising. "Where was Doyle? Where the hell was he when . . ."

"He did good. Don't start on Doyle."

"But if he hadn't . . ."

Julie leaned close. "He got Parker. Now I got Parker. But keep your mouth shut about that."

Michael listened, disbelieving, as Julie told him what Doyle had done. That his first thought was Johnny and Moon when he saw them both down . . . Moon's got a good chance, by the way . . . so Doyle jumped in the Mercedes, went to help them, haul them out of there, but Moon waved him off and said get to that boat, go help Michael. Doyle is Doyle, so he argues. Moon threatens to shoot him if he won't shut up and go.

"He left Johnny?"

"Johnny would have told him the same. But by this time," said Julie, "you're already down and the girl . . . she don't care if she burns as long as she can get one hit on Parker . . . she's in there blasting away at him. Parker sees the firemen coming, he's going to get shot or get caught. He throws in the towel. Doyle sees all this too. He figures the firemen don't need him, he'll only get in the way. So like I would, he goes after Parker. Like I would, he wants to kill him. But Doyle, unlike me, stops and uses his head. The guy you want to dump on took Parker alive."

"Where? Where's Parker now?"

"Trunk of your car. The airport by now. My guys, Doyle, and a guy you don't know, name's Yahya, they're taking him back to New York."

Michael reached for his sleeve. "I want him, Julie."

"You listening? We got him."

"I mean him and me. Alone in a room. As soon as I'm—"

"Hey, this isn't a fucking schoolyard, Mike. You don't get a rematch on this one."

He kept watching the doorway, expecting to see Megan. He kept seeing her in his mind, inside that burning boat, thinking only of him, trying to get Parker before Parker got him. The more he thought about that, as proud as he was of her, he was that much ashamed of himself. He'd done nothing. Worse, thanks to him, she was hurt, scarred, and homeless.

A woman from admitting came in after breakfast. Breakfast was a soft-boiled egg. A nurse had to feed him.

"Do you have an address for Miss Cole?" asked the woman.

"Her only address was her boat. Give her bill to me, if that's what you're asking."

"What I'm asking is where she might be. She was scheduled for some tests but she got dressed and walked out."

"When was this?"

"Around two in the morning."

"She's been gone all this time? She's out there alone?"

Two nurses had to restrain him.

Fat Julie came in one more time.

He brought a message from Moon. "Moon said behave. He said Lena Mayfield's coming down to make sure you do."

An indifferent shrug. Michael stared at his bandaged hands.

"Hey, what's with you?" Julie asked him. "You did your best. You can't stand it that you weren't a hero?"

"Julie . . . would you please look for Megan?"

"We'll find her. Moon already asked me."

"Thank you."

"You're welcome. Answer my question."

"I should have done more. I should have done better."

"Like Moon did for example?"

"Like he taught me to do."

"Except Moon didn't do shit. It was Moon's new lady who clocked Parker's Jap and hammered that guy from the subway. It was her who kept Moon from bleeding to death. You think it bothers Moon that a woman saved his ass?"

"Lena is Moon's new lady?"

"Get better, Michael. While you're at it, grow up."

More than a week went by. The three burn patients had been released. Michael had the ward to himself.

Jake's friend, Marty Hennessy, flew up to see him. The visit was official. He was looking for leads on where Parker might be. Michael said he didn't know, but Hennessy saw the truth in his eyes. He had already spoken to Julie. He'd seen it in Julie's eyes as well.

"I want him, Mike," he said. "But at least I want a body. Tell Giordano I at least want a body this time."

Hennessy left, said he'd look in on Moon and he'd look in on Johnny. On the day of his visit, the charge against Moon was dropped. Michael didn't know why until some flowers were delivered later that day. The card was signed "Marty." The note said, "You owe me."

Johnny G. remained in a coma, mostly. There were one or two times when he seemed to respond to voices but not to light and not to pain. His condition was all the more worrisome to Julie because Bart Hobbs had died in the meantime.

But Moon was released over the objections of Dr. Berman. An embolism, most likely a blood clot, had been pretty much confirmed. It could shut down an artery at any time. Lena took him home to the Taylor House. She told Michael she'd stay on until Moon makes up his mind.

"Makes up his mind about what?"

"Whether to be a damned fool and kill himself. Or whether he knows a good woman when he sees one."

They could not find Megan.

All Julie knew for sure was that she'd gone back to Woods Hole. She was seen, that day, on the six A.M. ferry. Bandaged eye, burned clothes, limping. No question it was her. That same morning, she tried to charter a sailboat. They saw she was a mess, wouldn't let her. No one saw her after that.

That was on Saturday. On the following Friday, a dentist from Falmouth came to Woods Hole to do some work on his boat. The boat was missing. Two days later, it was found, drifting, down off New London.

Michael's skin went cold. "What does the Coast Guard think happened?"

A hesitant shrug. "They asked . . . could she have iced herself."

"No way. Not Megan."

"They only asked because . . ." He groped for better words, finding none. "Is it true she's not right in the head?"

"Who the hell said that? Doyle?"

"Hey! Doyle's out breaking his ass trying to find her when he should be attending to business. We're not done settling up for Jake."

"Yeah." Michael let out a breath. "I know."

"You ready to look at what I got?"

"I'm ready."

Julie opened the briefcase he brought with him. Michael recognized it as Doyle's. A small charred hole had been punched through one end. From it, Julie drew out Johnny's notebook, the AdChem annual report, and a sheet with a list of names and numbers on it. This last was a transcription of Arnie Aaronson's list. The original had been in Michael's pocket when the ambulance brought him here.

"How'd you get that?" he asked.

"Like I said, someone had to attend to business."

He reached into the briefcase again and produced a pin-bound document of perhaps two hundred pages, double-spaced, on legal sheets with line numbers running down the right margin. Julie placed it on Michael's chest. Michael's left thumb was free of dressing. He used it to scan through the pages.

The document was another transcription. Of an interview . . . a deposition . . . an interrogation. Q's and A's ran down the left margin. Many of the questions were repeated several times. The language often seemed stilted, the syntax awkward. Many of the answers were halting, fragmented, agonized but, in time, all answers were always completed.

"This is Parker?" Michael asked.

Julie nodded. "Anyone doubts it, it's also on videotape."

"Who's this asking the questions? This isn't you."

"Guy named Yahya I mentioned. He's better at it."

The document was a blueprint of Rast's entire network. It listed every location where the counterfeits were produced and how they were distributed. It listed dozens of people, men and women who were on his payroll, and what services they had provided. Several were high-placed executives with rival firms.

Julie sat at his bedside while Michael read through the transcript. He read parts of it twice, in particular the section on Bronwyn Kelsey and what else she had done for them. On at least two occasions she had lived with other men who were suspected of cheating the Baron. Both men were soon murdered. Their deaths were made to look like street crimes. Michael had to pause, for a time, to clear his mind before he went on.

He knew, by the end, that he would never get his hands on Philip Parker. Four times, in the last ten pages, Parker had begged to die.

He closed the document.

"Marty Hennessy wants a body."

"I know."

"Will he get one?"

"He'll get the parts he needs."

Michael stared, for a while, at the photo in the AdChem brochure.

"We do this my way," he said to the gangster. "Not yours."

"Split the difference," said Julie. "We do it Johnny's way."

Fat Julie had brought Doyle's Priva-Fone with him. Julie handling the dialing. Fallon placed calls to each of the seven names on Arnie Aaronson's list. He spoke only to their secretaries. He left identical messages for each.

Five called him back within the hour. The sixth called him from an airplane en route to London. The seventh called from his vacation home on St. Croix. He read a prepared statement to each of the seven. Included were items from Johnny G.'s notebook and several from Parker's confession.

At its end, he asked that each of them meet with his respective chief executive. He would give them four hours. At the end of that time, he and the seven CEOs would meet by way of a conference call.

"Will they call you?" asked Julie Giordano.

"Sure."

"Their lawyers will let them?"

Michael nodded. "The lawyers will be listening. They'll need to know how much we have."

Fat Julie began pacing the ward. "Let me understand this," he said. "These guys are all crooks?"

"Not at all. Not the way you mean."

"How many ways are there?"

The answer Michael gave him was, he felt sure, essentially what Aaronson had told Doyle. They're trying to run companies. They're doing their best. They've all skirted the law, or built plants in countries where they could buy the law, because that's how you get done what you're in business to do. Illegal is not the same as wrong. It's certainly not the same as evil.

"Michael . . . are they all making counterfeit drugs or not?"

"Yes and no."

They're not, he explained. At least not willfully. But in many if not all of their plants, there is theft of ingredients, theft of finished product, and massive product overruns that never show up on the books. These men, these seven CEOs, know that it's happening in each of their firms. Not on the scale of AdChem, perhaps, but it happens. As Aaronson said, they try to contain it. They'll try to contain this as well.

Julie left him alone. If it's going to be a four-hour wait, he said, he'll go upstairs and sit with Johnny.

The conference call took place after lunch. It took twenty minutes to make all the connections. Most had a hollow sound. Michael knew that they had him on speaker phones, some of which had been set up in boardrooms.

"First I'll read a list of names," Michael told them. "They're on your payroll but they've also been on Rast's. If they're listening to this, you might want to ask them to leave."

He read the names. He heard gasps and denials and the shuffling of chairs. He heard "Out," "Just go," and "Go wait in my office." He thought he heard the sound of a face being slapped.

Michael did his best to put the remaining listeners at ease. He blamed none of them, he said, for what happened to Arnie. It would also save time if they would put thoughts of extortion out of their minds. He had no wish to go public. He wanted nothing for himself.

All he wanted was this. One way or the other, they would undertake to buy AdChem out. He didn't care who bought what

or how they would split it up. He didn't care whether they ran
it or shut it down as long as they put their own managers in
place within hours of AdChem agreeing to sell.

"Do you care what we offer?" asked one of the voices.

"Per share? The fifty-two-week high plus one dollar. Except
for the shorts, I want nobody burned."

"The family owns seventy percent," said another. "Who says
they'll sell?"

"They will. They'll want to be out of this."

"When we tell them what you're threatening to publish?"

"Uh-huh."

"That's illegal, Michael."

"That's why you have lawyers."

In fact, thought Michael, it's why most of these guys play golf.
More deals like this are made on golf courses . . . because they're
hard to bug . . . than in all the boardrooms put together.

"Michael . . . you're aware, are you not, that the FBI is already
interested in AdChem?"

"They don't have what I have."

"To say nothing," someone added, "of the SEC, the New York
police, and especially the FDA."

"That's why you know senators. Just get it done, gentlemen."

A long and hollow silence.

"But leave the FDA to me," Michael added.

Parker, in his tortured deposition, had named more than that
list of executives. He identified nearly a dozen men and women
who were in the employ of the Food and Drug Administration.
The few names he had given to Johnny—Turkel and a couple
more—were only AdChem's first cracks in the door. Those few
had recruited the others.

Michael would help the FDA clean house. It would be done
quietly. In return, he would ask for certain changes in policy, in
particular those that Johnny G. had found noxious. The agency
would agree to pose no obstacle to the dismantling of AdChem.
The current director would have to resign.

Johnny G. will have to be satisfied. This was not quite the
nuking he probably had in mind but in the long run it was better.
But let's hope, thought Michael, that it won't be Johnny's legacy.

*   *   *

"When these guys buy the stock," asked Julie Giordano, "it goes up, right? Not down."

"Up."

"So I lose my ass? That's my end in this?"

"You and Doyle both. Let that be a lesson, you prick. You were going to go into the business."

"That was . . . that was only a flight of fancy."

Fallon couldn't help smiling. "A flight of fancy? Fat Julie Giordano says he has flights of fancy?"

Julie reddened. "You want another kind of flight? I'll throw you out that fucking window."

"Ah . . . I might have another idea."

"I'm listening."

"Later. Let's get this rolling first."

"Mike . . . we haven't talked about Rast."

"You had Parker. Rast is mine."

"Except he's gone. He's back in Germany behind some moat."

"I know."

"So you'll do what? Fly over there with a Louisville Slugger?"

No answer.

"You thought about that, didn't you. You give me crap about flights of fancy and, meanwhile, you been laying there dreaming how you're gonna pound some old man into dog shit."

Michael had to look away.

"Forget it, Mike. It just isn't in you."

Another week passed. The bandages on his hands had been removed. Two-a-day sessions with a therapist were quickly restoring their function. The arm and shoulder were healing nicely. The bullet near his kidney had not been removed. The surgeon had decided it could wait. The knee might not need surgery after all. Dr. Berman found Michael in the day room. He told him that he could go home.

Myra Lovelace came with a change of clothing. A nurse helped Michael dress. His right arm was in a sling. He told Myra that he'd take a cab later. He wanted to go sit with Johnny for a while. He found Brendan Doyle already there. Doyle had come unannounced.

"He knows me," said Doyle, excited. "He knows who I am."

"You're sure? How can you tell?"

"Look at his right hand."

Fallon did. Johnny G., no mistake, was giving him the finger.

"Say you're sorry," said Doyle.

They had walked back to Michael's room.

Michael knew this was coming. "We should give Julie a call. Tell him what Johnny just did."

"After you say you're sorry."

He took a breath. "Brendan, I am. I thought the worst of you, I was wrong. I won't ever doubt you again."

"Let's not go crazy here, Michael."

Doyle said nothing more as Michael, using his one good arm, gathered up his belongings. Doyle stood at the window, staring out.

"Something else on your mind?" asked Michael.

"I got a phone call. I've been deciding whether to tell you."

A knot tightened in his stomach. "Megan?"

Doyle shook his head. "It's Rast's wife. The Countess."

He could breathe again. "What about her?"

"She asked to see you. She wants you to come to Munich."

47

Moon was on the telephone when Michael arrived at the Taylor House. He was asking for flight information. Doyle had told him.

Lena Mayfield stood in the doorway, her arms folded.

"You'll go," she said to Moon, "over my dead body."

The Countess had sent a driver. He met them at the Munich-Reim airport.

He was an older man. He said his name was Manfred. He came alone.

"That's so we let down our guard," whispered Lena.

Moon doubted that there was much danger for now. He saw no loitering muscle at the airport, no pursuit cars waiting outside. All the same, he checked the front seat before letting Manfred climb back behind the wheel. He found no hidden weapons. Nor did the chauffeur seem to care whether Moon or Michael might be armed. He did call ahead, however, as the limousine reached the gates of Schloss Scharnhorst.

Schloss Scharnhorst was not what Michael had expected. There wasn't any moat. Just a big house of stucco and stone. The style was German Baroque. The stucco was painted in a soft rose color. It seemed a woman's sort of house.

"This place have a dungeon?" asked a sour Lena Mayfield.

He didn't answer. He was scanning the curtained windows, half expecting to see Rast peering out from behind the folds. Old man or not, he knew what he would do if he got close to him.

"This is dumb, Michael," said Lena. "This is major league dumb."

Moon grumbled quietly. She had hardly let up since they drove out of Edgartown. On the plane coming over, he tried pretending to sleep. That did no good either. Every ten minutes, Lena would nudge him just to make sure he wasn't dead.

The Countess, alerted by Manfred, stood waiting on the steps of her home. Michael recognized her at once. Doyle had given him a copy of her profile. She was tall, quite thin, about seventy years old, but her face was largely unlined. She was dressed in a business suit and wore a choker of pearls. She offered no greeting. Only a look of mild surprise on seeing Lena and a small nod of acceptance. She turned and walked up toward her door, which opened to admit her by an unseen hand. Moon and Michael exchanged glances but they followed.

The room off to the left was a library. Several men, mostly older, sat staring at the visitors through doors that had been left fully open.

"Our board of directors," said the Countess. Michael recognized all of them. Most of them were family. The Countess made no move to enter.

"My family is an old one, Mr. Fallon," she said. "It has known defeat. It has never known disgrace. On my honor, no person in that room was aware of my husband's activities."

Fallon only looked at her.

"Up these stairs," said the Countess. "Follow me, if you will."

She paused near a room at the top. A man was standing guard.

"This is Heinrich, my nephew," said the Countess. "The Baron has been ill. Heinrich has been attending to him. It is time, in fact, for the Baron's medication."

Heinrich reached to open the door. Fallon saw the Baron at once. He was seated in a chair, a blanket wrapped around him, his chin against his chest. Both hands were visible. They were trembling as with palsy. One cheek bore a large fading bruise. His lower lip had been split although that too was healing. He seemed unaware of their presence.

"My husband has given an account of himself," said the Countess. "It was not well received. You speak German, I believe, Mr. Fallon?"

"My friends do not."

She made a gesture with her hand. It said that conversing in German was not her intention. "Do you know the word *Verrater?*"

"It's . . . one who betrays."

"And of course you know the word for 'bigamy.' It is exactly the same in English."

Michael did not understand the reference. Moon cleared his throat.

"Rasmussen had an American wife," Moon told him. "I don't think he ever divorced her."

"Just so," said the Countess. "Heinrich? His medicine, please?"

Heinrich reached into his pocket. He produced a velvet box of the type used for bracelets. The Countess opened it. It contained a syringe. She approached her husband. She knelt before his chair and spoke over her shoulder to Fallon.

"I do hope I have the right medication. He's been taking so many, you know."

She shook the Baron's leg.

"Herr Baron? Franzy? Mr. Fallon is here to see you."

The words penetrated, but slowly.

"And Mr. Moon as well. And a Mrs. . . . ."

"Mayfield. Don't mind me."

Rast's chin came up. His eyes began to widen. He now seemed so terribly old to Michael. That this man could have defeated Jake Fallon . . .

The Countess waited until she saw recognition in her husband's eyes. Now, satisfied that she did, and that she saw the beginnings of terror, she slid the needle into his thigh. She pressed the plunger with her thumb.

The Baron's mouth, and eyes, opened wide. One leg went into spasm, then the other. And now his whole body went rigid as if struck by an electrical charge. He slid to the floor. His body relaxed, slightly, then went rigid again. His lips peeled back from his teeth. His mouth formed a frozen grin. He made mewing sounds.

"What's German for 'strychnine'?" Moon asked the Countess.

"One word for it is *Scheidung,* Mr. Moon."
The Baron began to squeal. It took him ten minutes to die.
"Will you be staying for lunch?" asked the Countess.

Michael had declined. The Countess had walked with them back to the car. Only then, and only slightly, had her composure begun to abandon her. She reached to touch his arm. Her lower lip quivered. But she said not a word. Manfred drove them back to the airport.
"I think that was an apology," said Moon.
Lena Mayfield shook her head.
"Then what was it?" he asked.
"It was more like . . . she wanted to say why she married him. She just couldn't."
"Why did she?"
"Rich folks get lonely too," said Lena.
As they waited for their flight, Lena found a German-English dictionary.
"*Scheidung* doesn't mean 'strychnine,' " she said to Moon. "It means 'divorce.' "
"I think that was the lady's point," said Moon.

AdChem would be divided seven ways. Some companies bought more of it than others. It would be some months before a deal of this magnitude could be completed in all particulars but the management change was immediate.
The new owners agreed, at Michael's suggestion, on the need for a common security system. He knew just the firm to handle it. A contract was signed with Giordano Security Services, Inc. Fat Julie Giordano was chairman of the board. Mohammed Yahya was senior vice president for intelligence. He was terribly proud of his new business cards.
The presidency would remain vacant until such time as Mr. John Anthony Giordano was well enough to assume that office. Brendan Doyle, Esquire, was named executive vice president for legal affairs.
In the long run the firm would be funded by the seven. The source of immediate funding, however, would be through fines to be levied against a list of executives who were formerly in the

employ of both AdChem and Lehman-Stone. The fines were in
the amount of their total net worth. Fat Julie was charged with
collecting.

Frampton Childress was under indictment already. The FBI
claimed that it had broken the case. Two agents named Mowbray
and Phipps were singled out for their diligence. The charges
against Childress, however, involved only the smuggling of veterinary medicines and evasion of taxes. Evidence relating to human
medicines would never reach the public.

On a jogging path near the Jefferson Memorial, Avery Bellows
put a gun to his temple and pulled the trigger. Victor Turkel had
indeed left the country. He first flew to Panama where he kept
his money, then worked his way north to Costa Rica. Two weeks
later, in the town of Limon, he was murdered by two children
who wanted his watch.

Brendan Doyle, once again, paid an unannounced visit to Martha's Vineyard. And again, he had the look of a man with something on his mind. It was a look he'd had, it seemed to Michael,
every time they'd ever talked about his mother.

Michael knew, in his heart, that she was dead. Whether she
died out West, whether she never left New York alive, Michael
didn't know. Maybe Rast had her killed, or maybe, like his father,
she took her own life. Whatever the truth was, Doyle and Moon
and especially Jake had been trying to protect him from it since
he was twelve years old.

"We need to talk, Michael," said the lawyer.

"Listen . . . Brendan . . ."

"You better sit down."

Fallon shook his head. "Brendan, look. I told you that I trust
you. I guess I want to say that if there's something you know
. . . and you've felt that you shouldn't tell me . . . I can live
without knowing it myself."

Doyle blinked. A look of confusion.

"Brendan . . . let it lie. Let's just go on from here, okay?"

Doyle scratched his head. "You don't want to know about
Megan?"

Fallon felt his blood go cold.

"She's alive, Mike. I think we found her."

48

He did not need to sit down.

He had tried, these past weeks, to believe that she was alive. But afraid of the answer, he had not asked.

"You have to understand," Doyle was saying, "when you send out a skip-tracer, you can't expect him to hunt in the dark. He's got to learn all he can."

"Brendan . . . where is she?"

"Because no one disappears completely. Sooner or later, they'll contact a relative, a friend, and you have to know who these people are."

"Brendan . . ."

"We think she's in Mexico."

Doyle wanted him to hear how they traced her. Michael didn't care how.

"You'll listen," said Doyle. "I have my reasons."

The tracer, in fact, had found only one relative. But Megan would not have called him. Nor did she seem to have any close friends. The tracer, Eddie Larkin, had come up empty.

Finally, on a hunch, he checked with the telephone company. Given that the girl knew at least three of the victims who'd been taken to the hospital that night, and had practically lived with one of them, maybe she could not resist calling to see how they were. Maybe there was a record of a call from New London.

There were two. One on Saturday, one on Sunday of Memorial Day weekend.

There had been many such calls that weekend. Many people had suffered burns. The volunteer who worked the phones could not remember who called about whom. But she said that a woman had called several times since and as recently as a week ago. She had asked, each time, about the same three men.

The telephone records showed calls on those days from Mexico. They were placed from a town called Campeche on the Yucatan Peninsula.

"But . . . why would she go there?" Michael asked.

"She's talked about it. The Oceanographic Institute, Woods Hole, has been doing a series of digs down there. There's this comet that hit near where she's—"

"She's with them? With a diving expedition?"

"She's alone. The next dig's not until the fall."

"Well . . . what's she doing? How does she live?"

"She's got an income, Mike. Not big, but enough."

"I'm going down there. I'll fly down tomorrow."

"Michael . . . there are things I think you should know."

Whatever it was, Fallon didn't want to hear it. Not from Doyle. He would go to Campeche. He would find it. She would tell him or not. It would be strictly up to her.

"She'll run from you, Michael. And this time she might hurt herself."

"You don't know her that well. You don't know her at all."

Doyle only sighed. He raised his hands in surrender.

"What if . . . you just told me a little?"

Michael asked this question as he packed a bag.

"There isn't any little."

"Then never mind."

"Michael, this is dumb. Why should I know and not you?"

"Then just . . . tell me the basics. Tell it slow. If I ask you to stop . . ."

"That's fucking ridiculous, Michael."

"I know. But do it anyway."

* * *

"Would you believe it ties in with drugs?" Doyle asked gently. "Not hard drugs. Drugs from drugstores and doctors."

Michael believed it. She hated when he took pills. She was glad when he stopped. He'd assumed that she might have been hooked at one time.

"Aged twelve through twenty," blurted Doyle, "she was in an institution."

Fallon blinked. "For substance abuse? At age twelve?"

"It's a place in Virginia."

He waited for Michael to stop him. Michael didn't. Doyle threw up his hands.

"Mike, there's no slow way to say this. It's a place for the criminally insane."

Doyle had refused to play the game any longer. He reached into his briefcase, a new one, and pulled out a nine by twelve envelope. He handed it to Michael.

"Read it, don't read it, that's up to you. Just don't kill the messenger," he said.

The report was from Edward J. Larkin Associates. Its contents broke Michael's heart.

Her name wasn't Cole. It was Anderson until she changed it. Cole had been her mother's maiden name. Sixteen years ago, her mother was murdered. She was hacked to death as she slept. Megan was charged with the crime and found not guilty by reason of insanity. She was committed for an indefinite period.

Her father, Warren Anderson, owned a small chain of drugstores based in Newport News, Virginia. He testified at the trial that his daughter had been almost totally out of control for the two years prior to the murder. She was a drug user at ten, perhaps even before that. A quantity of drugs, morphine in particular, and certain hallucinogenics and other psychoactive compounds had disappeared from his stocks. He was sure that she'd taken them. But he made a mistake. He tried to protect her.

His daughter, he said, was an addict at eleven. She was sexually promiscuous, sleeping with grown men to get money for more drugs. She even, to his horror, offered herself to him if he would bring her what she needed from his pharmacy.

The father was away when it happened. Mother and daughter were home. Megan claimed to have awakened the next morning and found her mother hacked to death. She got dressed and went to school. She mentioned to a teacher that her mother was dead. The teacher called the police. The teacher later testified that Megan seemed numb, detached, unaffected. The police had her examined. They found a multitude of drugs in her system. Megan denied that she took them. The examination also confirmed that she had indeed been sexually active. Megan denied that as well. She then accused her father of murdering her mother.

Fallon had to stop reading. He could barely see.

"It gets worse," Doyle said quietly. "But then it gets better."

Fallon swallowed hard. "How does a thing like this get better?"

"Give me. Give it here."

Doyle found a section he had marked.

"These three pages," Doyle told him, "say how she said she saw him do it. Her description of the weapon, the blows, matched the physical evidence exactly. Except her father had an alibi. He was way up in Richmond at his other store. So if Megan was right about where her mother got chopped and how many times, it had to have been her who did it, right? On top, they found blood in Megan's shower where she'd tried to wash it off and more on her bedsheets. She claimed it was there when she woke up."

Fallon couldn't look. Doyle poked him.

"Anything I just said ring a bell?"

"Brendan . . ."

"She saw him do it, Michael. First she says she was asleep and then later she says she saw him do it. When faced with the contradiction, she said she saw him in her mind."

Fallon still didn't get it. Doyle turned more pages. "Read what Larkin says there."

Eddie Larkin believed her. So, for that matter, had at least one detective and a psychiatrist at the Virginia asylum. But Megan, by the time she was committed, wasn't sure whether she killed her mother or not. For almost two years after that, she was essentially catatonic.

Over time, the psychiatrist came to believe that the father, Warren Anderson, had been systematically drugging her, and then molesting her, *unknown* to her, for a period of at least three years.

Fallon was stunned. Doyle took the document out of his hands.

"This same shrink," he said, "also asserted that she seemed genuinely clairvoyant. That's how she saw her mother being murdered. He didn't know whether this was something she was born with or whether it was some accident of circuitry caused by some combination of all the drugs she'd been fed."

"Who says she didn't take them herself?" asked Fallon.

"That's the good news. The shrink said that she was unable to recognize any of the drugs she was supposed to have been taking. When deliberately left alone with them, she ignored them. Any junkie would have scarfed a few down but this kid, at that time, would not have known drugs if they bit her on the ass."

"Then why was she kept there eight years?"

"You won't like the answer."

"Brendan, I don't like a single word of this."

"They wanted to study her."

"Study what? The psychic thing?"

Doyle nodded. "And a couple of them, they—" He grimaced.

"Finish, Brendan."

"It's not important."

"Brendan . . . a couple of them what?"

"They, um, saw that Megan was a nice-looking kid. They thought maybe her father had the right idea."

Michael now understood all those showers.

And why sex, as she put it, was not her sport. He might well have been her first since she was freed. Her first, at least, in which she knew what she was doing.

He began to understand, just a little, that first night when she came to the Taylor House. How she could be there, having sex with him, without really being there at all. Maybe, with all that damage, it was a thing her mind had taught itself to do. To just not be there when it happened.

In the end, said Larkin's report, a lawyer got her out. The shrink had blown the whistle. The lawyer filed suit against the hospital and against the father who had remarried some Richmond bimbo within a year of his wife's death.

"That bimbo was his Richmond alibi?"

"You got it."

"His first wife, Megan's mother, caught on to what he was doing with Megan?"

"That's what Larkin thinks. No way to prove it."

"What happened with the lawsuit?"

"The father had already sold his drugstores. He skipped town but the hospital settled. Two male nurses went to jail. The settlement bought her that boat and a small annuity. The shrink taught her to sail it. He got her tutors to help her catch up. He even taught her how to dance."

"This shrink . . . was his name Sheldon Greenberg, by any chance?"

"His name was Waxman. He passed away."

"Oh."

"Who's Sheldon Greenberg?"

"No one. Never mind."

"Brendan?"

"Yeah, Mike."

"I want to hire Eddie Larkin."

"You already have. You think I'm paying for this?"

"Fine. I want him to find Warren Anderson for me."

Doyle told him that Anderson was dead. An automobile accident, six years ago in Denver. And that the bimbo had already divorced him by then. Only the last part was true. Megan's father was very much alive and he had a new drugstore. He lived in a town just outside New Orleans.

Doyle had shown the report to Moon. He wanted to know, in Moon's opinion, whether Michael could handle this right now or whether they should leave well enough alone.

Moon said, "Don't keep it from him. He has a right. And he won't be mad that you know all this. But don't show him this last page, the one with her father's address. Leave that last page with me."

"Hey, Moon . . ."

"Lena has kin down south. She's talked about wanting to see them."

"Moon, don't do this."

"Anderson's how old now . . . my age?"

"A little younger. Middle fifties."

"I'd say he's lived long enough."

Lena Mayfield agreed to stay on at the Taylor House. But only if Moon stayed as well, and only if he promised to eat right and start acting like a gentleman his age. Moon promised that he would.

But he also pointed out that Lena had been cheated of her Memorial Day vacation. He suggested a long quiet drive, just the two of them. Down to Selma, Alabama for a start. He said it seemed only proper that a gentleman such as he should present himself to her kin.

That done, he told her, he would like to push on to New Orleans. Lena liked that idea. She'd always had a yen, she said, to see the Big Easy, try some of the food it's famous for. Moon said he had a bit of business to see to in a town near there. After that, they'd have plenty of time to visit.

49

Michael found her on the Yucatan in the town of Campeche.

For three days he only watched her. Except for the eye patch she wore, and her hair cut short because so much had been burned, she looked just as she did on the day he first saw her. Cutoff jeans, deck shoes, a loose-fitting blouse tied off at the waist.

She had bought an old boat, it was small, too small to live on but it would do to sail out to the diving grounds. She had rented a room in an old Spanish house that offered bed and breakfast at a modest price.

On the evening of the third day, he received the call he'd been waiting for. The next morning, an hour after sunrise, he walked to the waterfront where she kept her boat. With his right hand, the other still in a sling, he loosened both of her lines and set it adrift. The tide took it out and westward, roughly in the direction of Texas.

He hurried to the little bodega where she stopped each morning to buy the bread and fruit that would be her lunch. It was not yet open. He stood at the door, touching his palms to the frame. He turned, walked a block away, and waited.

At last, she came. She arrived as the bodega was opening. She waved hello to a sidewalk vendor and reached with that hand for the door. She stopped. She stopped cold. She stood there for ten seconds, twenty. And now she turned her head, this way and that. And there it was, for anyone to see. Megan knew that he'd been there, no doubt in the world.

But now she seemed ready to run. She started back, not down to her boat, but back the way she came. No, Megan. Go to the dock. Go see what's down at the dock.

One hand wiped her cheeks as if brushing away tears. She turned and slowly walked in that direction. He watched as she reached the old jetty where she'd tied up her boat. She saw it. It was nearly a quarter mile out. She stood there, frustrated, hands on her hips as a new and larger boat dropped sail and luffed into the space that had been hers.

Two young men, deeply bronzed, stood on the foredeck. One of them had a bow line in his hand. He called her, asked her to catch it. She did. He hopped into the surf and approached her.

"Are you Megan?" Michael heard him ask.

She wiped her eyes. A tentative nod.

"All yours," he said. "Happy birthday." He and his companion turned and walked off toward the town.

She stood there, frozen, for what seemed a full minute. At one point, he saw that she was counting on her fingers, trying to figure the date. She stopped on four. The Fourth of July.

Fallon couldn't stand it any longer. He kicked off his shoes and walked down to the jetty.

"Nice boat," he said.

"Damn you, Michael." She wouldn't turn.

"Cheoy Lee ketch. Forty-four. They were out of thirty-fours."

"Who was that boy who knew me?"

"He didn't. He delivers boats, that's all. He brought this one all the way from Miami."

She still didn't get it.

"It's yours, Megan. The papers should be up on the chart table."

She said nothing. She didn't move.

"I picked a new name for her. Go look at the transom."

Nothing.

"I named it *Fallon in Love*."

That almost made her turn.

"And I had them design a spinnaker with a big red heart and an arrow through it. It says, 'Michael & Megan' in letters eight feet high."

A disbelieving groan. "Michael . . . tell me you didn't."

"Okay, I didn't. You still have an unlisted boat."

Her chest rose and fell. She glanced back at him now with her one good eye. It lingered for a moment on the sling he wore and on his hands where pink new skin had grown over the burns. She winced at the sight. But she wouldn't look up at his face. She turned away and she sat, cross-legged, in the sand.

"Megan . . . it's over. Come home."

"You know about me, don't you?"

"That's over too."

"It won't ever be over."

"Megan . . ."

"And look at us now. Look at me. This eye patch will make it even worse."

He knew what she meant. No more getting lost in the crowd. But it was nonsense. Berman says give them six months and she'll have mostly full sight in that eye and no scars. Well . . . maybe one little scar at the corner. In the meantime, however, an eye patch on a beautiful lady sailor was about the most irresistible thing he'd ever seen.

"Michael, I don't want your boat."

"It's not mine. You accepted delivery."

"And I don't want your pity."

"That's what you think? I'm here because I feel sorry for you?"

"Michael . . . it won't work. Sooner or later, you'll start to wonder about me."

"*Start* to wonder? Megan . . . what's left?"

"Things like . . . whether I really did kill my mother."

"You didn't. End of discussion."

"Then things like . . . these trances. How many more Taylor Houses have I wandered through? How many men, like you, have I climbed into bed with?"

"We're going to compare sex lives? Okay, mine started with Mary Beth . . ."

"It's not funny, Michael."

"Okay, how many?"

"None. But you'll wonder if I even know. Someday you'll get mad at me. You'll use that to hurt me."

Oh, boy.

"Moon? What do I say to a dumb thing like that?"

"Take her out for a sail."

"She'll want to go catch her own boat."

"Accidents happen. Ram it."

That wasn't Moon. That sounded more like Jake.

"Uncle Jake?"

"Michael . . . you talk too much. Hold her."

"If I do, I might never let go."

"You're beginning to get the idea."

But he couldn't. She knew that he wanted to reach out and grab her. He knew that she'd only twist away. A wonderful relationship, not long on surprises. He lowered himself to her side and touched his right hand to her knee. He wanted her to be able to feel him. He wanted her to be able to listen.

"Since this whole thing began," he said slowly, quietly, "I've done just two things right. One was going to Woods Hole that day. The day that I met you."

Her eyes welled up again.

"The second thing, Megan, was loving you. Whether you feel that way or not, whether you come home with me or not, I'm going to love you for the rest of my life."

Her small body shuddered. She traced one finger in the sand. Several moments went by before she could speak.

"You said six months?" she asked him at last.

"Um . . . what?"

"You said something about six months."

Oh, for Pete's sake.

"No, Megan. Dr. Berman said that. What *I* had in mind was forever."

"I'll try it, Michael. I'll try for six months."

He reached for her. She did not resist. She buried her face against his chest. He held her, tightly, with his one good arm.

"Six months for starters," he whispered. He touched his lips to her hair. "We'll try it six months at a time."